SHE WHO CHOSE WAR

Cover art by Christian Bentulan
Map design by Madison Rene

ISBN 979-8-9884246-0-4 (paperback)
ISBN 979-8-9884246-1-1 (ebook)

www.MadisonReneAuthor.com

Published by Jade Quill Press

In loving memory of my dear Granny~
Not a day goes by that I don't miss you so much.

KATSAO
KOHARI
THOMANI
SANEN
ZENOCH
ANANSI
YONA SHORE
SILOS PEAKS MINE
DALTIUM
IVALIA
VELSPIRE
LIVASHIRE
SALLAIS
SOLARIS
MALABRIA
PORT KYANOS
BRIMON
KRYSTOPOLIS
SANVOLK
BLACK RIVER
MT. SKIA COAL MINE
ELFIN SPRING
PALTHESI
ASTURIA
VENOS
LUNUCA
KIKIONI

EASTERN SEA

DANAECA

SHE WHO CHOSE WAR

MADISON RENE

JADE QUILL PRESS

CHAPTER 1

Nevia was late, and the water was cold.

Gooseflesh prickled her bare arms as she shuddered, drawing them across her breasts. She couldn't keep her teeth from chattering. Just when she thought she was acclimating, a torrent of water poured over her head, drenching the platinum waves of her hair and plastering them to her face in thick sheets.

"Elante, please," she rasped, shaking the hair away from her face and blinking back water droplets. Her gaze met with her handmaiden's, whose slender, youthful face reflected nothing. The servant girl wasted no time in running a scrubbing brush down the length of Nevia's back, the bristles coarse and prickly against her tender skin.

"I am sorry for the lack of accommodations, Your Highness. Had you been here an hour ago, the water would still be pleasant," she chirped. "But there is no time to reheat it before you must join your husband for the festival."

The bristles grazed along the base of Nevia's spine and dove over a tattoo of the legendary roc bird upon her left shoulder, the mark serving as one of the many reminders that Nevia wasn't from there. That she had lived another life before becoming empress of the Androvich Empire.

The gleaming tub of rose gold was spacious, allowing her plenty of room to stretch her legs, toes peeking out from underneath the thick layer of peony-fragranced bath foam. Warm sunlight poured from the open windows, casting a ray of light through the pale pink privacy screen surrounding the bath and onto the form of her handmaiden. The servant's long dark hair was plaited, brushed to one side to fall down to her waist. Freckles adorned her hairline and nose, and the wrinkles around her eyes indicated that she knew joy. Elante was one of her favorite people and most cherished friend within the empire, even if such a relationship was considered improper between handmaiden and empress.

The bath was brief, and soon enough Nevia found herself led back to her adjoined room, freezing despite the warm summer rays that kissed her skin. She rubbed her slender fingers along her sides as Elante tugged undergarments over her head. Briefly their hands met, Elante's pallid skin contrasting with the empress' tanned complexion—another stark reminder that Nevia was a foreigner.

Hanging from a hook on her wardrobe door was her attire selected for the festival. She was unable to mask her glee when her gaze fell upon it: a beautiful gown woven from the finest emerald velvet, embroidered with golden flowers and tiny glass beads which reflected the light so that they glistened. Her fitted bodice was cut low and spun of silk in a matching emerald, with open bell sleeves that cascaded down to her waist. It was festive, lively, and beautiful—everything that an empress needed for Saavis, the longest day of the year.

She was guided over to her dressing table for her hair to be styled, bare feet padding along the smooth bamboo floors. Carefully she tucked her emerald gown around her so that she didn't wrinkle the fine material, settling herself into the armchair she would take up residence in for some time. Her thick blonde hair was wild and unruly. She would've felt sorry for Elante having to suffer with styling it had she not known she would pay retribution. While it wasn't Elante's intention to be harsh, their lack of time would cause her to work swiftly and likely with less care as time would have permitted.

"Really," Elante murmured, running a comb through the front sides of Nevia's hair, which saw the most distress. "I wish you would consider wearing your silken night scarf, Your Highness. It would prevent a great deal of pain and distress."

"I can never get it on," Nevia protested.

A few more scratches of the comb before Elante set it down on the table in defeat. "That is why you have a handmaiden to help you."

A laugh escaped Nevia as Elante brushed against her left side, retrieving an iron from a basket of hot coals to begin styling. She wrapped a small section of hair around the cylindrical iron, waited for several seconds before releasing the strands, and placed it back for reheating in the start of a tedious dance. Such was reserved only for the most special occasions.

"And what a wonderful handmaiden you are." Nevia turned to offer Elante a smile, resulting in her handmaiden adjusting the position of her head. "What would I do without you?"

Elante's cheeks were tinted by the praise. "Well, for starters, you would always be wearing that braid. And His Imperial Highness would not be showcasing you to all of the lords and ladies quite so frequently."

"You're quite right about the first. I love my braid," Nevia confessed. "Though I'm not sure about that last one. I think my homely appearance would be all the more reason that Darius would showcase me."

Elante snorted and then hissed, accidentally catching the tip of her finger on the hot iron. There had always been a casual ease between them, perhaps because Nevia wasn't born into nobility and understood a life outside finery. She was in her twenty-second year, eight years Nevia's junior, yet the two had much in common and always enjoyed one another's company.

"So," Elante started, hands hard at work, brow creased in concentration. "Are you looking forward to the festivities today?"

A sigh escaped the empress, the tug from the hair at her nape restricting her from bowing her head. Saavis was the most important celebration of the year; a grand occasion across all of Danaeca. People gathered from far and wide to celebrate the birth of Gaia and the annual slumber of the goddess, Saava. It was mostly tradition by then; hardly anyone referred to the myths surrounding the creation of Gaia, and yet the festivities remained. It was a time of joy: to embrace vitality and forget pain, sorrow, and hatred.

"To be honest, I don't find this to be the most joyous of occasions. It's nice to see the people happy, but I feel this entire day is a farce, and I don't enjoy having to put on a show for the Five Lords."

Elante paused in her motions, seeming thoughtful. "Do they not love you, Your Highness?"

"No, that they do not. But, not only that, they also do their best to jab at Darius for choosing me, a primitive clanswoman from the north, to be his bride, when instead it should've been one of the far-off princesses that could have earned him an alliance."

There was another tug, this one not nearly as gentle. "It must be very upsetting to you."

"It isn't that which troubles me," Nevia protested, even if it was partly true. "It's seeing how much it bothers him. He pretends not to care, because he married for love and he's proud of that, but I see the pain in his eyes, the shame. This happens every time we are at these dinners, and I hate it."

"Maybe it is time that tradition changes then," Elante supplied.

The empress unclenched the fists that had been wrinkling her skirt. Change took a great deal of time in the empire; she had discovered that all too quickly.

"I think it wouldn't be such a great bother to the lords if I were a noble, or even a native to the empire," Nevia admitted, "but the fact that I'm just a peasant from Zenoch troubles them greatly. I think. I don't know."

"But you have adjusted to our culture marvelously over these past two years of your marriage, Your Highness." Elante beamed at her in the mirror. "I am sure it was very difficult to adopt our way of life, with traditions differing drastically from your own."

Nevia glanced down at her lap as Elante worked at the back of her head. It was true: the adjustment had been a challenge for her. Back home she would scour the forests, tucking away wood for fires and berries to dry for the winter, wearing the same plain clothing for days on end. She would aid the Katsao clan with fierce devotion. She was an outcast in the eyes of the the imperials, so to accept her as their *empress* had been challenging. While some had grown to accept and love her, the lords of the five imperial countries were not so readily swayed.

"I have done what I can, but I can never change the color of my skin or blend in to this society. I will never be one of them, and many hearts are hardened to differences."

Choosing not to answer, Elante rubbed her palms with sweet-smelling almond oil to work into Nevia's hair, gently caressing and fluffing the freshly styled curls to make them shine. Upon looking in the mirror Nevia hardly recognized herself. She looked regal, fit to be a figure of authority, fulfilling the silent role of the emperor's wife. Whenever she had opened her mouth to speak, there were always disapproving murmurs and shakes of the head, so she learned to refrain from doing so.

Nevia started to reach for her hair, but Elante caught her hand. "They will last longer if you look and not touch," she explained. "And I think you would like for it to remain looking decent through dinner."

The empress smiled up at her handmaiden. "But Elante, I thought that's what you were for. You could fix it up for me again between now and dinner."

Elante raised her hands and backed up in mock alarm. "Oh no, I don't get paid enough to work on *that* behemoth more than once per day!"

Both women giggled, the empress rising from her seat. Elante knelt to begin fluffing her petticoats.

"Since I'm such a handful," Nevia teased, "how about you take the rest of the day off?"

Elante winced, looking as though she'd been stricken. "But, Your Highness, who will—"

"I'm sure that I can manage," she reassured. "After all, I was able to take care of myself for years. I think I can get through one day without your care. Wouldn't you like the spend the day with your family instead of tending to my every need and whimsy?"

"I am always honored to care for you." Elante ran her hands down her own worn skirt, ankles covered to maintain modesty. "Though I will confess, I haven't seen my sister in a while, and she has a new baby that I have yet to meet—"

"Then go!"

Elante's nervousness morphed into giddiness. She offered a low curtsy to her empress, dark locks brushing the floor. "Thank you so very much, milady. You have my gratitude."

"As you have mine. Always." Nevia knelt alongside Elante and affectionately tucked a lock of hair behind her servant's ear. The two rose together, holding hands. "I would never have survived the brutality of immigrating here if it had not been for your friendship."

Elante's smile shone brighter than stars, hands squeezing Nevia's tightly in return. Finally Nevia released her and shooed her off. "Now go on, get! Be with your family!"

Elante appeared nervous as she traipsed out of the parlor and down the hall, the empress shortly behind her. Guards were stationed at every entrance in the rich Velspirian palace halls, backs against the doorframes wearing their usual dull, lifeless expression.

Overhead crystal chandeliers illuminated the way, west-facing windows providing very little morning light. Nevia's shadow bounced along the familial portraits on the textured wall, the sound of her heels masked by the burgundy runner along the floor.

The guardsmen in the foyer acknowledged the empress with a bow, before stepping aside and opening both double doors for her. A pool of brilliant natural light engulfed and momentarily blinded her. Outside it was already warm, a rush of summer air rustling through her curled hair and caressing her nape. She drew in the delicious scent of honeysuckle.

Along the winding cobblestone pathway awaited the royal chariot, its lacquered wood a deep ebony with two mares hitched to the front to match. Gold trim adorned the doorframe, glistening radiantly in the sun. A footman awaited her, flourishing a respectful bow before extending a hand to her. She hated being waited on, but it was customary and it would've been a grave insult to refuse him. She grasped his gloved hand and hitched up the front of her skirt, hoisting herself gracefully up the steps and into the coach.

A bored yawn greeted her as she entered. She glanced up to see Darius already seated casually, one elbow hanging out the window. His chocolate eyes met hers evenly.

"You're late."

The door to the coach snapped shut behind her, leaving the two alone. Nevia's painted lips tightened into a thin line as she took up the seat alongside him. Darius was dressed in similar splendor: black pants matched his hair, his jacket resembling spun gold. Green accents adorned his sleeves and mandarin collar, the perfect companion to Nevia's attire. Someone must have caught a glimpse of Nevia's gown and coordinated the emperor's clothing to match. She couldn't help thinking that Elante may have had something to do with it.

"No, you're just early." She elbowed him in the ribs, offering him a playful smile, which he returned with more of a grimace. She looped her arm into his, leaning her head against his strong shoulder as the coach rolled into motion. His muscles tensed under her cheek, and even his attempt at masking his discomfort by lacing his fingers through hers was unsuccessful. "Something is on your mind," she observed.

Darius' long bangs fell over his forehead. "I hate these gatherings."

"I know, and I do, too." She nuzzled her nose into his arm, not realizing until too late that she was smearing face powder onto his sleeve. "But we will do fine. We always do. And at least we have each other."

He gave her a sideways glance, offering a sad kind of smile before kissing her on the temple. "The lords always press and pry. I do not like having to be on the defensive or pretend."

"Then don't pretend. Just be yourself."

"It is not that simple." Darius sighed irritably, shifting away from his wife and straightening his fallen bangs to the side.

"'Myself' is not what the people expect from their emperor, especially the Five Lords."

Nevia shook her head. "Then just forget what the Five Lords want for once. You yourself have said how impossible they are to please."

The carriage rolled onward, the bumps in the cobblestone path jostling the pair. The birdsong of chickadees echoed through the carriage, but even that failed to thaw the ice that encased Nevia's heart with their conversation.

Darius gripped her hand tightly, all of the playfulness in his expression gone. "Nevia, I love you, and you know that I respect you in every way"—Nevia recoiled, waiting for the rub—"but please trust me when I say that you do not fully understand the complexity of the situation. The Five Lords are my seniors, the rulers of the five countries that make up this very empire. They have been serving my father for as long as I have been alive, and they expect a man like him to rule. But I'm not my father; I've made that painfully clear over these past two years, and they do not particularly take kindly to this. There are whispers behind my back, most of which are not good."

Nevia returned his gaze coolly, irritation starting to simmer under the surface. "You shouldn't care what people say."

"I *have* to care," he snapped. "The empire depends on it. If the lords conspire, who am I to stop them from using their vested power to overthrow me and ruin everything that my father has built, everything that I have been struggling to maintain?"

Nevia folded her arms over her chest and leaned back in her seat, gaze boring into the back of the charioteer's head. She found it impossible to speak with her husband when he became fixed on his failures. "Your father was not perfect. He had many flaws. You are a better man than he is."

"Many would disagree with you," he said tersely. "While he may not have been a kind man, he was an exceptional ruler."

"But you need kindness to rule a nation."

"You need authority and respect to rule a nation, Nevia. There is a difference. I don't expect you to understand."

"Then what would you have me do?" She threw her hands in the air, voice rising an octave. "What *can* I do?!"

"Absolutely nothing!" he shouted back in equal fervor. "You've already done too much by being here! Speaking only makes it worse. Just try to be quiet, and for the love of the goddess please just try to be one of us. That's all I ask."

A pained silence followed; the quiet before the storm. Nevia drew her lips into a narrow line, gaze blank as she blinked back moisture accumulating in her eyes. She folded her hands primly in her lap, back straightening in her seat. He started to reach for her hand, remorse gripping him, but she recoiled from his touch.

"Neve, I—"

"I understand, Your Highness. You are ashamed of my presence. It is fine; I have known this for a while."

A frustrated growl escaped Darius as he gripped her shoulders and turned her to face him. "Absolutely not. I am ashamed at myself, my own actions and decisions." He shook his head. "Making you my wife was the best thing that I ever did. You're not responsible for the backwards way that these people think and behave, my selfish decisions for putting you into such an unfair position."

"I understand." The lie easily escaped her lips; she did not understand at all.

Sorrow clouded his gaze, his finger running down her cheek.

"Let's just do what needs to be done today," she said, withdrawing from his caress, ignoring the pain etched on his face. "You be the cold, calculated dictator that you feel your people need, and I will be the silent, pretty empress that is just an object for you to control."

"You are putting words in my mouth now," Darius snapped. "You are being very unfair and cruel to me, Nevia."

"*I* am being cruel?!"

"You don't know how hard this is! I am torn between being two people."

"Then maybe you need to stop and decide who you really are," Nevia shot back.

A pang of guilt tore at her chest at the look of shock that crossed Darius' face, but it did not last very long. "If you just be yourself, maybe the people will learn to respect you more. Switching between your two personas only garners mistrust and disrespect. It makes you look like you don't know who you are or what you're doing."

"But it's the truth," he murmured darkly. "I don't know what I'm doing anymore."

Nevia was at a loss for words.

The coach groaned to a halt. The sounds of music and laughter flooded their cabin, filling the uncomfortable silence that once encased them.

"The central square, Your Excellencies," the footman chirped, opening the door and extending out his hand for Nevia.

The empress felt the brush of Darius' fingers on her forearm, as though silently asking her to wait, but she ignored him. She didn't lift her head, refusing to see the hurt in his eyes, or cater to the desire to make amends. While she felt bad that she wounded him, *he* wounded her, too. She knew that she was unwelcome in the empire, but to hear it come from her own husband's mouth? It was too low of a blow, one that she didn't want to forgive—at least not yet.

She allowed the footman to guide her down the steps, into the sunshine and the heart of the festival that greeted her with raucous cheers.

CHAPTER 2

The relentless summer sun poured onto the empress, platinum curls glistening. She didn't wait for Darius to exit the carriage, or even await an escort. For a brief moment she wanted to simply be Nevia: a woman enjoying the festival, just like everyone else, without imperial eyes spying her every movement.

She watched as happy couples walked arm-in-arm in the central square, dressed their best and smiling. The cheer was contagious, and Nevia found that her negative mindset couldn't survive long.

The central square symbolized the heart of Velspire, the imperial capital nestled along the eastern coast of Ivalia. Storefronts lined either side of the street, old buildings which survived the test of time by standing for over a century. Behind them lined the tall spires of factories, plumes of smoke billowing into the air and cascading across the warm summer breeze. The air was not clean in Velspire, a well-known fact amongst them. It was an industrial city, housing the majority of the empire's factories and production. Smog filled the air at all hours of the day, yet today the sky seemed less hazy, the air a little bit clearer. Most factory work was suspended that day, in honor of the celebration of the planet's birth.

Vendors from far and wide gathered in the capital city to offer their finest wares. A peddler nearby showcased his wide array of brocades from the Feishin Kingdom across the Eastern Sea, while another offered elbluma, pastries native to the southern country of Lunuca. The scent of the cream-filled pastries made her stomach rumble and mouth salivate, and perhaps she would have stopped to make a purchase had there not been a line of two dozen patrons.

The majority of stands were similarly packed, eager customers crowding around to examine fine wares or compete in a bottle-toss challenge. Nevia scoffed as she watched a group of grown men attempt to toss their hard-earned gold coins into the fine hole of a glass bottle neck. It appalled her that it was legal to allow people to gamble their wealth in exchange for a promised prize should they succeed in sinking a coin in one of the bottles.

Music flooded her ears as she delved further into the heart of the square, her vision greeted by a wall of bodies obscuring the musicians from view. She managed to wind her way between two school-aged children, no older than eleven years of age. They wore wide smiles, and it didn't take Nevia long to see why. Standing upon the dais, before the fountain and statue of Saava, were a troupe of performers, each dressed in vibrant golds, greens, and pinks. They brought fine, uplifting music to life, making Nevia wish that Darius was there so that she could drag him into the center and force him into a dance. She could make out the clarinet, flute, and violin being played, along with a variety of drums and tambourines.

Patrons cheered, showering the feet of musicians with gold coins and whooping laughter. A young couple moved toward the front, swinging and dancing with the music. Much of the crowd began clapping in rhythm, the couple spinning faster and faster.

The moment of joy was swiftly stolen from her when her gaze flickered to the helmets of imperial soldiers. She should've been glad to see them, as it was indeed unsafe and unwise for the empress to wander the streets alone. But she relished in being herself, just for a moment, and she wasn't yet ready to give it up. She backed away from the soldiers that were doubtlessly looking for her, blending into a cluster of women in brilliant-colored skirts and getting sucked into a crowd that observed brooches consisting of a rare variety of gemstones.

A sigh escaped Nevia, her ice-blue eyes falling on a fire opal the size of a gold coin before moving on. She cursed herself inwardly for her foolishness, for her mad desire to be free from her title, but she was unable to persuade herself to return.

As she passed by a stand of exotic fruits and a woman trying to vend fresh fish, Nevia's attention fell on a stand of wind instruments. She approached the table, following a small, portly man bemused by a trumpet that was nearly as large as he was. All of the instruments were beautiful, but none caught her as finely as the neat row of flutes did. The majority was made from strong tonewoods in a variety of hues, with adornments which made Nevia's own pale boxwood flute seem rudimentary at best. Many were trimmed with silver and gold, some with the imperial seal stamped on them.

"I can engrave your initials, or even your full name if you'd like," a voice piped up, startling Nevia from her reverie and causing her hand to fall from a lovely blackwood flute. She hesitated before reaching out for it again.

"It's lovely," she remarked, running her fingers along the grooves of the smooth wood, the polish that sealed the instrument pristinely. It took her a moment to realize the jade mouthpiece was authentic. "Are they imported?"

The salesman was young, perhaps no older than twenty years of age, with blond hair that curled around his ears. His features suggested he was not native to the empire, or at least not inherently. "They are from the Feishin Kingdom. Jade can only be found there."

"Oh, I see." She picked it up, weighing it, calculating. Yes, she could see herself playing this fine instrument. She wondered if it would sound similar to her flute back at home. She brought it close to her lips to test, but then thought better of it.

"You thinking for a gift, or for yourself?" The salesman's smile ignited his deep blue eyes.

Nevia shook her head, gingerly placing the flute back down. "No, for myself. I love to play."

"Ah, I do as well, though I love many wind instruments." The blond salesman roved from the table to rummage through crates stacked precariously to the side. Packing paper and silks streamed around him before he procured a long, thin instrument wrapped in a silk scarf. His hands moved gingerly over the material as he returned before her, meticulously unraveling the silk to unveil another flute, its beauty stealing Nevia's breath away. "I wonder if this one may interest you."

It was red, made from either the very rare cocuswood or rosewood—Nevia could not tell which—and had engraved cherry blossoms down its face. A pink metallic trim adorned the flute, adding to its elegance. The empress began reaching for it before she could stop herself.

"Lovely, isn't it?" He held it out for her to examine. "The finest flute in my possession, made from the rare cocuswood, found only in Iddlegaard these days. Took me a while to scour it. You won't find another like it this far east."

Ah, so it *was* cocuswood. "It's beautiful." Nevia turned the instrument in her hands, her fingerprints leaving smudges along the glossy, smooth finish. "How much?"

The youth ran his tongue across his upper lip, contemplative. It seemed that either he never considered having it up for sale, or simply didn't know what to ask for it. "Seven-thousand ocres."

It was Nevia's turn to act surprised. That was at least triple the value that she had anticipated. She dropped the flute to the table, lips pursing into a frown. Was she being cheated because she was empress? That hardly seemed fair. "Does that not seem high to you?"

"May be the only flute of its kind that I'll ever see. Imports like this don't come every day."

Her frown deepened. It was not that she couldn't afford it, but its purchase was frivolous—and unnecessary. Despite this, Nevia found herself reaching for her coin pouch, dropping a large sum of golden coins clattering on the table. He reacted quickly, ensnaring a few before they bounced to the ground. He dipped his head in gratitude, before steepling his hands to create a triangle that he brought to his chest. Her heart fluttered, recognizing the common greeting from her native land that she hadn't seen in so long. He wrapped the flute back up in its pink scarf, sheathing it in a thin black box before handing it to her.

Purchase tucked under her arm, Nevia resumed scouring the festival. She had been meandering the streets for an hour, and was certain that her husband and royal guards were quite beside themselves with worry. She knew that she should find them, but she was having a fine time keeping to herself and exploring. Part of her secretly did not want to face Darius, dreading the expression that she would have to put on when it came time to make a public address, let alone the dinner with the Five Lords.

Nevia was so distracted by her own thoughts that she gasped when a pale hand shot out, clasping her wrist tightly and yanking her into an abandoned alleyway between buildings. The stench made her eyes water, filth and human waste outlying the streets, black flies flittering around and batting at her face.

"What gives you the right?" Nevia demanded, but fell short at the sight of her assailant: a middle-aged woman, hair as white as an elder's. Studded piercings adorned her face in several places, tattoos extending over the length of her arms and what was exposed of her chest. What startled Nevia most was her pink irises which bore into her soul. The empress could feel the fine hairs on her arms stand on end, and she didn't think she was imagining things when the eyes of the woman seemed to ignite with newfound energy.

Like magic.

CHAPTER 3

“ You're a seer,” Nevia gasped, realization dawning on her. She had only heard whispers of the seers, individuals born with unusual characteristics and believed to wield the gift of foresight. It was rumored they were demon-touched and bequeathed terrible curses wherever they went. When discovered, they were sentenced to death. This tradition had been upheld for centuries, yet Nevia didn't believe in this precautionary measure. No ill omen seemed to exude from the woman standing before her; the thought of burning her at the stake to cleanse the world seemed like utter rubbish.

The seer outstretched her palms, willing the empress to offer her hands. A warmth permeated from them, which culminated and grew until it enveloped the pair. The raucous laughter and clatter from the festival began to fade, basking them in silence, as if in a stasis separating them from both time and space. The dank alleyway dissolved in whorls of smoke and a faint shimmer of rose dust, encapsulating them in mystical energy.

"Nevia Bylilly of Zenoch." The seer's voice came out high and gravely. "You have been destined for great things, to become the hero that will deliver Danaeca from its path of death."

"Who are you?" Nevia asked, panic rising in her throat.

The seer closed her eyes, nostrils flaring from her petite nose. "I have many names, but you may call me Yune. I have been searching for you, Nevia Bylilly. An audience with the empress is hard to come by."

Nevia blinked, taken aback by the seer's untowardness. "I suppose abducting me in the central square is easier than scheduling an appointment." Despite her harshness, Nevia did not try to escape, too mesmerized by the energy that Yune was drawing and expending, energy that ran across her hands like dancing threads willed to life.

The seer unveiled her pupil-less gaze, focused on something unseen, as if into a plane beyond their own.

"You will have to make impossible decisions to be on the path of life, making sacrifices that will leave you broken." Her voice wavered, and she drew in a rattling breath. The color in her lips shifted from white to blue, and Nevia wondered if she was being deprived of oxygen. "You will choose war, your reward a sea of soulless bodies, a coastline whose stains will never be washed away.

You will unite bonds once severed, bringing prosperity and peace. They will sing your praises for ages to come. But you will see hardship, Nevia of Zenoch, hardship unlike any. Love will betray you, and your own heart will become your enemy."

Yune shook violently, and for a brief moment her magic lapsed, sounds piercing their stasis. Nevia's eyes widened in alarm as she began to withdraw her hands, yet Yune only clung tighter. "You will have to make the correct choice if you wish to save Danaeca from a catastrophic end," she rasped. "Befriend Queen Arethusa, for her path is intertwined with yours. Aid her . . . and she will aid you."

"The Feishin queen?" Nevia blinked. "I have never even met her."

Focus seemed to return to Yune's gaze, looking at Nevia now instead of through her. "You will."

The glow of her eyes faded, along with her energy. In an instant the silence was filled by the festival garble they'd left behind, shouts and clatter assaulting Nevia's ears. She blinked, glancing around the square in a daze, before allowing her attention to fall back onto the seer. The woman was kneeling, eyes closed, body convulsing violently as her eyes rolled back into her head. She would've collapsed fully to the muck-stained cobblestone had Nevia not sprung to catch her. The seer's head lolled against her arm as her seizure ceased, eyes clenched tight.

A chill hung over Nevia, despite the stagnant tepid air in the stench-filled alley. Nevia didn't know whether to believe a word the seer said, though understood she believed the message to be dire for Nevia to hear, regardless of the risks.

Or costs.

"Neve?"

Cold dread filled Nevia as her back stiffened, Darius' voice causing nervous energy to ricochet within her. Her immediate impulse was to hide this woman, this seer who risked much to deliver such a prophecy to her. But she knew it was too late as Darius rounded the corner, his boots clicking ceremoniously on the streets. She turned to see one of his dark brows arch in curiosity, the gold of his mandarin collar shimmering in the sunlight. "What are you doing, and who is this?"

"She's. . . ." The words died in Nevia's throat as her husband knelt beside her, shoulder brushing her own as he peered into the face of the unconscious woman. "I think she's dying. We need to get her to a doctor, and fast."

He didn't appear to be listening. His face darkened as his hand flickered over to the woman's wrist, pulling up her sleeve and letting out a hiss of disdain. The tattoo of an eye resided there, and Nevia did not need to study it long to know what it meant. Among those born with the gift of foresight, there were those who survived, banding together into a nomadic group that swept over Danaeca and honed their skills underneath the head shaman, Maestra Annika. Even if Nevia tried to deny this woman's magical affinity, the tattoo would condemn her to damnation. Her eyes fluttered closed as Darius forcefully threw her wrist down.

"A seer," he practically spat, gaze flickering up into Nevia's shocked face. "What did she tell you?"

Footfalls sounded from around the corner. Clearly Darius didn't come alone. Her gaze faltered, shifting to the folds of Yune's pale-blue gown.

"It was nothing."

It was far from nothing, but Nevia would spare him the details. Words that would cause nothing but trouble, and perhaps only shorten the duration between Yune's capture and execution. Her response was enough, as Darius was swift to signal to the guards behind them to take the seer and dispose of her in the prisons.

"She should be sent to the infirmary instead," Nevia insisted, fingers digging into Yune's shoulders before the guards could snatch her away. "She expended a lot of her energy, and is now weak. At the very least let her heal and—"

"And what? Burn her then?" Darius' voice was cold and calculating, causing a chill to quiver down her spine. The woman was ripped from Nevia's limp arms, the guard pitiless as he haphazardly flung her over his shoulder and strode away. Nevia watched as they went, wishing to say more, do more, and yet she was capable of nothing. No defense could be offered against those who practiced magic fully knowing of the law. Yune would now be subject to paying for her crimes.

Crimes that she committed to help Nevia.

It surprised her when Darius tenderly lifted her from the ground, his strong arms wrapping around her and bringing her to stand against his side. She didn't protest, couldn't find it in her to do so, and walked along numbly as she allowed her feet to follow Darius from the narrow, darkened alleyway back into the liveliness of the square, people wall-to-wall and barely allowing enough room to breathe. Whispers met their backs, and it took Nevia a long moment to realize they were due to the public affection Darius displayed by holding her close, yet it didn't stop him. She finally turned her gaze up to her husband, taking in his jaw concealed by his closely trimmed beard, and, finally, the warm chocolate-brown eyes that melted her insides.

Finally she spoke, voice raw. "Will they punish me?"

He stole a glance at her, footsteps even. "Should they?"

"I don't know."

A moment's silence lapsed before he stopped. His grip on her tightened as he whirled her around to face him. She sniffed, eyes red from tears.

"Neve." His grip was firm, but not unkind, matching his even tone. "You are not the one that performed magic. Whatever happened back there wasn't your fault."

"She was caught giving me a prophecy, though, so I feel partly accountable." She could not hold his gaze, instead bowing her head. "She had a warning for me, and maybe—maybe she knew the risks of being caught, but decided to sacrifice her own life to give me this message?"

Darius looked contemplative. His lips grazed Nevia's temple, planting a kiss along the soft, fine curls residing there. "I'll admit that I haven't cared to learn very much about them, but I think it is a dark art that can lead to trouble. Even if what they claim is false, a person's own will can make it true, and find themselves fulfilling a prophecy that never would have come to pass." He released Nevia, running a hand over his velvet coat. "So, in that sense, I am glad that she found you. Had she not, I fear what other kind of chaos her messages could've created if left to continue preaching."

Nevia winced, shocked by his callousness, even if his words should've been perfectly reasonable. Ignoring her reaction, he wrapped her in a tight embrace. "It's okay, Neve. It's not your fault." His breath tickled her ear. "Don't blame yourself."

She let out a quivering breath, wrapping her arms around her husband and burying her face into his shoulder. He was right; she knew he was, and yet still she felt accountable.

"So she completed giving you a prophecy, then?"

Nevia froze, heart aflutter. The portent. It brought her much anguish, but she'd momentarily forgotten its impact on her from the guilt she burdened herself with. "Yes, but I'm sure that it was false." Nevia shook her head sadly. "It did not make sense."

"What was it?"

She forced a false smile onto her lips and planted a kiss on his cheek. He appeared nearly as anxious as she felt, running his hand through his bangs and fidgeting, as he often did when troubled. "Nothing worth fretting over." She grabbed his hand and patted it. "Now, what sort of fun have you been up to without me?"

Darius seemed hesitant to let the subject drop, yet he relented and humored her. "Well, none, because I have been searching for you."

"Oh." She tucked her hair behind her ear nervously, noticing her curls were already coming apart. "I apologize for keeping you from your festivities, then."

He waved a hand, offering Nevia one of his sideways smirks. "No matter. Nothing that you can't make up for in due time, I'm certain."

"What did you have in mind?" she asked playfully, falling in step with him, slipping her hand into his. He brought her hand up to his lips and kissed it, eyes brightening with mischief. It was nice to see this side of Darius again, the one that was livelier, brighter. The man that she'd fallen in love with three years ago in the forest bordering Zenoch, and still loved dearly to this day. In that moment Nevia forgave him, their prior fight dissolving into the depths of the past as she basked in the warmth of this moment, which only grew warmer when the emperor swooped down to kiss her.

Nevia closed her eyes, savoring the feeling of his lips against hers. She splayed her hands across his chest, leaning into the kiss with earnest. The heat from her sun-baked neck traveled lower and into her stomach, the tight knots softening to butterflies as Darius wrapped his arm around her, drawing her closer, his hand ensnaring her thick mess of hair.

For a solitary moment it was just the two of them: the emperor and his empress. Nevia wished it could be like this forever, but all too soon they were interrupted by the rustling of chainmail. Her body grew limp in Darius' embrace, arms slipping from around his neck. A member of their imperial guard, who stood several paces away, cleared his throat.

"Erm, Your Imperial Highnesses." The guard tugged at his mandarin collar, clearly uncomfortable. "Lord Verrine is here to see you."

Darius drew Nevia away as if scalded. Waving at them from behind the guard stood a short man with long, blond curls, an obnoxious smile plastered on his angular, pallid face. His brown eyes glittered as they fell upon the couple, and his head bobbed, more insulting than courteous.

"Your Majesties." His voice was laced with oil as he flourished a dramatic bow. Swiftly he moved towards Darius, clasping his hand in both of his own. Nevia sucked in a breath, holding in any retort as she inclined her head respectfully in greeting. Despite how much Nevia loathed the man, Verrine Livirius, Lord of Ivalia, deserved respect, and she wouldn't dishonor her husband as to refuse Verrine this courtesy.

Darius' smile resembled a grimace, hands clenched tightly at his sides. A muscle at his temple twitched. "I trust that you have been well, Verrine?"

Verrine's serpentine smile widened. "Quite well, Your Excellency. The goddess has smiled upon us and bestowed us with

Her blessings this past winter. As you are doubtless already aware, our crops are looking promising this year."

"Very good." Darius offered him a curt nod, placing his hand behind the small of his wife's back, fingers splayed against her side. The movement wasn't missed, the lord's eyes darting to Nevia's waist before meeting her eyes. His smile remained in place, yet his eyes narrowed.

"We should be going back to the festivities, as should you, my lord," Nevia said tautly, hand resting against Darius' chest. "It was lovely seeing you."

She well knew it was not her place to dismiss him, and such was undoubtedly rude, but she hardly cared. She was more than ready to be rid of him.

Bemusement glittered in Verrine's eyes. "Well, it was lovely seeing you both prior to this evening's dinner." He adjusted his violet top hat, blond curls bouncing. "I look forward to the address that you give the people this fine summer solstice. I bid you adieu—"

"Wait"—Nevia reached out, her fingers catching his velvet cape.

"Yes, my lady?"

Her heart beat frantically in her chest as she swallowed down the panic. "Were you not looking for us? What was it that you wished to discuss?"

Another poison-laced smile greeted her. "Ah, yes, that. Well, it can wait until our delightful meal back at the palace. I don't wish to take away from any of the, ah, *fun,* that you two are having."

Nevia's bit the inside of her cheek, her fingers slipping from his cloak as he saluted the pair and turned to leave, sunlight pouring onto his shoulders. Two Ivalian guards tailed him, their boots ringing against the cobblestone—an ominous march.

Of course, it was just like Verrine to withhold vital information and ruin the festival.

It's just Verrine being Verrine, Nevia told herself as they wove their way through the square, the scent of fried cinnamon dough wafting through the air. *This is just his way. There's nothing that he could say or do that would truly impact me or make a difference.*

Nevia felt Darius' hand envelop hers, their fingers intertwining. She lifted her head to offer him a smile, but he wasn't looking at her, his attention diverted to the thousands gathered in the central square, a sea of brightly-colored garments and parasols. Nevia's breath hitched in her throat. That was a lot of people. Never did she think she'd get used to being the center of attention to so many.

A trumpet blared to life, silencing the lively chatter. The imperial anthem was played, announcing their arrival. Finally the trumpeter brought the instrument from his rotund lips, crying out in a hoarse bellow: "LONG LIVE THE EMPEROR AND HIS EMPRESS!"

The crowd parted and cleared a pathway to the ancient fountain, its clear waters sparkling under the relentless sun. The golden statue of the goddess stared down at them, judging, observing. Garments shuffled as all fell into a bow for their sovereigns. Such a display of respect was expected, but it still made Nevia uncomfortable.

He continued to hold her hand, despite knowing full well that such was inappropriate in public, and the judgment that he would earn. He loved her, and in that moment all of Nevia's fears of the prophecy ebbed away. He never could betray her.

Whatever came next, she knew it would never come to that.

CHAPTER 4

❝Citizens of Velspire!" Darius boomed over the crowd, standing on the wide, circular dais with arms spread wide. Saava's fountain gurgled at their backs, flanked by two imperial guardsmen with hands pressed at their sides. "Thank you all for gathering here today, where we celebrate the longest day of the year, a day of life, of love, and prosperity. Prosperity we have been granted for nearly forty years since my father, the late Emperor Rufus, secured this empire through tears and blood. Never shall we allow his sacrifices—and those of the brave men of our empire—be in vain. We shall remember them each and every day, and, most importantly, we shall do it in unity on this Saavis.

"As many of you are aware," he continued, "we have accomplished much since my father built this empire. Trade has been secured between our lands and the country of Sallais, something long in the making. With this came more jobs and opportunities. Our economy is stronger than it has ever been, as is our network of physicians working hard to better our understanding of science, and of the world.

"And yet, despite this nation stronger than ever, our borders more open than ever before, our hearts have not grown at the same rate. As a result, the people still struggle."

Murmurs broke the silence. Nevia watched as a man near the dais leaned in to whisper into the ear of his companion, and she caught the words "Zenoch" and "primal folk" in the same sentence. She forced herself to glance away, raging heart pounding.

"Let us not turn away from our neighbors, from our companions in humanity," Darius continued. "Let these people migrate into our society, and embrace them with open arms. Allow their children to attend schools without fear of judgment and discrimination."

The flicker of metal catching the light caught Nevia's eye, tearing her attention from Darius' speech and into the crowd. All faces were somber, absorbed in the emperor's speech, no one moving beyond a simple sway or scratch of a limb. A frown furrowed her brow, reasoning that it must've been the glint of someone's jewelry.

"Without generous hearts we don't have what it takes to be a prosperous nation, something that I hope to change during my reign—"

It glinted again, only this time closer to the dais.

A flicker of maroon robes disappeared into a cluster of young women, who seemed none the wiser. Nevia's fingers began fumbling at her waist, subtly unleashing the dagger which she kept concealed in her sash. She never left the palace unprepared—a learned impulse from living in the north.

"So, dear families and friends, I ask that you please consider joining me in—"

It all happened so quickly. Gasps echoed through the crowd, along with sickening gurgles as a man collapsed behind Darius on the dais, bleeding freely. A jagged knife rolled from his hand and landed at Darius' feet. Crimson splatters emblazoned Nevia's emerald dress, her own dagger resting in her palm. It was not her weapon, however, that created this mess, but that of the imperial guard behind them.

The guardsman strode forward, removing his sword from the assassin's chest with a squelch. A coppery tang permeated the air, and a pool of blood grew along the dais before dribbling down the side.

"My pardon, Your Imperial Highness," the guard said to the pale-faced Darius. "This man snuck through the crowds with a weapon and charged forward. He was trying to assassinate you."

"That was a mistake," Darius said evenly. And yet, despite his bravado, the color had not returned to his cheeks. After a moment of insensible, continuous nodding, Darius clapped the guardsman on the shoulder. "Well done, Gregor. I owe you my life."

The guard, clearly pleased, bowed lowly with a hand hovering over his heart. "It is merely my job, Your Imperial Highness."

The other guard scurried forward to remove the body, and it wasn't until they rolled him over that Nevia gave a start. She must have started to sway on the spot, as Darius threw out a hand to steady her.

"That is all for now," Darius said to the audience. "Please, let not this unfortunate event tarnish your joy, and continue with the festivities as planned. May the goddess smile upon you all. Thank you."

A chant of "LONG LIVE THE EMPEROR!" followed, but he was barely paying attention as he led Nevia off the dais and away from prying eyes, to which she did not protest. Her head was spinning both from horror and fear.

"Are you alright?" he asked finally.

Nevia cast a glance over her shoulder; two guards flanked their backs, which was understandable given their tenacious situation. She bit her lip, giving one swift nod before leaning into his side, whispering, "I knew that man. He's—he was a friend of my father's."

An uncomfortable silence lapsed between them, the grip on Nevia's arm tightening as he led her from the festivities and toward their chariot. Perhaps he'd lost the celebratory spirit, though more likely he sought privacy for them to speak. He ignored the bewildered footman as he wrenched open one of the doors of their ride, emerging in without so much as a backward glance at his wife. Shooting the footman an apologetic glance, she slipped beside him. Where she sought comfort, however, she was greeted with anger, his eyes ablaze.

"Do not *ever* repeat what you just told me."

A shiver went down Nevia's spine as she gripped her arms. "Of what, the incident?"

His gloves crunched from being clenched so tightly. "No. Of knowing the man that tried to kill me. Do not speak of it. Ever. Never again."

Something feral kindled underneath her skin, and she didn't know what overcame her when she blurted: "Mind telling me why you're silencing me?"

"A man from Zenoch just tried to assassinate me, Nevia. Me, not you, which makes things even worse because you share his heritage. And, on top of it, you know him. Imagine what sort of talk would arise if it were to become public knowledge. Just don't, don't say it again. Draw no connections to the man or yourself. I beg of you."

His insinuation filled her with sudden horror. "You don't think that I—I had something to do with this, do you?"

Darius ran a hand down the length of his face. "No, of course I don't, but the lords will. And if they turn against you, Neve"—his somber, chocolate eyes turned to her—"even I, with all of my power, cannot stop them from what they might do to you."

CHAPTER 5

The orchestra's lively music resounded through the golden halls of the imperial palace, flooding the corridor where Nevia stood waiting. She glittered in the dim candlelight, bedecked in her form-fitted evening gown of shimmering gold, train cascading along the tiled floor. Her pale hair had been twisted into a knot on the back of her head, tiny braids feeding into it while loose curls bounced playfully against her cheeks. A golden circlet rested atop her head, rubies sparkling like crystalized blood.

Nevia eyed the elaborate dining table from around the corner. Enough food was set to feed half of Velspire, yet only seven would be seated to dine that night, five of which already present at the table: finely dressed men, their brightly-colored suits emblazoned with their countries' emblems upon their chests. At the heart of the table a bowl of assorted fruit was placed, a display of wealth and abundance. Golden platters of bread rolls, meats, glazed nuts, and cheese were set at each end of the banquet, with bottles of their finest wine chilling in ice-filled basins. Silk napkins spun from the finest saffron fibers adorned each place at the table, along with cutlery and plates accented with gold.

"Your Highness."

She spun on heel to behold a man no taller than herself, blue eyes twinkling as they met her gaze. He offered her a soft bow, robes made from indigo linen sweeping the tile. "Might I be so bold as to state that you are the loveliest woman in the empire tonight?"

A laugh escaped Nevia. She cupped the man's cheeks in her palms, reaching on tiptoe to kiss the top of his smooth, bald head.

"You are too kind, Father." Her smile was genial. "But it is not the title of the most lovely I seek tonight. It is gaining approval I need. Darius takes the brunt of my shortcomings, and my heritage seems to be an exceptional thorn in his side lately."

"The blame, my dear, is not yours to bear." He reached for her hands and clasped them, his calloused and coarse in contrast to her own. "Darius knew the sacrifices that he was making by choosing to wed for love instead of status. He wanted to display unity, to weave our nations together. I believe Darius is wise beyond his years, thinking in ways that traditionalists aren't ready for."

Nevia shook her head, curls caressing her blushed cheekbones. "There may be some merit to your words, but is it not my responsibility to adapt to this society, to become one of them?"

"You owe it to yourself to be true to your heart. Let the people learn to love you for it, including your husband." He brought a hand to cup her cheek. "You are doing me proud, Nevia. I am sure your mother would agree with me."

A pained smile stretched her soft lips as she nuzzled her cheek into her father's hand. "Thank you, Father. This means . . . means a lot to me."

Footsteps sounded from around the corner, causing them both to look over. The emperor flashed brilliantly white teeth at them, his garments replaced from the festival finery to a golden suit embellished with burgundy accents. "Ah, there you are, my dear wife." He pressed a kiss to her temple and wrapped an arm around her stiff shoulders before offering his father-in-law a respectful nod. "Hello, Eja. I trust that you enjoyed the festivities in the square this afternoon?"

The elderly man gave a soft bow in return, folding his arms in his robes. "It was good, my son. I thank you." He lifted his head and pressed a kiss on both of Nevia's cheeks twice, a Zenochian custom. "Remember what I said, my dear girl. Have a good evening."

Nevia felt Darius cringe, as though the gesture personally offended him. She tucked her hand in the crook of her husband's elbow, allowing him to guide her into the dining room, watching as Darius gave her father a smile.

No, not a smile. A sneer. A threat. A warning.

When they turned the corner he dipped his head close to hers, lips pressing against her ear. "What *did* he say?"

Nevia was taken aback by his irritation. "Later, dear. For now, let us focus on being the emperor and empress the people expect and get through this dinner, shall we?" She offered him a genuine smile, and she truly meant the words that next slid from her lips. "Despite the challenges . . . I am glad to be standing by your side through it all."

His lips drew into a thin line, jaw clenched as she allowed her lips to graze his cheek, short beard scratching her chin. He responded by wiping away traces of her lipstick, not even looking her way. He'd slid behind his other mask again: his best impersonation of the ruler that he felt the Five Lords expected. Nevia hated this version of her husband, but she closed her mouth and merely smiled, because that was what she was supposed to do.

The music stopped as they emerged through the double doors, their shadows illuminated by the candles held in brackets along the walls. The Five Lords rose from their seats at the table upon their entrance, bowing their heads in respect. Light reflected their jewels and finery, which Nevia guessed was their best to impress their emperor.

"Greetings, Lords of the Androvich Empire," Darius' tone rang with authority in the silent chamber. "It brings me great joy that you could arrive and celebrate Saavis with us once again this year."

Darius led Nevia around the table, a servant pulling out a chair for her before doing the same for the emperor. As she sat her gaze met with that of Verrine, his narrow, serpentine eyes glittering with amusement.

"The pleasure is ours!" An energetic voice boomed from across the table, a jovial lord with short-cropped gray hair slinking back into his chair. Out of them all, Vladios of Malabria had always been her favorite, despite his reputation of drowning his miseries in liquor and failing to be sober, even in court. The corners of his eyes crinkled as he offered her a smile, short beard wrinkling around the edges of his mouth. "My dear empress, how good it is to see you again! Pray tell, how have you been? Have you been home to Zenoch over these past couple of years?"

Her smile fell at the mention of Zenoch, all breath leaving her lungs. Home . . . she hadn't thought of the northern mountain country as home in so long. Her lips grew numb, and the circlet about her forehead grew suddenly heavy.

"No, she hasn't, Vladios," Darius answered in her stead, as if she was incapable—or unauthorized—of speaking for herself.

The edges of her lips quirked downward, fingers flexing underneath the table. The eyes of several lords fell on her, as if they could detect her irritation threatening to escape and were eager to see what would happen next. She lowered her gaze to the tablecloth and silently dipped her head in assent.

"I see." Sorrow laced the lord's voice. "Well, over autumn, perhaps. Or maybe in the spring. It would do you good, I think, to smell the mountain air again and let your old acquaintances see that we didn't have you for supper, after all. You should take her, Sire."

A frown furrowed Darius' brow as his goblet was filled with wine by the servant over his shoulder. "Perhaps, though I will confess that I am not all too eager to get anywhere near the mountain range after what happened today."

Of course, the assassination attempt. Nevia grew silent, feeling that her own husband, who echoed sentiments of unity, was discriminating against all of Zenoch. Because one man tried to kill him, he didn't want to visit their lands. Her home. This buried a knife deep in her chest, a wound that none could see but still ached.

"Ah, but nothing came of it!" Vladios remarked. "You're here, and where is the assassin? Dead, so I would say the joke's on him. Would you not agree, Torquil?" He elbowed a tall, slender lord, whose long auburn hair framed his angular face, making him appear older than he was. He carefully folded his bony hands on the table.

"I think it was a disturbing development," Torquil responded. "I do not like that such an action was boldly made during your address to the people, Your Imperial Highness, especially one of unity, no less. This attempt will prompt more, as he has set an example that others will surely follow."

A throat was cleared further down the table; a rotund man with near-white hair and a curling mustache glanced up at them with beady dark eyes. This man was Lord Roark, of the central imperial country of Daltium. "Well, assassination attempts aren't exactly new. They happen all the time. The chief difference was that it happened so boldly, in front of everyone, and that the would-be assassin managed to come so close to his victim despite security measures."

Nevia fidgeted in her seat. Why would this man, a Zenochian trader who was an old acquaintance of her father, lash out against Darius in the middle of a peace speech? The kind man who once crafted a dreamcatcher with her favored turquoise beads specifically for her didn't seem capable of murdering her husband. It just did not make sense, and it troubled her.

"You seem lost in thought," Verrine observed, eyeing Nevia over a servant offering him fruit. "What have you to say on this matter, Your Highness?"

A test, one that Nevia would have to tread lightly upon to avoid unwanted scrutiny. Her palms snagged on the golden sequins of her gown. "I think it disturbing that my husband was nearly killed this afternoon," she said tersely. "And that my favorite dress is now tainted with that man's blood."

Lord Roark nodded solemnly. "Of course, this must have been deeply upsetting to you, Empress Nevia. I am very sorry that you had to witness such bloodshed firsthand, as well as the near assassination of your husband."

"Thank you, Lord Roark," Nevia said, relieved that he was sympathizing rather than laying blame. "It was rattling, but I will recover. Time heals all wounds."

Roark nodded, quickly shifting his attention to the servant about to walk away with a tray of caramelized nuts.

"I only find it troubling," Verrine began, shifting his attention on Darius, "that the assassin was Zenochian, a nation you were trying to aid in your very speech. We haven't had issues with those savages for some time. Why strike now? I would especially think that they would be at peace with us, given that our very own empress is one of them."

Nevia visibly winced, unable to contain her irritation at Verrine's insolence. Savages. . . . The Zenochians were *not* savages—far from it. Their way of life differed vastly from imperial customs, but that did not make them uncivilized by any means.

"We also don't know if he was acting alone or if this was but one body in a developing movement," Torquil added, hands steepled in front of him. "The guard's blow was lethal, so unfortunately no questions can be asked of the assassin."

The fifth lord who remained silent up until this point glanced up. "Do we know his identity?"

Lord Remus governed the southeast country of Sanvolk, the mountainous region within the empire. An observer with silent demeanor and passive face—it wouldn't have been surprising if he outwitted them all in brilliance.

"That hasn't been determined yet," Darius said, perhaps too fast, gaze flickering toward Nevia in warning. "But my plan is to reach out to a few of Zenoch's chiefs to see if we can determine which clan he is from. Just because one clan has a quarrel with us doesn't mean they all do."

A terse silence followed Darius' words as they all resumed their meal. Darius' face contorted as though his roasted vegetables had turned rancid, eventually allowing his focus to fall on Lord Torquil to his left.

"It has been a while, Lord Torquil." Darius paused to drink deeply from his golden goblet, eyes locked onto Torquil from over the rim. "You were always my father's favorite, and it saddens me that I haven't seen you since his passing."

The lord's knuckles turned white around his fork. He seemed composed enough, but Nevia knew the lord well enough to understand the arch of his brow and set of his thin lips suggested it was a struggle. "I apologize for my absence, Your Imperial Highness. It has been difficult to get away from home. There have been pressing matters in Asturia which have required me. While my wife does well at handling my affairs while I am away, I have felt it prudent to stay and do my part. I hope that my presence hasn't been missed too greatly."

"I'm afraid it has."

The orchestra continued with merriment, lively music from violins and flutes echoing off the ivory walls. Servants swept around the table, offering more food to fill emptying plates. Nevia helped herself to a slice of roast beef, sawing into the juicy flesh with her knife. Darius' plate remained untouched, hands folded in front of him. His attention remained riveted on Torquil. "I assume you won't mind my asking what kind of difficult matters you've been encountering at home? Not civil unrest, I hope?"

Torquil's hand fell as he reached for a dinner roll. "Nothing that I haven't been able to handle."

A tilt of Darius' head suggested that he sought more information, but none came. Torquil proceeded to slather his roll with an unhealthy amount of butter before taking a slow, savory bite. The emperor's lip curled in disdain—he did not like being ignored.

"If you need reinforcements, I have the entire imperial military ready to assist." He glanced at his own plate dismally, as though the very sight of food sickened him. "I am happy to support Asturia in any way that you need."

"You have my thanks, Your Highness." Torquil's voice was taut. "We have everything that we require, but I will remember your kind offer should my situation change in the future."

Their exchanges and pleasantries went on for some time like this, and despite the sometimes heated questions, Nevia thought things were going rather well, and was relieved when the assassination attempt wasn't brought up again. A glass of red wine was poured to Nevia's right, the servant's dark curls brushing against the empress' shoulders as she shifted away. Nevia murmured her thanks, wrapping her fingers around the smooth glass and bringing it to her lips. It was both tart and sweet, the perfect balance.

A throat was cleared across the table. Nevia glanced up to find Verrine staring intently at her, holding a wine glass of his own. He had the same sickening smile plastered to his face, raising the glass as if for emphasis. It took her a moment to realize his grip didn't match her own, the lord only holding it between finger and thumb. Nevia bit her lip; she had forgotten, instead having grasped it with the entirety of her hand. Another imperial custom. There were so many to remember, and many that she still was learning. Silently she adjusted her grip, before tenderly placing the glass back on the table and folding her hands primly in her lap. She felt humiliated and already wished to be excused from the table.

The orchestra began a peaceful rhythm, replacing vibrant, lively violins. Harp strings created a comfortable, slow atmosphere, as if the musicians adjusted the pace of the music to the meal. Verrine, Torquil, and Roark were engaged in heavy conversation pertaining to the Asturian summer diving squad and who would make the team, while Darius and Remus were discussing the mining industry in Sanvolk. Nevia absorbed fragments of each conversation, yet neither interested her. She sipped at her soup in silence, the final course of their meal. Leeks and carrots swam on the bowl's surface, the aroma of fresh rosemary and thyme filling her nostrils. She was grateful that the spotlight was not on her—for once.

Vladios, too, fell silent, well into his third glass of wine for the evening. If the alcohol was getting to his head, he did a clever job of concealing it. The empress shot Darius a smirk as Vladios accepted another glass from the attending servant, but he didn't notice, his attention solely fixated on what Remus was saying, causing Nevia to lean in and listen, as well.

"So you're saying that there were no survivors?" Darius' voice was dubious.

"Not very many," Remus responded. "The collapse of the mine was devastating and its news has traveled fast. I am surprised that you hadn't known of it before now."

Darius lifted his gaze, meeting that of his wife. "I have been so busy with other matters here in the capital that I'm afraid this accident hadn't met my ears."

Remus heaved a sigh, his fingers reaching for his goblet. "It only happened two days ago, so the incident hasn't made headlines in the papers yet," he admitted, "but apparently the collapse of the Mt. Skia Coal Mine left thousands missing, the majority of which is assumed to be dead. The mine went down at least a thousand feet into the ground, and many, many months went into digging it."

From across the table Lord Vladios let out a heady sigh. "Even with the labor force needed, which we no longer have, it would probably take six to eight months to uncover that kind of ground again."

Nevia pushed back her bowl of soup, sitting back in her seat. Thousands of coal miners, likely dead. The news numbed her, and it seemed from Darius' paleness he too felt its blow.

"How many operating mines do we have left?" A tone of urgency inflected Darius' voice.

Remus appeared hesitant. "About three operations in total, Your Highness, but none produce nearly as much as the Mt. Skia Coal Mine in Sanvolk. This is going to cut our coal production to roughly a third of what it was."

Alarm flickered across Darius' face, his knuckles turning white as he clasped his hands together.

"As I'm sure you're aware at this point," Remus continued, "that is nowhere near enough to get us through the winter, especially if we are to provide aid to the neighboring countries in Danaeca, as you already pledged."

Darius sat back in his seat, running a thumb and forefinger over his short-cropped beard. "This news is troubling." He turned toward Roark. "And how is your new coal mine coming along? When do you suppose you can start production?"

"Relatively soon, Your Highness," Roark said. "My hope is to have operations running at the start of winter, but it is a small mine with limited resources. I suspect we would only be able to provide coal enough for maybe half the homes in Velspire, if being generous."

"What about instigating withholding measures on coal usage?" Vladios offered. "We could ration our supply, stretch our coal well into the winter, and maybe even have some to share with neighboring countries as a result."

"No, I will not compromise what belongs to the people in order to divvy out more resources to other countries," Darius replied sternly. "That would be unfair, and would put undue hardship on our already hard-working imperial families. There must be another solution to this problem."

"Adding to what His Excellency said," Verrine spoke up, "instigating a limitation on resources would only create anxiety in the people, further raising red flags that something is wrong and not having enough fuel to go around."

"What do you suggest, then?" Nevia asked.

All fell silent, even the orchestra as they shuffled on the stage to begin the next piece. This one was slow and melodramatic, once again following their pace.

"Well, I have one suggestion," Torquil said, hesitant. "But I am not sure it will get us anywhere, or be of any particular use." All eyes fell on the auburn-haired lord, whose gaze fell to the table under such scrutiny. "We could see about investing in some of the Feishin Kingdom's resources. You know, their everlasting core shards."

Tension filled the table. Vladios busied himself with arranging his plate in a ridiculous fashion, while Remus excused himself from the table. Looks were exchanged among the remaining men.

"Very little is known about these core shards," Darius said warily. "Rumor has it that they're everlasting and don't burn out, but no one in Danaeca has ever seen them, let alone been able to prove that they exist."

The core shards. . . . Nevia had indeed heard of them. A fabled resource burrowed deep within the heart of the Feishin Kingdom, an island located across the Eastern Sea which kept to themselves. The shards' existence came to light after one of their guardsman returned from holiday after visiting his Feishin mother. The story remained dubious, even if there was little reason to foster such a lie. Little was known about the country's affairs since they declared themselves independent of Danaeca a little over a hundred years ago, and visitors were not welcomed, making confirmation of the shards difficult.

"It's a vital resource if it never burns out." Verrine splayed his palms on the table as he rose from his chair. "And I think it's time the world knew about this material, if it indeed exists. It isn't something that the Feishin Kingdom should keep to themselves."

"Well, the Feishin Kingdom, while independent, still shares a sea with us," Nevia said, "maybe its queen would consider sharing her resources if she knew the dire circumstances we're in."

"I'm not convinced this would change her mind," Darius spoke warily. "But I suppose you all are right. A conversation with Queen Arethusa wouldn't hurt."

The lords seemed to pretend that Nevia wasn't there as they further discussed the shortage, which was just fine with her. Remus returned to the table, neatly dabbing at his mouth with a napkin as he inquired as to what he missed, and Vladios, in his own words, filled him in on the details. "Since the Feishin Kingdom has magical crystals we're going to go over there and ask their queen to share. It's only fair. If *you* had magic, wouldn't *you* share, Remus?"

Remus merely blinked, alarmed, wiping stray strands of wispy gray hair from his eyes and surprising everyone when he poured himself another glass of wine. He seemed distressed, though whether from the coal situation or Vladios remained uncertain. "Magic is outlawed in the empire."

"They aren't really magic," Verrine drawled with an eye roll. "Please. It's just some kind of energy source that the Feishin Kingdom is hoarding."

The dinner conversation droned on well into the late hours of the night, the empress' back aching from sitting so rigidly throughout the evening. When she was convinced that her presence wouldn't be missed, she silently slid from her seat and began to move from the banquet table. Only Remus took notice of her. "Retiring for the night, Empress?"

"I believe so," Nevia responded, dipping her head. "It has been a rather long day, and my head is paining me."

"I blame the wine!" Vladios interjected, now on his fifth glass.

Both spared him a glance, before Remus turned back to her. "Well, then I pray that you have a good night. It was wonderful to be graced with your presence, Your Imperial Highness."

The fact that he'd acknowledged her with such honorifics warmed her heart, a display that he truly viewed her as his empress.

She offered him a genial smile. "Thank you, Lord Remus. The pleasure was all mine."

She allowed her hands to graze Darius' shoulders, daring to sweep a kiss on his cheekbone before shifting away. For a moment they merely stared at one another, before irritation crawled under her skin. He pursed his lips and looked away from her.

"Goodnight," she offered, expectantly.

He barely waved a hand in acknowledgement, once more turning to Verrine. The lord of Ivalia offered her a wiry smile, one that she didn't give him the satisfaction of returning. He seemed to be savoring her rejection.

Nevia smoothed her hands over her hips, trying to conceal her disappointment as she drew in a shuddering breath. She turned and glided over the checkered tiles of the dining hall, her train of shimmering gold slinking behind her.

"You know," she heard Vladios say from the doorway, followed by a hiccup, "you could've at least kissed her goodnight."

CHAPTER 6

It felt strange and yet wonderful to tend to herself for once, with Elante still away with her family for the festivities. While a bath sounded heavenly, Nevia felt too tired to fetch hot water, thus she made do by simply changing out of her formal attire, allowing her gown to slink onto the hardwood floor in a heap around her ankles. She felt her hairpins free themselves as she tugged her cotton nightgown over her head, causing her thick tresses to tumble over her shoulders. She ran her fingers through her hair numbly, lips pursed into a pout as she exercised feelings of resentment toward Darius. She didn't know what she expected from him; maybe a kiss goodnight, as Vladios so boldly suggested, or a reassuring smile or pat on the shoulder. A deep sigh escaped her as she flung herself on the plush bedspread, her weight sinking into the soft mattress.

Darius was two sides of a coin, torn between duty and love. Perhaps it was a shortcoming of his that he conducted himself in this manner, or maybe it was Nevia's own failure that she didn't operate similarly. Her mother had always taught her to be true to herself, and it was something she held close to her heart, regardless of the ire it garnered.

The gentle evening breeze rustled the sheers of the twin windows along the eastern wall, carrying with it the scent of honeysuckle from the gardens below. Her thoughts soon became jumbled, one thought blurring into the next as sleep threatened to claim her. She didn't even have time to slip under the sheets before drifting off into slumber.

Nevia hadn't heard Darius enter. Her dream had her tracking the legendary roc bird, traversing the depths of a cavern adorned with crystals shining like fluorescent green lanterns. The rocky terrain had started to give way under her feet, and that was when she felt Darius' weight on the mattress shift her toward the center of the bed. She inhaled sharply, body and mind returning to the present. She didn't feel like interacting with him, not after what happened. Soon she felt his warmth curl around her. A shiver coursed through her, partly from the cold, but mostly from his touch.

Nevia felt his finger run down the length of her spine. Caressing, coaxing.

"Mmm," she murmured, feigning sleepiness. "Can't it wait till morning? I'm rather tired."

"I'm afraid it can't."

Nevia rolled onto her back, nearly crushing him, arms folded under her breasts as she peered into his face. His brown eyes were tender, sorrow etched into his features and the set of his jaw. No longer did he wear the finery from the dinner, instead dressed in simple trousers and nothing more.

He brought a hand to cup her cheek, and her anger ebbed away. In that moment his imperial title was nowhere to be seen. He was simply Darius—the man she loved.

"I am so sorry for how I treated you." His voice was low, dark lashes batting as his gaze faltered. "You were trying to be sweet and I shoved you away. You deserved way more than that, Neve. I have wronged you terribly."

Nevia bit her lip, keeping her hands to herself despite how much she desired to intwine them into his attractive dark hair. "With me you are one way in private, and a very different way in front of others, especially around the Five Lords. Do you really have to be so two-faced? It's hurtful."

Darius grimaced while propping himself onto an elbow. His hand traveled from her cheek and strayed to her abdomen, tracing one long stroke after another with his finger. "I don't know how else to be, Neve. I'm trying, really I am, but I know that they have expectations of me, and I'm failing in most of those."

"I think you're overcomplicating things all the time," she said, ignoring the aching yearning in the pit of her stomach from his touch. "Just, maybe try? Be yourself?"

"I don't think they will accept it," he said somberly. "I . . . guess I never thought through how I was going to pursue our marriage as well as fulfill the expectations of the people, and I'm sorry, Neve."

"You've been doing this balancing act for years," Nevia interjected. "Surely I thought you would've learned how by now, but it feels like you've just gotten worse."

Darius hung his head in defeat. "You're right, I have. But I will not stop trying. I will always continue to try. Will you forgive your foolish husband, and allow me one more chance?"

The incline of his head gave her pause, the way that his bangs clumped together and fell forward into his face. Nevia's anger could not hold out against his charismatic charm, and she found herself cupping his face, raising herself to press her soft lips on his own.

The emperor's breath hitched, his lips inviting as he returned her passion with equal fervor. His hand fled from her stomach and entangled into her hair, fingers locking into her soft strands as he drew her closer. The butterflies in her stomach had been freed, now permitted to flutter through her entire core as she wrapped her arms around his neck, deepening the kiss and pulling him down toward her. Very soon she found herself cocooned in his arms, cradling her entire body close to his bare chest.

Their arms and legs tangled, their kisses growing more desperate. Nevia pressed a hand against Darius' smooth back as he coated her neck with kisses, his tongue running down the hollow of her throat before he pressed a kiss against it. His hands roved the length of her thighs, underneath the sheer fabric of her nightgown, traveling along her smooth bronze skin and grasping her round hips. He caressed them tenderly as he drew her closer against his form, their hip bones grinding together. The throb within her lower torso intensified, her longing culminating as she threw herself against him, letting out a soft moan as he stroked her inner thigh, slowly running his hand further up to her core.

With garments cast aside, their tender flesh connected, it was only her and him, two souls intertwined as one. All titles, and everyone, could wait. It was only them that mattered in that moment as their bodies pressed together, sharing a bond they reserved for only one another.

CHAPTER 7

Dawn's first light poured forth from the windows, casting long, radiant beams along their discarded clothing and onto the sleeping forms entangled under the covers. Nevia lay awake, taking in the sandalwood scent of her beloved beside her. Her head rested on his strong, muscular bicep, her arms tucked against his chest. A soft smile played on her lips at the realization that he'd held her the entire night.

He planted a kiss on the top of her head, causing her to stir.

"Sorry," he murmured, stroking the soft skin between her shoulder blades. "I didn't mean to wake you."

She kissed his cheek in response. "I was already awake." He turned his head, forcing their lips to meet. Freeing her arms, she wrapped them around his torso, pressing her breasts to his chest. "I was just thinking about the day we first met."

He stroked her hair, finally murmuring under his breath: "When I had nearly mistaken you for a deer and shot at you."

A coarse laugh escaped her. "Right, yes, and then you were angry because I made you lose your prey."

"And then we spent half the day talking about how wrong hunting for sport was."

"We only spent ten minutes on the subject. We then talked about dreams and politics, and that was when I fell in love with you."

He pressed her tight against him, and she could feel the thrum of his heartbeat under her cheek. "And I fell in love with you the moment you tried to stop me from pursuing that deer."

They continued to lie there for half an hour, reminiscing about the past and discussing their dreams for the future. Darius craned his neck to catch a glimpse of the grandfather clock propped against the wall and let out a reluctant sigh. "I have to go soon. I need to speak with the council about our upcoming voyage."

"I know." She proceeded to run her fingers through his hair. "But at least we won't have to contend with the lords anymore."

She felt Darius grow still in her embrace, causing her to lift her head. His chocolate eyes were glazed and unfocused, the edges of his mouth tugged into a frown.

She sat up, disheveled locks tumbling over her breasts. "What is it?"

"Well, about that"—his gaze darted across the room, avoiding her—"Verrine proposed to come along."

"He *what?!*"

"And I, being the kind, generous emperor that I am, agreed."

"Why on earth would you do that?!"

Darius finally looked her way as she wrenched herself from his grasp, instead folding her arms with a scowl. He let out a sigh, allowing his hand to fall. "I was being sarcastic. He didn't exactly give me a choice. I tried to insist that we didn't need him, but he wouldn't take no for an answer."

"You know that he's just going to make your life miserable, don't you?" Her expression was pleading. "He's the worst of them all."

"You're right, he is." His affirmation surprised her. "Which is why I must tread with caution. He is always putting me to the test, and this will undoubtedly be the ultimate one. I must be cautious on how I handle this particular situation. You know that he's great at causing a ruckus."

Nevia looked down. "You're going to have to pretend you loathe me again, aren't you?"

"Oh, Neve, Neve, Neve." He breathed her name, wrapping his arms around her shoulders and drawing her close, ignoring her hesitation. "You know how much I love you, don't you?"

"Not enough to prove it to the lords, it seems."

She didn't mean for the scathing words to escape her lips, but they did before she could stop them. Immediately she regretted it.

His gaze darkened and grip slackened. "Do you not remember our conversation at all from last night? I'm trying, and I will continue to try. I just ask that you please . . . please be patient with me. Especially on this trip. I am feeling a lot of pressure right now."

"Why now, and not before?"

He shifted under her weight, leaving her on the satin sheets as he rose from the bed. She watched the muscles in his shoulders grow taut as he threw open her wardrobe, searching for something to wear. Finally he settled on a robe of deep burgundy, one of the few garments that belonged to him within her armoire. "It's nothing worthy of discussion."

Nevia fumbled for words, watching him dress not helping matters. She crawled to the side of the bed, crossing one leg over the other.

"I'll try."

Dark eyes met with hers. "Try what?"

"To be patient. I'll try to accept that you're working through a lot of pressure and learning to balance an empire and your wife."

His expression softened, relief evident. He padded over to her, running a hand through her web of hair before kissing her. She wrapped her arms around his neck, drawing him closer and deepening their kiss. A chuckle escaped his throat as he threw out a hand to steady himself, lips moving from hers as they brushed noses affectionately.

"Thank you, Neve. For your patience, but most of all for believing in me."

His whiskers grazed her cheek as he left her side, sweeping across the room and toward the doorframe. The door swung open as he begun to reach for it, and from where Nevia sat she recognized Elante's high pitched laugh, the familiar lilt of her voice. Quickly she snatched up her forgotten nightgown from the floor, yanking it over her head gracelessly before her handmaiden stepped past the emperor and entered.

"Good morning, milady." Her smile was bright, dark locks neatly tucked into her usual braid as she dipped into a curtsy. "I trust that you were well last night without me?"

Nevia hugged her knees to her chest, recalling the details of last night. Heat rose to her cheeks as her thoughts fled to her and Darius' passionate lovemaking, but that was not what Elante was asking. "Quite well, thank you, but I still need you by my side. Especially after you see what I did to my hair."

Elante lifted her head marginally before her jaw fell in horror. "Milady! Whatever did you do?! That will take hours to arrange!"

"I'm . . . sorry?"

Her handmaiden stood there fussing, muttering to herself that only the empress could get her hair in such a state. "I'm going to need a raise if I'm going to continue taming this wild mane of yours."

Nevia laughed, piercing through Elante's irritation, and allowing a smile to replace her scorn.

"Okay, I forgive you," Elante teased. "But please consider wearing the nightcap, please? For me?"

"It would probably come off in the night, anyway," Nevia insisted.

"Highly unlikely." Elante's lips pursed, but she didn't continue the argument. She dragged Nevia up and away, behind the rice paper dressing screen where she selected her garments. The empress crossed her arms over her bosom as Elante prepared the laces on a midnight-blue gown, a chill coursing through her. Her gaze traced the whorls and petals on the thin, translucent screen, a faint light filtering through and kissing her skin.

"Will you be coming with me?" Nevia asked finally.

Elante drew the dress over Nevia's head in one swift, skillful motion before her nimble fingers deftly laced the back of the bodice. The empress jerked whenever Elante tightened a lace. "Where to, milady?"

Hesitation crawled under Nevia's skin, wondering how much would be wise to share with her, despite how much she trusted her. Apart from Darius, Elante was her best friend. Never would Elante dream of betraying her or compromising her safety, but that didn't mean word of their predicament wouldn't spread, especially within the gossip circle of royal servants.

"To the Feishin Kingdom," Nevia responded simply. Much to her relief, Elante didn't inquire further, the handmaiden's brow furrowed in concentration as she perfected the knot at the top of her bodice.

"I didn't know that you were leaving," she said. "When will you depart? I should prepare your belongings for travel."

"That I don't know," she responded, shaking her head. "But I believe as soon as possible."

"I see."

The tugging ceased, Elante having finalized her hard work and permitting Nevia to move freely. She stretched her arms over her head, shaking out her mane before walking out from behind the screen.

Elante shifted her braid off her shoulder, dark eyes fixing on her friend. "Well, worry not, milady. I will have a trunk prepared for you within the hour, so that is ready for you whenever you do decide to set off." Her smile wrinkled the corners of her mouth. "And I would be delighted to accompany you, of course. I will go wherever you go."

Nevia reached to squeeze Elante's hand, yielding a grateful smile. It would be a relief to know that Elante would be there, regardless of what Verrine did. And if Darius failed at balancing his allegiances again, which she secretly knew he would.

CHAPTER 8

After three weeks had passed without word from the Feishin queen, Darius and his council chose to depart for the island. Nevia did not think it wise to encroach the Feishin Kingdom without first awaiting correspondence from Queen Arethusa, but her opinion fell on deaf ears.

Seaspray kissed Nevia's face as she stood upon the deck of The *Dauntless*, their trusty vessel for the voyage. Her paint peeled on the sides of the splintering bow, and yet despite her haggard appearance she was a dependable ship.

The shrill cry of seagulls filled the air, wings outstretched as they circled the ship, enthusiastically seeking their next meal. The rhythmic rise and fall of the ocean waves soothed Nevia's frayed nerves, her gaze falling out to the sparking cerulean sea which stretched on for what seemed like forever. How she adored the ocean—it rejuvenated her soul.

She turned from the ship's railing and wrapped her arms around herself, hands coursing down the length of her sheer shawl. The air was much cooler over the waters than on land.

"Cold, milady?"

Darius came up alongside her, shedding his own cloak to wrap about her, with a tenderness that suggested she was as fragile as a flower. The soft burgundy velvet smelled of sandalwood, much like him, and brought with it a warmth that blossomed within her heart. She shifted a smile in his direction, their gazes locking before he stole a glance at her lips.

Before he could act on this impulse to kiss her, a throat cleared behind them.

"It *is* a rather chilly day, isn't it?"

Verrine stood directly behind them; Nevia suspected he took it upon himself to follow them, as it seemed that was where he was always found. The folds of his violet cloak flowed over the faded wooden planks as he strode to join them at Darius' side. He drew in a sharp breath of salty air. "I have always loved sailing, don't you? We should make some time to do something pleasurable while we are out here, make a vacation of this. Do you not agree, Your Highness?"

Darius flinched, and momentarily Nevia wondered if the sea spray managed to reach him. "That does sound like an extraordinary idea"—his tone reflected otherwise—"though sadly

I won't have as much free time as I'd like. I need to focus on what terms to negotiate with the Feishin queen. If I come in without any expectation it will be all too simple for her to play me like a fiddle."

A pleasant smile lingered on Verrine's lips. "I would be happy to help you with that! That's why I'm here, remember?"

Nevia rolled her eyes, her mood for pleasantries spoiled rotten. She shrugged off Darius's cloak and extended it to him, head bowed lest her irritation show. "I will see you later." She didn't lift her head once as she shuffled belowdecks, not wanting to see Verrine's smile or hear his snide remarks. He'd won her husband over, and she would now be cast aside.

Again. Like always.

The ship swayed amidst the ocean's turbulent waves, and the empress threw a hand against the wall to steady herself. She could feel the wrinkles of the nautical wallpaper underneath her fingertips, the warmth of the lanterns illuminating sketches of anchors and lighthouses. Nevia was grateful that the sea didn't make her stomach lurch, a plague all too common with the fine ladies of the imperial court as she discovered last year in the companionship of high nobility. Only Nevia and Lady Vera, Lord Roark's wife, were able to withstand the voyage without needing a basin everywhere they went. It made for a rather unpleasant journey for everyone.

Her room was the one she'd always used when aboard the ship. The door's rusty hinges screamed in protest as she swung it open, revealing a lone window draped with gray curtains. A trunk with her belongings rested at the foot of the bed, pinewood floorboards exposed save for a faded mauve rug in the heart of the room, its pile short. Nevia gave a start when her boot collided with a moving object in the center of the rug, which groaned in response and shifted. Nevia's features contorted with concern as she knelt by the heap, realizing with sudden horror that it was Elante. She pressed a hand to her forehead; it was clammy and cold with sweat.

"I'm sorry, milady," she whispered, closing her eyes tightly. "I can't handle the motion."

"Shhhhhh," Nevia urged, helping her handmaiden into her lap, stroking her damp, loose strands away from her face. "Don't worry. Here, let me help you."

Elante, too weak to protest, allowed Nevia to heave her off the floor. The empress was grateful for her handmaiden's slight figure's making it possible for her to hobble to the mattress and set her down on the creaky thing. She fluffed the pillow and tucked it under Elante's head.

"This is wrong." A croaky laugh escaped Elante's throat. "This is your bed. I couldn't possibly—"

"No one has to know." Nevia sharply tucked the cotton quilt on either side of her. "You tend to me when I am sick, after all."

"Yes, because you're my lady!"

"But I'm also your friend," Nevia reminded her. "And today I'm going to take care of you."

"But it's so very wrong!"

"Not if I say it isn't."

It seemed that Elante couldn't come up with a protest to *that*, much to Nevia's satisfaction. Besides, taking care of Elante quieted her restless mind, her thoughts of Darius and Verrine fading into the background. She seized a tin pitcher of water from the nightstand and poured a glass for her handmaiden. "Now, I will go fetch you a basin. Do you need anything else while I'm away?"

The young woman drank deeply, draining her glass in record time. She leaned back against the pillow. "A strong plank, maybe? Something to render me unconscious for the remainder of our trip?"

Nevia punched her shoulder playfully, causing her servant to laugh—how she adored that laugh.

"Right, so a basin, but I'll bring some tea too." She backed towards the doorway. "Don't go anywhere. I'll be right back."

Ghastly pale, Elante closed her eyes, fingers twisting the edge of the quilt. "Trust me, you have nothing to worry about in that regard."

CHAPTER 9

Nevia chose to allow Elante to rest in her room, instead retreating to Darius' quarters for the night. He certainly did not mind the company of his wife in his bed, though he was curious what prompted her to stay.

"The sea isn't treating Elante well," she explained simply, leaving him on the bed to slip on her robe. "So she is staying in my room."

His dark brows knitted together into a frown, propping himself on his elbow. "Don't the servants have their own quarters that she could rest in?"

Nevia shrugged on her slippers. "I'm sure they do, but not as comfortable, and this way I can check in and make sure she is taken care of."

The empress didn't stay long enough to see Darius' lips thin, or the anger that contorted his expression. Instead she slipped off to the kitchens, procuring a tin platter of porridge and tea for Elante and making haste to her bedroom.

The stench of sickness assaulted Nevia's nostrils the moment she opened the door, her handmaiden's sallow face a sickly shade of green. Nevia sucked in a breath, wasting no time in cranking open a window, forcing the glass frame forward and allowing the saltwater breeze to fumigate the space. She feared the scent of the sea may further nauseate her friend, but she was willing to risk it.

Elante managed to push herself up the length of the pine headboard, forcing a smile to stretch her pale, cracked lips. "Good morning, milady. I don't suppose we're nearly there?"

The empress allowed her weight to sink on the mattress alongside her, the bedsprings groaning in protest. She stroked her dark hair from her face, then reached for the damp cloth that she had left along the bedside table to blot at her forehead.

"It will be a bit still, I'm afraid," Nevia said with remorse. "We likely won't be there until tomorrow evening. But you will be better soon. Once you get used to the rocking it won't be so bad."

A groan was the only response that Nevia received, her handmaiden plopping against the pillows dramatically. The empress ignored this, instead lifting the bowl of porridge. It was still hot, the aroma of maple and cream filling her nostrils. "I have something for you."

Her handmaiden perked up slightly, glancing over her nose at the bowl within her mistress' hands. Her dark eyes roved from the bowl to Nevia's face, considering. Finally she extended her hands, cupping them to accept the meal.

The slurps and sips as she downed the contents of the bowl were music to Nevia's ears. Color seeped back into Elante's cheeks, replacing their once sickly hue. She swiped her mouth with the back of her hand, her tongue tracing her lower lip. "You are too good to me, Empress. Few nobles would offer their servant such accommodation."

"You are more than just my servant." Nevia leaned forward and wrapping her arms around Elante's tiny frame, pressing their foreheads together. "You are my best friend, too."

For a moment the young woman looked as though she might cry. "And you're mine," she whispered back. "But it would be grossly inappropriate for a woman of your position to be friends with a lowly servant such as me."

"Well, I'm doing a pretty good job at breaking the mold." Nevia snatched the empty bowl from Elante's lap with a wink. "Being best friends with my handmaiden shouldn't be too much of a stretch."

Long shadows danced around the room, the pale orange glow fading from the window as the sun rose higher. Nevia swept over to her trunk, shuffling through her belongings. She pushed aside shoes and a hairbrush, finally procuring a simple cotton dress, one of her only garments that didn't require someone to lace up the back for her.

"Is Verrine behaving himself?" Elante asked, face pointed at the ceiling to avert her gaze. Nevia made it no secret that she disdained the lord.

"So far, so good," Nevia tugged at the waist of her gown, trying to get the princess seams to lay flat against her ribcage. Her fingers ran along the length of her ruffled neckline, which swept low to reveal a fair amount of cleavage and any jewels that she chose to wear. "He's behaving as well as a serpent can: flicking his tongue and hissing every now and again. So far he hasn't bitten anyone, but I'm certain that this is only a matter of time."

"Milady, *really.*"

"I'm being serious! Have you not seen the length of his tongue?!"

Giggles from the bed caused Nevia to crack a grin. She procured one of her favorite sapphire necklaces from her jewelry box, lifting her blonde waves to fasten it around her neck. The silver swan-shaped pendent lay perfectly between the outline of her breasts. "But seriously, I'm sure that he has some fine qualities. I have only been fortunate enough to see his serpentine ones. He doesn't like me."

"I'm not so sure that he doesn't like you"—Nevia didn't have to see her handmaiden's face to know that she was frowning—"I think he perceives you as a threat, so he doesn't know how to handle you except with a sharp tongue."

"I didn't know that you were a Verrine fan, Elante."

Elante sighed, rolling onto her side. "It's not that. I just think he could be your ally if you let him in."

Nevia's stomach hurt. She didn't want to think about the Ivalian lord any longer.

"You should get some rest," Nevia suggested, eager to leave the conversation behind. She stole a glance toward her handmaiden; she looked so small and fragile, one hand curled on the pillow beside her head. While her complexion was much improved, her face appeared sallower than usual.

"Thank you again, Your Highness." Elante's eyes fluttered closed. "You are too good to me."

The empress felt her heart swell. She brushed Elante's hair behind her ear. "I am only doing what you would do for me."

The warm evening air greeted the empress as she emerged above decks. Her pale blue skirts brushed against the faded lifeboats, only a minimal breadth away from the railing. Their worn wooden planks had once been a nice shade of blue, yet now stood sun-bleached, paint peeling along the edges. Thick hempen rope snaked across the floor and trailed down a trapdoor, leading to what Nevia assumed were the sailor's quarters—an escape rope, she identified.

At the ship's bow stood her husband. The folds of his cloak billowed in the sea breeze, his broad shoulders taut as he gripped the ship's railing. She noticed him tense as she drew a step forward.

Nevia swallowed the lump in her throat. "If my calculations are correct, we should arrive at the island this afternoon. Is that true?"

His gaze didn't waver from the sea. "It is. The wind has been at our backs. We should be there in a matter of hours."

A relieved sigh escaped Nevia, grateful that Elante would soon be free of her suffering. She strode over and rested her head against his shoulder, folding her arms neatly around the crook of his elbow. "That's good. Elante has been so sick."

The emperor drew in a sharp breath and pinched the bridge of his nose, drawing her gaze upward. Fury pinched his brows together, his temple twitching. "When will you start behaving like an empress and stop waiting on your servants?"

Nevia recoiled from the malice in his tone. "What?" Surely she misheard him. She knew that it was inappropriate for her to tend to her handmaiden, but didn't think it would earn her such ire.

"I said," he repeated, tone cold enough to freeze water, "when will you start behaving like my empress? You are making a fool of yourself. You might not care, but *I* do. It has been the talk of everyone throughout this voyage. How do you think that makes you look, makes *me* look?"

"You're concerned about your *image* when Elante is sick?"

"Your image, my image. It is the same difference." He waved a hand irritably. "I have been patient with you, Nevia. I understand this is a different culture, and your role as empress is very different from how you were raised in your backwater tribe"—Nevia winced at the casual slur—"but you have been here for two years now. At this point you should understand how a person of your status must behave and what is expected of you."

"What's wrong with caring for my servant?! What ill does it display on my character?" Nevia demanded, her voice rising in anger.

A sharp clang filled the air as his heavily jeweled hand clashed against the metal railing. "It displays that you're weak, and that I'm even weaker for making you my empress!"

"Then maybe you should've thought about that before you married me!"

A deadly silence fell after her callous words. Nevia was too late to realize the gravity of her mistake. She grasped his arm but he wrenched himself free, gaze penetrating the rise and fall of the limitless sea.

"Darius, I—"

"Don't." His voice was deathly low "Don't criticize my decision to wed you. I hear it from everyone else, and I don't need you to start."

"Darius, listen—"

"No. You made it clear. I don't need or want to hear more from you."

Nevia wrenched his arm from his side, fingers digging into his bicep. She desperately fought to make him face her. "You know that I didn't really mean it like that."

"I said *stop!*" He tried to escape her grasp, but Nevia wouldn't yield. They struggled, arms interlocked. Nevia finally grasped the front of his tunic and wrenched him close. If he would just *look* at her, only listen to her! Finally Darius' gaze met hers, a cold flame kindling within his eyes, snuffing out the warmth that Nevia adored. The rubies on his fingers flickered in the sunlight as he raised his hand, bringing it down to strike her face with such force that she couldn't help reeling back. Her hand fled to her cheek, her flesh angry and hot under her fingertips. Tears began to well in her eyes, not from pain but shock. Darius' lips tightened, face contorted with cold fury.

"Don't ever question my decisions again."

His velvet cloak brushed her side as he spun on heel, leaving her without another word. Her legs buckled out from under her as she slid down the metal railing, rust snagging at the fine latticework of her bodice. She drew her knees to her chest, rocking back and forth and letting out a strangled cry.

Never had he crossed that unspoken boundary between them: to physically do her harm. Seldom did he ever raise his voice, but to strike her? She knew that she'd pushed him too far—but he'd gone too far, too.

CHAPTER 10

The island of the Feishin Kingdom glittered to life as the imperial ship coursed toward the shoreline. Tips of the city's colorful onion-dome rooftops soared into the clouds above the stone wall surrounding the kingdom. The setting sun cast a golden halo around the island, the sky painted shades of pink and sherbet orange. Lampposts illuminated the docks, and it wasn't until they drew closer that Nevia realized they weren't lit by flame but instead narrow wire encased in glass orbs, technology that the empress had never seen.

Their ship had barely docked when they were surrounded by Feishin guards, dressed in black leathers and turquoise tunics. The Feishin emblem of a lotus and three orbs rested upon the left breast of every man and woman. Both genders wore their hair long, carefully tied back from their pallid, angular faces and dark eyes.

One of the women in uniform approached their ramp, hand on her hip. Her dark red ponytail swayed over the shield on her back. "Greetings, travelers. What is your business in the Feishin Kingdom?"

The rhythmic tapping of a cane answered. A portly man no taller than Nevia hobbled down the ramp to greet her. His balding head was concealed by a maroon cap, his burgundy imperial uniform accompanied by a golden robe suggested he was a high-ranking member of Darius' court. He had been advising Darius ever since he became emperor, as he had done with his father before him.

"Hello, noble guardian," Prometheus greeted, neither friendly or warm. "I am Sir Prometheus Volchek, advisor to His Imperial Highness Emperor Darius Androvich the Second. We hail from the Androvich Empire in desire for an audience with Her Royal Majesty Queen Arethusa."

The female guard's eyes flickered toward the ship, where Nevia and Darius stood waiting.

"I was not expecting members of the empire," she murmured lowly. "Her Majesty has not informed us that you would be arriving."

"Ah." Prometheus snatched off his cap and begun wringing it in his gnarled hands. "My apologies. We notified Her Majesty of our arrival via letter weeks ago, but perhaps we made better time than the post. We sincerely apologize for the surprise, but surely she would not mind indulging in a quick conference of a matter of grave importance?"

"A grave matter?" the woman repeated. "Pray tell, what is this grave matter that could be so important?" Her tone reeked of sarcasm.

A harsh, high laugh escaped Verrine, whom had remained on the deck until then. His boots clicked along the ramp as he fell alongside Prometheus, his smile flickering with malice. "Mmmm, I am afraid that information is private." He looked down the bridge of his nose at the Feishin guard, expression dour. "It is only for Her Majesty and her royal council to hear, which I'd assume is not you?"

The woman's lip curled upward into a sneer, exposing bared teeth. "Let me remind you that you will not be entering our land unless you can convince me to let you through. So, despite my *lowly* rank, I suggest that you humor *me,* as I'm the one standing between you and an audience with the queen right now."

Nevia couldn't help but grin as she watched Verrine squirm, the smile fading from his face. "But of course. I suppose you must protect your country from invaders and the like."

Her expression hardened. "We take border security very seriously here."

"Yes, yes, I can see that." Verrine lobbed his head to the side. "Very well, allow me to indulge you: Danaeca is currently in the middle of an energy crisis, and we wish to confer with the queen on energy sources of her own, as well as seek aid for those suffering within our continent."

Her brows furrowed as she processed the information. "Wait here. I must confer with my colleagues."

The Feishin guards spoke in hushed tones, in clicks and sounds unfamiliar to Nevia. She realized that they must've been speaking in their native tongue, Tolsi, which none onboard would've understood even if their words could be heard.

After several tense moments the female guard strode back to Prometheus and Verrine, hands clasped behind her back. "We accept your proposal to speak with Her Majesty." She gestured towards the large green gates behind her. "You are welcome guests to the Feishin Kingdom. Let us escort you to the Wind Palace, where Her Majesty will be informed of your presence."

Leaving the crew and servants on board, the four followed a pair of Feishin guards along the winding path, beyond the oxidized copper gate and into the dusk-covered city. Lampposts illuminated their walk every few yards, which Nevia was grateful for lest she stumble on a patch of overgrowth that wound its way through the path of mortared clay bricks. Civilians traversed the streets clad in garments that gave Nevia a start. Both men and women were dressed in trousers and brightly colored tunics, something which would've garnered great disapproval in the empire for both flamboyance and immodesty.

They were brought to a halt before a carriage with no horses, its steel painted a light shade of gray. The front jutted outward, though Nevia was uncertain on what such a compartment would be used for. Curious glances were exchanged between Verrine and Darius, though neither man said a word.

A Feishin guard opened one of the doors for them, revealing seats of black velvet on either side. Prometheus and Verrine were the first to take the social cues and enter, finally followed by Darius and Nevia. The fuchsia drape along the window rustled as the door was closed behind them, which Nevia wasted no time in throwing open. She could feel the carriage shift as more weight was loaded in front of them, followed by the light hum of machinery. The carriage began to lurch forward, homes scrolling past their window, along with a carriage fashioned exactly as their own. Nevia saw their two escorts sitting in the front of their carriage in a rectangular box seat, one clutching and steering a wheel before him. A frown furrowed her brow; what curious machinery this was.

"The Feishin people have technological advancements beyond our own, Your Highness," Prometheus reminded her, as if detecting her thoughts.

"Incredible," Nevia breathed.

They traversed through several shopping and residential districts before rolling to a halt in front of a gate not unlike the one barring entrance at the coast, its arching base scrawled with weathered writing in Tolsi.

" 'Pass with a heart of peace and understanding,' " Verrine cited, glancing up at the loops and scrawls of the text. "It is a famous Feishin proverb."

"Interesting." Darius folded his arms over his chest. "How old is it?"

The door to their coach was opened, allowing them to pour out into the manicured gardens of the Wind Palace. Verrine's nose scrunched in confusion at Darius' question, smoothing down his coat's lapels as his boots met with thin blades of grass. "The gate or the writing, milord?"

"Well, both."

"Hundreds of years, at least. I cannot be too certain, really." Verrine spun to one of their escorts, tapping him on the shoulder until he glowered. "Hey, erm, I don't know your name."

The frown on the escort's face deepened, lines etching themselves on his youthful face. "My name is Itari."

Verrine's face brightened as he gave Itari's shoulder a tight squeeze, the latter looking like he wanted to crawl away and die. "Ah, good! Itari! How old is the gate and the inscription?"

His hooded eyes roved the length of the quote, rereading it before providing an answer. "It was inscribed by our ancestors about a millennium ago," he explained. "The founder of our nation wanted this island to be one of peace, free from the wars that waged within Danaeca and the famine that came in its wake. King Feishin, The First King, believed through a heart of understanding, compassion, and peace that anything could be achieved."

"I did not ask for a history lesson," Verrine harrumphed. "I only wanted to know how old it was."

Itari's eyes flickered with raw emotion, but he held his tongue to Verrine's abrasiveness. Instead he strode away, throwing down a latch and causing sounds of gears to come to life. The gate slowly opened, its doors retreating inward to grant them passage.

They passed blossoming trees, stray pink petals fluttering daintily in the evening air. The Wind Palace was perched upon the tallest hill on the island, with no protection from the winds that would grace the coast. Its pale ivory walls reflected the amber light from the surrounding lampposts. Elegant sheers rustled within the arching window frames, the scent of jasmine and green tea wafting through the garden.

Greeting them was a woman in a sweeping gown of turquoise, her gray hair pinned high and waist cinched by a dark violet obi belt. Their escort shuffled forth, blurting a quick line in their language before understanding dawned on her face. She turned to the newcomers with a wide smile. Welcoming at first sight, but dangerous upon further examination.

"Welcome, imperial friends, to the Feishin Kingdom." She folded her arms into her bell sleeves as she spoke.

"Thank you for the warm welcome and accepting our arrival on such short notice." Prometheus strode forward, drawing himself to full height. "We are pleased to be here in your beautiful kingdom."

He promptly introduced himself and the others, to which the woman responded with a courteous dip of the head. The silver ornaments on her belt clinked with her movement, jade earrings catching the edges of her collar.

"My name is Rumaar Teniel, Prime Minister to the queen. It is a pleasure to meet you." She held out her hand, which Prometheus accepted awkwardly, being unfamiliar with the Feishin greeting of a friendly handshake.

"It is a pleasure, Lady Teniel," he replied. "We look forward to our stay. And once more, I apologize for arriving prior to our communications. A message was hastily sent out after the summer solstice, but it seemed either intercepted or delayed—"

The woman's smile didn't falter. "Oh, no, it was received." Nevia had the chilling feeling that the smile would linger even if she spoon-fed them poison. "Her Majesty just felt it best to keep the correspondence confidential. Most are not aware of your communication."

"Your discretion is appreciated," Darius spoke up, edging closer to the pair. "Since you are aware of our predicament, an audience with Her Majesty sooner rather than later would be greatly appreciated."

"That can be arranged." Teniel waved a hand to dismiss Itari before clasping the folds of her long gown, leading them inside. "You will have to forgive me for asking you to wait in the hall while I prepare the queen for your audience. It should not be long." Her sharp gaze collided with Darius. "Unless, of course, you require rest or refreshments before meeting with Her Majesty?"

"No, we will be fine," Darius spoke quickly. "I would like to see the queen as soon as possible."

With a curt nod, they were brought inside, passing halls bedecked with murals from various periods in history, some seeming to date back to The First King. Nevia was particularly drawn to a tapestry depicting a battle between warrior and dragon, whorls of blue, violet, and crimson surrounding them. The domed ceilings yawned high above their heads, held up by ivory-colored columns made from the same marble as the flooring.

They were brought to a halt before twin oaken doors, magnificent in height and nearly twice as tall as Nevia.

"If you will excuse me." Teniel's voice permeated Nevia's thoughts, snapping her from her awe. "I will inform the queen and be back momentarily."

CHAPTER 11

Nevia's footsteps echoed across the tapestry-covered walls of the throne room, passing by polished golden statues of revered Feishin deities on either side of the cerulean-blue runner. The room was massive, twice that of the empire's own council room. The walk felt as if it stretched miles to reach the other side to the dais, where a pearl throne perched atop marble steps awaited them.

The Feishin queen sat regally upon her throne, the flecks of silver adorning her deep burgundy hair like fine wire. Her stern angular features were accentuated by the twist of her ruby-red lips, sharp eyes of the deepest hue of ebony watching them as they approached.

Teniel bowed lowly before the queen before flourishing a hand in the direction of the imperials.

"Your Majesty," she greeted. "I have brought the emperor and his entourage."

Nevia hitched up her silken skirts and paid her respects to the Feishin queen by dipping into a low curtsy. Verrine and Darius seemed to settle for a respectful tilt of their heads, their left fist against their hearts. Both were more customary gestures in Danaeca. The queen's dark eyes glittered as she settled them onto Darius, her tongue running over the edge of her teeth.

The queen crossed her legs, dainty bare foot dangling. "Welcome, Darius, to the Feishin Kingdom. I don't believe that you have ever stepped foot onto Feishin soil before, have you?"

Darius shook his head. "No, Your Majesty," he responded. "My father has come to visit you and your shores, but never I. I apologize for not having come sooner."

The queen casually waved her hand. "It's quite alright. I am sure that you have had plenty to do after your coronation and your father's untimely passing. And then there's your marriage which coincided with all of it." At this, she offered Nevia a genial smile. "I believe that was the last time I saw you both: on your wedding day. I appreciated the invitation. Not many in Danaeca think of me in their affairs."

"That is unfortunate," Darius said, to which the queen merely shrugged.

"It is understandable. I keep to myself, and it is only natural for many to find me unapproachable. Not you, it seems, especially seeing as you've invited yourself to the kingdom."

Darius locked gazes with the Feishin queen, and Nevia wasn't certain if he was being challenged by that statement, the intensity of their staring contest radiating from them like a campfire at full burn.

It was Verrine that broke the uncomfortable silence between leaders. "We invited ourselves with good reason, Queen Arethusa." The queen snapped her head in Verrine's direction, as though she'd forgotten he was there. "We are suffering a crisis in Danaeca and are in desperate need of your assistance."

"Yes . . . the coal shortage." The queen's polished red nails clicked together as she clapped her hands, garnering the attention of her handmaidens. They bowed lowly to the queen and began shuffling themselves out of the grand entrance, filing between Nevia and the others. The guards at either side of the dais remained, and the way they shifted suggested they had no intention of leaving.

Arethusa flung her legs and rose, dark leather coat unfurling down the length of her back, brushing her ankles. She tossed her head to the side carelessly. "Pray tell, Darius: what do you think caused the coal shortage this year? This has never happened in the history of your father's reign. What changed to lead to such a crisis?"

All eyes fell on Darius, who fumbled to answer. He looked to Prometheus as if seeking his council, but the elderly advisor remained silent. "A disaster occurred in our most productive mine, and to make things worse we have stretched ourselves too thin," he confessed. "My empire has lent support to surrounding countries within Danaeca that have been unable to help themselves. We have tried to strengthen our relations with our neighbors and provide the resources they lack but desperately need, but this has proven to be impossible given the mine collapse. Not only will we fail to provide for our neighbors, but we will not even be able to keep our own homes warm this winter."

Arethusa pondered Darius' words, a pencil-thin eyebrow arched. "It sounds very much like you have created a mess for yourself, and instead of confessing to your mistake and suffer its consequences you want me to come in and fix it. Is that right?"

Darius' fists unfurled. The statement certainly struck a chord.

"And in your letter"—she flourished a hand—"you expressed an interest in Nephyl, the material that we recently discovered at the heart of my country."

"You mean the core of *our* planet," Darius corrected coarsely.

Arethusa smiled, exposing white teeth that were a perfect contrast to her deep lips. "No, young emperor, I mean *my* country. The material was found while mining for minerals, having been pushed up from the heart of Gaia. My scientists were unable to identify the material, determining it has never been seen before. We believe it is a gift from the gods themselves, something to reward our efforts of unity and peace within our kingdom."

"A gift." Darius scoffed, folding his muscular arms across his chest. "More like you found it surfacing from the core of the planet, and it happened to occur on your island, nothing more."

She waggled a finger to silence him, which he had the smarts to do. "Do *not* belittle the gods," she warned. "This is precisely why you found yourself in this predicament, and why you will always struggle in Danaeca. You and your people think yourselves higher than divine law, sneering down at blessings and allowing your greed to control you. Unlike you, however, we have kept our greed in check. We have only taken what we need, and no more. We could choose to mine deeper for this material, to sell it, trade it, grow prosperous from it, but we have deliberately chosen not to." She stepped down from the dais so that she stood a mere few feet from Darius, a head shorter than he.

"Excuse me, Your Majesty." The empress didn't know what overcame her when she decided to interject, arresting the attention of everyone in the room. Arethusa's intense gaze fell upon her like a strike, the darkness of her eyes engulfing her. Nevia's tongue felt like cotton in her mouth. "This may be foolish, but what are these core shards, really? We have only heard the rumors."

Arethusa merely stared as though she'd grown an additional head. "I suppose it couldn't hurt to indulge you in this: it is a material that possesses tireless energy, believed to be charged with the life of the planet itself. A small shard can provide energy for locomotives and heaters, provide lighting, and more. The Nephyl that we've extracted has served all of our needs, and will continue to do so for as long as my people continue to follow the principles that govern this land."

Nevia frowned, realizing that Arethusa was quite devout to her own narrative. She now understood why the Feishin Kingdom was so segregated from the rest of society. They *wanted* to be segregated because they believed everyone else was corrupt. Such a dangerous and yet contagious mentality. She shot a glance toward her husband, wondering what his next move would be. They barely scratched the surface of this negotiation, but it appeared the queen was shooting it down before it even began.

The Ivalian lord shuffled forward, the soles of his boots soundless as they sank into the plush runner. "If you don't mind my saying so," Verrine voiced hesitantly, the first time Nevia witnessed him anything other than arrogant, "your statement was riddled with propositions and carries no facts. There may be no truth to anything you're saying. We have no proof that this was from any divine being, let alone the gods which you worship."

The disdain in Verrine's voice at the idea of her gods was undeniable. While differing from their own beliefs, such disapproval should've been concealed, Nevia thought. Arethusa's eyes burned like freshly ignited coal as they bore into Verrine.

"There is more to faith than proof and hard facts. Sometimes you must follow what is in here"—she placed a hand against her heart—"with the evidence presented to you. That is proof enough."

Darius shifted uncomfortably. He, too, must have realized things were turning south quickly. "I am loathe to ask this of you, Your Majesty, when I have done nothing to gain your favor and have little to offer in return, but I come pleading for you to help us. We are looking at a very cold winter without your assistance. People will starve and freeze. Many lives will be lost, and we will have to refuse aid to those countries that were depending on us.

"We come to you not as another country, but as other humans seeking help from those that have the means of supporting us. Yes, I have made many mistakes during my reign. I have promised help when I should not. But I have a good heart, and it is my sincere wish to help everyone, most especially those unable to help themselves."

The emperor dropped to one knee, chin lowered to his chest. He knelt there humbly, lowering himself into subservience before the monarch. The queen's pallid visage softened as she looked down the bridge of her small, pointed nose at the emperor.

"It is my belief," he continued, "that you also have a good heart, Your Majesty. You display it with your every action in bringing your people the best mode of living that you possibly can, not seeking revenge over the death of your husband at the hands of the Zenochians and instead choosing peace and forgiveness, embracing the Feishin ways to the fullest and maintaining prosperity for your people through your selflessness."

Her lips twisted into a grimace, causing Nevia to cringe. Bringing up the queen's late husband, King Athilan, was a dangerous move, and yet the tears that dampened the queen's eyes were without malice. Darius kept his head bowed, not allowing himself to see if he were making progress.

"Please don't let my faith in you be in vain. Come through for me and I promise that I will be there for you in return."

A dangerous promise in a world of politics, and Arethusa must've known it, too. The queen stooped down and gripped Darius' chin, slender fingers grazing over his short-cropped beard as she tilted his head to meet his eye. Hers glittered; not from cruelty, but unshed tears.

"I will not need anything from you," she said lowly, "my people have everything that we need, and it will continue to be this way so long as we do not meddle in the affairs of careless men who seek vengeance and fruitless conquest by warlords. However, I can see that you speak with a sincere heart, and I am touched by your words. I have underestimated you, young emperor. You are not your father's son, as I had once assumed, and I like that."

Darius' throat bobbed, the color of hope flooding his face. The queen ran her tongue over her bottom lip, contemplating, considering.

"Come with me." The queen released his chin and rose, her leathers brushing his cheek. "I want to show you something."

They all moved to follow when she paused, shoulders stiffening. "This is only for the emperor's and empress' eyes. I ask that the rest of you stay where you are."

"I am afraid that I must insist on accompanying you," Prometheus blurted. "I am here to keep His Highness safe, and it would be unacceptable for me to allow him out of my sight, alone and unaccompanied by an imperial guard."

Arethusa turned around to face the advisor, deep wrinkles creasing her forehead. "If I wished him harm he would already be dead. No harm will come to him."

A chill coursed through Nevia's spine at Arethusa's bold claim, how casually she assumed she could discard the emperor at a whim. A confidence emanated from her; a woman who knew her place in the world. She was Arethusa, queen of the Feishin Kingdom, and everyone loved and respected her for it. Nevia's intimidation by the queen shifted to admiration, wishing that she too could exude a similar air.

"I trust her," Nevia said, words slicing through the tension like a knife. "I will go, if Darius will not."

A deep scowl lined the emperor's face as his gaze flickered over toward her, vein bulging at his temple. She recognized that look. He was irritated with her—again. But instead of cowering, Nevia held her head high, meeting his gaze with a tilt of her chin. A silent challenge.

"Very well," Darius said at last. "We will accompany you. Lead the way."

She beckoned for them to follow her across the chamber, the queen's coat offering little to conceal the swell of her hips. As they strode from the throne room one of the queen's handmaidens awaited them. She sported a red slipper in either hand and knelt before the queen, slipping them over her bare feet. The queen barely acknowledged her presence, offering a simple nod of thanks before continuing.

"The mine is located directly beneath the palace," she explained to them.

They wove through corridors lined with elaborate, colorful silk tapestries, through another hall where the scent of fried dough wafted through the air, indicating the kitchens were nearby. At the end of a long, otherwise un-noteworthy corridor lay a stone platform situated in the center of a cold, barren chamber and encapsulated by a brass railing. An attendant stood sentinel over a lever with gears and switches, and upon approaching Nevia noticed a rope tethered at the base of the platform to some mechanism above, the darkness concealing it from view.

The ground swayed under the empress' feet as she followed the queen onto the platform. She braced against the railing, fearful that its tether would snap at any given moment and send her plunging into the depths below. Darius gave her a sideways glance, shuffling into the corner and folding his arms across his chest. She could've sworn the tug of his lips suggested amusement.

"Your Majesty." The attendant bowed deeply from the waist. "Will you be traveling to the excavation site?"

"Yes," she responded. "Take us there at once."

The attendant's gloved hands curled around the lever. "Please hold on to the railing. The descent can get a little bumpy."

The platform jerked, and Nevia's knuckles turned white from her tense grip. The sterile white chamber surrounding them disappeared as they sank through the floor, replaced by sheets of stone and jutting rock. Soon the light above became a distant beacon overhead, the party encased in darkness save for twin lanterns on either side of the railing.

The air was moist and thick here, the scent earthy and carrying a musty odor. The chasm seemed to stretch on infinitely, until the clinks of pickaxes met their ears, the faint glow of small lights illuminating the cavern below. The attendant cranked the lever, slowing their descent until they came to a jolting stop.

Beyond the railing a narrow tunnel stretched onward, its decline delving deeper into the earth. Lanterns along the walls illuminated the space, making visible the earthen walls and dirt-smeared faces of the men and women hard at work, elegant features concealed by a thick layer of grime. They wore headgear outfitted with glass-capped headlamps seemingly powered by Feishin technology, something Nevia knew to be dangerous normally with an open flame if they encountered any gases.

The laborers didn't acknowledge their presence as the three walked past, the ground rickety and uneven under their feet. To their left were buckets filled to the brim with iridescent, uncut opals that caught the lantern's light and shone like rainbows. Their beauty stole Nevia's breath away.

Eventually the tunnel's mouth yawned wider, opening up into a chasm that shimmered like an enchanting sea of green lanterns. It took Nevia a moment to realize there were no torches; the glow emanated from the walls themselves.

Before them stretched a deep crevice, green shards protruding from the rocky terrain. Their intense glow illuminated Nevia's bronze face as she sucked in a breath, awestruck. The material's pattern was similar to quartz crystals—the shape, the opacity— but Nevia didn't have to be a scientist to know that their composition was drastically different. The crystals poured forth from the crevice and stretched along the walls, as though the earth underneath could not contain it from spilling and infecting the ground above. At her side was her husband, his face illuminated a sickly, eery shade of green and struck with awe.

"Only authorized personnel are permitted here," Arethusa explained. "Few have seen the natural occurrence of Nephyl, so consider yourselves lucky. This is what we found at the heart of our island, our blessed source of energy for the past decade."

"It's"—Darius glided his hand along a wall glazed over with Nephyl—"more beautiful than anything I've ever seen."

CHAPTER 12

A smile crept over Arethusa's lips as she watched the emperor, enraptured by his surroundings as though he was a child.

"It's quite the sight to behold," Arethusa agreed. "Perhaps, with the combined efforts of your nation, you too will be gifted with this limitless energy one day."

Darius' gaze flickered onto the queen. "Perhaps," he obliged, his tone dubious. "But nothing like this has ever been recorded anywhere in Danaeca. I think it may be something that only can be found here. Perhaps it is your positioning on the globe that grants you access in reaching Gaia's core. Nonetheless"—his gaze fled back to the protruding shards—"this is an incredible discovery. You truly should share this with the world. This could change the way we live our lives. It could change everything."

"Nephyl is a gift from the gods," Arethusa responded coolly. "Do you share gifts when they're given to you?"

"Sometimes." Darius set his jaw. "Especially those that would be for the greater good."

A chill filled the cavern as a momentary, uncomfortable silence washed over them. When Arethusa next spoke, her words were laced with a lethal calm. "You haven't demonstrated that yet."

Nevia let out her breath. "Forgive us, Your Majesty. We just are marveling over this incredible material, and we want to help the world evolve, much as your kingdom has evolved over the span of the past decade. This technology, those automatic, horseless carriages—"

"Automobiles," Arethusa corrected.

"Yes, yes, of course." Nevia nodded enthusiastically, excitement building. "Isn't it a part of your principles to help others? Can you really justify keeping this a secret from the rest of the world?"

She was treading on dangerous ground, which would either get them somewhere or backfire, but Nevia felt they had little to lose. They were already doomed to fail; it couldn't get much worse.

"There is more to it than that, Empress." Pain laced the queen's face as she closed her eyes, and for a moment Nevia saw her true age behind the graceful beauty, the six decades that lined her face. A queen who had endured great hardship over her reign and still continued to show up, to see her people happy. "I firmly believe that this is the same energy that fuels our world, the very life force of Gaia. Do you really think mankind, as selfish as it is, would be satisfied with a fraction to fill their needs, or would they see this as a means to gain wealth, fame, and power? Where would it end?"

Her words rang with truth, even if Nevia wished to deny the uglier side of humanity. The queen rested a slender hand on the empress's shoulder, gaze somber. "If I were to share this wealth with the world, wars would break out. People would fight and kill for this power. Nephyl would be extracted faster than it can accumulate, until there is nothing left to fuel the planet. I fear—I fear that revealing this material may sentence the death of Gaia, a responsibility I do not wish to shoulder. Surely you cannot blame me for my hesitation?"

It seemed that Arethusa *had* considered sharing the wealth, but saw the consequences of doing so. Nevia dipped her head, unable to meet Arethusa's eye any longer. Suddenly she felt small and ashamed for being there, thinking that they could ask for this substance to solve their problems.

The shard's inner light danced off Arethusa's angular features as she turned to the emperor. "I'm sorry that I cannot help you in the manner that you'd hoped, but I trust that you understand the delicate position I am in. I must proceed with the utmost caution, and I can't have Nephyl leave the island. We do, however, have emergency stores of coal. Not enough for all your needs, but enough to fill two of our freight ships which could set sail on your heels tomorrow."

Disappointment shadowed Darius' face as his shoulders slumped. Perhaps, despite the risks, Darius hoped that Arethusa would sympathize with his predicament and come to his aid. Even still, he would need to display some amount of gratitude for her generosity. He dipped his head.

"This. . . ." He hesitated, searching for the words. "Is quite the honor, Your Majesty. I am humbled by your generosity. Thank you."

A simple nod was all Arethusa offered, withdrawing her hands to fold them in her wide bell sleeves.

"We can offer payment for the coal," Nevia said quickly. "This is so very much appreciated, and will help us tremendously."

She bowed, platinum hair shifting over her shoulders. The emperor remained rigid at her side, though finally followed into bending into a bow from the waist. "I echo my wife's sentiments. We're very grateful for this aid. Though I am saddened that I will no longer be able to stay good to my promises to our neighboring countries, it was my own mistake. I can't expect you to fix my problems for me."

"We all make them, young emperor," she reassured. "I certainly have, as did my late husband."

Her expression grew solemn, Nevia's quickly following suit. She understood that the late Feishin king was a sensitive topic for her, and she was not going to further pry and cause her more grief.

"Thank you," Darius said at last. "I just hope that the rest of the continent will be as understanding as you."

They strode back the way that they came, the three of them wholly silent save for their footfalls that would occasionally scrape against granite. The empress fell in step with her husband, trying to meet his eye, and when she did it surprised her to see a glimmer of determination kindled within them. She offered him a smile, and it felt as if a weight of iron was lifted from her heart when he returned it. The emperor snatched up her hand and tenderly brought it to his lips, thawing something frozen inside her. While she had yet to fully forgive him for striking her, she could finally envision them forging a path forward. Perhaps they would be able to have a long conversation that evening to sort things out. She was certain the tension of their situation contributed to their earlier outburst, no matter how unjust the outcome was.

Nevia drew closer to Darius, willing him to wrap an arm around her. He pinned her against his side, his beard snagging on her thick tresses. Hope bloomed in her chest that everything would go back to the way it had been, especially since a compromise with Queen Arethusa had been struck.

They found the rest of their entourage waiting for them in the foyer of the Wind Palace. A chill hung in the crisp evening air, sending a shiver down the empress' spine. Upon sight Prometheus visibly relaxed, glee evident on his face, and against one of the other marble pillars stood Verrine, seemingly bored as his gaze traced the latticework along the ceiling's edge. He kicked off the pillar as they approached, raising a single brow in question toward Darius.

The disappointment on Darius' face was brief but evident. A slight shake of the emperor's head was all the confirmation that Verrine needed to twist his lips into a frown and dip his head with understanding.

Arethusa cast off her leather coat and shoes, handing both to her handmaiden. She was none the wiser to the exchanges that occurred behind her. The red satin of her pants hugged her curves as she glided up the steps, her movements slow and deliberate. Once seated upon the throne, she flung one leg over the other, fingernails scratching the invisible layer of lacquer upon the armrests. She turned a critical eye on them.

"Use this gift well," she said. "I wish you a prosperous reign, young emperor. I will have Sara escort you back to your rooms, and will send word for our cargo ships to be loaded and deported to your shores. Will you be needing any further accommodations for the voyage back to Danaeca?"

Darius shared an uncertain look with Prometheus. The advisor piped up in his stead. "No, we should have everything that we require, Your Highness, but I thank you for your hospitality. The ship is in sound condition."

"Very good, then." She clapped her hands together and a young serving girl appeared from seemingly nowhere and folded herself on the ground before the Feishin queen. "Please take our guests back to their quarters and ensure that they have everything they need. Further, gather a parcel of fresh fruit for them as a parting gift."

Nevia felt Darius' fingers slip into hers as they departed from the throne room, snaking around the palace as they were led to a set of rooms. Nevia withdrew her hand to part ways, but was surprised when Darius' grip only tightened.

"Will you come to my room?" he asked. "Please?"

Nevia sucked in a breath, thinking, chewing on her lower lip. Prometheus passed by in the background, quiet and meek, while Verrine gave Nevia a surreptitious look as he too went past. The soft folds of the brocade curtain partitioning her room from the hall caressed her fingers as her hand fell.

"Yes, I will be right there," she responded. "I just need to get my things."

Darius nodded, expression tight. Concern wove its way around her heart. What was he not saying?

Puzzled, Nevia went into the small, cramped room assigned to her. The space lacked adornments, with a single mat on the floor for sleeping and a worn desk pressed against the opposite wall. Her thoughts were so jumbled that she let out a cry of surprise when she noticed movement in the corner. This in turn made her handmaiden jump, dropping her pincushion and the empress' silk nightgown in a heap on the floor. The rickety chair in front of the desk groaned slightly as Elante collapsed back, pressing a hand to her heart.

"Honestly, Empress." She slumped over to retrieve the nightgown, setting it back in her lap to finish mending a seam. "You gave me quite the fright." Her needle punctured the fine fibers, and she didn't think it was a coincidence when she yanked the thread so forcefully it snapped.

Finally she lifted her head and shot Nevia a sympathetic look. "Your cheek looks painful."

Nevia had almost forgotten about the mark that Darius' outburst left, fingers fluttering up to caress her cheekbone. Her gaze flickered about the rudimentary room in search of a mirror, only to find none, the closest being the surface of water within a clear pitcher. The swelling had gone down, replaced by an angry purple bruise.

"Is it really that bad?"

Elante sighed defeatedly, setting the gown aside to rummage through Nevia's trunk, searching her belongings until she procured a cylindrical tin of ointment. Unscrewing the lid released the pungent fragrances of arnica and calendula into the air. A simple wave of Elante's hand was all the guidance that Nevia needed to seat herself upon the wooden trunk, slumping over as her handmaiden dabbed ointment over her bruise with a pinky.

"I'm surprised that the Feishin queen didn't ask you about it," Elante admitted. "I think it's pretty obvious what happened."

Nevia blinked. "And what do you think that is?"

"That he hit you." A bitterness filled Elante's tone, her cheeks flushing with fury. "Something happened on that ship. You were upset and not yourself ever since. And he hasn't been himself either. It isn't really my place to say more, except that I'm so sorry, Your Highness. I am sorry for what he did to you."

The empress could only stare ahead stonily. Were the circumstances really that obvious, or did Elante simply know her almost as well as she knew herself? Did everyone else figure it out as readily?

"That . . . isn't what happened." The lie escaped Nevia's lips so easily that it startled her. "I tumbled over Darius' belongings in the dark and slammed my cheek on the trunk. I'm embarrassed that you think he struck me."

She cursed herself inwardly for the haughty tone that she took on. Elante's expression only grew more somber as she tended to the bruise. As she drew away, her work complete, Nevia caught her hand and pulled Elante so that she faced her. Concern widened the handmaiden's brown eyes.

"Don't repeat this to anyone," she whispered. "Please. For my sake."

The way Elante pursed her lips made Nevia think she'd refuse, but instead she let out a long, frustrated sigh, slamming the tin of ointment on the pine desk.

"He should never do it again," she said with such loathing that it made Nevia's chest burst with affection and terror. Her thoughts were a jumbled mess. If Elante knew that he'd done it because of her. . . . Nevia shuddered at the thought.

Stifling the chill that coursed through her, the empress rose, hands wringing each other. "He wanted to see me, so I'd better go and see what he wants."

Elante raised a brow. "You're not going to change first?" She gestured toward the pale blue nightgown. Nevia stared at it a moment, thinking she should, but instead shook her head.

"No, too many people will see me immodest down the hall."

All the breath left Nevia's lungs as Elante threw her arms around her in one final embrace, drawing in Elante's warm scents of citrus and cinder. She swallowed back tears that threatened to surface, emotions from the previous day threatening to lay claim to her. Finally she pulled away, drawing in a shaky breath before leaving the room swiftly and stalking down the hall to her husband.

CHAPTER 13

The brocade curtain to Darius' room was drawn wide, making it easy for her to find him along the corridor of matching curtains. His legs were folded underneath him on his sleeping mat, scrolls of worn paper scattered in front of him. His maroon jacket had been discarded onto the sitting cushion beside him, leaving only his white undershirt, v-neck cut low and exposing his chest. He turned to glance at her, chocolate eyes devoid of their usual warmth.

"Neve." He snatched up one of the scrolls and coiled it before she could steal a glance at its contents. "I'm really glad that you came. Thank you."

Her hands remained clasped in front of her, chin held high. "I figured it must be important if you had a need for me," she responded, unable to keep the chill from her tone.

If it bothered Darius, he didn't let it show. He kicked out his legs and patted the mat, gesturing for her to sit alongside him. Her hands flexed irritably at her sides, but eventually she allowed herself to sit, yet maintained as much distance between them as possible.

He only moved closer. "I assume that you must be mad at me."

Nevia could've laughed. Mad? That barely scratched the surface of her emotions. She folded her arms. "I am hurt."

He exhaled sharply. "I figured that it was something like that."

Something unleashed inside of her, emotions pouring forth in a torrential downpour. "You told me off, Darius. You *hit* me. How was I supposed to take that? What were you thinking?"

Silence. Nevia dared herself to glance up, and was surprised to find Darius' face buried in his hand, shoulders sinking. His form shuddered, and it didn't take long for Nevia to realize that he was sobbing.

She bit her lip in irritation, and yet guilt gnawed at her insides like a relentless itch. Was she to comfort him? But how could she, when he was the one who brought this upon himself? She held her hands together in her lap, suppressing the wild urge to stroke his back or soothe him. She curled her lips inward, forcing herself to remain silent.

"You're right," Darius said weakly. "I am losing my way, and in the end I am going to end up hurting everyone. Most especially you. I am a worthless ruler and an even worse husband."

Nevia swallowed, mouth dry. She turned her face away from him.

"The pressure that is being placed upon me, Neve, you cannot imagine. Verrine has threatened to challenge my position as emperor."

"He cannot do that."

"Yes, he actually can, if the lords feel that I am making unfit decisions they have the power to force my abdication and appoint a new ruler, and he has reminded me every step of the way that I have been making numerous bad decisions. The coal shortage is but one of them, my promises to help Danaeca being another."

"Also your marriage?"

His silence told her everything she needed to know. She shook her head and started to rise, but was halted when Darius grasped her knee, willing her to stay.

"He thinks that I should've sought a marriage alliance with Queen Arethusa's daughter, Princess Mila. That way we would've woven bonds with the Feishin Kingdom, strengthened our position, and carved a pathway for technological advancements akin to that of the kingdom."

"But she's barely of age!" Nevia seethed. "She's only, what, fifteen?"

"Sixteen last month," Darius corrected, as if this made a great difference. "What's more is that he's telling me it isn't too late."

Nevia's heart threatened to stop. "What, divorce me?"

Darius looked pensive, perhaps knowing that he would receive Nevia's ire if he didn't proceed cautiously. "Well, he's been reminding me that polygamy is commonplace and acceptable here in the Feishin Kingdom—"

"*What?!*"

His fingers dug deeper into her knee, as though sensing her irritation. When she began to wrench herself from his grasp he braced her shoulder and drew her close. Nevia blinked. How she hated herself for finding his face so helpless, so lovable, in that particular moment.

"I reminded him that *I* don't believe in it, and that it goes against my marriage vows to you," he told her in desperation, willing her eyes to meet his. "I could never do that to you, Neve. I respect you too much."

Her heart skipped a beat, feeling suddenly lightheaded. This was not the conversation she anticipated.

His hand left her knee and found her back, as he began lazily tracing a finger along the length of her spine. Her breath hitched, muscles tensing under his touch. In a moment he froze, and Nevia willed herself to steal a glance at him. His expression was tender, his fingers barely grazing her voile sleeves as he reached to brush her cheek, the one that Elante carefully treated with arnica ointment. "I just want you to understand the immense pressure that I am under. They think every choice I make is wrong, that I should start making better choices, and quickly. I love you, Neve, with everything that I am, and yet I have to admit that my decision to wed you was selfish. I was thinking only of myself and my love for you, how much I adored you, how much I wanted you always by my side." He paused, reaching for her chin and turning her head. For a long moment he studied her, as if searching for something. "You felt the same, right? You wanted me as much as I wanted you?"

"Of course," Nevia answered, perhaps too quickly. Her eyelids fluttered closed. "And I still want you. The real you. But, Darius, this has to stop. You cannot berate yourself and desire to be one man, while also being another. My heart cannot take much more of it, and you're going to end up hurting yourself more than you'll hurt me."

Arms encircled her as he pressed her against his side, his heartbeat frantic underneath his thin shirt. His nose grazed her ear, breath tickling the crease of her neck as he whispered: "Can you give me one more chance?"

His seductive tone made her toes curl in her boots, yet she couldn't stifle her annoyance. This same request had been made of her many times over, again and again.

His gentle kisses made their way along her collar bone, traveling along her throat and behind her ear. Eventually his lips hovered a mere fraction from her own, as if seeking permission. Acceptance. Forgiveness.

Her will broke. She threw herself into his arms, pressing her lips against his. He crushed her body against his own as if desperate, their kiss deepening, tongues intertwining between rasped breaths. The empress drew in a shaky breath, resting her cheek in the crook of his neck, arms wrapped around him as a brought her in his lap. She ran her tongue along her chapped lips.

"I forgive you," she said. "But please, please think about what I said."

Darius held her gingerly, one hand entangling into her thick platinum mane as he gently rocked the two of them. "I promise that I will. I will not fail you."

His hands roved up her back, and she felt his fingers slip between the laces securing her bodice at her back. She pressed a kiss to his throat.

"There isn't much privacy here. These walls and curtains are so thin—"

"Do you think I care?" His tone was filled with amusement and hunger. At this Nevia smiled, looking up into the face of the man that she adored and fell in love with.

"This is the version of you that I'd like to see more of."

His calloused palms cupped her flushed cheeks, his gaze consuming her with its intensity. "Then this is who I will be." His hands glided down her neck and over her shoulders, allowing her unlaced bodice to slither to the ground. "For you, Neve, I will be anything."

CHAPTER 14

The journey back was smooth and uneventful. Nevia saw very little of Verrine, and she couldn't have been more pleased, even if it was unlike him to keep to himself. Occasionally he would traipse past her in search of Darius, or when he saw Nevia alongside him his eyes would narrow and he would stalk away. If Darius noticed, he didn't react.

Their shipment of coal arrived on Velspire's docks shortly after them, and crews had already been arranged to unload the cargo and begin distribution within the empire. They were still graced with the heat waves of late summer, thus their need for coal was limited to their usage for cooking and gas lamps. Signs of their shortage were still under wraps, but that soon would change when the winter winds would sweep from the north, when more civilians retreated to the warmth of their homes and would burn hearths that required coal. That was when everything would catch up with them—the shortage, the collapsed mine, and Darius' promise. It would only reflect poorly on them.

The heavy draperies of Nevia's sitting parlor in the Velspirian Palace remained drawn, shunning the late morning sun and casting the room in darkness. Flinging them open, she basked in the sunlight that pooled onto her. Below the bay window her vision was greeted by the vibrant hues hydrangeas and tiger lilies of the palatial gardens, their sweet fragrance wafting on the light summer breeze. The warmth of the sight and ample sunlight caressed her face as her eyelids fell. She drew in a sharp breath as she lifted the jade mouthpiece of her new cocuswood flute to her lips, and blew.

The tone was elegant, beautiful, and powerful. The flute in her hands was unlike any she had ever played. Liveliness filled her soul and fueled her fingers as she allowed herself to play a song of joy. A song of birth, life, and vitality. Nevia felt her soul bind to her music as she swayed to it softly, her ivory skirt sweeping across the redwood floorboards.

Soon her song was finished, and she allowed herself a moment to even her breaths. She nearly jumped from her skin, however, when clapping resounded from behind her. Sitting crosslegged on her rose-patterned ottoman was her husband, eyes warm and inviting. Her heart swelled to see him, and a certain pride filled her to know she had played just for him. The flute clattered on the windowsill as she gingerly set it down, gliding across the room to wrap her arms tightly around his shoulders. She drew in the warm scent of sandalwood on him.

"Hello, my love." Her words fell short when she noticed his shoulders tighten, body growing stiff in her embrace. She allowed her arms to lower. "Are you okay?"

He kept his face cleverly hidden, chin tucked against her shoulder, the pearls of her neckline brushing against his beard. "Of course!" His tone was filled with exuberance that Nevia immediately detected as false. "Am I not allowed to come listen to my wife play?"

"No, no it's not that, it's just, I—"

She pulled herself away, searching his face. Her gaze was unable to study him long, however, as he pressed his lips to hers. They were warm and tender. Soon she forgot about the hesitation on his face as he embraced her, one hand tangling up into her web of curls.

"It's not often that you come listen to me play," she said finally, breathless once more.

Darius gave her a knowing smile. His arms drew her into his lap, pulling her in close. "You don't give me the chance to hear you often."

His lips brushing her earlobe sent a warm quiver down her spine. She lazily traced her finger along his hand, the lines creasing his weathered palm. "I should play more often like I used to."

"Yes, you really should. It brings me joy to see you happy."

She looked up into his face to offer him a smile, but her efforts were lost at the expression on his face. He looked worn, exhausted, and defeated.

"Okay, I know something happened." Her ice-blue eyes were stern. "Why are you really here? I doubt it was so you could hear me play."

He shifted uncomfortably, though it had nothing to do with her weight on his lap. His eyes darted to the bay window, as if to seek refuge where it didn't exist.

"You read me like a book, Neve. I did want to come here to listen to you play, but it wasn't the sole reason I sought you out. I wanted to reassure you that everything will be okay. Everything will be over quickly and we'll have a prosperous winter."

She shot him a dubious look. "Oh, that's very kind of you." Her brow arched with suspicion. "But why bring this up? I wasn't worried."

A hand raked through his smooth dark bangs as he let out a long, forceful breath. "He said that I shouldn't tell you, that you wouldn't understand—"

"Who said?" Nevia's voice rose an octave. Darius' arms slackened, allowing her to rise and begin pacing, her footfalls as loud as her raging heart. He continued to sit there in dumbfounded silence, fidgeting with a button on his coat's sleeve. "Darius, what is it that you aren't supposed to tell me?"

The emperor looked tortured, torn between duty and love. *As he always has been,* Nevia thought bitterly. *As he always will be.*

"Verrine. He, well, he understands that you see politics through a different lens, and that this news would distress rather than help you. It would be better if this was left unsaid, but—"

"But?!"

"But I disagree. I think it is your right to know. You are my empress and my wife; I want to be open with you."

Nevia stopped pacing, eyes falling on her husband. Gratitude flowed through her, his desire for honesty pacifying her. She went to his side and filled her hands with his. "Tell me."

He stared into her eyes, the color drawn from his face. "We still won't have enough resources for this winter," he said hesitantly. "The coal shortage runs deeper than we calculated, and winter draws ever closer."

"Oh." Nevia's chin drooped, crestfallen.

"But I have found a solution, so you need not worry. Everything will be fine."

Nevia raised a brow, awaiting further explanation, but none came. Carefully he averted her gaze, instead allowing his attention to rest on Nevia's parakeet, Kiya, perched in a cage outside her window.

"That's good, then, isn't it?" She tilted her head. "Did you want to talk about this solution, or . . . ?"

"Not really, no, but you're going to find out one way or another, and probably better from me than from the newspaper." He threw his long legs out before him, locking his ankles together as he affixed one of his most intense stares on his wife. "We're going to be procuring some core shards from the Feishin Kingdom. It's the only way we'll survive."

Nevia's eyes narrowed. "Really." It was a statement, not a question. "After the Feishin queen denied your request? Were you able to appeal to her and change her mind?"

"Well, no, she is unaware that I came to this decision."

"So you're going to take it by force?" Nevia's voice rose again. "And, pray tell, how do you plan on doing that? A massive stone wall surrounds the island, and there's tons of guards on the shores. There is absolutely no way to sneak into the Feishin Kingdom, not to mention the mine is at the heart of her palace. You're going to start a war, Darius, and that is foolish."

Darius rose from his seat, feet scuffing the floorboards. "You're right, I *am* going to start a war, but not in the way that you think."

What little color was left in Nevia's face drained, her blood running like sludge in her veins. "What do you mean?"

He tucked his arms behind his back, striding up to the window and gazing down into the garden. "Nothing can stop what is happening now. It is only a matter of time."

"What are you talking about?" She marched up to him, hands fleeing to his shoulders and forcing him to spin around and face her. He met her gaze with tortured eyes, pain lancing his features. "What. Did. You. Do?"

He glanced warily at her flute on the sill, then back at her. "An assault is being made on Zenoch in the Feishin Kingdom's name.

Zenoch will retaliate for this unwarranted strike, and the rest is history."

"You mean you are provoking Zenoch?! In Feishin's name?!"

"It's the only way, Neve. Once they are engaged in conflict, her troops will be divided. Everything will be in disarray. It will be easy to invade the Feishin Kingdom to protect the citizens, and from there we can infiltrate her mine and reveal the core shards to the public, which will be outraged that she kept such a vital resource secret."

"So you're sowing discord, just so you can have what you want?"

"It's the only way," Darius repeated stiffly. "I don't love this plan anymore than you do—"

"No, I *hate* this plan."

"I do, too."

"But you're doing it! I never would!"

Darius threw his hands up in defeat. "Those who wield power have to make difficult decisions for the greater good. This is the only way, Neve, but it's going to be okay. You don't have to get involved, and it will be over before you know it."

Nevia shook her head, shrinking away from her husband. "No, you are starting a war, one which may become global. All for something that you want. You earned Queen Arethusa's respect, her trust, and you would betray her in this way?" Fury turned to despair as she let out a frustrated cry, dragging her fingers through her roots. "You cannot do this, Darius. This isn't like you. What about unifying Danaeca, the world? This was your vision, and you're going against everything that you believe in, that I believe in."

He winced as though struck. "Perhaps my goals were foolish. I cannot undo what has been done, but I can change the future. I must now do what is in the best interest of my empire, and if it is to become a man that I despise, then so be it. Please, Neve, I beg of you: understand."

She couldn't believe her ears; this was madness. "I can never understand. This is *wrong*, and you know it. You're saving your people, but at what cost? So many people are going to die because of you. Besides, who would believe that the Feishin Kingdom would attack an unprovoked country anyway? How could you convince the people that it was the Feishin Kingdom and not you who attacked? The Feishin people are pacifists."

"Because I'm influential," Darius said at last. "Because I have demonstrated that I want peace and unity, and Arethusa's reputation already precedes her. She has a country with closed-off borders, with rumors of secret technology that she won't share with the world. Everyone also knows she's become bitter since her husband's death in Zenoch. A Feishin attack against Zenoch would make plenty of sense to the people."

What horrible, poisonous lies! Nevia cringed and recoiled from this man, an emperor that she no longer recognized. She only could see a venomous snake in his place, ready to sink his fangs into innocent victims rather than work through his problems with the dignity and grace that he once exuded.

"Verrine put you up to this." Nevia's fingernails dug into her palms. She strode to his side and gripped his shoulders. A muscle twitched at his temple, jaw rigid as though pained. "Do not let him start a war through you," Nevia warned. "He is manipulating you. Don't you see that?"

"You never gave him a chance. You've hated him from the beginning. He's tried to befriend you, but you sneer and jab at him and are unwilling to work through anything."

"Don't you turn this on me and change the subject!" Nevia snapped. "Do not, do not, *do not* start a war! I won't let you!"

The color drained from Darius' face. "Oh?" His voice lowered dangerously. "And how do you intend to do that?"

Nevia allowed her arms to fall and fixed her chin. "I will tell them. Will tell everyone what you are doing, and that it was you. It would ruin *your* reputation, and backfire on you."

"You wouldn't do that to me." He took both her hands into his. "Nevia, we are a united front; we are a team. Do not choose a side other than mine."

Her eyes, twin chips of ice, kindled with determination. "I already have. I will not let you get away with this despicable sabotage."

The hands encasing hers stilled, his gaze flickering with an unreadable emotion. His lips curled into an ugly sneer. "If you do this, you will regret it, Nevia. Mark my words." Releasing her hands he took a step back. "Verrine was right, but I didn't want him to be. I had more faith in you than this. He told me what I should do with you if this were to happen."

Nevia arched a brow. "Oh? To slap me again? To vilify me?"

He drew himself to full height, everything about his posture intimidating. "No." The thick malice behind his words caused her to wince. "Something worse. Far worse. You will *not* cross me, Nevia."

Nevia managed a glare. "I am not afraid of you."

His cold exterior ignited with flames, and for a moment Nevia thought he would indeed strike her again. She squinted, bracing for impact, but to her surprise the blow did not come. She cracked an eye open and witnessed him spinning on heel to exit the parlor, footfalls echoing in his wake.

"You should be."

A threat. A promise.

His words cut deeper than his hand ever could.

Trembling, she backed into the window, fingers trailing to the polished sill behind her. She felt her wrist brush against something that rolled. The moment she realized what was happening there was no time to react. Hands swiped at empty air as her lovely flute fell, the dark red wood shattered as it met with the brick path below. Nevia gasped, throwing one hand over her mouth, her grip on the sill the only thing keeping her from plummeting through the window with it.

The most beautiful item that she'd ever owned: fractured, not unlike her own heart.

CHAPTER 15

The scent of freshly brewed coffee wafted through Ardan's tent, steaming mug untouched on his desk. His shoulders ached and neck burned as he poured his attention into a report on the latest recruits to their hunting party. The assignment was past due, and he knew the head huntsman of the Sanen clan, Ro'Orda would be displeased at the delay. A sigh escaped Ardan as he sat back numbly in his chair, stretching his long legs out beneath his desk. Sometimes he hated being the chief's second. It was a great honor, but with said honor came many headaches and an ever-growing pile of responsibilities, aging him beyond his thirty-one years. His dark hair, full-length and brushing his shoulder on the left side of his head and shaved on the right, had not yet grayed from stress however, so he must have been doing something right.

Finally he set his quill to rest alongside his report, pausing long enough to take a swig from his mug. The warmth of the coffee spread through his throat and into his soul. Despite autumn's late arrival, the insulated leather tent, with a well-stoked fire at its center, was chilled. Having lived in the far northern mountain range of Zenoch all of his life, he didn't know what traditional summer was. He'd heard of sun-baked days, of listening to the ocean waves rolling off the rocks of the coastline, of the temperature being so hot that sweat would bead down your chin. Such things seemed like a mere fairytale to Ardan as he sat there, swathed in thick furs and woolen clothes amidst the mountains. Perhaps one day he would be able to experience other climates for himself, but he did not foresee leaving Zenoch anytime soon. Traversing the mountainsides was arduous at best, deadly at worst. They were nestled there: an encampment in the valley between two steep cliffs. This was, for the most part, fine with him. He wasn't much for adventure.

He stifled an inward groan as he leaned forward, back muscles burning in protest. There was not much left for him to write. He only needed to record progress on Trevir's snow bear slaughter and—

The tent flap began to flutter, his mug rattling on the desk. Ardan allowed his quill to linger too long on the parchment, ink blotting over his scrawled text. He couldn't deny the muffled din that met his ears as dread settled in the pit of his stomach.

An avalanche—and it was nearby.

"Well, shit," Ardan blurted, darting to the entrance and snatching his nearby spear. He threw open the tent flap and bolted outside.

The tent on the hill overlooked the entire encampment, colorful tents dotting the snow-covered valley with mountains flanking them on either side.   His gaze quickly fell on a horrendous sight: a sheet of white resembling an entire mountain crumbled before his eyes, tumbling with a fierce roar and slamming down into the valley that they called home. The rushing snow gained momentum, barreling down at dangerous speed as it consumed all in its path. Ardan recoiled as he watched an entire outpost be flattened, the guardsmen's steel-tipped spears dipping underneath the wave of snow as it carted them away. Dread coursed through him.

He shifted to face the two patrolmen stationed outside his tent. Their normally tanned faces were pasty white, and it looked as though the simplest breeze would be enough to knock them over with the way they swayed on the spot.

"We have to do something!" Ardan boomed, twirling his spear as if preparing to take an enemy head-on, but the enemy was Mother Nature herself: a force impossible to reckon with.

The patrolmen had more sense, and one turned to him with pitying eyes. "And what would you have us do? Stop the avalanche?"

Ardan gritted his teeth in protest, yet he knew that the patrolman spoke true. No one could stop an avalanche; all they could do was allow it to run its course and pray that survivors could be plucked from the aftermath. But Ardan knew that survivors would be slim—hardly anyone caught in an avalanche lived to tell the tale.

Ardan clapped the patrolman on the shoulder. "I'm going to get everyone out. I suggest you do the same." Ardan ducked out of view, skipping down the hillside and weaving his way deeper into the valley, racing against time itself.

Tendrils of smoke greeted him, cries echoing in the chaos. A blur of his clansmen and women frantically darted about, gathering up belongings and children, seeking refuge from the oncoming disaster. Ardan grasped the nearest man by the coat and thrust him in the direction whence he came. "To my tent! Now! Up the hill!"

Horror-filled eyes met his, followed by a nod. He scurried away, abandoning his belongings in a heap. There was no time to waste; death would encompass them in a matter of minutes, a window not long enough to collect anything but one's self in hopes of escaping Fate.

He barked a similar order to every person he passed, his words often falling upon ears deafened by shock. It seemed, however, that everyone was starting to understand the gravity of the situation. What once was a crowded encampment began to disperse as a trail of clansmen retreated to the safety of higher elevation, Ardan's tent a beacon of hope against the inbound cloud of death. The majority of stragglers consisted of elderly individuals challenged by the snow, or young family units who tarried, refusing to leave their loved ones behind.

A tent flap in front of Ardan jutted open, and out stomped a woman bedecked in thick winter gear like himself, with fiery wild hair flowing down her back. Freckles adorned her small round nose and cheeks, despite never getting the full intensity of the sun. Eyes the shade of emeralds bore into him, flashing dangerously at his approach.

"What are you still doing here?!" she shouted. "You're going to die!"

She rounded on him, gloved hands splaying against his chest in an attempt to shove him. "If we both don't make it out of here, who will lead the clan?"

Ardan couldn't help cracking a grin. They were staring death in the face, and her concern was her people—always her people.

"I intend for the both of us to lead, Risanna, as we have for years."

Risanna opened her mouth to protest, but the deafening rumble of snow overpowered her. He watched as the wall of death made it to the base of the mountain, barreling over everything it touched.

They had to flee. Now.

The vibrations of the encroaching snow shook them as they dashed toward the hill. *This is it,* Ardan thought dully, heart threatening to rip free from his chest as his feet kicked up snow.

I'm going to die here. If I had known, I would have worn my best suit.

Every ounce of his adrenaline was expended as his legs surged him forward. All the air escaped his lungs when unsteady footing claimed his balance, tossing him face-first into the snow. Fatigue seized his muscles when he ordered them to raise him. His shaking biceps nearly prevented him from rising when, to his surprise, Risanna's arms gathered him and helped him to resume scrambling to safety.

Rushing cold air chilled his sweat as he looked up, the white-dapped hill and cliff before him inviting and intimidating. It provided a safe haven from the avalanche, yet there was no way they could scale it in time. He barely noticed Risanna surge past him, arms pumping at her sides as she launched herself, coursing through the air as her legs swung to gain purchase on the steep incline. Without further consideration Ardan followed suit. He gained as much purchase as possible with freezing fingers onto the icy cliffside, gasping for one more breath as snow sprayed his back. It worked! The wall rumbled past below.

A quivering sigh escaped Ardan's snow-plastered lips, his body easing back against the ice-glazed hill in relief. They'd made it. They survived. He could hardly believe it, and it took his body even longer to accept this. He shakily rose to his knees, glancing over at the chief.

"Are you all right?" he asked.

Risanna lifted herself, meeting Ardan's gaze darkly before glancing toward the clearing that was the valley. "It's gone." Her tone was flat and lifeless. "Everything that we worked so hard on. The home that we built. . . ."

Never had Ardan seen his fearless leader so broken, so utterly shattered inside than now when she slammed her fist into the ice and let out a cry of helplessness and intermittent swearing in their native tongue. Her red hair had fallen from its tie, falling in a sheet across the left side of her face.

Ardan wasn't quite certain what to do. He crawled to her side and rested his hand overtop hers. She swatted it away, jabbing her spear into the ground to allow herself to rise on shaking knees. Mutely she stood and stared out into the new landscape that had once been their home, Ardan following suit. All he could repeatedly ask himself was "How? Why them?"

As if in answer, a blast echoed over the mountain, striking fear in Ardan's heart. His head swiveled to glance over his shoulder. Across the great distance east, he saw a peak begin to crumble. Another avalanche. A frown furrowed his brow. This was unnatural and improbable—if not impossible. Never had this happened in Zenoch's recorded history, and it didn't seem likely that two avalanches could occur at nearly the same time, so far apart.

His frown deepened. This started to seem more sinister than a mere fluke of nature. It was true that avalanches can and did occur by exterior forces, but not in this manner.

It seemed man-made, intentional.

An act of war.

CHAPTER 16

News of the avalanche echoed to every corner of Velspire, and with it the same lie: that the Feishin Kingdom struck against several of Zenoch's clans, for reasons unspecified but presumed to relate to the late Feishin king's death. Murmurs from the guards at every turn, the whispers of the kitchen staff passing meals to the servants—every time she heard them, Nevia cringed.

The empress stood outside a frosted glass window of the communal music room, watching as a carriage bearing the Ivalian insignia rolled to a halt before the palace gates. Verrine emerged with his familiar violet suit and bouncy blond curls, flashing a smile to the sentries at the entrance and waving in that casual, arrogant manner of his. Nevia wanted nothing more than to punch him.

A gentle rap at the door partially arrested her attention from the window. "Can you believe this?" Nevia blurted, folding her arms. "He's back for more blood, I would presume. Why can't he focus on his own country and leave Darius in charge of running an empire?"

Silence ensued, followed by a slight, quiet squeak. "I—I don't know, Your Imperial Highness. I just came to offer you bread and wine."

Nevia's voluminous burgundy skirt whipped as she whirled around. Before her stood a small, short serving girl. She carried a silver platter bedecked with refreshments, a befuddled expression etched on her face.

"Where is Elante?"

The serving girl swallowed, placing the tray gingerly on the table in front of the unlit fireplace. "I—I can't say for sure, Your Highness."

"Is she ill?" Nevia further pressed, coaxing her.

"I don't think?" The serving girl slumped her shoulders, smoothing back strands of black hair. "I haven't seen her since yesterday, so I am not sure."

Nevia tilted her head. "Since yesterday?" The sound of her heels echoed along the hardwood floor as she approached, glowering upon the servant. "She's not anywhere in the servant's quarters?"

"No, Your Imperial Highness. I don't know where she is." The girl sniffed, refusing to lift her head. "Maybe she is visiting her family? On holiday?"

None of these suggestions satisfied Nevia, but interrogating further would do no good, and she didn't wish to terrify the girl more than she already had. "Very well, that will be all. Thank you."

Relief flooded the girl's face at her dismissal. She offered another curtsy before scurrying from the room at top speed.

The empress sighed, allowing herself to sag into her chair as she considered the bread and wine. It shouldn't have bothered her to receive the replacement girl, but Elante never failed to appear. She was always there, rain or shine, sick or not. In her bones she could feel something was amiss. She picked up the glass of red wine, swirling it before bringing it to her lips.

She wouldn't have left without saying goodbye.

She placed the goblet down and rose to her feet. She knew who would have answers.

Her footsteps rung rhythmically through the corridor, heartbeat quick to match. She glided down a long, curving flight of steps before arriving in the foyer. The sound of Verrine's high-pitched laughter carried from the great hall, arresting her attention, and turning the corner she found Darius standing beside a column, the lord of Ivalia at his side. The soft curves of their shoulders suggested an ease about their conversation. The couple's eyes met, and Darius' genuine smile quickly faded. She saw the recognition flicker in his eyes. He knew why she came.

Verrine whirled around, his smile growing wider as his eyes narrowed into slits. A sneer, one she was all too accustomed with. Nevia balled her hands into fists at her sides, clenching her jaw so tightly it hurt.

"Nevia," Darius greeted. "Have you decided to join us? Our conversation will probably be of little interest; we are discussing our hunting party for next month."

"No," Nevia said, with such malice it scared her. "I need to speak with you"—she shot a glare towards the Ivalian lord—"alone."

Verrine's lips curled upward, eyes glittering as if awaiting a spectacle. The emperor's hand fled to his short-cropped beard, musing over her request.

"Very well, I suppose that I could indulge my wife briefly." Darius rested a hand on the small of her back, escorting her from the room. He nodded toward Verrine. "If you will excuse me."

Both were silent as they walked, the false pretense of a perfectly normal couple. Nevia folded her hands primly in front of her as they went, barely able to think straight from the fury coursing through her veins.

Once Darius closed the twin oaken doors of his study, Nevia wasted no time in rounding on him. "Elante is gone. Why? Where is she?"

The emperor collapsed into the chair at his desk, leaning back casually and folding his arms over his chest. A mocking slant of his lips matched the lilt of his voice. "Oh, Neve, Neve, Neve. Where do I begin?"

Her heart hammered in her chest, her glare as sharp as twin daggers. "You're behind it, aren't you?!"

Darius raised a hand, either in defense or silence. Perhaps both. "Calm. Actions have consequences. I thought you knew that by now."

"What are you talking about?"

Darius leaned back in his seat, tucking his hand into his breast pocket and procuring a worn, yellowed envelope. She noticed the imperial wax seal broken along the edge, a scrawl of familiar handwriting on the front. Her handwriting. Cold dread filled her body, immediately realizing what he held.

"I had placed a halt on all correspondence leaving the palace" —he unfurled the parchment in his hands, grip so tight she thought it would rip—"until Prometheus could oversee everything. This ended up in his hands the night after I unveiled my plans to you. And I can't help but wonder: did you think that I'm a windbag of empty threats? I warned you, Neve. I told you that you shouldn't choose any side but mine. But alas, you had to go behind my back and betray me."

Her hands fell dully at her sides, no words able to rectify the grave mistake she'd made.

"This *is* treason, you know." He crossed the ornate area rug to the fireplace on the opposite end of the room, its wood alight with flame. "This is proof enough to have you hanged. It would please everyone, after all, since they—and *you*—remind me that this is what I get for marrying a foreigner with no loyalty to the Androvich Empire."

Her eyes burned as she watched him shake out her letter, clear his throat, and read: " 'To Her Royal Majesty, Queen Arethusa. It pains me to deliver you the news that His Imperial Highness, Emperor Darius Androvich the Second, intends to betray you. He is sending out a military troop as I write this, posing as your own men and women to lead an assault on Zenoch in your name. It will be presented as an act of vengeance for the death of the late King Athilan, and a demand that the clan chiefs pay proper compensation for your loss. My belief is that he intends to use this war as a means to justify an invasion on your kingdom, one which will allow him to seize the core shards he so desperately seeks.' "

He crumbled the letter in his fist, vehemence claiming him. To her surprise he chuckled the ball of parchment into the flames. They licked the paper eagerly, ready to devour every condemning word that Nevia had written.

When he turned to face her, his eyes were glazed with unshed tears. "How could you? Nevia, I love you. I always have, always will. I thought that we were on the same side; how could you go behind my back like this?"

Remorse dug its claws into her soul. She had wounded him. Clearly he hadn't taken her seriously when she claimed that she would stop him, much like she hadn't thought he would seriously punish her.

"What you are doing is wrong." Her gaze flickered to the fire, watching as the rest of her letter turned to blackened ash. "I cannot in clear conscience stand by and watch as you make two innocent nations kill each other, all for your personal gain and glory."

"No, Neve, that is where you are wrong"—he squeezed his eyes shut—"I don't intend to gain glory for myself. I intend to save my country, and those countries that are relying on me. The Feishin queen is wrong for hoarding such a resource that should be benefitting the entire world. Don't you see that?"

He crossed the room in three quick strides and gripped her shoulders, fingertips digging painfully into her upper arms. "This is the only way. I am just trying to save everyone and do what I think is best."

"Best?" Nevia snapped out of her reverie and looked Darius in the eye, his gaze surprisingly soft and forlorn. "How do you think this is best? Do you know how many lives would be lost? And Arethusa trusted you . . . how wrong she was."

"And how wrong I was," he stated, expression darkening, "for I trusted *you*."

His words cut deeper than any blade. Nevia bit her lip, forcing her face away. Darius ignored her and continued. "I let your servant girl go. It was improper for a handmaiden to be so close to her empress, for you to wait on her as you did. Besides, I think she is a bad influence on you. I know that she doesn't like me. But worry not. No harm will come to her. I merely dismissed her; I didn't have her tried for any crime."

"But—but she is my friend." Nevia spread her arms in front of her, feeling small and helpless. "And now she is gone. Do you know how few friends I have here?"

His eyes shone without sympathy. "Well, maybe this will just give you an incentive to make new friends. Maybe start making yourself feel like you belong here and ally yourself with the empire in more than your marriage-earned title."

Nevia backed away from him, shaking her head. "I must go to her, bring her back."

"I wouldn't advise that." Darius shrugged. "I dismissed her this time. Who is to say that I won't dismiss her more violently next time? More permanently?"

The threat drew something ferocious from within her. "You wouldn't dare—"

"Oh, but I would." Darius' smile was sinister. "In fact, you go to her at all and I will personally see to it that she suffers. You brought this upon yourself, Nevia. You only have yourself to blame."

"Then I will tell the world what kind of monster you've become!"

Nevia spun on her heel to march herself out of the study, but was wrenched back as Darius seized her by her sash. Gripping her arms tightly, he threw her against the wall, pressing her against it so roughly that she bit her lip to conceal a whimper.

"You want a monster?" Something ugly revealed itself in his face, fierce and despicable. "I can be one."

His hot breath beat on her face, causing her to turn her head away. "You have seen nothing. Go back to being my wife, the empress that you are supposed to be, and all this can end. But continue challenging me and I swear, Nevia, I will start taking everything from you that you love. Piece by piece. You will *not* backstab and humiliate me like this again. I will not tolerate it."

Nevia shuddered in fear and hurt. "You already have taken everything that I love."

His frown deepened. He lowered his arm, releasing her from restraint which resulted in her sliding down the length of the wall, crumbling into a miserable heap on the ground. Darkness contorted Darius' gaze as he turned pitiless eyes upon his wife. He shook his head and stalked off.

"This isn't what I wanted at all."

His footsteps faded into the hall, the doors slamming shut behind him. Her pride hadn't been willing to give him the satisfaction of seeing her cry, but now that she was alone the tears forced themselves free. Fingernails clawed at the tiled floor as she crawled closer to the hearth, seeking comfort from the flames to thaw the ice that now encased her aching heart.

This wasn't what she wanted.

CHAPTER 17

The soft tinkle of wind chimes echoed through the dining space, pink drapes billowing in front of open windows. The Feishin queen's legs were tucked neatly under her as she knelt at the head of the dining table with her children on either side: the fair Princess Mila, a young woman blooming into a fine lady of the royal court, and the silent Crown Prince Qirin, who would one day succeed his mother in the responsibilities of the throne.

She lifted her porcelain cup to her lips, closing her eyes as she took in the sweet aroma of honey ginger tea. She drew in a sip, listening and knowing that her movements were being mirrored— at least by one of her children.

Mila sat primly on her knees similar to her mother, her slender fingers wrapped carefully around a steaming cup. An ornamental hairpin of pearls and jade held her deep red hair high atop her head, clothing pressed and proper for a lady. Across from her sat her brother, four years her senior, yet his manners fell gravely behind hers. He sat with legs crossed, disheveled black hair spilling over his shoulders. He swished a bowl of soup, oblivious to his mother's stare.

"Now then," Arethusa started, head swiveling, "do either of you remember the Prayer of the Wanderer?"

Excitement bubbled in the visage of the young woman, lips pursing as her cheeks dimpled with a smile. She fidgeted, directing Arethusa's attention on to her. "Yes, Mila?"

The princess cleared her throat, rising gracefully in one fluid motion and placing her folded hands across her slight chest.

"Oh ye who have fallen astray, whose eyes have left the stars,
Take heart, for your path forward is always within.
Stay swift and sure, seek Zian's good fortune, and your spirit will guide the way."

Arethusa beamed at her daughter's recitation as she applauded, red lacquered nails gleaming in the sunlight. "Excellent, Mila! You have been working hard on your studies, I see."

The prince swirled his soup, watching a green onion spin on its amber surface. Like a young child he thought danger wouldn't see him if he didn't look at it. Sadly, he failed in avoiding his mother's scrutiny.

"Have you thought more about Liana's marriage proposal?" Arethusa prodded.

The prince rolled his eyes. "I knew this would come up sooner or later." He lowered the bowl and rubbed his temple. "Mother, I have no feelings for the girl. She is kind and gentle, but very clumsy, and I know that she does not care very much for me."

"But Qirin! She barely knows you. Give her time and I am sure that love would blossom between you two," Arethusa coaxed.

The prince looked down into his soup as though it had been poisoned.

"That I highly doubt," Qirin stated flatly. "She loves another. I believe they are already in a rather . . . *intimate* relationship, if any of the rumors hold true."

His little sister snorted, a stark contrast to her previous poise. "And the rumors say that you fancy the men, so what does that mean? That it's true?"

He shot her a glare, which caused her to giggle wildly.

"She wants Lord Jing, which is quite fine with me," he continued, returning his attention to the queen. "I do not wish to meddle in their affairs or be a third wheel in their relationship. That sounds too messy to me, and nothing good will come of it."

A frown furrowed Arethusa's brow. "Well, have you spoken with her about it?"

"No, that wouldn't be appropriate," Qirin responded tersely. "Especially if she is under pressure from her parents to wed me and become the crown princess. I don't think they would understand that her heart pulls her elsewhere."

The queen looked thoughtful. Her gaze lifted to the window, the gardens in full bloom and visible outside. "How very considerate of you," she said softly. "And I don't suppose that there is someone else that catches your eye, as well? Is that why you are being so, ah, generous?"

Qirin's silence spoke volumes. Suddenly he became interested in his untouched tea, which had long gone cold.

Before Arethusa could inquire who the lucky woman was, urgent footsteps approached the lounge and three guards rounded the corner, their shields reflecting the artificial light from the lanterns above.

"Urgent news from the docks, Your Majesty. We are under attack!"

Arethusa blinked in bewilderment, shifting in her seat casually. The words took a moment to sink in. "What's that now?" Her tone was too soft, too easy given the circumstances.

"We are under attack, your Majesty! Zenochians."

Color drained from the queen's face at the mention of Zenoch, the murderers of her husband. The lines along her face etched themselves deeper as she frowned, and her hands balled into fists on her thighs.

"Why are they here?" She rose sharply, low-cut crimson robes pooling around her formed leather pants.

"They said they want to take down the nation of hypocrites," one of the guards said with a shrug. "We are not retaliating, but maintaining a line of defense. They have killed all of the sentries at the city gates, Your Majesty. They have entered the kingdom."

Arethusa's eyes stung. Hypocrites? She shook her head in an attempt to clear her confusion.

"But I don't understand," she murmured, as if to herself.

"Your orders, Your Majesty?" the guard prompted, gently trying to coax the queen from her daze.

"Send reinforcements," she commanded, certainty returning to her tone. "And tell the person in charge of the assault that I would like to speak with them. I am sure that this is some kind of misunderstanding that we can better smooth over with words than swords."

The guard opened his mouth for rebuttal, but instead offered his queen a low bow and scurried away.

A shudder coursed through Arethusa, gooseflesh pricking on her exposed arms. This was unprecedented; there hadn't been an attack on her country since the kingdom was founded a millennium ago. A hand rested on her shoulder belonging to Qirin, her son's dark eyes a perfect match to her own.

"It will be okay." His tone was strong and assertive, for a moment reminding Arethusa of her beloved Athilan who now resided beyond the mortal plane. "If anyone can fix this, it's you."

She pressed her cheek against his hand. "Thank you, my son. Secure the palace, and stay safe. I will go meet this Zenochian brute who thinks he can storm in here and take the lives of my people needlessly."

Khatalia brushed thick blonde hair over her shoulder. She'd known that the Feishins were arrogant fools, but how much so astounded her. Negotiating with her after they had brutally killed so many in Zenoch? The audacity! She scoffed, slamming her weathered spear into the grassy earth.

"Settle things with words." Khatalia spat at the guard's feet who suggested such a notion. "Say that to the hundreds of my clansmen that died thanks to your handiwork."

The Feishin guard's face remained expressionless, dark eyes conveying nothing. The Feishin Kingdom considered themselves a pacifist nation, to which Khatalia couldn't be more disgusted. What a devious, conniving demon that slept under the guise of tranquility! A fierce roar escaped Khatalia's throat as she plunged her spear into the guard's chest, running him clean through his leather armor. A whimper escaped the guard's lips before he fell lifeless to a kneeling position. Khatalia merely shrugged him off and flung him to the ground, crimson blood pooling at her feet.

Her bloodied spearhead shimmering like rubies in the midmorning sun, she turned to face the men and women donning the Feishin Kingdom's colors of turquoise and black before her.

"Are you all really going to keep pretending to be pacifists?" She laughed humorlessly. "You sicken me. I will have no remorse killing every last one of you, even if you don't fight back. After what you demolished, what you've done—"

Tears blurred her vision, painful memories flooding her of the encampment that had once been her home. The avalanche swept across her home in the blink of an eye, destroying everything that she cared about without warning. She would never forget the moment where she had burrowed a hole in the snow, finding *her* moments before death claimed her. Reiya . . . her beloved wife, gone, just like the rest of her clan, including her son, her parents, and best of friends. She wouldn't even be able to find their bodies to give them a proper ceremony, not unless she wanted to dig for an eternity.

No longer was she chief of the Kohari. She was simply Khatalia, with only a handful of survivors at her side.

Khatalia was determined to make the Feishin Kingdom pay dearly for their sins against humanity—and to all of the gods that watched them.

She relentlessly cut through those that barred her, barreling through the Feishin line with a ferocity that shouldn't have befitted a single woman. Three guards attempted to apprehend her, one getting so far as to disarm her, the spear rolling across the ground and being claimed by another. She whipped around, head-butted her assailant and, grasping his shoulder, tossed him into one of his compatriots. She whirled around and sharply kicked into the chest of another, forcing him into the shields of two guards behind him.

The handful of her companions stood in a V-formation behind her, steeling themselves for combat with their simple hand-axes and spears should the need arise. Khatalia, however, was a force to be reckoned with, and so far she had done an impressive job at leading the assault. That, and the Feishin guards offered little resistance, making it simple for them to gain traction in the pacifist kingdom.

The sounds of death echoed through the cobblestone streets, a sound once foreign to the country. Blood splattered Khatalia's tanned face as her spear cleaved through the royal guard Itari's chest. He clutched the spear with both hands as his weight sagged onto the cool metal. With a haggard breath Itari freed himself from the length of her weapon, falling onto his back and failing to rise again.

"Cowards." Khatalia's footfalls echoed on the stone as she marched forward. She glowered at his fallen form. "Pitiful, the lot of you. Death is too generous of a sentence for what you've done to my people. My family. Why, I should—"

"ENOUGH!"

The commanding voice boomed through the blood-drenched streets, the sounds of combat ceasing and unveiling a newfound silence. Khatalia whirled around to find the wall of Feishin shields part, allowing an opening for none other than the Feishin queen herself. She held her head high, expression haughty. Her sharp gaze flickered from Khatalia to the lifeless form of her guardsman.

"What is the meaning of your senseless slaughter?" Her voice was as deadly as venom. "You have invaded my land and killed my people senselessly. Are you mentally unstable?"

Khatalia let out a hollow breath, her lips curling up into a sneer. She swiveled her spear in her hand and marched up to the Feishin queen, intention behind her movements. The guards drew their shields, ready to sacrifice their lives for their sovereign, but Arethusa raised her hand to halt them, eyes never leaving Khatalia's.

"You killed my family!" Khatalia's voice cracked as her shoulders quivered, a sob threatening to break through her coarse exterior. "You killed everyone that meant something to me, leaving my clan in shambles!"

She gestured behind her, throwing an arm to emphasize her handful of clansmen. "This is all that is left! Everyone else is gone. Hundreds, *hundreds,* all dead because of YOU!"

Her clenched fists shook with raw emotion, silent tears rolling down her dirt-stained, hardened face. Emotional pain radiated from her, softening the gazes of the Feishin guards around her. All, except for the queen, who seemed unmoved by Khatalia's anguish.

"I do not kill," she said calmly. "You must be mistaken. We of the Feishin Kingdom are pacifists. Have you seen any of my guards retaliate against your ruthless bloodshed?"

"It's all lies!" Khatalia pointed her spear directly at Arethusa's heart. "This is all a facade so that people think you are a great queen. Well, you are filth, and I will make you pay."

"You are grieving," Arethusa said, without kindness. "You have lost everyone dear to you, and you want to make me hurt, as you hurt—"

"You're damn right, I do!"

"But killing my men and women won't bring your family back." Arethusa folded her arms in her wide sleeves. "Nor will it ease your broken heart. Let us calmly talk things over in my home. We will use words, not steel."

Khatalia's green eyes were sharp and feral. "No! I will go nowhere with you! Your kingdom will fall. I will see to it!"

A disheartened sigh escaped the queen. Red strands flew as she shook her head dismally. "I see there will be no reasoning with you. Very well; I have no choice but to stop you. I cannot have you killing any more innocents." Her eyes narrowed into slits. "I am very disappointed in you."

A shrill battle cry escaped Khatalia as she charged, aiming to plunge her spear clean through Arethusa's heart. Instead of piercing through her fine robes of satin, however, the tip of her spear clanged against steel. The soldier at Arethusa's right gritted her teeth, parrying the blow with all her strength. Khatalia set her lips into a thin line, considering the defense before sending her boot into the female guard's gut, knocking the wind from her and forcing her back.

Something sharp pierced the delicate flesh of Khatalia's neck, pain radiating from the point. Her fingers fled to a small dart at the site, but grasping it failed. Her fingers were failing, her limbs growing numb and heavy. Her vision blurred as she swayed, struggling to maintain her balance. Slurred speech came out instead of intended cursing.

"Rest," Arethusa's voice echoed, sounding far away. "You will be sent home, and I ask that you do not return. If you do, you will become well antiquated with my dungeons underground."

Khatalia growled, feebly grabbing for Arethusa's face before slumping forward. Her face met with the cobblestone path, a searing pain lancing up the bridge of her nose. Her vision swam before her, the edges growing dark.

Darker.

Until everything faded to nothing.

CHAPTER 18

The cool autumn breeze caressed Nevia's cheeks. The green leaves of maple trees were shifting to vibrant shades of rust and fiery-red, a reminder that very soon fires would need to be kindled. Coal would need to be burned, and that is when their shortage would need to be revealed to the people and give way to consequences.

Or everything went according to Darius' plan and their lives were made exceedingly comfortable by the core shards that didn't belong to them.

The empress sat crosslegged underneath one of the maple trees, alone as she often was since Elante was exiled from the palace and her life. The beat of dozens of wings caused Nevia to glance up at a flock of grackles migrating south to warmer climates; how she longed to join them.

Soft chirping drew her gaze from the sky and onto her own bird: Kiya, a bright-green parakeet that Darius gifted her when they were first together, all those years ago.

Back when he was a different man, Nevia thought bitterly, swinging open Kiya's cage and letting her flutter into her palm. Kiya took the bait, its kiwi-green wings outstretched, searching her hand for food. Once certain that the empress offered no sustenance, it twisted its neck, gazing up into the enormous blue sky. Nevia's gaze followed.

"You're thinking what I'm thinking, aren't you?" Kiya began to preen her hair draped over her cheek. "So close to freedom, and yet so very far. It's lonesome here, isn't it?"

Cupping her hands, she threw them upward and spread them so that Kiya would have no choice but to beat its wings. Fluttering stronger, before Kiya shakily took off into the sky, joining its brethren on the migration south.

"Be free."

A tear stung Nevia's eye as she watched her pet soar beyond sight, for a moment allowing her imagination to follow. To pretend that she, too, was free.

A flicker of movement from her peripheral vision at the palace gates to her right arrested her attention. Two imperial soldiers rushed to the gate from the cobblestone street, speaking in urgent, panicked words with the sentries before darting through the gate and into the palace.

A frown furrowed Nevia's brow. How curious. She began to move toward the sentry at the gate, a question on her tongue, when she heard Prometheus' voice echo from behind her, emerging from the palace as he clambered down the steps.

"Is she still alive?"

He marched towards the gate alongside the two men, moving faster than Nevia had ever seen him do, sweat gleaming on his bald head.

"Yes, but she is rather weak. She remains in custody until we are able to gather more details. She"—the guard faltered, casting a sideways glance at the advisor—"isn't exactly in a condition to relay what happened."

Nevia approached them, barring their path to the gates, hands clasped neatly in front of her. "What's happening here?"

The trio looked up in surprise. Prometheus grasped Nevia's upper arm and shook his head, as though she was a nuisance. "There is no time for me to explain now. You will learn the details later. Right now, I must go to the docks."

"Why?"

"Later." He dismissed her with a wave, moving past her and following the two soldiers through the palace gates. They halted in front of an awaiting carriage, Prometheus reaching with a gnarled hand for the box's handle, yet halting when he realized the empress was still behind him.

"I *am* coming." There was no hesitation in her tone.

A sigh escaped the man as he slowly turned, the many folds and wrinkles upon his face deepening as he frowned. "The emperor would be displeased if you were to involve yourself."

"That's fine, he can be displeased all he wants," Nevia said coldly, uncaring. "Let's be on our way."

The two filed into the carriage, the door snapping closed behind them. She gathered the many layers of her linen skirt around herself, watching as Prometheus strummed his fingers on the windowsill with a somber gaze turned outside. Their bodies jolted and swayed as the horses began to trot.

"Prometheus," Nevia pleaded, growing tired of being ignored. "What is the situation?"

Silence followed her words. For a while she thought he wasn't going to tell her. A deep sigh escaped him as he folded his hands against his chest and caved. "A longboat arrived, crudely crafted. We believe it is of Zenochian make."

Nevia raised a brow. "And this requires your immediate attention? Why not allow customs to handle the situation?"

"Because the captain was bound to the helm, gagged and in awful condition. It seems that she has been this way for two days."

Nevia's eyes widened. She could only imagine the captain's state if what he said was true. "But I don't understand. How was she able to navigate from Zenoch if bound and gagged to the helm? Why would someone do this to her? What would be the point—"

Prometheus threw his hands in the air. "Your guess is as good as mine, Empress. I only have the same information I shared with you. I'm going to find out more. I thought that you were coming to do the same."

The empress fell silent. No further words were exchanged between them.

It felt that their ride lasted far too long, and Prometheus practically kicked open the door when the carriage halted at last. The navy-blue cloak fastened about Prometheus's shoulders streamed in the steady oceanic wind as they rushed for the docks, where a cluster of imperial soldiers stood before the supposed Zenochian ship, their backs to them. It wasn't until they came closer that Nevia realized they were circling around a woman not far from death.

Nevia bit her lip, the sight horrific yet she couldn't avert her gaze. The woman's blonde hair was matted and crusted with blood, the sides of her mouth chafed and split. Her face was peeling and reddened from the sun. What horrified Nevia most was the gauntness of her cheeks, her sunken eyes. With no food or water, left to roast under the relentless sun for two days—that she still lived was a wonder.

Prometheus bent over the woman and uttered soft words that Nevia couldn't hear, resting a hand against her sunburnt skin. The clanswoman leaned in to his touch, exhausted and too weak to maintain her grip on a canteen, courtesy of a nearby guardsman, if gauging how he gently retrieved it and stuffed it back in his pouch.

Nevia drew a hesitant step forward, all eyes falling on her. "This woman must be brought under the care of our medical personnel immediately."

No one responded to her command, gazes dazed and unmoved. The soldier with the canteen winced as he stared down at the binds entwining her chaffed wrists together. The other imperial soldiers merely loitered, clearly disinterested in honoring the request of their empress.

"Did you hear what I said?" Nevia snapped. "Now! Take her to the palace!"

Grunting, the soldier nearest her drew a knife from his belt, the blade catching the sunlight as it clove through her bindings in a single movement. Nevia's lip curled in disgust; they should not have bound her when she was clearly so close to death. She had already suffered enough.

The blonde's head bobbed upward, swollen eyes lifting to the empress. Her face was terrible to look at, and yet Nevia steeled herself to maintain eye contact. "Please help." Her words escaped as a gravelly whisper. "My family, my clan—everyone."

A frown pinched Nevia's brow. "Who are you? You are from Zenoch?"

The woman dipped her head, yet was unable to lift it again. She collapsed, strength diminished, against the soldier who unbound her, his youthful face schooled into indifference as he threw her body over his shoulder and rose. From his expression, he still could not decide whether to treat her as a guest, patient, or prisoner.

"Take the carriage," Nevia said flatly. "We'll find our own way back."

"Your Highness." The soldier bowed, the only member of the imperial guard ready and willing to follow her command. They marched past her as they left the docks.

Nevia jerked her head in the direction of the vessel. Like Prometheus had stated, it was of very rough make by hands unused to crafting such a large vessel, or not having the time to craft one properly. Crudely fashioned with a lone sail and roughly sawn boards, it was not likely to last long on weathering seas.

Tearing her eyes away, she turned her attention onto a lingering sentry, burgundy cap being wrung in his gloved hands. "Has anyone searched the ship?"

"There were four others aboard, Your Highness," he answered. "Two of them dead, while the others are in critical condition."

"See to it that they receive immediate medical care, as well," Nevia said. "Hopefully we can nurse them back to health and learn more about why this happened."

"If—if it helps at all," the guard offered hesitantly, "the lookout noticed a ship moving from the east. He estimated it was moving at ten knots. The winds were gracious."

Nevia ran a dry tongue over her lips. "From the east." She shook her head. "That doesn't make sense. She is from Zenoch—"

"We think so," Prometheus corrected. "We don't know that for sure."

"Why would she be coming from the east?" She turned back to the guard, whose Adam's apple bobbed underneath his uniform's mandarin collar. "Was it just to dock, or . . . ?"

He shook his head. "No, it had been sailing due west since it was sighted. Normally, ships from the north come from a different angle than this one."

Another curious piece to the incomplete puzzle. Nevia shook her head. "That doesn't make any sense."

"No, it doesn't," the guard agreed. "I'm sorry I couldn't be of more help."

The empress felt a hand rest on her shoulder. Prometheus fell in step alongside her, sorrow wrinkling his weathered brow. "We should go back and fill in His Highness on the details we have managed to procure so far. With the goddess' fortune, the woman will awaken after some proper nourishment and rest and provide us with more answers."

Nevia nodded in assent, a sense of dread coursing through her veins as she watched two more figures being hauled from the vessel and ushered into another carriage. She didn't want to think too long about how they fared.

"I hope so, too, Prometheus."

"Whoever did this will come to justice," he reassured her.

She tried to smile but faltered, knowing deep down that this was somehow Darius' doing.

CHAPTER 19

"Her name is Khatalia Alasa," Darius said outside the infirmary door, where Prometheus and Nevia awaited news of the clanswoman survivor. His expression held indifference. Was it pain? Angst? Remorse? Nevia's fist curled at her side; she hoped it was the last. "She says she is well enough to speak with us, if you all are ready."

Prometheus gave a solemn nod. "Khatalia Alasa . . . isn't she one of Zenoch's chiefs?"

"Yes." Darius sighed, rubbing his temple. "She lost the majority of her clan during the avalanche assault, and the rest of it on her . . . voyage here."

Nevia glared daggers at Darius's back. He carefully avoided all eye contact with his wife as he threw open the door of the infirmary, forcing her to remain silent.

Shuttered windows framed the small, narrow bed where Khatalia rested. Sunflowers in full bloom were neatly perched on her nightstand, though Nevia was clueless as to who would bequeath them to the chieftain.

Despite being under the care of the empire's finest physicians, she still appeared far from hale. Her lips were no longer cracked, however, and the hollowness of her cheeks ebbed away. She impaled them with her slow, steady green-eyed gaze. Her hands, wrapped in narrow strips of yellowed gauze, clutched the blankets tightly at her sides. She didn't seem happy to see them.

"Khatalia." Darius voice held an uncharacteristic tenderness. "I'd like you to meet my wife Nevia, and my advisor Prometheus Volchek."

She jerked her head, eyes still red and puffy. It took Nevia a moment to realize that this was not the aftermath of her condition, but rather that the woman had been crying.

"I met them earlier," she said, voice clearer than previously, "on the dock where your men tied me up. Your wife saved me. I owe her my life."

A pause lingered, before Darius nodded. "Yes, it was her quick thinking that probably saved you from an untimely death. I'm sorry my men reacted the way they did. There was little understanding why you were bound to the helm when you arrived."

"It doesn't really matter. I failed them all anyway." Khatalia weighed her words, as if wondering if she really wanted to know the answer to her question, before adding, "They're dead, aren't they? The last of my kin?"

Darius nodded grimly, smoothing his coat as he slid into the chair at Khatalia's bedside and patting her hand. "I'm afraid they didn't make the journey. I am so sorry . . . . . If you had been out at sea much longer, the doctor says that you wouldn't have, either."

Khatalia hung her head, shoulders sagging in despair. Her sorrow quickly morphed to anger, however, as she brought a fist to slam down onto the nightstand, rattling the vase at her bandaged knuckles.

"Those damn, good for nothing, lowlife royals!"

The woman's outburst caused Nevia to retreat, alarmed. The empress shot a glance at Prometheus, whose expression was as worried and grim as hers.

Darius dipped his head. "You have suffered a great loss, to which you have my greatest condolences."

"You have no idea."

She buried her face in her hands, drawing in deep breaths as sobs enveloped her.

"When you can, please tell us what happened." Darius placed a hand gently on Khatalia's knee. "We are here to help you."

Nevia scoffed, disgusted. Thankfully no one was paying any attention to her. If Khatalia knew the truth. . . .

"The snow started falling." Khatalia's calloused hand slid into Darius', squeezing his fingers so tight that her knuckles turned white. "I was with the other survivors when it happened. We were out hunting. Heard the avalanche and made it back as quickly as we could, but we were too late. Our entire clan was annihilated. My wife, Reiya, my son, Ayan. . . . We were making our way south to the Sanen clan when we found the Feishin military launching a cannonball at another mountain, causing yet another avalanche. We killed them, fed them to my wolves, and set sail for the Feishin Kingdom to do the same to their savage queen."

Nevia winced at the brutality behind Khatalia's words, yet still pitied the woman and could hardly blame her. She lost everyone that she cared for in the assault on their country. Seeking retribution was only natural.

"Once there, we made them pay. A life for a life, though no amount of life could ever amount to those lost in the avalanche that day." Khatalia hung her head, letting out a slow, labored breath. "One minute I'm talking to the Feishin Fiend, the next I'm waking up bound to the helm in the middle of the ocean, my companions tied up similarly on deck. I didn't know where we were heading, or how long I'd been out at sea, but I couldn't break free, couldn't do anything. So I followed the stars, sailing due west, hoping to find help at some port. I knew if I tried to go back to

Zenoch there would be a chance that no one would be left alive to help. The south was our best bet for survival."

Darius gripped her shoulder with his free hand. "You did the right thing. I am glad that you were able to navigate the seas. What an awful experience you must've been through."

"Not as terrible as what my clansmen suffered."

Her words initiated a long silence. Nevia glanced between Darius and Khatalia, chewing on her tongue to prevent it from stating the truth. If Nevia told Khatalia who really was behind the death of her kin, there was no telling how the chieftain would respond. She had already made a show of killing anyone in her path in the Feishin Kingdom; what would stop her from attempting to slay everyone in the room? Suddenly, an alternate idea struck her.

"You said that the Feishin military was present?" Nevia asked, to which Khatalia responded with a painful nod. "That's odd because the Feishin are pacifists; they haven't had a military in hundreds of years."

Maybe she couldn't tell the truth, but she could poke holes in their conclusions. The emperor's lips drew into a thin line, and his dark gaze flickered toward Nevia, irises dancing with menacing flame. She merely smiled serenely at him. *Let him sweat a little,* she thought. Not only did she feel satisfied, but she reveled in it.

"It was all a ruse." Khatalia resumed staring at her blanketed feet. "The pacifism, the lack of troops. She still has guards and trained soldiers. Her nation is so secretive; I'm sure she's had a military all along."

"Lady Khatalia has a fair point." Prometheus slid his spectacles up the bridge of his long, crooked nose. Nevia wouldn't have been surprised if it'd been broken and improperly set at least once in his lifetime. "It is quite plausible that she had troops under special military training, and that no one was aware of their existence or would question the possibility because they're openly against war."

"But that seems all wrong," Nevia said, shaking her head. "Queen Arethusa is proud of the peace they attained, having sacrificed much to obtain it. Why would she risk all of that now on an assault?" She strode forward, hands grasping the iron footboard of the infirmary bed. "You killed dozens of her guards, and yet she didn't kill you when she easily could have. No one knew that you were there; it would've been simple if she is indeed a killer, as you say she is, but instead she pardoned you and let you live—"

"She tied me to the helm for two damn days!"

"Well, yes, that is true. But, to be fair, you killed dozens of her people."

"You're saying that her dozens lost was excessive for the hundreds, if not thousands, that she killed?" Khatalia's nostrils flared, her fierce glare clashing with Nevia's calm gaze.

"No." Nevia let out a sigh. It was her only shot at poking a hole in the theory; she had to make sure it was big enough. "I am just saying, how do we know it was really her that called the shots?"

"Maybe because Khatalia saw Feishin military at the base of the mountain?" Irritation culminating made Darius' tone terse. "Isn't that enough evidence for you?"

"Anyone could don uniforms."

Another long silence yawned. Darius' eyes were locked dangerously on her. A second warning, one she wasn't foolish enough to miss.

"What did the soldiers look like?" Prometheus asked. "Their physical traits could be a telltale sign."

All eyes fell on the chieftain, whose gaze fell to her fidgeting hands in her lap under the pressure. They were calloused and cracked around her nail beds. "I honestly don't remember," she confessed. "Black hair, fair skin. I am sure that they wore the Feishin Kingdom's emblem on their uniforms, and they wore their country's colors."

"That part wouldn't necessarily matter, dear," Prometheus said tenderly. "We don't doubt that they were Feishin uniforms. The empress is merely suggesting that a source other than Feishin soldiers were wearing them."

"Oh." Khatalia folded her arms. "In that case, I have no idea, but I can only assume they were who they said they were."

"And why would anyone lie about it?" Darius further added. "That makes very little sense to me."

"Maybe someone who wants to go to war with the Feishin Kingdom but are too cowardly to start the war themselves," Nevia shot.

Darius' jaw clenched, a muscle twitching at his temple.

The expression on Prometheus' face was unreadable. Curiosity arced one of his bushy gray brows. "That . . . is an interesting theory, Your Imperial Highness. But there is not enough evidence to suggest such. Right now eyewitnesses are all that we have to go on, and unfortunately their bodies cannot be inspected or confirmed as Feishin because they have been, erm, mutilated. Is that correct, Lady Khatalia?"

Khatalia's gaze met Prometheus. "They were eaten, yeah."

"Right." Nevia could've sworn that she saw Prometheus shudder. "So until we have more evidence that this was sabotage, I believe that we should keep speculation pocketed and stick with the facts."

"I agree with you, Prometheus," said Darius, a finality to his tone. The emperor rose from Khatalia's bedside, offering Nevia a smug grin. Darius won, and he knew it. Nevia refused to look at him, the sight too much for her to stomach.

"Well, if we're finished here, I'd best take my leave." Nevia spun on heel and gravitated toward the door, nauseated by the deception and foul play. "Rest well, Khatalia. And again, you have my greatest condolences for your loss. If there is anything that I can do to make your stay more comfortable, please don't hesitate to ask."

The chieftain leaned back against her pillow, letting out a long sigh. "I just need space to mourn and think." She closed her eyes. "But thanks for your hospitality. It's appreciated."

Nevia gave a swift nod and exited the room, before anyone could summon her back. Darius would be livid after her bold insinuations. Her paces matched her racing heart as she strode down the familiar halls of the palace to her private set of rooms, locking the door behind her despite the armed sentry posted behind it.

Her private suites had once been a place she seldom frequented. Now she was there every day and night. It had been months since she shared a room with Darius, avoiding even glancing in the direction of his quarters. Everything about him made her recoil; sometimes she didn't even know what she'd seen in him all those years ago when they first met.

She moved toward her canopied bed, its pale rosemary wood bedposts and pink silken spread beckoning her. The soft mattress cocooned her and offered comfort in a world that only caused her pain. More and more she became a recluse, skipping out on formal dinners and councils between neighboring countries. She didn't trust herself to keep her mouth shut. If the truth made others she cared for suffer by Darius' hand, staying in solitude seemed to be the answer.

And yet, she knew that she would need to fight to get the truth out in some manner or another. If Darius had a Zenochian chief on his side, she feared what sort of rally he could start against the Feishin Kingdom.

And now he had the proof he needed to display Arethusa's barbarism: Khatalia's mistreatment.

A groan escaped Nevia as she placed a cool hand over her eyes. The situation was going from bad to worse. She knew what she needed to do, but neither Darius nor she was going to like it.

CHAPTER 20

Hunting season peaked, the sport cherished within the Androvich Empire. Men would travel far and wide across the imperial countries to seek out the best hunting grounds for deer and wild boar. The forests along the western side of the Black River were by far the best, and wealthy imperial men would travel in parties to go on hunting expeditions.

Nevia watched from her window as her husband strode alongside Verrine, preparing for one such expedition. Darius's hand fell on the Ivalia lord's shoulder as they both met with their steeds and mounted.

Feigning sorrow to see her husband go couldn't have been farther from the truth. Her opportune moment to shed light on the truth presented itself. For her plan to work, however, she had to rely on the populace to side with her, otherwise her risk would be for naught—and she would pay the price dearly.

Nevia shuddered, trying not to think of the consequences of her failure. The benefit of success far outweighed the risk: the war would cease. Darius would likely be deposed, but she couldn't afford to feel sorry for him. Sympathy was partly what got her to this point. For that, Nevia could only blame herself.

For the first time since Elante's departure, Nevia called upon her new servant to dress her. The young serving girl was suspicious at Nevia's allowance, yet did as she was told without question, selecting for her empress a gown of shimmering black sequins, its bodice perfectly fitted and accentuating the curves of her breasts and hips. Silver beading adorned the V-neckline of her gown, as well as the train that followed her. She was beautiful, stunning, and intimidating all in one breath—precisely the image she sought that day.

Nevia twisted in front of her dressing mirror, taking in her image as if staring upon a stranger. Finally, she nodded with approval. "You've done well. Thank you. This very much matches what I had in mind."

The girl bowed in response to the empress' praise, her plain brown dress dusting the polished floorboards. "The pleasure is all mine, Your Imperial Highness."

The empress' gaze softened as she turned to face the girl, realizing just how young she truly was. Her face was round with youth and was further accentuated by her short, chin-length bob.

Her slight figure suggested she hadn't yet bloomed into womanhood, perhaps no older than fourteen. "What is your name, child?"

"Faye, Your Highness."

"Well then, Faye, I am happy to have your service. I hope that you have a pleasant day."

Recognizing the dismissal, the serving girl squeaked her gratitude and slipped out as silent as a mouse. This left Nevia alone with her thoughts, fidgeting with a crudely fashioned roc of turquoise and wood beads. Outside Zenoch this ornament held little significance, yet within it was customary for the groom to handcraft and present his bride-to-be with their Kindred Spirit, in Nevia's case a roc. Despite it being an alien concept, Darius made it for her himself, knowing that tradition was important to her and professing his undying love in her and his own way.

A hot tear wound its way down her cheek and beaded at her pointed chin. Furiously she swung open a bureau drawer and threw it inside. A wing broke off from the impact. The man she'd known and fallen in love with was gone; only the second face of him remained, and that was a man she could never come to love, no matter how hard she tried.

And she had tried, so very hard.

She strode through the palace with lifted shoulders and an air of authority, not bothering to glance at any of her subjects as they extended pleasantries toward her. Her train swept along the maroon carpet of the winding stairwell, fingertips barely touching the banister in her descent. Before her, pacing in the otherwise vacant foyer, was her father, the natural lighting dancing off the folds of his weathered, bronze face. His heavy footfalls eased when he saw her, a warm smile igniting his familiar blue eyes. At the foot of the stairs he reached for her, the empress' hands slipping into his effortlessly.

"Have the preparations been made?" she asked breathlessly.

Her father nodded. "Everything has gone according to plan, just as you asked, my dear. Everyone is awaiting you."

"And Darius is none the wiser?"

"As far as I am aware, yes. His hunting party left Velspire three hours ago."

"Good. Everything *is* going according to plan, then."

Nevia's father tilted his head, running a hand down her chilled arm. The heat bled into her skin. "Don't be so afraid, my dear."

For a heartbeat Nevia thought that her father had gone senile. "Oh, you're right. I'm just about to tell the country that their emperor is a conniving ruler that undermined the Feishin Kingdom for its resources. Absolutely. Nothing to be afraid of at all." Her voice dripped with sarcasm.

A sigh escaped her father. "Your audience views you as their empress, a figure with utmost authority. Your nervous energy is contagious. Sway them. Show your authority and confidence, and they will respect what you have to say, but waver and you have lost the battle before it even started."

"You make this all sound easy, but what I'm about to do is treason. I don't know how I am not supposed to be nervous."

He squeezed her hand until her fingers grew numb. "Because you know what you're doing is right. You are saving thousands of lives, bringing justice. I am proud of you, as your people will be. You will do well, Nevia. Just believe in your own inner light. It will guide you."

Nevia opened her mouth—to thank him, to say she loved him, anything at all—but he was already leaving her side to retreat to the confines of the limitless library. She threw out a hand. "Wait!"

He turned, eyes twinkling. Her mouth suddenly went dry. "Aren't you coming with me?"

Slowly he shook his head, bracing a hand on a column of books to his right. "No, my dear. It is important that you do this alone. My presence will only be a reminder that you aren't one of them. You need to be empress right now, and for that you need to forsake your roots. This is important."

Nevia wanted to argue that he was wrong, but deep down she knew he spoke truth. Her heritage had posed a complication since she arrived, and it wasn't going to change anytime soon. Especially if her father was at her side, cheering her on.

From this point on she would have to walk alone—and she was terrified.

But instead of letting it show, she held her chin high as she walked into the light, allowing herself to be led away in a chariot before the palace gates to the central square, where an assembly had formed for an emergency announcement from Her Imperial Highness.

Sunlight from the afternoon sun poured over Nevia's face as she exited the coach, a lithe guard with striking red hair extended a gloved hand to her. He flashed a smile, his dark, narrow eyes warm and distinctly Feishin. "We have arrived, Your Highness."

Nevia accepted his hand, allowing herself to be guided into the expectant eyes of hundreds that followed her every movement. She swallowed, momentarily hesitant, but her father's words echoed inside her mind, reminding to have confidence and believe in herself. She lifted her chin, refusing to be intimidated. Imperial soldiers awaited her a few paces away, removing their caps and bowing at her approach. This prompted the citizenry to lower their chins and place their hats before them, paying their respects to the empress who walked amidst them, as one of them.

A calm settled over her. These were her people too, not just Darius'. She had every right to lead them as he did. Between the parted crowd she strode, up to the same dais where they stood all those months ago at the Saavis festival, when Darius gave his speech on unity and was nearly assassinated. From unity to initiating a war in a mere matter of months—the thought made her heart ache further.

"Dearest citizens," Nevia began, fixing her gaze on a point in the distance. "Thank you all for answering my summon on such short notice. It is a matter of grave urgency which I gather you all today, one which cannot be delayed a moment longer. I strongly urge every one of you to spread this information far and wide. Danaeca deserves peace, truth, and justice.

"When I said my marriage vows to Emperor Darius, not only did I promise my life to him, but I also dedicated my life to you, my people. I disowned my heritage to serve you all as Empress, and I stand here proud of that decision. When you are in pain I grieve, and when I see you suffer I want to do everything in my power to fix it."

Nevia finally dared to glance at her audience. So far they appeared captivated, drawn in to what she had to say. Many nodded in assent.

"A coal shortage has been kept from you," she said gravely. "Emperor Darius didn't want you to worry, which I commend. He shouldered this burden himself, but in doing so the stress of this matter clouded his judgment and morality."

A few frowns tailed her speech, murmurs breaking into the once-silent audience. Nevia attempted to school her face into calm, proceeding as if nothing was wrong.

"The Feishin Kingdom harbors a resource that His Imperial Highness views as essential for the empire's survival in this upcoming winter. In response, he has entered negotiations with the Feishin queen."

More excited murmurs. She watched a young man lean into a peasant woman with a babe, excitedly whispering something in her ear. Hope ignited her soft features, tenderly rocking the sleeping babe in her supple arms.

"The negotiations did not go as hoped. However, Emperor Darius still feels that this material is vital, so he has proceeded down a path he felt would yield the least amount of repercussions. With imperial soldiers donning Feishin uniforms, he sent an assault on Zenoch, making it appear that they wish harm upon the nation. He sabotaged the kingdom."

Gasps and angry murmurs followed this declaration, which was to be expected. She raised a hand to calm the raging crowd and spoke louder over the din.

"This has allowed us to rally forces against the Feishin Kingdom for striking an ally, creating an all-out war. This will allow the Feishin government, which relied on pacifism and isolation instead of combat, to crumble. Emperor Darius will easily acquire what it is he seeks and come out unscathed. I have expressed disapproval of this, but he is adamant on his decision.

"It is up to you, the people, to share this information, and together we must put a stop to Emperor Darius' tyranny! To reunite Danaeca once and for all!"

She gripped the podium with both hands, face stoic, awaiting applause that never came. Only confusion and unrest echoed amidst her audience, none displaying the enthusiasm that she admonished—and expected. Darius always garnered approval from his audience; where did she go wrong?

"What material is it that His Imperial Highness wants from the Feishin Kingdom?" one man asked.

"How do you know all of this for sure?"

"Why would His Excellency lie to us? Why do you have to go behind his back?"

"This is some power grab, isn't it? You're not really one of us."

The protests grew sharper, louder, with more vehemence as they mounted. Nevia's kohl eyeliner smudged as she rubbed her eye. She just told them the truth, and they denied it? Frustrated, she slammed her fist on the podium before her.

"I have nothing to gain from lying to you!" Desperation and hysteria inflected her tone. This was all wrong. She'd lost her nerve, as well as her audience. "Please, you must listen to me. I am speaking out against my husband at great personal risk to myself. You don't know what I had to go through to get this message to you."

"You're nothing but a treacherous heathen from the mountains!" a woman cried, slipping off her shoe to toss at the empress. It bounced off the podium's steel surface, but it was enough to prompt an imperial soldier to draw closer to her side.

"Your Highness," he uttered tensely above the roar of the crowd. "I think this meeting isn't quite what any of us were expecting."

"You think?" She didn't try masking the sarcasm in her voice, laughing bitterly. Her credibility disseminated like dandelion fluff, but it hardly mattered. She already lost. Word would get back to Darius, and he would be livid.

"You're asking us to betray our emperor, the one who gave you your crown?" a man jabbed. "This is nothing but sabotage, a well-crafted lie so you can maintain the throne for yourself."

"Maybe she is in league with the Feishin queen," another said, waggling a finger at the empress. "After all, I hear that women have greater authority than men there."

"Silence!" Nevia demanded, pounding her fist again on the podium. Trying to call for order did no good. No one would listen. Loose articles of clothing were being flung at her as missiles, as well as a shower of insults.

"Death to the heathen!" one woman screamed, tossing a baguette at the podium.

It struck Nevia's calf, the empress too stunned and shocked to react. She looked down at the vengeful woman with a pierced heart. Others began to charge forth as well with makeshift weapons, though the flicker of a knife in the crowd arrested her attention. A sword too was unsheathed beside her, causing her to squeeze her eyes shut tight. She thought her own guards had also decided to turn on her.

They might as well, she thought bitterly. *I'm as good as dead anyway.*

A guard gripped her upper arm and brought her to his side, his touch firm but not unkind. "You need to leave, Your Highness!"

Two guards leapt before her, swords extended, fending off her assailants with parries and strikes, while another, the redheaded soldier from the coach, held her close to his side, eyes urgent and pleading. A painful realization suddenly hit her: only a dozen soldiers accompanied her to the central square when they were surrounded by an audience of hundreds. She didn't think there would be any need for more.

How naive, how foolish. There was a very real possibility that she would be killed by the very people she sought to protect.

The guard's lips moved, yet his words failed to reach her. Irritated, he gave her arm a strong yank and forced her to move. She stumbled after him. The angry cries and clash of weapons resounded from behind her.

"Are you going to kill me?" she asked weakly. He couldn't help but stop, brows knitted together.

"Your Highness, I must insist you stop this foolishness. I'm going to save you. You are my empress and I believe in your cause."

She blinked, eyes wide, before noticing that they were being charged by a ragged man, dagger in hand. The guard gripped her arms, twisting her to spare her from the assailant's blade and instead taking the blow, steel embedding into his shoulder. He clenched his jaw as he whipped around, taking his attacker by surprise and slashing at his chest with terrifying precision. A sickening gurgle escaped the assailant's lips as he fell limp to the ground. Nevia couldn't withhold her scream.

Three more pursuers charged at her guard. His shoulder wound bled freely, and with each parrying blow it seemed the wound only worsened. He grunted, throwing off one of the angry attackers who aimed a knife at the empress.

"Go! I'll hold them off!"

Fear stabbed at Nevia's heart. "But you'll die—"

"I said GO!"

Nevia shot a glance in the direction of her chariot, hidden behind a cluster of steel factories, their smoke pluming into the smog-covered sky. She was still several blocks away, and there was no doubt that she would encounter more angry citizens wishing her death. Yet if she stayed they both would die, and she couldn't let this man perish in vain. Her lips met with the scratchy red whiskers on his cheek, causing his eyes to widen in surprise.

"Thank you, truly, for believing in me."

He barely managed a smile before a man with a pitchfork charged at him. It stabbed into his armored side, not meeting flesh but knocking the breath free from his lungs and causing him to stagger back. She feared for his life at the hands of the angry mob, the sheer number of them, but there was nothing she could do. Sniffling, she gathered her train in her arms and fled, scurrying down the cobblestone path as fast as her legs would carry her.

It wasn't long before heavy feet pounded behind her. Someone managed to get past her guard and was now close. Biting back panic, she tore off her shoes to run faster, chucking them over her shoulder. Pain laced her feet, cuts and bruises making purchase on them from the coarse stone.

Her chariot loomed into view at the outskirts of the square, its door with the golden imperial insignia ever beckoning. Hair wrenched free streamed about her face. The driver twisted in alarm at the sight of her—and beyond her.

"Jump up!" He extended his hand. She reached for it, but was yanked back by hands encircling her waist. Body pinned against a stranger, she screamed and attempted to break free from her assailant to no avail. Cold fingers pressed against her throat, strangulating her and silencing her scream. No air could escape or enter her lungs. She threw herself into her assailant, the back of her head meeting with his forehead. The man swore darkly under his breath, yet his grip held firm.

Her desperation only grew. The driver shouted something, but her senses were failing her; she couldn't manage to focus on his words. The corners of her vision grew dark. She twisted and wriggled. Finally her hands found his bearded face. Her thumbs pressed into his eye sockets, causing the man to scream and immediately release her. Air was renewed to her lungs as she collapsed forward, hands splayed against the multicolored stone underfoot. Her vision sharpened, but she was still lightheaded.

"Zenochian bitch!" he screamed, making a grab for a fistful of her hair.

Nevia yanked her head forward against the pain, allowing tufts of hair to be pulled free from the roots to make her escape. Her scalp screamed in agony, but she was not going to die here. If not for herself, for the Feishin guard who sacrificed himself for her, who believed in her. Perhaps he truly felt she could save his homeland—if she survived.

"Get me out of here," she murmured at the driver's side, tears stinging her eyes. The driver didn't have to be told twice. He shook the reigns, and the horses stole them away from the square homeward.

Nevia sat beside him as the cool air eased her wounds, even if the nearby factory smoke stung at her nostrils. She sniffed, blotting tears that streamed from her eyes.

This was her coup de grace, her last stand against Darius, her only chance at ending the atrocious calamity he started.

And she failed.

CHAPTER 21

When Nevia asked to be taken away, she somehow hadn't envisioned the palace. Her heart sank as she watched the familiar steel gates loom into view: the bars that had become her prison and, simultaneously, her sanctuary. Thankfully the mob did not follow, the gates of the palace tranquil. The sentries' stoic faces contorted at the sight of Nevia's torn dress and disheveled hair. Spears seeming to grow slack in their palms, they broke protocol and yelled to open the gates. The iron doors creaked open, allowing the chariot to enter the imperial gardens.

The chariot's wheels jolted backward after grinding to a halt. Nevia lifted what remained of her gown and leapt off the driver's bench with unladylike conduct, yet would have been acceptable back home in Zenoch. She felt eyes upon her, but chose to ignore them. Their opinion of her didn't matter right then. Inside many more eyes feel on her as she marched up the winding flight of stairs, unspoken questions lighting their eyes. They knew it wasn't their place to ask. One of the few times that being empress had its perks.

Androvich family portraits greeted her as she rushed through the west wing corridor. Nevia cried out in surprise as she collided with a mess of blonde locks and burly muscles, stumbling back on her tattered train. Strong arms fled to hold her steady, protecting her from taking a tumble down the steps.

"Empress." It was the Zenochian chieftain, Khatalia. Her biceps bulged as she yanked Nevia away from the stairs' edge. "What the hell happened to you? You look like shit."

Nevia lowered her face, uncertain of what to say, where to even begin. "I tried to make something right, but I only made a mess of things." A shiver coursed through her body, the gravity of her actions starting to sink in. As far as the public was concerned, she was a traitor. In the eyes of the court she would be no better. "I need to leave. I have to get away from here before Darius gets back."

A bushy brow rose. "I don't understand you."

"I'm sorry." Nevia withdrew from the chieftain's grip, the lent strength that she provided. "I can't explain everything right now, but just know that Darius has been lying to you. About everything."

"What are you talking about?"

Nevia's heart grew louder in her ears. "It was all Darius. He wanted to invade the Feishin Kingdom, so he staged the attack. He's the one that killed your family." The words fled her lungs in a single breath, causing her to sway on her feet. "I'm sorry. I wanted to tell you sooner, but I was threatened not to. I couldn't say anything in front of him."

Confusion clouded Khatalia's face, her nose wrinkling in concentration. Nevia should've waited around, and perhaps with more time she would've, but she had to make her escape while she still could.

Khatalia's footsteps echoed along the corridor, following her. "You blame your husband for killing my clan?"

"I'm sorry!" Nevia waved a hand and broke into a sprint, fleeing to her suite to gather her things.

In anticipation of her arrival a fire had been kindled, bed neatly made and throw pillows fluffed. Khatalia approached, stopping suffocatingly close.

"You need to explain." It was a command, not a request.

Nevia sighed, gesturing toward the bed. "I need to pack. You can sit there while I explain everything."

The chieftain's weight sank into the pink, plush duvet while Nevia scrambled to find a bag, any bag, and began to shove her most precious belongings inside. Her broken flute, a necklace gifted by her mother long ago, and several articles of practical clothing lacking the frills and finery of most her wardrobe. When she sat back on her heels to look into the face of the chieftain, she could read the intensity burning within her emerald eyes, the pain of her lost loved ones.

Nevia hesitated, weighing which would hurt Khatalia more: confirming the truth, or allowing her hatred for the Feishin queen to fester. She decided the truth was necessary, no matter how much it pained her.

She recounted everything starting from their journey to the Feishin Kingdom. Of the core shards that Queen Arethusa zealously protected, as well as Darius' plan to sabotage the country. Khatalia slammed a fist onto the solid oaken face of Nevia's nightstand, knocking over a petunia-filled vase and spilling water onto her lap and the floor.

"That conniving bastard!" Khatalia glared at Nevia, seething. "So that foolish queen was telling the truth."

"I couldn't stop him. I tried to dissuade him, but he was determined, and threatened that if I got in his way I would pay dearly. I know he means it."

"He is so sick," Khatalia murmured. "Playing god with the lives of others. He actually pretended to feel sorry for my loss!"

"I think he was being genuine." Nevia rubbed her head. "He's a very complicated man. I don't think he's wholly evil, but he has lost his way."

Khatalia's head whipped to Nevia so fast that she thought her neck would snap. "Only an evil man could do this without remorse."

Deep inside, Nevia felt Khatalia was right.

Rising, she slipped behind her privacy screen to climb out of the tatters of her formal gown, replacing it with a simple tunic and pants. She layered on her warmest coat and sank her feet into the fleece-lined boots she'd brought from her Zenochian home. Fully clad in her gear, she strung a bow over her chest and seized a quiver of arrow from against her wardrobe. They were intended for hunting, but Nevia had no qualms in repurposing them for her escape. Her aim was not good, but, even if she could maim, that would suffice.

Sharp green eyes surveyed her as she emerged. "Where are you going?" Khatalia's question made her halt.

"I-I honestly don't know, but I can't let him find me here."

"You should try to stop him," Khatalia insisted. "You might be the only one that can."

"I already tried. If you don't remember, that's how I got myself into this mess."

Khatalia shook her head impatiently. "No, I mean, you couldn't reach your people. But how about my brethren? They don't know the truth, and they deserve to know. Risanna would want to know."

Nevia tilted her head. "Who's Risanna?"

"The chief of Sanen. Right now they're probably planning how to get back at the Feishin Kingdom, like I did. And with my retelling of accounts here and how I was tied to a bloody helm, I'm sure that your *husband* is rallying all the clans to get what he's after. We can't let him get away with this. He deserves a public execution for what he's done."

A shudder coursed through Nevia. Perhaps it was true, but she didn't like to entertain the thought. Evil or not, Darius was still her husband, a man she couldn't yet bring herself to hate. Nevia's head spun. "I don't know. Trying to get to Zenoch and cross those mountains sounds impossible."

"No, it isn't. And I'll be there to help you."

"What?"

"You didn't think I was going to sit here in the home of my family's murderer while he wages war against pacifists, did you?"

"W-well, um, no, not exactly."

"So I'm coming with you." Khatalia folded her arms triumphantly. "I know those mountains. You would probably starve or freeze to death without an escort."

While guilt gnawed at her, relief simultaneously settled in. Thoughts of being alone was frightening, yet having a comrade at her side who would hold her hand through it all changed everything for her. Maybe she *would* stand a chance of providing her testimony to the other clans.

Nevia swung her satchel over her shoulder, adjusting the shoulder straps to accommodate her. "You have my thanks, Khatalia."

The chieftain winked. "Don't mention it."

With a heavy heart, Nevia cast one final gaze around the room. So many memories surrounded her, and too many belongings.

The thought of leaving brought her less joy than she once thought it would. As an afterthought Nevia shoved her jewelry box's contents into her satchel, thinking they could be sold later if the two were in need of coin. Mentally she bid her beloved music corner farewell, along with her favorite rocking chair before the fire.

The door rattled on its hinges, snapping Nevia from her reverie. Both women leapt in alarm as the emperor emerged. He flung his black cloak to the side, a deep scowl etched in his face. His dark gaze flickered toward the dying hearth.

"Darius." Nevia blanched.

His chocolate eyes met hers; never had they felt so devoid of warmth.

"Going somewhere, Neve?"

CHAPTER 22

“What are you doing here?” Nevia blurted. “You were going hunting, weren’t you?”

Darius shook his head, clearly unamused. “Of course I was. I had to come back because I forgot my father’s compass, but was a bit surprised when I found an angry mob marching up the streets of Velspire demanding the death of their empress.”

Nevia swallowed hard and met his gaze evenly, wondering if he, too, wished for the death of his empress. His expression revealed nothing.

“Really?” She could’ve cursed herself at the fragility of her tone.

He folded his arms over his chest, lips twisting in disbelief. “You didn’t know?”

Nevia shrugged. "I mean, it's nothing new to me. They've wanted me dead for a very long time."

"Generally they haven't been quite so bold as to cry it through the streets with pitchforks and torches."

"Maybe they saw an opportunity while you were away."

"Maybe." He closed the door behind him, cloaking their words from the sentries stationed outside. He pressed his back against it, gaze focused on Nevia as though she was a delightful treat. "Though I am hard-pressed to know who found the opportunity: you, or them."

He knows, Nevia thought, heart sinking. *He knows everything, and he has come back to kill me.* Nevia opened her mouth to speak, to feebly offer her apologies and defend herself, but was cut off by the booming voice of the chieftain beside her.

"You. Sick. Bastard!"

They had all but forgotten Khatalia's presence. In a blur Khatalia rushed forward, wasting no time when backhanding the emperor across the face, knuckles colliding with his cheekbone. His cheek grew an angry shade of pink, his fingers rising to meet the swelling flesh.

"Khatalia," he blurted, but was interrupted when Khatalia struck him again. Nevia cringed at the sound of his jaw snap.

"You have a lot of nerve lying to my face!" the chieftain roared. "Traitorous, conniving, backstabbing monster! You threaten your wife, betray the Feishin queen, mislead *me.* I killed dozens of innocent lives in the Feishin Kingdom all for your lies and ruthless deception!"

His lips drew into a thin line. "That sounds like your problem, not mine."

Nevia gritted her teeth at the sound of a third strike.

"I would advise caution about making too much noise," he warned, a deathly chill permeating his voice. "There are sentries posted right outside this door. They may . . . get the wrong idea if they hear what is going on."

"Oh, they'll get the right idea, all right." Khatalia grasped the front of Darius' burgundy collar and drew his face so close her spittle flecked his beard. "They will see your blood coat the walls of this room when I'm done!"

This was going from bad to worse, and Nevia could envision Khatalia ripping Darius apart limb from limb without intervention. As such, she drew a step forward and placed a hand on the chieftain's bicep. "Khatalia, please. Stop this."

The chieftain ignored her.

"That would be a bad idea. It's only going to paint your friend there even more of a traitor," Darius commented, a smirk aimed at Nevia quirking the edges of his lips. "Not that I really care right now. After all that I did, everything that we talked about, you still had to do things your own way. Stab me in the back and twist the blade when I wasn't looking, hmm?"

"I had to do what was right," was her only reply.

"Wounding me was what you felt was right?!" Darius threw Khatalia's hand aside, sidestepping the chieftain and taking two long strides to stand before his wife. She flinched and turned her face away upon feeling his hot breath beating down on her face.

"I gave you multiple chances, Nevia." His fingers dug painfully into her jaw as he gripped her chin and forced her head to the side to whisper in her ear. "You have hurt me for the last time. For this I will—"

His threat ended with a grunt and a smash, body slumping forward into her. Nevia let out a yelp as she fell backward under his weight, tripping over the rug and falling to the ground alongside her chair. Broken pottery shards lay on the carpet, the roots of the fern bare and exposed. Nevia shrugged the unconscious emperor off and shot a glare at Khatalia overhead, who brushed soil from her palms over her thighs. The chief merely shrugged.

"I was tired of listening to him prattle."

The door of Nevia's suite burst open, the commotion attracting the sentries at last. Long steel spears in hand, their gazes traveled hesitantly from Darius, unconscious, to the two women. That was all Khatalia needed. Nevia watched as the chieftain disarmed one of the guards with a spin faster than her eyes could follow. The other sentry rounded on her, but before he could land a strike his head was slammed into the opposite wall. He collapsed to the ground beside his unconscious emperor.

Nevia's eyes widened, staring down at the three unconscious men in disbelief. Khatalia snatched up one of their spears and offered a hand to the empress to spring to her feet.

"Remind me to never get on your bad side. You're scary when you're mad."

Khatalia shook her head, letting go to retrieve the empress' satchel. "It's called combat training. You haven't seen me mad yet. Mad was when I was in the Feishin Kingdom."

Nevia bit her lip. If this wasn't angry, she didn't want to see what was.

"Before we go, though, I'm going to finish off the bastard—"

Khatalia twirled her spear, preparing to run the emperor through the chest. Fear dove into Nevia as she ran between the two, arms outstretched. "Wait! You can't!"

Khatalia seethed, teeth bared. "This man threatened you, Nevia. He'd just as soon have you killed."

"But he didn't."

"He didn't have the chance."

"But even still, don't kill him." Nevia shook her head frantically. "I think someone else is behind his actions. Please. He's my husband."

Khatalia's gaze softened a fraction, frown remaining. She pointed the tip of her spear at Darius' broad back "But he's a shitty husband."

"I know, but even still. . . ."

A sigh escaped Khatalia, lowering her spear and bounding toward the door. "Fine. He's yours to kill when you're ready. Let's go, then. No sense in waiting till they wake up and having to knock 'em out again . . . unless you want to."

"Um, no, that's okay," Nevia said, perhaps too quickly.

The two women burst through the door appearing disheveled and troubled, garnering the attention of servants and sentries outside. Nevia kept her paces quick and even, falling in step with Khatalia as they made their way downstairs. Despite looking suspect, no one had reason to apprehend her yet. She hoped they were able to escape the palace before everyone was on high alert.

"I need to get my father," Nevia said. "He'll surely be in danger if I leave him here. Darius hates him."

The chieftain's gaze scanned the hall for security. "Where is he?"

"At this hour I have no idea. If I were to guess I would say in his set of rooms. He doesn't get out much."

Nevia prayed it was true, as they didn't have much time to explore.

The palace was a maze Nevia had long-since memorized. The expansive library entrance greeted them, the archway adorned with ancient texts. Khatalia stopped, impressed. The vast expanse of bookshelves filling the massive space beyond the entrance was devoured by her intense gaze. Nevia didn't allow her to linger long, tugging on her arm and together rounded a corner to enter a short hall guarded by two sentries.

Without knocking, Nevia pushed open the door to her father's set of rooms, poking her head into the ever-empty sitting parlor, where guests could have been entertained—if he ever had any. The room was in disarray, poorly stacked books and loose papers littering every surface. Alongside a worn leather recliner by the fireplace—her father's favorite spot, where she would often find him crafting leather goods as a pastime—a bone-handled pocket knife lay on a coffee table. Nevia glanced around, noticing the coals had long since cooled, resulting in a chill being present in the air.

"Father?"

Nevia carefully tread through the mess, trying not to further scatter papers to the best of her ability.

The chieftain leaned on the doorframe, its white paint worn and peeling. "He's not here?"

Nevia ignored her, bursting into his bedroom and sending another stack of papers bustling about. The bed was unkempt, sheets bunched and draped haphazardly over the mattress. The curtains were drawn to reveal the gardens below and the encroaching darkness tinting the evening sky.

A hand rested on Nevia's shoulder, causing her to tense. Khatalia's eyes were gentle as they fell on the empress, understanding etched in her face. "He's not here." The chief echoed the words that already took residence in Nevia's head. "We must not linger. He could be anywhere."

"But I can't leave without him." Panic raked its way through her chest. "He will be harmed in my place if I leave."

"And he'll still be harmed if we stay here and get caught." Khatalia stepped around a crate of wooden peelings towards the door, their purpose unbeknownst to them. "Come on, do him proud and change the fate of the world. That's your job right now."

The empress' mind whirled. Everything was happening too quickly. "He could be gathering more supplies," Nevia murmured. "For one of his many projects. He's a leatherworker, and—"

"And we'd be wasting valuable time wandering around for a phantom," Khatalia interjected. She gripped Nevia's arm, leading her from the wreckage of her father's suite. "We will try to find him later. But for now, you need to leave."

Before they could exit the room, however, two sentries appeared, barring their path with crossed spears.

"Halt," one said with remorse, refusing to meet Nevia's gaze. "In the name of His Imperial Highness, both of you are under arrest for treason."

Khatalia chuckled darkly, cracking her knuckles at the challenge. "Yeah, not today, sorry."

Within a blur of movement Khatalia retrieved her spear and ran the unfortunate man through. He crumbled to the ground, gurgling something before stilling, hand clutched at his side where he was pierced.

"Don't kill them," Nevia pleaded. "Please. Even if misguided, they are still my people."

In Khatalia's hesitation, the remaining guard dove forward. He didn't, however, engage Khatalia, whose spear was braced and ready. Instead he struck Nevia, unarmed and vulnerable. The cold steel penetrated her left shoulder, pain searing down her arm and radiating through her chest. The sentry trembled as he held her there, pinning her against the wall.

"I'm sorry, but we've been commanded to bring you to His Highness, dead or alive."

Nevia could tell his apology was sincere, and for that she was grateful. She closed her eyes against the pain, feeling warm blood trail down her fingertips.

As the weapon was wrenched free the pain further intensified, blood flowing profusely from her wound. She sank to her knees, hands fleeing to her shoulder in an attempt to stanch the bleeding. In her daze she could barely concentrate on the exchange between Khatalia and her attacker. Spears clashed once, twice, thrice, before Khatalia ran him clean through and cast his body aside. The chieftain's knees hit the tiled floor as her hands fled to Nevia, lips forming words she couldn't understand. The room came in and out of focus, and Nevia almost succumbed to the quiet darkness that beckoned until a stinging pain lanced the side of her face. Her visioned cleared.

"You need to stay with me," Khatalia said gruffly, hand out, ready to slap her again if needed. Tears welled in her eyes. "Focus."

She blinked, watching the chieftain rip some material from her father's blanket to make a bandage. Nevia groaned as pressure was applied to her shoulder.

"Got to stop the bleeding," Khatalia murmured. Her hands worked deftly, dressing the wound and wrapping leftover material around Nevia's body into a sling. The fabric was coarse against her torn flesh, yet the discomfort paled in comparison to the wound.

Nevia gripped her hand with her uninjured side. "You are a good friend to me."

"Save it."

The makeshift bandage did its part of stanching the bleeding, but the matter was not over yet. Khatalia heaved Nevia off the ground, but the empress sagged against Khatalia's chest, unable to support her weight. Nevia shook her head, face pale and skin clammy.

"Leave me. I will get you killed," she whispered. "He wants me, not you. Get out while you can."

"Oh, for the love of—hang on."

Khatalia stowed her stolen spear onto her back before swinging Nevia over her shoulder. The smooth steel of the spear collided with Nevia's forehead as Khatalia made off into a sprint, down the hall and toward the nearest exit. They barreled through a chamber, baffling the guards until cries echoed behind them with the drawing of blades. Nevia hung lifelessly over Khatalia's shoulder, barely coherent. She didn't recall how they had found themselves in the courtyard, standing before her lacquered chariot under the twilight sky. Khatalia untethered the mares before hoisting Nevia onto one, her stomach making impact on the horse's bare back. She wrapped her arms snugly around the mare's neck, leaning into its mane as her body slackened.

"Don't let them escape!"

Footsteps resounded behind them, their escape not yet purchased. Nevia's fingers threaded through her horse's mane, strands thick and coarse against her sticky, bloodied hands. Khatalia gave the backside of Nevia's horse a slap, forcing it into a canter.

No, she thought, forcing her mind to sharpen, to hold on for just a while longer. *I can't let go now. If I do, he will win. Don't let go.*

It was a thought, a promise that she swore herself to. They galloped through the city gates of Velspire and into the underlying forests, their pursuers losing them shortly after they entered the thickening wood. Nevia felt herself slump forward, static silence filling her ears before she went numb and cold inside.

Her consciousness slipped into oblivion.

CHAPTER 23

Plink, plank!

Cold droplets fell on Nevia's dirt-stained face, streaking down the apples of her cheeks and into her ears. She winced, nose wrinkled.

Plink, plink, plank!

Her vision swam in and out of focus as she finally willed her eyes open, the visage of a bronze-skinned woman looming over her, holding a canteen over her face. Irritation bridled under her skin, yet her limbs felt too heavy to swat her away.

"Oh, good, you're awake." Khatalia lowered the canteen, grinning. "You had me worried for a moment there. I thought that I lost you."

In response Nevia groaned, wriggling herself onto her good side. Her shoulder screamed in protest. She squeezed her eyes shut and drew in agonizing breaths.

A tender hand helped her into a more comfortable position and propped her head on her satchel.

"Don't move—you lost a lot of blood. The wound has finally clotted, and I can't have it opening up again. You need to be still for a while yet."

Memories of their narrow escape flooded her, from the encounter with Darius to the wound that left her incapacitated. Nevia let out a hollow breath, watching as it fogged the forest air. How far did they travel? Back in Velspire the foliage still had shades of red, gold, and orange adorning the ground, yet her surroundings were coated with a thick layer of fluffy snow, and overhead evergreens bowed their branches under heavy blankets of white.

"Where are we?"

"Just south of the mountains underlying Zenoch." Khatalia settled herself beside the empress, propping her elbows over her knees. "We have been traveling for a few days. We're close, but we can't scale the mountains yet, not with you in this condition. We need to wait till you're better."

Nevia wanted to cry. "We could be waiting a long time. If we don't get press on a full-on war will break out, and Zenoch will be fighting with the enemy as their ally."

"I know."

"So we have to go." Nevia grunted, pushing herself onto her uninjured side, elbow digging into the frozen soil. The blood rushed from her head, making her head swim. The dizziness failed to subside, and Khatalia patiently eased her back onto her makeshift bed, drawing up her cloak to Nevia's chin to serve as a blanket.

"No, we don't. I have sent word to Risanna of Sanen via a messenger bird explaining the situation. If all goes well, they should send aid."

Nevia shook her head. "You should've sent word about Darius."

"No, we need help, first and foremost. If I mentioned that ass, there's a chance they would smell a rat and choose to strand us. We will tell them in person. It'll go over much better that way."

Her eyes stung from unshed tears. "But Khatalia, we probably won't be able to tell them in person. Sending them a warning might have been the only way, and—"

Khatalia's palm slapped her cheek, earning a glare of defiance at the chieftain.

"Stop hitting me!"

"Stop being so damn pessimistic all the time! I can't stand it!" Khatalia shot to her feet. "Now stay still already. I'm going to find food. Move an inch and I'll bind you to a tree instead. You got me?"

Nevia pouted her lips, but did not doubt for a moment that Khatalia would stay true to her word.

"Good. I'll be back soon, then." She slung a pouch over her chest.

Nevia watched as the tall woman disappeared into the frosted trees, the crunch of her footsteps fading until all was silent. Eerily so. The birds had fled south for the winter, leaving nothing to greet Nevia except the sound of her own rattled breath and occasional rustling of branches, perhaps from a visiting squirrel or the wind.

And crackling . . . she noticed the crackling.

A fire roared a few yards away, its smoke pluming up into their foggy surroundings. Propping herself up again, Nevia wondered why she hadn't recognized the scent of charcoal sooner, as it was soon all she could smell. She craned her gaze skyward, taking in the trees surrounding her. Maples and elms were predominant, with clusters of evergreens. The fresh scent of pine occasionally drifted her way through the chilly breeze.

She hated being alone with only her torturous thoughts for company. She missed home—her true home in the north. The idea of returning should've filled her with joy instead of the gnawing dread in the pit of her stomach. Instead of returning citizens, they were coming as messengers of grim tidings. Nevia couldn't help wondering if they would believe her story or react as the people of Velspire had.

Darius entered the forefront of her mind, pain lacing its way across her chest like poison. Her best friend morphed into her worst enemy seemingly overnight. Nevia couldn't resist the tears that fell, sobs wracking through her entire being as she curled her knees in toward her torso. The seer's words returned to her, and in that moment Nevia realized the prophecy was real. This betrayal, this hurt, was exactly as described to her that day. She wracked her brain, trying to recall the rest of the prophecy, but her mind was too addled to remember. There was something about making the right choice when the time came . . . but what was that? Was she making the right choice in leaving? Should she have stayed? She shook her head in frustration. Everything hurt, and recognizing right from wrong felt like an impossible task.

Crunching snow announced Khatalia's return, a dead rabbit clutched in her fist. Specks of crimson dripped from her prey and stained the pure white snow. She slumped down beside the fire, her back to the empress, sifting through her things before procuring a jagged knife.

"You know, I never did thank you for saving my life."

No response came from Khatalia, only the sounds of skinning greeted her.

"You didn't have to do this," Nevia continued. "You had everything you needed. I was only a liability. By protecting me you could've gotten yourself killed. You still could. You're harboring a traitor."

Khatalia's work on the rabbit grew violent and messy, blood spraying in the direction of her face. The chieftain lowered her blade long enough to sift through sticks, searching through their firewood to procure the perfect spit for their dinner.

"I refuse to let another person die." Khatalia professed. "Too much blood has been shed under my watch, and I refuse for there to be more. Maybe I couldn't save Reiya or Ayan, or anyone else from my clan, but I can save you. And save you I will."

Khatalia's hands curled into fists, making Nevia wish to be there to comfort her. The acceptance of death was never easy, but to this extent, this kind of intimate loss . . . Nevia didn't know how she found the strength to even go on.

Khatalia's entire frame shook. "I killed so many, even as they calmly told me they didn't do it. But I didn't listen, because I am a fool. I have always been a fool. So utterly, horrifically, HOPELESSLY STUPID!"

She kicked out at the snow, the flames flickering weakly before roaring back to life. Nevia didn't trust herself to speak, thinking that no words were appropriate for how Khatalia was feeling. The chieftain jerked the skinned rabbit through the spit and tossed it over the fire for roasting, hands trembling as she worked.

Summoning her courage, Nevia dared to prop herself on her elbow and finally spoke.

"You were a victim here, just like the rest of us. If you're blaming yourself, you could blame me even more. I'm married to the monster whose responsible for all of this, and I did nothing to stop him."

"But you tried," Khatalia spat hoarsely. "You did everything you could. It's silly to lay more blame on yourself."

"Don't you see it's the same for you, too? You were led to believe your clan was slaughtered by the Feishin Kingdom. You retaliated with what you knew—"

"The people didn't even try to defend themselves!" Khatalia turned to face her, tears trailing down blood-stained cheeks. "I killed innocents, Nevia. That doesn't make me proud! And that doesn't make me a thing like you. Stop trying to compare us. You're just making it worse."

The air suddenly felt colder. Nevia shuddered as she lay back on the ground, breathing deep to keep her emotions in check. The scent of roasting meat merged with burning wood made Nevia's stomach rumble. How long had it been since she last ate? Nevia ran her tongue over dry lips.

"What is our plan, then?" she dared ask, puncturing the hanging silence.

Khatalia sniffed the air, her gaze afar into the forest beyond. "First we need to get to Zenoch. I overheard the emperor discussing a unified front to storm the Feishin Kingdom. I agreed to help, and stupidly told him the other chiefs would help, too."

"And they will." Nevia bit the inside of her cheek. "If Darius gets to them first."

"That is *exactly* what I am afraid of."

"Getting to them is going to be difficult." Nevia allowed her gaze to follow Khatalia's into the forest, lifting above the tall, impenetrable tree trunks toward the horizon. She could barely make out the snowcapped mountains through the fog, and knew they would need to traverse them to accomplish their goal. "Your best bet is to leave me. I'm going to just slow you down."

An irritated growl came from Khatalia as she rotated the roasting rabbit. "Nice try, but I'm not letting you die. If I was going to do that, I would've left you back at the palace the moment you told me the truth." She craned her neck to glance at the empress. "Which, come to think of it, I didn't thank you for. Thank you for being honest with me when it would've been easier to lie."

Nevia dropped her gaze from the chieftain's scrutiny. "It was the right thing to do."

"Not many do the right thing when presented with the easier way out."

The words seared a hole in Nevia's stomach, yet she knew it to be true.

All too well.

"How will your help know how to find us?" Nevia asked, glad to change the subject. "And is it reliable? Could the message be compromised?"

Khatalia pinched the bridge of her nose. "The message is in code. None but the other chiefs will be able to understand it, so even if the message were confiscated no harm could to come to us." Her gaze meandered to their meal. "But I do worry if they will find us. We're not exactly stationary. A lot of it is going to be up to the gods' grace, and chance."

Nevia winced, but not from the pain. She rested her head back against her sack of clothing serving as a makeshift pillow, lumpy and uncomfortable at the base of her skull.

"Then we have a long road ahead of us."

Khatalia yanked one of the rabbit's legs free from its socket.

"The road was long the moment you stood up against that bastard."

CHAPTER 24

The wind intensified as they walked. Aching cold clawed at Nevia as she forced her steed onward, one hoof in front of the other. Her teeth chattered, her toes numb and curled in her fur-lined boots, and her face felt burnt by cold fire from the exposure to the elements. Their tracks were covered almost as quickly as they were laid, the blizzard blowing a new blanket of snow in their wake.

"It's a good thing that it's storming," Khatalia had told her when Nevia suggested traveling once the blizzard subsided. "It'll be harder for the imperials to track us."

"Or anyone else," Nevia recalled mumbling, but Khatalia's only response was a smack to her horse's backside, urging it forward.

That was six hours ago, and they had been traveling ever since.

The movement kept the horses warm, but it did little for Nevia and Khatalia. Nevia glanced over toward her companion, whose head was held regally over her shoulders, back as stiff as a board. If Khatalia was cold, she didn't show it. Nevia refused to complain either, having suffered worse weather in her past. She forced herself to sit upright, her aching thighs braced against her horse's sides while maintaining her balance on its bare back.

The dull ache in her shoulder reminded her that only two weeks ago she had been on the brink of death. Her father's woolen blanket, once used to blot her wound, now served as her sling, hugging her arm to her chest. The lack of mobility grew cumbersome, but it was her only saving grace from reopening the wound.

The snow obscured their view, and Nevia occasionally questioned the direction. Now and again she would catch a glimpse of the mountain range beyond the horizon, reassuring her that they still traveled north. Without the landmark, she was certain that they would've lost their way long ago. Even the stars could not provide assistance, the cloud-covered nights barring any hope of navigation.

The trees grew sparse, maple and elm trees replaced by the occasional evergreen laden by blankets of white snow. Relief flooded her when Khatalia came to a halt beside her, Nevia urging her horse to do the same.

"The horses need water and to graze, and we need to warm ourselves," Khatalia said, giving her steed a gentle pat on the flank. "Can you help me gather wood for a fire?"

Nevia nodded, grateful to finally make herself useful. She swung a leg over her horse, inhaling the scent of freshly fallen snow and pine and she shook out the stiffness that settled inside her joints and muscles.

Her boots crunched underfoot as she sought out imprints in the snow-covered terrain. Any fallen tree limbs would be buried and she would consider herself blessed by the goddess if she found any wood not saturated and useless to them. She would have to meander farther, yet was loathe to do so. Visibility was poor. The duo was swept in a swirl of white air, not unlike the inside of a snow globe, and she feared that she would be lost for good if the horses, scratching their hooves in search of buried grass and leaves, left her sight.

A thin line of pines standing several paces away attracted her. She would rather sever fresh limbs than risk getting lost over scanning for fallen ones.

The bark was brittle, easily peeling under Nevia's fingers and leaving sticky sap in their wake. She applied force to the thick branches she could easily reach, but none gave way. She had no way of separating them from the trunk. She would have to climb and get closer.

The sling dug uncomfortably into the crease of her neck, a reminder that it would be impossible to climb. That is, at least with the sling.

It took longer than expected for her to unravel. The knotted fabric proved difficult with fingers sticky and numb from cold. Finally she was able to free her arm, securing the remnants of her father's blanket in the folds of her tunic. Slowly Nevia eased her weight onto one of the lower-hanging branches, and reached up to scale higher. The movement made her shoulder scream, but she grit her teeth and bore with it.

Finally she found a branch that she thought would be suitable, and she knelt to procure her knife, tucked safely in the confines of her boot. It took a fair amount of sawing, but eventually the limb was weak enough to be broken and dropped to the ground. Shouts echoed below her after the branch fell, causing her breath to hitch in her throat.

The voice definitely did not belong to Khatalia. Could it be her friends? Nevia craned her head to peer out between the branches to spot burgundy uniforms against a sea of white, causing her heart to sink in despair. The empress swore to herself, stealing a glance down at the ground, ever distant. She could climb higher and try to wait until they left, but if spotted she would surely be caught. Squeezing her eyes tight, she leapt, legs flailing through the air before making impact. The plush snow broke her fall, yet it didn't spare her from the searing pain which shot up her shins.

She hissed, but didn't allow herself time to recover as she sprinted off.

Swords unsheathed behind her. "Hey, you there! Halt in the name of His Imperial Highness!"

Oh, not again, Nevia thought, footfalls matching her pounding heart as she bolted.

Their horses were passive and exactly where she'd left them, yet the chieftain was nowhere to be seen. An arrow soared past Nevia, causing her to duck, but it flew wide and missed her entirely. That was when the strangled whinny resounded through the air, followed by the collapse of her beautiful ebony mare.

No, Nevia thought, horrified. *They weren't aiming for me, but for our escape.*

Khatalia returned with a bundle of branches in her arms in time to see their predicament: Nevia, pale-faced and terrified, the fallen horse, and a half-dozen men that approached with swords raised high and clinking armor.

"How can they even see in this damn storm?!" Khatalia blurted, the branches tumbling into the all-encompassing snow as she spurred herself into action. Arms encircled Nevia's waist as the chieftain flung her onto the back of her horse, mounting behind her. She hurriedly clicked her tongue and jabbing her heels into the mare's side to flee from their pursuers. Losing their supplies was nothing in comparison to losing their lives.

Several bowstrings snapped, a torrent of arrows showering down on them. One narrowly missed the empress' wounded shoulder, instead slashing across the tender flesh of her upper arm.

Another arrow struck true, embedding into the neck of their majestic steed. Nevia shrieked in horror as they stumbled, falling to the ground in a combined heap. The mare's warm blood soaked into Nevia's pants as it flailed to right itself, the weight of the horse sending all of the air to escape her lungs. Khatalia's strong arms tucked underneath hers and hauled her free from under the weakening horse. Nevia shook all over—another life lost because of her.

Footsteps and yells sounded from behind them. The imperial soldiers were drawing close. Khatalia swore darkly, arms still encircling the shaking empress. She shoved Nevia away brusquely, as a mother bird would force her fledgling from the nest. "Go on ahead! I'll slow them down."

Nevia blinked, staring at her friend as though she were mad, but she knew nothing would persuade her from charging them head-on. Spear raised overhead, Khatalia's strong, sturdy frame ventured off, devoured by the blizzard. Khatalia seemed so ready to tackle the odds of numbers and nature itself that perhaps she could indeed win both battles. A shiver coursed through Nevia; she was, once again, very alone.

The empress stole a glance toward the mountains. They were inching closer; with luck she could reach them before the sun set. She could complete the quest that they set out to do, yet that would mean one more person dying for her. She couldn't allow that.

Nevia's fingers wrapped around the hilt of her dagger, the leather giving way under the pressure that she applied. She turned and ran—not toward the mountains, but away from them.

I'm sorry, Khatalia. I'm going to disobey you one more time.

It did not take long for her to find Khatalia engaged in battle with two imperial soldiers, her spear interlocked with one's sword. The chieftain's face furrowed in concentration as she applied her weight behind her weapon, boots sliding over the icy terrain. Another soldier made a motion to stab her from the side and catch her unaware, but she was faster. Khatalia lunged at him, spear running clean through his side.

Nevia felt hands grasp her forearms. She wrenched forward, but the guard's grip was relentless. Khatalia's eyes clashed with Nevia's, the chieftain not even trying to mask her fury. In that moment of weakness an assailant slammed the hilt of his sword into the base of Khatalia's skull. With a grunt Khatalia fell, her knees collapsing to the ground, hands splayed before her. The guard marched forward, hands brandishing his claymore as he raised the blade's sharp tip directly above Khatalia's heart.

Choked sobs escaped Nevia's throat as she viciously fought to free herself, back pressed against the broad, solid chest of the imperial soldier that claimed her. The man's muscles rippled, his arm pinning her to him. Try as she might, she could not get free, being left at the mercy of fate as she watched the death of her friend unfold before her eyes.

The blade rose, then started to fall.

CHAPTER 25

When Nevia expected to hear the meaty piercing of flesh, she instead heard a shrill canine howl. One first, then others joined.

Distracted, the soldier halted his execution long enough for Khatalia to take action. She rolled onto her back, swinging her body to clamp her hands around his sword by the blade. The sharp steel bit into her palms, slicing clean through her leather gloves and leaving streaks of crimson to drench the fleece-lined cuffs. Her arms shook with an unrelenting grip as the two fought over custody of the weapon, but Khatalia managed to wrench it from the surprised soldier's grasp. She kicked out, both heels slamming into her assailant's torso. A hacking cough escaped his lungs as he stumbled and doubled over, clearly in pain.

Unbeknownst to him, this action sentenced him to death. Khatalia flung the sword aside and braced his head in her bloodied hands and sharply twisted, snapping his neck in a single fluid motion. The resulting crack made Nevia wince and force her gaze away. Though she was no longer a stranger to death, she hated seeing it, especially when involving men who once served her loyally.

In a whirlwind of howls and loud panting, four enormous silver hounds padded toward them. They were majestic, larger than any wolf that Nevia had seen, with dual-toned fur coats of white and silver. They looked as soft as a rabbit, yet more ferocious than a grizzly, with sharp canines glinting underneath a thick layer of saliva. Eyes darkened with hunger met hers, which she quickly lowered. Meeting the gaze of a wolf was considered a challenge, one she knew she would not win.

A throaty growl escaped from the hound nearest Nevia, causing her to shrink back against her captor. The hounds paused, seemingly sizing up their foe, before they leapt forward at breakneck speed. They charged toward the imperial soldiers without mercy. While indeed majestic, they were as hideous as monsters when attacking with such brutality. A hound with white paws pounced upon an imperial soldier and raked its claws across his face while prone, the soldiers cries and pleas useless against the creature. It sank its teeth into the man's neck, blood jetting from the wound and staining the wolf's pristine coat.

The wolf turned, pink tongue lapping at blood dripping from its jaw. Its eyes met with Nevia once more, causing her to squirm. While she was grateful that the silver hounds saved Khatalia, she wasn't so certain they wouldn't be next on the menu. It sprang, not toward her, but her captor. The man screamed, having no choice but to release Nevia as the beast sank its fangs into his thick, sturdy arm, shortly thereafter aiming for his jugular. Nevia was swift to bolt, not wanting to be next. Even still, she could almost taste the tangy scent of copper that permeated the air.

A whistle came from Khatalia, and all hounds immediately froze. Some were fighting, others snarling, and others still, sickeningly, eating their fresh kill. They padded toward her, heads hung low. Their motions were deliberate, mechanical, as if she had placed them under a trance and under her control. Maybe they were.

It took a moment for Nevia to realize that the danger had passed, when these hounds—presumably some breed of wolf— were nuzzling Khatalia in greeting, like an old friend.

"Do they . . ." Nevia started, shaking her head in disbelief of what she was witnessing. "Do they know you?"

"Indeed, they do know her."

Nevia spun, meeting the gaze of a tall, lithe man close to her age. Dark sleek hair brushed the right side of his bronze face, a long, jagged scar tracing from his ear and disappearing underneath his thick fur collar. She wondered how far it traveled. Wrinkles lined his hazel eyes, and within them sat a sadness that only death's witness could harbor. Immediately Nevia pitied him. She lowered her gaze in shame, as if seeing a vulnerability not meant for her, even though she knew nothing about him. While she did not raise her gaze, she felt his eyes linger, causing her to gulp back her nerves.

"Well, it's about damn time, Ardan!" Khatalia barked. The entourage of wolves followed as she stalked over to him, many salivating as if awaiting reward for a job well done. "What took you so long? Need a fresh set of face paint before coming?"

Nevia dared to jerk her head upward, and was grateful when the man's attention was diverted from her. He blinked, visibly wounded by Khatalia's abrasiveness.

"You're welcome for saving your life," the hazel-eyed man grumbled, stabbing his spear into the snow with more force than necessary. "Looks like I came at the perfect moment, if I may say so myself."

Four more figures loomed into view from the surrounding whiteout. Each stood taller than Nevia, a spear or a two-handed axe clutched or slung over their backs. They didn't smile, yet were not unpleasant, merely curious, and, perhaps, apprehensive. Their eyes shifted uneasily from Khatalia to Nevia, bronze-skinned yet a stranger.

"Khatalia, who is this that you have brought with you? Is she of your clan?" Ardan's eyes latched onto Nevia's again, assessing. She forced herself to meet his soul-penetrating gaze, one which bore into her very soul, leaving her to feel vulnerable and exposed.

"No, all of my clansmen died. This is Nevia Bylilly of the Androvich Empire."

Ardan's eyes widened, stepping back as though scalded. Was she really that abhorrent?

"You mean *the* empress?!"

Heat flushed Nevia's cheeks as she sheepishly turned her face downward, feeling shy from all of the eyes resting on her, expecting her to say something, to give answers she didn't have. She inwardly cursed herself; why was she feeling withdrawn now, when she'd been given much larger audiences before? Perhaps it was the fear, the way they recoiled from her.

Nevia shook her head. It didn't matter. Or at least that was what she reassured herself.

"I am, or was," Nevia responded at last. "I have no idea what I am now that I've betrayed the emperor and escaped the country."

Bringing herself to meet their gazes in turn, she could see Ardan blinking, staring as if she'd sprouted a second head. Nevia shifted her weight onto her other foot; why wouldn't he stop staring at her?

"Why would you do that?" he blurted, turning to Khatalia abruptly to add: "What is she talking about?"

Khatalia growled under her breath, kneeling before one of the hounds to burrow her fingers into its plush coat—a rewarding scratch. The canine whined in approval.

"It's a long story, too long to discuss here," Khatalia responded tersely. "Let's get back to your people. Get her warm and fed, and her wound dressed. She can share the story, but it'll make sense in Risanna's presence. No need having to reiterate the same story again and again."

Gratitude flooded Nevia, and she reached over to squeeze Khatalia's arm. Reiterating the tale was akin to exposing some deep forbidden part of herself.

Ardan looked like he wanted to retort, but instead grunted and leaned into his spear. "Fine. But it's getting dark. We should camp at the base of the cliffs, and then scale at first light tomorrow."

"But there will probably be more of them," Nevia insisted. "I know Darius. He would've sent his entire entourage after me if he wanted me enough."

Yet that was the key question that she'd been asking herself: did he want her enough?

"She's right," Khatalia agreed. "We have to press on through the night. We're already dead if we decide to linger here when we've already been tracked by them once."

Ardan chewed his lower lip, casting a sideways glance at the peaks. Though they grew larger over the duration of Nevia's journey, they still looked so far away. "Let's see how far we can get," Ardan relented. "But it would be suicide to scale the cliffs when we can't see. With this blizzard and the darkness, it would be impossible."

"Difficult," Khatalia corrected. "But not impossible."

The two locked eyes, a silent battle of contesting wills. It was finally Ardan who lost, shrugging as he wrenched his spear from the ground. "Come on, then. It's not getting any earlier while we stand around bickering."

CHAPTER 26

Nevia's legs were numb from cold and fatigue, their long trek taking its toll on her. Seldom did they stop for water or a nibble of dried meat and bread, just enough to fuel their bodies and stave off starvation. Her hunger had long since dissolved into an agitated knot in the pit of her stomach, occasionally causing a wave of nausea to wash over her. Trying not to think about her current predicament helped, as well as laying her musings of the prophecy to rest. Instead she learned to preoccupy her mind with humming songs, most of which were imperial in origin. She fell in love with the harps and strings used in Velspire, and quickly became a fan of Gabriela Vaanis, a famous composer heralding from Sanvolk. She had been fortunate enough to meet the woman once in a concert, and she was delighted that her bright demeanor was as contagious as her music.

They paused at the mouth of the mountains, the peaks soaring high into the sky, their tips invisible due to a thick fog cloud hovering above them. A narrow path cut between two cliffs, winding between the mountains and snaking up, up, nearly vertical. With such a steep hike Nevia was uncertain if she would be capable of the challenge.

Ardan shifted his pack onto his other shoulder, throwing an irritated look toward Khatalia who stood at Nevia's side.

"I think we should stop here," he said. "The hounds are tired, as are you both. The chances of being found up here are slim to none."

The chieftain shoved past Ardan, craning her neck to stare up at their path. The cold wind bit at her cheeks, tousling her loose tresses and turning her nose red. "We haven't a moment to waste. We have to keep going." She willed herself onward, marching up to the steep, icy incline and beginning her ascent.

Nevia didn't know what came over her when she drew a step forward and placed a hand on Ardan's shoulder. He looked about as shocked as she felt. "Hey, it's okay. We'll just climb a little ways before resting for the night. I'm sure that we can all make it that far." This close-up, she noticed his hazel eyes were predominately green with flecks of gold. To her surprise he laughed, causing her to recoil and withdraw her hand. "What?"

He wiped at his nose with the back of his hand. "Oh, nothing. It's just ironic, really, that an empress of the flatlands is telling a northerner it's okay to scale his mountain home."

She couldn't tell if he was mocking her. She folded her arms across her chest, fixating him with her sternest glare. "It was my home once, too, before I became empress."

At this he attempted to sober himself, clapping her on the back and following her lead as they started their own ascent. "But yes, you're right, of course. A short ways in, then we'll rest. We don't want to become frozen statues, after all."

Again, Nevia couldn't tell if he was mocking her.

The temperature declined further as they scaled the path. Nevia gritted her teeth as she forced herself along. Her toes had long since gone numb, as would her hands had she not kept them buried in the recesses of her coat. She tucked her cheeks into the thick folds of her scarf, but it did little to stave off the cold. Her face hurt, her eyes burned. Even her lungs screamed with every breath of chilled air.

Darkness had fully set in by the time they stopped, Ardan declaring that they would lose someone if they kept going. Nevia braced a hand against the cliffside, breathing hard and suddenly feeling dizzy. She felt an arm circle her waist, and for a moment she thought it was Khatalia. It surprised her to glance up into Ardan's face beside her. His cheeks were red from cold, brow creased with worry. He clutched her against his side, and for a moment she felt compelled to bury her face into his chest, desirous to absorb his warmth.

She allowed herself to lean into Ardan as he guided her up the steep path, one arm woven around her waist while his other hand braced his spear turned walking stick. Nevia had to admit that he was much stronger than he looked.

"Thank you." Her voice came out softer than intended.

The wind howled in answer, his dark locks on the unshaven side of his head caressing her cheek.

"What made you leave?" he asked instead, gaze falling on her. "You were empress: you had all of this power laid out in front of you. I promised Khatalia that you wouldn't have to explain your story until we came back, but the curiosity is eating at me. You were in such a good position, and now your own husband is hunting you like livestock."

She lost her footing, and would have stumbled to her knees had she not been held her upright. "I think we should wait until we arrive," she agreed. "It's too long of a story."

"It's just a simple question," Ardan countered. "Why leave it all behind?"

She closed her eyes, frozen eyelashes brushing against her skin. "Because I was a prisoner in my own home, and I couldn't sit by idly while pain and suffering was inflicted upon others, Feishins and Zenochians alike."

His brow knitted together, as if attempting to put together the pieces Nevia laid out for him. "Very well, I'll let you explain it all once we get there. But I have so many questions."

"And you will get your answers in due time."

They were silent the rest of the way.

They halted at a flat sheet of bedrock a short distance away from the narrow path which they tread. It opened out to the cliff face, allowing a massive drop should they take a tumble off the ledge.

"I'll get a fire going," Ardan offered, leaving Nevia's side for the first time in hours. The empress instead meandered over to Khatalia, bumping her shoulder into the chieftain playfully. Khatalia glanced over at her, expression wary, before Nevia pressed into her, burrowing her face into the crook of her shoulder. Khatalia rolled her eyes, uttering a string of offensive words, some of which Nevia didn't even know, before wrenching off her own coat and tossing it over Nevia's shoulders.

"No, don't, you'll freeze—"

"Fire, now!" Khatalia barked to the others, tugging at the threadbare gloves sheltering Nevia's hands and placing them against her own neck to warm her. Khatalia's flesh felt scalding, and Nevia would've wrenched herself away had she not known she was trying to save her from being frostbitten.

"I didn't know you were this cold," Khatalia murmured.

Nevia could feel Khatalia's pulse beating furiously under her frozen fingertips. She couldn't help but smile. "You're really sweet."

"No, I'm saving your life. The bare minimum to being a decent human being."

"But you've risked yourself so many times for me." Nevia cupped her hand on Khatalia's neck, and an uncertainty flickered in Khatalia's gaze, as if to gauge whether she should be flattered or angry. "You haven't had to. Thank you. You are a true friend, Khatalia."

Khatalia growled in frustration, wrapping her hands around Nevia's wrists and pulling her away. "Like I told you before, I'm not letting another person die on my watch."

Nevia's smile widened. Despite her gruffness, Nevia could tell that she cared.

Ardan dropped a stocked armful of branches in front of them, leaning them against each other in a hasty circle as another clansman helped to place uneven, gathered stones.

"Where did those come from?" Nevia asked weakly, gesturing towards the branches in the makeshift fire pit with fingers she now could feel.

"Didn't think we'd enter the mountains unprepared, did you?" He threw her a wink. "A little survival trick. We had them with us. Not being prepared is how you die in the mountains. Lesson number one."

"Oh, please, that's just common sense." Khatalia rolled her eyes, releasing Nevia as she leapt up to start helping. It probably took twenty minutes before the flames roared to life, and all six clansmen and women huddled close, ripping off their soaked hats, scarves, and gloves to warm themselves.

Never had Nevia felt so grateful for warmth. She pulled off her boots and stockings, allowing her feet to soak in the radiating heat. Contentment escaped her in the form of a sigh, a sense of security enveloping her.

Khatalia cast a wary glance over her shoulder down the cliff face.

"We are too visible," she warned. "Everyone and their mother could see us."

Ardan shot her a withering look, his long shadow dancing behind him. "We don't have a choice. We need to rest and recoup."

Khatalia opened her mouth to protest, but instead shoved a piece of bread into it, gnashing her teeth violently. A clansman passed a loaf of bread around the fire, Nevia accepting her share of bread and dried meat when it was offered. Each, thankfully, had their own water skein, which they all drank from deeply.

"You seem like a leader." Nevia turned her attention toward Ardan. "Are you one of the clan chiefs?"

Ardan glanced up from the fire's trance. "Hmm?" He took another swig from his skein. When Nevia continued to stare at him he let out a sigh, wiping his mouth with the back of his hand.

"No, I'm Risanna's second-in-command, so close to chief, but not quite."

"Does that mean you would be chief when she passes?" Nevia asked.

Ardan's eyebrows crept up. "What a morbid sense of curiosity you have."

Khatalia laughed, clapping Nevia on the shoulder. "I think she is trying to figure out how to replace you."

"I am *not!*" Nevia retorted, shoving Khatalia away. Heat and color flooded her cheeks, only this time it wasn't from the fire. "I was merely curious how it worked in his clan, that's all. Don't make me sound so bad!"

The chieftain only roared harder with laughter. Ardan rolled his eyes. "Don't mind her. She just likes making people sound bad."

"I don't make people sound like anything. It's the people that do it themselves."

"Whatever." Ardan waved a hand dismissively, before returning his attention to Nevia. "But no, I am merely second-in-command, who aids the chieftain in anything that she requires, and rule in her absence. Should something happen to the chief, it would be her appointed heir that would take the place of chief."

Nevia nodded, curling her knees in to her chest. "You seem like you have the makings for a leader."

Ardan blinked before looking away, taking a sudden fascination in the wolves that piled themselves together to keep warm.

"He refused."

The words came from one of the others, a narrow woman with blonde hair plaited far down her back.

Surprise dawned on Nevia's face. "What?"

"Risanna tried to choose him as heir"—the clanswoman shot a glance at Ardan, who did his best to ignore them—"but he wanted no part in leadership. He said he wasn't worthy."

"Why would you say that?" Nevia asked. "You would do well."

Ardan adjusted his coat, agitation seeping into his jerky movements. "Let's not hash this out. It doesn't matter. Like you, I have my own story that I don't feel like sharing." He rose to his feet. "I'm going to make sure the wolves are fed, find them something. Best that the rest of you get some sleep. Take watches."

Without another word Ardan shrugged on his gloves, moved past the sleeping wolves and trudged on, boots crunching on the icy path. Nevia somberly watched him go.

"Is he going to find anything up here?" Nevia asked, to which Khatalia merely shrugged.

"He'll figure it out," Khatalia responded, prodding the fire with a stick. "Now come, we should get some rest."

The group was indeed prepared, with packs and leather-skin bedrolls. They only had one each, but it was decided that two should take watch at a time, leaving plenty for everyone. Nevia did her part and helped to unfurl the bedrolls as far from the ledge as possible. Goodness knew she'd hate for someone to roll off the cliff in the night.

The others wasted no time in setting their weapons aside, kicking off their boots and allowing their bedrolls to envelop them. Nevia did the same. She was surprised by the warmth that engulfed her, the leather serving as her shield from the harsh elements, the layers of sheep's wool nestling her in cozy warmth.

Khatalia slipped in a bedroll nearby, her arm serving as her pillow. For a while Nevia stared at her back, the broad shoulders that bore the weight of her fallen people. Her messy blonde hair, having not been graced with a brush for over a week, was entangled in snares. Nevia's hair probably didn't look much better.

Her eyelids grew heavy, the warming light of the fire dancing off her face. For the first time in so long, she felt warm.

And safe.

CHAPTER 27

The rest of their journey was predominately silent. They were hardly protected from the cold gusts that swept along the narrow path, Nevia clenching her teeth and folding her coat tightly about herself whenever the winds would sweep through them. After hours of walking she'd found Ardan slow his pace to be trekking alongside her. She mostly ignored him, running her gloved hands through her tangled web of hair in an attempt to smooth it enough to plait. She felt his eyes on her for what seemed like an eternity, before she finally succumbed and turned to face him.

"What?"

Ardan shrugged. "What do you mean?"

"You've been staring at me for the past hour. Is there something that you wanted to say?"

He smirked in an annoying fashion that made her want to both blush and smack him. Tossing his pack over his shoulder, he finally turned his gaze from her to the path beyond.

"Oh, I was just thinking about your backstory."

A frown furrowed her brow. "My backstory?"

"Well, everyone has one, and yours in particular intrigues me. You came from a clan of your own, from what, the west? Ended up marrying not only an imperial brat, but the emperor himself. Wound up as empress. Now you're here, fighting for your life in the brutality of the snowy peaks, escaping the country that you worked so hard to become empress of. That has to be one wild ride, and I'm dying to know more."

It was Nevia's turn to laugh. "You make me sound so interesting."

"But you are," Ardan insisted. "It's not every day that I meet nobility."

"Well, if we're playing the nobility card," Nevia drawled, savoring the moment of toying with him, "it might be best not to stare at me as if I'm some serving wench on display. It's kind of rude."

"I would never dream of it."

His smile suggested otherwise.

The walk was becoming easier with the distraction of conversation, her thoughts diverted from the muscles burning her thighs. "And secondly, you probably shouldn't ask me so many questions, especially when I already told you that I would tell you what happened in due time."

Ardan's mouth opened, hazel eyes thoughtful. "Well, actually, I wasn't asking about that story. I was more interested in yours. Like, how was it, leaving your old life behind to learn the customs and traditions of imperial life, and to become a figurehead of the nation?"

The question gave Nevia pause. She had never been asked this before. No one had ever stopped to consider what it had been like for her, to leave one way of life to embrace another. It was simply expected that she adapt, to become what she was intended to be.

Her pace slowed, Ardan matching. "It was very hard," Nevia croaked. "I had to leave my faith, my culture, my nationality. I've had to pretend to dislike the nation from which I was raised, to be ashamed of my heritage and embody being an imperial through and through. It has been hard, and often I messed up, and no one understands."

Concern contorted his features. "I can't say that I empathize," he said. "But I can *sympathize*. No one should have to feel ashamed of their heritage or who they are. It sounds like you've had to become a whole new person for the role."

"I have!" Nevia's eyes widened, realizing she exuded more passion than intended. Ardan nodded grimly in understanding.

"Well, then, I am glad that you left, if for that reason alone."

"That actually had nothing to do with it," Nevia said, and for a moment she wondered if she were speaking a lie. She had been telling herself that she had no choice, that she had to stand up for what was right. But was it true? Was there not more to her decision?

"I see." Ardan looked thoughtful. "Then the empire has a stronger empress than I gave them credit for."

The rest of their four-day journey went on like this. Walking until they could no longer feel their bodies, resting, and walking again. They rested for night—sleepless nights—and then they were back up again by dawn.

It wasn't until noontime on the fourth day that hope was on the horizon as Ardan halted in front of them and pointed to a valley below.

Multicolored tents stood out against the stark whiteness of the valley, homes that had been erected in haste and yet could withstand the harshest of elements. Nevia knew all too well about the nomadic life, traveling with the seasons and game, pitching tents every few months or whenever the muse to relocate would strike. The homes were simple, and yet it was just that: home. Nothing comforted Nevia more than the sight of her childhood, a life that she had long since left behind to adopt her title—and a doomed marriage.

Ardan spread an arm along the valley. "Welcome to the home of the Sanen clan!"

Down the snowy slope they traipsed as they made it into the valley. People were milling about, their heads covered by thick woolen caps draped over their ears and foreheads. Some of the more prepared ones even wore woolen scarfs, concealing the majority of their face, save for their identical blue eyes that trailed the newcomers at their approach.

They halted before two individuals heavily engaged in conversation. A man leaned casually on his spear while listening to a woman sporting wild, curly red hair. She stopped talking as her gaze flickered on to Ardan, then Khatalia. Their eyes met briefly before the two women rushed each other and embraced tightly.

"Never do that again!" The redhead punched Khatalia in the shoulder, and for the first time since Nevia met the chieftain Khatalia offered a true smile. Nevia came to stand several paces away, holding her arms at her sides awkwardly. Khatalia approached and wrapped an arm about the empress' shoulders as if they were old friends. "This is Nevia Bylilly."

Nevia ducked her head in greeting. "Hello."

The woman's face lips drew tight as she took a step forward. "Emperor Darius' wife."

The redhead's scrutiny made Nevia cringe.

"Well, um, yes. Kind of. I am more of a possession than his wife, I'd say." Nevia shrugged, the words ridiculous and yet she believed to be entirely true. "I don't even know what we are anymore."

In answer, she held out her hand to Nevia. "Name's Risanna, chief of Sanen. Welcome to our camp."

"Pleased to meet you, Lady Risanna."

Khatalia cleared her throat nearby, arresting everyone's attention. "We took great pains to make it here to you today," Khatalia explained. "Nevia has a very important message to deliver."

"Is that right?" Risanna gestured with an arm toward her tent. While simple in nature, the pluming smoke suggested it would be toasty warm inside, with a fire going at its heart.

"Well, come, you should warm yourselves and get comfortable. I am sure that your journey was an exhausting one. Would you like to rest for the night and share your news in the morning?"

"It can't wait," Nevia said abruptly, wringing her fingers in front of her. "I'm sorry. It's just . . . imperative that you know as soon as possible."

Risanna gave a curt nod in understanding, and whistled to garner someone's attention. From the two spears fastened to the individual's back, Nevia would've guessed it was a guardsmen or someone who watched over the clan. While kin, she was unfamiliar with the workings of the Sanen clan, and if they differed from that of Katsao.

"Start a pot of tea for my second and me, as well as our two guests"—she carelessly gestured toward Khatalia and Nevia—"and gather some food. They are probably half-starved after journeying straight through the mountains. Only a fool would do that."

By the way that Khatalia smiled wryly, Nevia would've thought the statement was a compliment.

The pair followed Risanna and Ardan into the circular tent, which was more spacious inside than it had appeared. A bedroll was cast to one side, with a cluster of colorful cushions encircling a round mat on the other. A fire crackled within an in-ground fire pit at the center of the room. While such a fire would be hazardous under normal circumstances, Nevia well knew that the design of these tents allowed for proper ventilation, with a hole in the tent's roof aligning perfectly with the fire pit. This allowed smoke to escape rather than build within the leather walls.

She dropped across from where Ardan sat, making herself comfortable on the plush cushion while folding her legs. Khatalia and Risanna remained at the tent flap momentarily, their loud voices carrying across the warmed space. Words were exchanged about trophies and armor before the two meandered out, leaving Ardan and Nevia alone.

In silence.

The firelight accentuated Ardan's exhausted features, illustrating fine lines that wrinkled his brow and the sides of his cheeks. His skin was sallower than when they had met, dark circles permanently fixated under his eyes. His gaze snapped over to Nevia as she studied him, a wry smile curving the side of his mouth. "Now look who's being rude."

"I didn't mean—I mean, not like *that.*" She cast her gaze upward, watching as plumes of smoke filtered to the outside.

His chuckle was soft and warm in response. "It's fine. I'm just messing with you. You know, you're so much fun to tease."

Nevia jerked her head, ready to retort, yet the words died in her throat. Their eyes locked, a genuine, easy smile worn on Ardan's gentle face. There was a tenderness and innocence, a familiar expression. Yes, she thought Darius once had this look, but her memories of who Darius used to be had become fuzzy. She started to question if he was anything but sinister all along, and maybe he concealed the truth from her too well.

"You watched your people die too, didn't you?" The question escaped her quicker than she could stop it. She watched as his expression shifted, eyes going dark and devoid of emotion. Immediately she regretted her words. "You don't have to answer. I'm sorry, I shouldn't have—"

"No, it's fine. You have a right to know." The soft tinkling against their tent suggested that it had started to snow. Ardan's gaze bore into the dancing flames, long shadow flickering against the tent wall.

"I was up on the hill when it all happened. I heard the roar, but it was too late. We warned who we could, but ultimately neither me or Risanna could stop the destruction. When a natural disaster strikes, you're just at the mercy of mother nature. And that is a very helpless feeling."

Nevia nodded, dipping her chin, the pain in his words carving wounds into her own heart. "I understand. It's hard watching people you care about be hurt when you can do nothing to help them." Her thoughts immediately flashed back to Elante and she shuddered, desiring nothing more than to repress the thought.

"Indeed, it is."

A quivering breath escaped Ardan. "We lost dozens, but that is nothing in comparison to what Khatalia has lost."

That was the hard truth. Nevia closed her eyes. She recalled the way that Khatalia carried herself, her broad shoulders sinking when she thought no one was looking. The pain that hid itself cleverly behind her burning eyes, the unshed tears that escaped through words in anger and ferocity. Immeasurable loss—Nevia couldn't even imagine what that would feel like.

"She is a strong woman," Nevia admitted.

"I never said that she wasn't." Ardan shifted to bring a knee to his ear. "The Feishin Kingdom must pay. These egregious acts cannot go unpunished."

Nevia bit her lip. Darius' influence had already crept over the clan. "Right. . . . About that." She smoothed down the hair she had been fidgeting with, making it into a braid despite its matted state. "It's not what it seems. The Feishin queen is innocent. Darius is the one that you have issues with."

He stared at her as though she was crazy. She returned the stare with equal intensity.

"I'm being serious."

"Is that why you're here and why he's hunting you?" Ardan shook his head. "Listen, we saw the uniforms. We know they were Feishin soldiers."

"They don't *have* soldiers. They're pacifists!"

"That's just what she wants us to think."

The tent flap opened and Risanna emerged, her face set in grim determination. Nevia hoped that it was Khatalia's mess of blonde hair that was behind Risanna, but instead it was another woman that she didn't know. A string of turquoise beads adorned thick strands of hair underneath a woolen cap, her thick coat wrapped tightly around her core by a leather belt.

"If you are well enough, Empress," Risanna started, folding her arms over her chest at full height, "we would like to hear your story. I hear that you went to great lengths to deliver it to us."

Here it was: the chance Nevia didn't think she would have. The empress drew in a breath, feeling suddenly dizzy with the walls of the tent seemingly closing in around her. She closed her eyes, concentrating on slowing her breath for a couple of rounds, and when she opened them, the room had stopped spinning. All eyes were trained on her.

"It started on Saavis, when we learned that there was a coal shortage that would plunge the Empire in its darkest winter."

CHAPTER 28

An audience of eight surrounded Nevia by the time she finished recounting her tale. Despite the temptation to gloss over the fine details, she refrained, instead sharing everything as she knew it: the core shards and the queen's insistence on hoarding them, Darius' change of heart and his corrupt motives, and how she felt the Ivalian lord played a role in this conquest.

The faces around her were grim. Fear, hurt, betrayal—all of these emotions came out in quiet seething, sometimes in fervent, powerful wrath. Risanna sat cross-legged at the head of the leather mat, pale lips drawn thin.

"That sick son of a bitch," the Sanen chief murmured. "This changes everything. If what you say is true, we've agreed to support a lowly, deceitful emperor in aggression against a peaceful nation that is wholly innocent. This disgusts me."

Ardan turned in surprise. "We have?"

Risanna dipped her head. "Yes, while you were away retrieving Khatalia and the empress, a message came from Emperor Darius. A unified attack is planned within two months, in an attempt to abolish the Feishin government. His aim is to transform the country into a democracy rather than a monarchy."

The empress' eyes glazed over as she stared once more at the opening in the ceiling, the sky darkening overhead. While it didn't surprise her that Darius would make such a power move, it made her stomach revolt nonetheless.

"He can't be allowed to do this," Nevia murmured. "The Feishin won't fight back. Their society will be annihilated."

"Well, what do you suggest then?" Irritation laced Risanna's words, not with her, she realized, but the entire situation. "Charge the empire? We'd be wiped out before we even cross the mountains."

"We could also warn the Feishin queen," Nevia offered. "Evacuate the civilians, and bolster their wall before Darius arrives."

"No amount of defense can protect them if they are unwilling to take out the threat at its source," Ardan reminded her, not unkindly. "The problem is less Darius' forces and more that the Feishin refuse to retaliate."

"So that's why we must do it for them."

Realization hit Nevia of what she had said after she spoke. Risanna sat mutely, fingers steepled under her chin. It was clear to see that calculations ran behind her eyes, but she didn't voice her opinion aloud.

"We would be vastly outnumbered alone," Ardan added. "But if we accrue allies from the other clans, and maybe even get some of the empire's own to side with us, the outcome could be very, very different, and not in Darius' favor."

A chill of icy air infiltrated as the tent flap was brushed aside, revealing a familiar mess of blonde hair and tattered coats. Khatalia brushed the snow from her pants, lips pale and drawn fine. The redness of her eyes didn't go undetected. Nevia surmised she had been crying.

"Sorry, didn't realize you guys were in the middle of something. I—I could go."

"Don't be ridiculous, Lia, come and sit down with us." Risanna shifted, patting the cushion beside her.

Khatalia trudged over to sit alongside her fellow chieftain, crossing her legs and removing her gloves. "So, what are we discussing?"

"How to reach potential allies with the truth," Nevia said. "Darius plans to invade the Feishin Kingdom in a matter of two months, and he has accrued allies within his empire and Zenoch to secure his victory."

Khatalia snorted. "That bastard. He doesn't even have to do all that to secure his victory. They aren't going to fight him. He just needs to get through their blasted wall and he's as good as claimed the place. Me and five were able to wipe out at least fifty members of the royal guard. An army's not going to have a hard time."

The redheaded chieftain clasped her hands over her head and stretched, head tilted to alleviate the tension in her neck. "Maybe we have our sights set too broadly. What if we were just to unite Zenoch against the empire? Like, how vast would his army truly be if we were to face the empire alone?"

From the pointed stare of Risanna's intense gaze, Nevia knew the question was directed towards her. "Well, he would have the support of the Five Lords and their military," Nevia said. "But I don't think he would involve other countries outside of the empire in this affair. Like said, he has no reason to secure that many allies. Maybe he has just made a show of seeking your support to make the situation more believable to the masses."

"That makes sense," Ardan agreed. "And if that is the case, we stand a bit more of a chance."

"That's a lot of ifs and maybes." Khatalia rubbed her eyes with the heel of her palm. "We need more information. As it stands we're just going to go to that rock in the sea and get ourselves killed."

The truth stung. Without knowing what they were up against, Nevia agreed it would be difficult to surmise what kind of battle they would head into and prepare themselves for.

"Our first conduct of business," Risanna continued, raising a finger for emphasis, "should be to reach out to the Feishin queen with our support and what we know. Second, we need to gather more information on the emperor's plan."

"I could gather information," Nevia offered. "They want me anyway. I'm sure they would be glad to take me back."

They all stared at her as though she were insane. Perhaps she was.

"No offense, but I barely got you out of there alive once," Khatalia said. "There's no way I'm getting you out a second time."

"I'm not a fighter. You don't need me for the war," Nevia further stated. She turned to Risanna imploringly. "I just came to share the truth. Well, escape for my life, actually, but that's beside the point. I can get information when I return, and send it back to you."

Risanna rose and began pacing, curls bouncing with every step. "There's no good choice," she admitted. "Either way you look at it, we're taking a risk. But it is much too risky to send Nevia back. She could be killed on sight. We'd be sending her straight into the lion's den."

"Agreed," Khatalia piped up.

"Me too," Ardan echoed.

Nevia sighed. She was outnumbered, yet a part of her was grateful. She didn't want to see Darius' face, or pretend to be anything other than disgusted with him and his choices. She did worry for her father, but there was nothing that she could do for him, even if she returned.

"Besides," Risanna continued. "We will need you to be our ambassador and spokesperson. You were a witness to the emperor's plot and you know the truth. You are a valuable asset if we want to win this war."

"Then I could try to recruit the Five Lords," Nevia said slowly.

Another moment of silence lapsed.

"How?" Khatalia asked, clearly doubtful. "You said yourself that one of them influenced the emperor's descent into madness."

A shudder coursed through Nevia as she envisioned his serpentine, conniving face. "Verrine, yes, and I wouldn't go to him. Some, I think, would be more receptive to what I have to say. Specifically Lord Vladios of Malabria. We have a good rapport."

"He could also give us information." Risanna was processing things slowly, starting to see the benefit of Nevia's proposition. "But would he risk treason on a whim based on your information? And what if he doesn't believe you? He would have you killed."

Nevia tried to make herself look brave, even if she felt far from it. "Everyone is taking risks here. Please, let me do this. If we succeed, it will greatly benefit us."

"And if we fail, you'll be tipping Darius off on what we're intending." Khatalia huffed. "I don't like it."

The empress fixed a cool stare on Risanna. "It's a risk that we have to take. Please."

Finally the chieftain broke. Her pacing ceased, arms folded. Her eyes studied the empress, as if gauging her seriousness and devotion.

"Alright, go to him. But if it doesn't work, get out fast."

"I'll go with her," Ardan said quickly.

"Me too," Khatalia echoed.

The redheaded chieftain hesitated. "I would rather you stay with me, Khatalia. I need you to help me form tactics and unite our clans. You have the most information on the Feishin Kingdom, after all."

A muscle twitched at Khatalia's temple. She shot Nevia a challenging glare, but eventually sighed in defeat.

"Okay. But Ardan"—she leaned forward, jabbing a finger directly between Ardan's eyes—"you let anything happen to her, and I personally gut you to feed your innards to my wolves. Got it?"

A playful grin tugged at his lips. "If you can catch me, sure, sounds like a plan."

"You both should leave tomorrow," Risanna declared. "Meanwhile, Khatalia and I will do what we can to secure alliances here in the north. We will all meet back here before heading to Feishin shores. Sound good?"

The empress's stomach twisted into a painful knot, yet she nodded solemnly.

Risanna marched over to Nevia's side and knelt, gingerly resting her hands on the empress' shoulders.

"Be safe, and may the gods aid you in this task. You are going to need all of the blessings that you can get."

Nevia was unable to hold her gaze. She knew this all too well.

CHAPTER 29

Entering imperial territory was far easier than the ascent into Zenoch. By descending the mountain, gravity relieved much of the heaviness from their packs. The only deficit was the difficult terrain. More than once they had to catch the other when they lost their footing on the slippery rocks, preventing an untimely death.

Ardan and Nevia spoke in great length over the duration of their journey, and Nevia found the second-in-command to be quite amicable. He shared a little about his family and clan, while Nevia opened up about the Katsao clan and her parents. The similarities comforted her, and she took delight in the fact that they were both stable hands back at home.

"Well, I sort of was a stable hand," Ardan explained. "We don't have horses, but we do have brydlewolves, and the process is kind of similar. Or, er, maybe it is more like shepherding sheep, now that I think about it."

The way his brows wrinkled in concentration brought a genuine smile to Nevia's face, not one of pretense or expectation but choice.

"This is so nice." When he shot her a befuddled look she further clarified. "I mean, talking about home. Sharing childhood memories. I haven't been able to speak freely about my time in Katsao ever since. . . ."

Her face fell as her voice faded into oblivion. She was grateful when Ardan didn't press, instead resting a hand of reassurance on her shoulder. She leaned into his touch. They shared no words, a silent understanding between them.

Upon wedding into the empire she'd been encouraged to embrace her new way of life and leave behind the old. For the most part it worked, but like any facet of an individual, the truth would sometimes surface when you least expected it. Shame had been entwined with her nationality, and so it felt both foreign—and amazing—to be able to so freely express it with Ardan.

"You should be able to talk about anything you'd like," Ardan said further into their walk, a stab in the bubble of silence beyond the crunches of their footsteps.

"Maybe, but that wasn't how things were."

And never would be, she realized. Through the clouded promise of a future where nationalities were meaningless, where race and culture were not a dividing barrier between peoples, she saw this. She should have realized it from the beginning when Darius first discussed change and sought to make a difference in the empire. It was all for naught. Perhaps Darius realized this, too.

On their eighth day of their journey they arrived within the imperial capital of Velspire. The sun painted vibrant magentas and lilacs against the twilit sky, trees coated with a thin glaze of ice, the occasional icicle dangling from low-hanging branches. While arriving in the capital would sacrifice an additional day, they felt it safer than risking being sought by bandits through the outskirts, where their existence was prevalent and people would frequently be mugged or, worse, go missing.

Tall spires greeted them as they dived deeper into the city, the cobblestone streets coated with thick freshly fallen snow heavily trodden by lively crowds which, to Nevia, was anything but normal for the hour. Individuals pressed against one another as they flocked from the marketplace to the newsstand, whispering conspiratorially to one another. It was enough to give Nevia pause when she caught the whispers of "execution" and "heathen's curse." She shot a glance over at Ardan, who seemed none the wiser, walking alongside her and admiring an old cathedral erected at least five centuries ago.

"Ardan." His hazel eyes fell on her, warm and inviting, and for a moment she found herself entranced by them. Eventually she broke free of his spell, shaking her head in an attempt to clear it. "Did you hear what those women said?"

"Was it about how gorgeous I look?"

She elbowed him hard in the ribs. "Very funny." Her smile was fleeting as she turned her head in an attempt to catch anything else, but she couldn't glean anything important.

The shadows of spears and feathers danced on the wall in which they stood before. Imperial soldiers marched forward, swords at their waists, and spread to surround the crowd as everyone seemed to flock toward the central square. Her brows rose high; something was happening, and she had to find out what it was.

"I need to check something," Nevia murmured aloud.

Ardan responded by catching her wrist, his thumb caressing her hand. "Okay," he responded. "What is it, and where to?"

"You can start heading to the outskirts of the city. I'll meet you there after I investigate."

His grip only tightened. People passed them in droves on either side without paying them any attention. Eery excitement lit the faces of many, inspiring a course of dread to wash over her. Her companion mirrored her concerned expression.

"What a foolish suggestion. You know that I'm coming with you."

Nevia's mouth opened, but no words came out. Drawing his hand into hers, she strode into the crowd, Ardan not leaving her side. What struck Nevia as particularly concerning was that everyone wore black—a mourning color, one predominately seen during memorials and executions.

An execution. Nevia's heart nearly stopped. There was going to be an execution. And yet, no public execution had occurred since she was empress. Executions were reserved for the gravest of offenses, generally those involving witchcraft or invoking evil forces. Seers and scholars of magic were often burned at the stake.

It's probably the seer from the square, Nevia thought grimly, lips in a straight line. She wished that she'd done something, could do something, but her hands were tied. This was the unfortunate price to pay for extending her message to Nevia.

Civilians pressed from all sides as they found themselves standing amidst them in the central square. From the rear Nevia couldn't discern what was happening, so she pressed forward, weaving her way through any opening to get closer to the front of the crowd. Upon the dais stood a cluster of imperial soldiers, stationary and stoic as they offered a formal salute, their burgundy caps coated with snow that had begun to come down heavier. Nevia's gaze flickered from the soldiers to the erected gallows, a hempen noose ready, beckoning its victim.

Nearby, Ardan leaned his head around a rather rotund woman to get a better look at what was happening, who screamed profanities at the dais in front of them.

"Maybe we should go." Nevia's stomach revolted, voice lost in the sea of chants and cries. "I don't really want to see this."

She started to move away, halting when she realized that Ardan wasn't following. His gaze was locked on the scene of the execution.

"That man is Zenochian."

Confusion arched Nevia's brow. "What?"

She leaned around him, and what she saw nearly caused her knees to give out. Two soldiers marched, each circling an arm of a wizened man whose bronze scalp gleamed in the torchlight to the gallows. For a moment she could only stare, unable to believe that she recognized the man. All reason left her when understanding sank in.

"Father," she said hoarsely.

Eja's hands were bound in front of him, his ankles shackled by chains so that any attempt to run would be futile. The imperial soldiers' faces were stony in discipline. An icy gust of wind blew, tousling Eja's woolen coat, his weathered face crinkling into a frown as he shielded his eyes by closing them.

Echoed cries throughout the crowd were quickly silenced. All about them garments shifted and rustled; the sea of onlookers sank to their knees. Nevia seethed as she caught sight of why. Marching onto the dais, hand raised to wave at the adoring crowd, was none other than Darius Androvich.

She clenched her jaw, hands balling into fists at her sides. An insistent tug on her arm from Ardan forced her to collapse onto one knee, despite her protest.

"You're going to stand out if you don't bow." he uttered through gritted teeth.

"I don't care. Let him find me."

His fingers dug painfully into her bicep. "You don't mean that."

He held her down just long enough for everyone to begin rising, allowing her to shoot upright. Her face was drawn tight, teeth bared, as she glared daggers at the man she once loved, who was now stripping everything from her.

Darius' bangs, parted to one side, caressed the edge of his face. He looked handsome and at ease—and evil.

"Greetings, people of Velspire!"

All remained silent, basking in whatever garbage Darius was willing to grace them with. Her gaze flickered from his hateful face to her father who stood stoically before the gallows. His eyes remained closed. A deeper age outlined his face, his once full form now withered and malnourished. Nevia could only wonder in horror what atrocities he'd been subjected to as punishment for her betrayal.

"This is sacrilege," Nevia hissed, leaning dangerously forward and receiving a quizzical glance from the woman standing in front of her.

"Nevia," Ardan warned, ready to seize her if she tried to move again, but she had to do something. Had to.

"You all are gathered here today to witness the execution of Eja Bylilly of Zenoch. He has been tried and found guilty of invoking dark magic to bewitch our dear empress, his daughter, forcing her to attempt a revolt against me. Eja, do you deny this claim?"

Panic dug its claws into the empress. She knew that Darius would try something after she left, but this was a low blow, even for him. She leaned forward, entering the personal space of the woman in front of them. Annoyed, the woman shifted away, a flock of teenagers replacing her. She should have been grateful for the cover so that neither Darius nor the guards took notice of her, but she didn't care. She wanted to be noticed. This execution was all a ruse—another foul play from Darius' hand. Her heart roared painfully as her attention shifted back to her father. The only inclination that he'd heard Darius was the flutter of his eyes as he fixed his son-in-law with a somber stare.

"No, what you say is true."

Darius dipped his head, dodging his gaze uncomfortably. Cries and chants echoed throughout the crowd, all silenced as he raised a hand and brought order. If he was enjoying this, he concealed it well underneath expressed sorrow. "The act of magic is forbidden in Danaeca, the crime punishable by death. You confess openly to know this, and still invoking forces beyond the physical world?"

Eja's expression remained stony. "Yes."

"Very well. As punishment for your crimes against the empire, you will be hanged to death. Consider it a mercy, as conspirators with magic are decreed to be burnt at the stake." Darius lifted his gaze, pity in his eyes. "May the goddess show mercy upon you on this day."

Nevia shoved a hand into Ardan's chest, forcing herself past him. This couldn't be happening. Her father couldn't be executed! She felt the wall of bodies closing in, pressing tighter around her the further she worked through the crowd. She inched closer to her father, breaths coming in cold rasps. She had to get to him—to save him from the fate she'd condemned him to.

The soldiers flanking Eja dragged him forward, to the plank that would be lowered out from underneath him. An eery silence filled the crowd, as if they all held their breaths in anticipation of the inevitable. She fought her way between a couple and found herself several feet from the dais, watching in horror as the noose was lowered over her father's head. The hempen rope was tightened around his neck with a solid yank. The soldier merely offered Eja one reassuring pat before leaving him there alone.

To die.

No longer could she resist action. She dove forward, but before she could scale the dais arms encircled her. Ardan's labored breaths were loud in her ear. She wriggled, struggling to free herself, to save her father before it was too late.

"Let me go! They're going to kill him!"

"And if I do they're just going to kill you, too," Ardan hissed. "We need to leave, Nevia. Nothing can be done for him now."

"No! I refuse to believe it!" Tears streaked her cheeks, her heart feeling like it would break in two. The seconds seemed to yawn on forever as Eja stood there, expressionless, gaze following the light snowfall that graced the smog-filled city. Taking it in—for the last time. She could've sworn, for one heartbeat, that his gaze met hers. His lips curved into the softest of smiles before moving, uttering something she couldn't hear. She reached out just as the platform went out from under his feet, her heart nearly stopping as his body shuddered violently.

A hand clamped over her mouth to stifle her scream.

Her strength faded, legs numb as she fell limply against Ardan. His grip remained firm as he pinned her close, whispering assurances that fell on deaf ears. Sobs wracked her entire body. She tried to avert her gaze away from her father's lifeless body dangling from the noose but couldn't. Ardan whipped her around to face him, tears streaking his own cheeks.

For a long moment he held her there, ignoring the negative attention they were attracting by displaying public affection. She wrapped her arms around his torso, clinging to him as if he was the only anchor tethering her to the present, her angst threatening to consume her.

Her father, her greatest cheerleader and dearest supporter, dead, his life taken by none other than her husband—because of her. He cleared her name and died for her. Her entire body shook in Ardan's arms. It didn't seem possible that she could get past this. That she could ever move on.

Nevia didn't remember Ardan weaving her from the crowd, returning her to the cobblestone streets and past the iron factory buildings as they made their leave. She didn't protest as he led her by the hand, outside the city into the outlying forest, southbound for Malabria. She felt like a small child. No words could console her, no thoughts able to enter her anguished mind. All she could do was replay the platform going out from underneath her father, watching as his body swayed limply in the winter wind. Again, and again.

Tears fell from her cheeks as she lowered her head, thinking shamefully: *It should've been me.*

CHAPTER 30

Raucous laughter echoed through The White Lotus, a bustling tavern at the heart of Malabria's capital city. The shadows of patrons lively from drink danced off the rustic wooden walls. It was the end of the work week, and after long, hard days, especially for those restoring the collapsed mine, a refresher was needed. Thus, miners found their way into the tavern, drinking away their pain and loneliness. Two bartenders behind the counter were kept very busy, sweat gleaming on their foreheads as they rushed from tap to customer, and back again. Four serving girls bustled about, providing pints of bubbling ale. Their voluminous matching skirts of crimson twirled about as they spun around tables as if in a dance.

Lord Vladios sat at a table in the rightmost corner of the entrance, perfectly situated between a bookcase and a window. He swirled his pint of ale before drinking deeply, dark eyes never leaving the serving girl nearest him, her rump in the air as she leaned over to scrub a table. Her long red curls bounced with her movements, along with other assets which he was quite fond of viewing.

Whenever anyone glanced his way he would tip his hat, shielding his face from view. Bundled in a black, worn cloak and a wide brimmed hat, few paid him any mind, and none recognized him as the lord of Malabria, something he greatly valued.

A sigh escaped him. Liquor far better than this was available in his private wares, and yet the company paled in comparison—the sole reason he came here.

Yes, the tavern was the place to be. It was Vladios' guilty pleasure, just as one would find solace along the mountains, streams, or coasts. He didn't see why his title should require him to make any sacrifices. If anything, it should've granted him *privileges* to pleasures which he wouldn't normally be privy.

"Oh, erm, miss—" He failed at stifling the hiccup that accompanied his words.

"Yes, sir?" The redhead stopped mid stroke to glance up, brown eyes wide and full of promise. The sight of her nearly took his breath away.

"Would you be a dear and get me a refill? Here's a nice tip for your trouble." He dropped more silver than necessary on his table with a clatter, shoving his pint closer to the edge of his table.

Confusion clouded her expression as her gaze flickered from the bouncing silver to the pint in his hands.

"Um, but sir, you have barely touched your beer."

Vladios glanced down, just as confused as she was. "Oh."

He took it, guzzling the bubbling amber liquid in record time. Finally he let out a loud sigh and slammed the tankard down with a satisfying smack.

"There. Now I'm done. Refill, please?"

It appeared that the table was the only thing protecting the serving girl from collapsing to the tiled floor. Glancing between him and the silver one more time, she swiftly glided over to his table and swiped the silver off, tucking it into her blouse for safekeeping. She made off with his tankard, red curls disappearing into the crowd.

Vladios sat back and smiled, pleased with his cleverness. It took him longer than it should've to realize that two figures in dark cloaks were watching him. Heat rose into his cheeks as he noticed them shuffle their way to his table.

"You don't mind some company, do you?"

That feminine voice. He recognized it, but from where? The figures slipped into two rickety chairs opposite him, and it wasn't until he saw the long, pale braid over one shoulder and bronze hands that went to lower her hood that he realized whose company he kept.

Vladios swallowed hard.

"To what do I owe the pleasure, Your Highness?" His tone was pinched. The empress fixated him with her blue eyes that bored deep within his soul. He cleared his throat nervously, then gestured to the tall, cloaked man beside her. "And who've you got here?"

"I have urgent matters to discuss with you," she said, tone low. She gestured toward the man beside her, who also lowered his hood to reveal equally tanned skin and dark hair which shone under the tavern' gleaming chandelier overhead. "And this is Ardan, my . . . friend."

She struggled on the word "friend," but Vladios was too stunned by her appearance to notice. The return of his tankard brought him back to the present, the serving girl averting her gaze as she spun on heel, wiping her hands on her apron as she went. Vladios' lips drew into a thin line of disapproval—and disappointment.

"This is . . . a surprise," Vladios managed, wiping the side of his tankard ceremoniously. "Though not unpleasant. I don't know if it's the ale talking, but what in Saava's name are you doing here? You know that you're wanted, do you not?"

He leaned forward. Nevia's expression betrayed nothing. Her hands were folded neatly on the table. Vladios couldn't help noticing that her eyes were red and swollen, as though she'd been crying.

"It's . . . complicated."

Her hands fled to her braid, fidgeting with the strands as her gaze flickered over the tavern and the other patrons. None of this was lost on Vladios; he knew the empress well enough to tell that she was exceptionally nervous, but, being the good man that he was, he didn't take advantage of this. Instead he arranged his face into that of sympathy.

"I see." His gaze flickered over toward the wall, where a steel-plated clock hung. It was nine o'clock at night, yet none of the patrons appeared ready to retire. Neither was he. "Well, I have all the time in the world, and it looks like they're not planning to close up shop anytime soon, so I'd say start talking. Would you like a drink?"

"Erm, no, I'm—"

"Here, I'll buy you one." He flagged down a bustling serving wench. The cute redhead didn't appear, much to his disappointment, but instead a woman with dark greasy hair in a braid approached the table. She placed her hands on her non-existent hips, her expression just shy of a scowl.

"Yes." It was a demand, not a question. Vladios calmly gestured toward Nevia.

"I'd like to buy the lady a drink. And you—erm, sorry, I already forgot your name—do you drink, too?"

Ardan opened his mouth to respond, but Vladios already made his decision as he continued: "Yes, yes, I'm feeling generous and will buy him a drink, too. The best the house has to offer."

The serving girl shot a glare toward Ardan and Nevia to see if they would protest. When they said nothing, however, she dipped her head and disappeared behind the counter.

"I'd like to keep my wits about me if I'm to have this conversation with you," Nevia said lowly.

At this Vladios couldn't help but laugh. Others jerked a glance their way, probably thinking the old man finally cracked. Vladios thought maybe they weren't wrong, especially since he was sitting with the empire's most wanted woman and was doing nothing to apprehend her, nor did he have any intention of doing so.

"Vladios. Please. I need your help, and I need you to pull yourself together so that we can talk." The urgency of her tone, the set of her jaw. He smoothed the front lapels of his jacket, smothering his humor with seriousness.

"You have my attention," he said smoothly. "Talk."

"First, I need you to promise me that not a word of this escapes to Darius."

Vladios arched a brow. "A tall order. It depends on what you share with me. He is my sovereign, and I but a humble servant— ah, thank you. Just set those down there."

Long, gangly arms extended two tankards over Nevia's head before being dropped down in front of them, foamy liquid sloshing over the side and pooling onto the table. Curiosity lighted

Ardan's eye as he studied the amber and white puddle. He dabbed his finger into it and brought it to his tongue, tasting it thoughtfully. Vladios deduced that Ardan had never tasted a beer before, much to his horror.

"Okay, I see your point." Nevia wrapped her hands around her ale. "You know the speech that I gave in the square?"

Vladios let out a sigh. "The one about Darius being a master manipulator trying to turn the whole continent against the Feishin Kingdom so that we may gain access to their resources? Yeah, I heard."

The grip on her tankard tightened. "Right. That one."

He gritted his teeth; this wasn't the kind of company he'd been hoping for, and he almost told Nevia as much when the empress continued.

"But there's more to it than that. Everything that I said—it's all true. I saw the mine, Vladios, and I saw the core shards. They are pure magic. They could change the world. There's so much potential there, and Darius sees it, too. He staged this so he could gain access to them."

Vladios turned a disinterested eye onto the empress. "And why should I believe you?"

"Because you are a good man with a kind soul. You know as well as I that leaders don't always make the best choices." She sat up straighter in her seat. "I need to stop this takeover from happening. The Feishin people are innocent. If Darius invades, he'll wipe the entire country clean to match his own vision, and it's going to involve more than just borrowing some core shards."

Vladios hummed and balanced on the chair's rear legs, pondering. Darius had shared with him a vision for the Feishin Kingdom, true enough, once the queen was forcefully ousted. While an odd discussion, he didn't think much of it at the time. Now, however, he could see the conversation in a new light, and it unsettled him.

"And you really think the emperor would stoop so low as to frame the Feishin Kingdom and annihilate the clans of Zenoch?" Vladios asked in disbelief.

The fall of an empty tankard turned all eyes to Ardan, who was wiping his mouth with the back of his hand. Apparently he enjoyed the liquor immensely. Under different circumstances Vladios would've beamed with pride.

"I was there when the avalanche hit," Ardan said. "I watched the women, men, and children buried alive in mountains of snow. I couldn't do anything to help. It was awful. Only a very cruel and conceited person would order such a thing."

Vladios' gaze softened. Something in him stirred, and, before he knew it, one of his large, heavily-ringed hands rested on Ardan's. "What you have faced was a calamity no man should have to bear," Vladios agreed. "Why do you feel so certain that it was Emperor Darius and not the Feishin queen? Do you not think that she bodes Zenoch ill after the death of her husband?"

"She knew it was an accident," Ardan said tightly. "It wasn't my father's intention to kill a well-meaning king. He was under the impression that he'd come with a weapon rather than a gift."

The empress looked befuddled. Her eyes shifted to her companion, question kindling in them, but didn't bring voice to it. Instead she turned to Vladios and stated: "I have no reason to make this up. You know me, Vladios; I would never do that. I loved Darius, but he's started down a dark path that I can't follow. It broke my heart to turn against him, but I couldn't stand by idly watching him go through with this. I have no proof that he's behind this, except for the confession he gave me. You just have to believe me."

The table was shaking, and it took Vladios a solid minute to realize that it was from his trembling hand. He forced it still, his free hand clamping over his wrist. For as long as he'd known Nevia, she was nothing other than kind, just, and fair. She had nothing to gain from laying the blame on the emperor, and he had to admit that it was auspicious timing, so shortly after Saavis and the discussion of the coal shortage—

"Say that I believe you, that what you say is true," Vladios started, palm flattening on the table. "What then? You think I can make him turn himself in and leave the Feishin Kingdom alone? Fat chance, my dear. And if that's what you're thinking then you're better off seducing him yourself with the proposal. My days of flattering him are long gone."

He took a very long draught. It burned his throat, yet filled his chest with a warm comfort he so desperately needed that escaped as a satisfied sigh.

Nevia drummed fingertips on the table impatiently. "Of course that isn't what I expect of you. What I'm hoping is that when the day of the invasion does come Malabria will take our side. We also need more information."

His eyes jerked up. "No way. I am not leaking military tactics. That is treason of the highest decree. I love my country and my empire; doing that would be foolish."

"But can you stomach an empire built on lies?" Nevia challenged. "Could you really sleep at night knowing that you supported him, suspecting foul play and sabotage brought the empire to its newfound glory?"

Vladios glared at her, not because he was angry, but because she was right. The seeds of doubt had been sown since Darius returned from the Feishin Kingdom, but he would never have voiced them. Instead he would've continued as he always had: head bent down, getting lost in drink and female company, and feeling shame that he went on without questioning what made their empire prosper.

She played him like a fiddle—and he didn't like it.

"You should go," he said gruffly, leaning back with his arms folded. "Someone could recognize us, and then it will all be over for you, as I'm not defending you."

"Please, Vladios." Something desperate and hungry clung to her voice, her eyes wide and tearful. "I don't think we can pull off this response without you."

"And what is this 'response'?"

She hesitated. "I can't tell you. Not unless I know that you're on my side, and with the way you've gone back and forth I don't think you can convince me now."

"Nevia, you know I've always liked you. You've brought something fresh to the empire that it has desperately needed—"

Nevia arched a brow. "But?"

"There is no 'but,' I'm just saying that I have a deep-rooted respect for you. Therefore I will further investigate what you said. But that is all. All that I will give you."

"And the information? We need to know who he's allied himself with, how he plans his invasion, and where he'll be during the siege."

Vladios just shook his head. "I will look into it."

His voice, however, was filled with doubt. It was the best answer that he would give her, and she seemed to know it, too. Nevia peeled herself from her chair and rose, hand fumbling in her pocket before procuring a few silver. Before she could drop it on the table, however, Vladios beat her to it by placing two fat golden coins on the worn wood.

"Just go, Nevia. Be safe and stay well."

Nevia gave him a swift nod, sorrow etched into her features. He wanted to cup her cheek, to reassure her, to express his pride in her decision to be the independent ruler that the empire needed, but he did nothing as he watched her walk away. Ardan remained behind, standing and polishing off the remaining beer.

"Thanks for that," Ardan said, tipping his head and leaving the lord speechless as he caught up with the empress.

Snow spun through the tavern door, melting the moment it hit the rubber mat. Vladios blinked from a waft of cold, dazedly looking at the empty mugs in front of him.

What the hell did I just agree to? he thought dully, pinching one of the golden coins between his forefinger and thumb, feeling the grooves etched along the thin surface.

"Damn it, Nevia," he murmured under his breath. He spun the coin and waited, holding his breath to see if it landed on heads or tails. "You're about to make me either a traitor or a hero."

CHAPTER 31

Over a week had passed after their visit with Vladios in Malabria, and, in hopes of persuading another lord to their cause, they picked up horses before setting off for Asturia. Nevia hung her head, fatigue starting to sink in. Not physical, but this time emotional. It had taken all of her willpower to suppress her grief while meeting with Vladios, and now she had nothing left to give. Often deep in the night the pain would wash over her anew, and tears of mourning would be shed.

Thankfully Ardan said very little, instead being the silent, reassuring presence that she needed, riding alongside her as they made their trek to the southernmost country within the empire. She shifted in her saddle uncomfortably, sore from the long hours on horseback each day. They often stopped for the horses to rest and refresh themselves, but it did little to ease the aches and bruises of travel. She wished that they could walk, but when she voiced this desire to Ardan he shook his head.

"Time is of the essence, Nevia," he had told her. "We have to press onward if we are to meet with the other lords before the siege. That's what you want, right?"

Of course it was. Time was not their ally in this war. They would need to make it to Asturia with all speed.

The terrain slowly shifted, the pockets of snow growing sparse as they ventured further south. The lands grew flatter, the trees thinner, and the chattering of birds, which had been absent within the northern territory for months, was persistent. Clearly those birds had come here. Nevia briefly wondered if Kiya, her beloved pet bird, was among the parakeets fluttering in the branches of an elm tree overhead.

The setting sun greeted them when Nevia's torturous thoughts got the better of her, the thoughts which persistently plagued her. Why did the goddess have to be so cruel as to take her father away? Why did Darius become such a monster? Tears threatened to escape her, yet she tried her best to smother them. They would be setting up camp soon, perhaps sooner than later if Ardan sensed her distress. As much as she tried to stifle these emotions, Ardan had become adept at reading her, which often resulted in tears and one too many cries into his shoulder.

"Life can be cruel sometimes," he voiced, dismounting and striding over toward Nevia with his steed.

He offered her a hand, to which she hesitated briefly before accepting. Accepting felt like admitting weakness, and she already felt so weak for feeling so broken inside.

"It does get better," Ardan reassured her.

A bitter laugh escaped her throat as she followed him to their chosen spot to camp for the night. The stars twinkled overhead in a perfect open sky, with no trees obscuring them from view.

"I somehow doubt that, but I thank you."

The light vanished from Ardan's eyes as they clashed with hers. "I speak from experience. It does, though the pain never goes away. But, neither will your memories of him. Both will now become a part of you, and it's up to you to decide whether it'll destroy you or make you become stronger, to live for both you and your father."

"It's not that simple," Nevia bemoaned. Then, she felt it: the heat rising to her eyes, the unwilling tears that began to blur her vision. She dropped to the ground, long blades of grass caressing her sides, fingers sinking into the silky tendrils that emerged from the earth. "He's all that I had left in this world. After Mom died, and Darius betrayed me, he was the only thing I had left to love, but with him gone, Ardan, what else is there?" She spread her arms wide, with as much pain as she could muster. "What else is there to live for if everyone I love has been taken from me?!"

The evening wind tousled his hair as he stalked over to her and knelt, taking both her hands into his.

"Nevia, listen to me." His tone burned with intensity, his eyes fierce when she finally met his gaze. "Your father loved you. He gave his life so you could live free. He wouldn't want you to waste away in your sorrow, or give up because he is no longer here. Wherever he is, he's out there rooting for you, and a part of him will always live inside you. It might seem hopeless, and the world might feel like it's caving in on you—"

"It does."

"But you have you have to keep going. You have to keep fighting. If you don't, then you're just letting Darius win, and I'm sure you nor your father want that."

His hands left hers, instead running up her arms, caressing her shoulders, her back, before wrapping her into a warm embrace. She pressed her cheek into his shoulder and sniffed, barely stifling the sob that threatened to escape.

"There will be time to grieve, and you deserve to take it," Ardan said at last. "But don't let it consume you. Please, if not for you, then for your country. For your people, for Khatalia. For me."

The tears began to flow then, Nevia no longer able to contain them. She cried and cried, and Ardan patiently held her, rocking her, caressing her hair and promising in her ear that it would be okay. That she would be okay, even if she didn't feel like it.

When her eyes were dried Nevia sat mutely, staring at her hands as Ardan set to work in building a fire. The evening air, despite the warmer climate, still carried with it a chill that crept into their bones. Once the flames roared to life he settled himself beside her, stretching out his legs and letting out a groan. He burrowed his face in his hands, hiding his exhaustion that Nevia knew was still there. She reached over and grasped his knee, giving it a gentle squeeze. He glanced at her hand briefly before snatching it, fingers intertwining, offering her a tender smile that made her heart feel slightly more whole. The scent of burnt wood wafted through the night air, plumes of smoke carrying off into the distance.

She sat numbly by the fire, bronze face illuminated by the fierce embers. A question had been burning within her ever since their discussion with Vladios, and finally she summed up the courage to bring it voice.

"So, Ardan, I was wondering—"

He lifted his face from the fire to meet her eye.

"Why did your father kill the Feishin king?"

A long, heady sigh followed her question. The fire crackled between them, tension as thick as the smoke in the air. Ardan rubbed his hands for warmth as if out of habit.

"It's a very long story," Ardan started.

Nevia bobbed her head. "It's fine, forget that I asked. I understand if it's private—"

"It was because of a misunderstanding."

Nevia folded her hands in her lap, surprised and yet grateful that he was entrusting her with this forbidden story.

"The Feishin king, King Athilan, came unescorted to learn the ways of our people. He was a devout believer in peace, and he thought that in further understanding others more universal peace could be attained. After Danaeca's many wars we were understandably wary, especially since the Feishin Kingdom was entirely cut off from the rest of the world. Word spread fast, and Risanna's sister, Ayla, said he was carrying a secret weapon, that she'd seen it glow in his belongings."

He closed his eyes, as if pained by the memory.

"It was a very long time ago. We were but teenagers then. Ayla meant no harm. The chief at the time—my father—took it very seriously. She showed him a sample that she'd snatched from his belongings. They wanted to explore its properties, so, they decided to destroy it. Ayla took it upon herself to snatch up a hammer and strike it, and that's when it happened. It retaliated upon impact, sending a course of energy to surge up her body. I wasn't there, but I heard it from my father. She lit up like a flame, and then fell, heart stopped. It killed her. Outraged and convinced that her theory was correct, my father poisoned the king.

"Later, we found out that we were gravely wrong. It wasn't a weapon, but a gift. A solution to our problems. On the coldest of days we would lose our most frail, elderly, infants, and those who were ill. This was a limitless source of energy, which the king had brought to help us, as a show of good faith. We didn't learn of this until the Feishin queen told us and demonstrated its use. But she, understandably, retracted her husband's gift, claiming that this was divine punishment for her husband sharing what was given to him without their gods' permission."

"The core shards," Nevia murmured.

Ardan blinked. "What?"

"The core shards—Nephyl—what we're going to war for." Her thoughts were spinning, blurting words faster than she could process them. "That must've been what the king had brought to share, and that is probably why Arethusa was so adamant against sharing it with others. Because—"

"Sharing it took her husband's life."

Goosebumps prickled Nevia's flesh. It made so much sense, all of it. Why Ardan didn't want to be chief, and why Arethusa was so adamant about sheltering the shards. Both shared a messy past of misunderstanding tied to grief, and she could hardly blame either for their position.

Ardan rose and dusted off his canvas pants at the fire's edge. The full moons rose higher in the sky with the hour. "It's late," he declared. "We should get some rest. We should be in the capital of Asturia soon, right?"

Nevia blinked back to reality. "Oh, right. Yes . . . we are only a handful of hours away now."

She smoothed down the patch of grass at her side, grateful that it was not snow that she would place her bedroll on. After nearly freezing to death when crossing the mountains, snow had grown distasteful to her. The fire started to fizzle out as darkness ensnared them.

Ardan and Nevia slipped into their bedrolls, both silent, as though their conversation erected a barrier between them. The shadow of his father's sins haunted his eyes, and Nevia could see the invisible weight it placed on his shoulders. There was so much she wanted to say, so many words of comfort left unspoken to die in her throat. She must've appeared troubled, as he came over to tousle her hair.

"Get some sleep. It's going to be a long day tomorrow," he said.

Their gazes locked, Nevia mesmerized by flecks of gold in his hazel eyes. He ran a thumb down the length of her cheek, hand finally resting at her chin. He tilted her head, bringing their faces within a fraction of each other. Nevia's breath hitched as she watched Ardan's gaze flicker toward her lips. She closed her eyes, attempting to stop the pounding in her chest and the irritating tug of fondness she felt toward him.

He leaned in, his nose brushing hers as their foreheads met. She tenderly brought a hand to caress his cheek before forcing them apart.

"Goodnight, Ardan," she whispered, rolling onto her side despite her body's protest. She pretended not to see the hurt in his eyes, or the disappointment etched on his face. Guilt clawed at her insides as he shifted away, returning to his bedroll and turning his back to her.

Guilt that she almost succumbed and kissed him.

Guilt that she chose to reject him.

CHAPTER 32

After a long journey lasting a fortnight in its entirety, Nevia and Ardan had finally arrived in Palthesi, the capital city of Asturia. The sky grew darker, suggesting only an hour of remaining daylight, but even still, Nevia was pleased. They had made it, and if all went according to plan they would secure an audience with Lord Torquil before the day's end and claim another one of Darius' allies as their own. War was like a game, one that Nevia took very seriously. They were all pawns on the board, and it was a scramble to see how many each side could claim before the game commenced.

The streets bustled with people, likely departing to nestle into their homes before darkness fell upon them. They passed two men clad in lavender uniforms, hair sleeked back and chins held high.

They were likely Asturian soldiers, causing her to don her cloak's hood. While she hadn't been recognized so far, she didn't want to press her luck. They slipped by silently, avoiding detection.

"Where do you want to go first?" Ardan asked beside her, causing her attention to divert from the potential threat. He looked as though he'd barely slept, featuring dark circles under his eyes with cheeks that were exceptionally gaunt. His dark hair hung in greasy sheets, reminding her that they hadn't properly bathed in days.

Despite their haggard appearance, she knew their next task with unnerving certainty. "We need to talk to Torquil."

Ardan bobbed his head in understanding, gaze flickering toward the buildings to his right. The streets were narrow, buildings nestled close together on either side. Their rooftops were colorful shades of orange, turquoise, and red, shingles pristine and well kept. Beige siding was outfitted with brightly colored shutters around the windows, coordinating with the rooftops.

"And do you know where this Torquil may be? Should we check the tavern?"

Nevia let out a hollow laugh, surprised when Ardan merely raised an eyebrow. He waited, silently, until the humor faded from Nevia's face, replaced by surprise. "You're serious, aren't you?"

"Isn't that where the lords often go in the evenings?"

A smirk crossed Nevia's face; she couldn't help chuckling again. Ardan's face shifted from expectant to frustrated.

"I don't find this funny."

"No, no, it's just Vladios was a very . . . special case. The tavern is the last place that you should normally find a lord. Torquil isn't like that at all." Nevia bit her lower lip, pondering. "He is probably in his manor somewhere, especially at this hour. Otherwise, I have no idea."

"Oh. I see. Well, I'll just follow your lead."

Nevia patted his forearm, gaze briefly flickering to his lips. Thoughts swarmed back to the night he'd tried to kiss her. Guilt gnawed at her stomach as they walked; she was grateful to have the horse's reins to fidget with.

The pair crossed a moat, water gurgling underfoot as their boots clapped harmoniously along the sturdy wooden slats topping the bridge. They followed a winding pathway cut between the trees to a hill where a stone mansion resided, larger than any building they'd passed so far. As they drew nearer, more of the establishment yawned into view, including fields which laborers tended and a mill grinding flour.

They hadn't even reached the steel gates fully when a uniformed man approached them. He bore the same lavender uniform as the soldiers in town, the Asturian colors with the imperial crest emblazoned on their left breast.

"Good day to you," the man greeted. "What business do you have on Lord Torquil's estate?"

The two exchanged glances before Nevia boldly stepped forward, hands clasped in front of her. "I'd like to request an audience with Lord Torquil."

The imperial guard eyed her, suspicion etched on his face. "I'm afraid that Lord Torquil doesn't see visitors unless there is an appointment. Are you in need of a council, or someone to settle a dispute? Perhaps I could refer you to the minister of public affairs instead."

"No." Nevia folded her arms over her chest, bringing herself to full height, which was difficult when feeling small and inferior. "His empress requests an audience immediately. I need to speak with him as soon as possible."

The guard's suspicion paled in comparison to the surprise now reflected on his face. His jaw slackened before he collected himself into a bow. "Yes, of course, Your Imperial Highness. You must, erm, forgive me. I didn't recognize you with your, erm, ah . . . yes. Right this way."

"Are all imperial soldiers this incompetent?" Ardan asked, louder than necessary.

Nevia shot him a dark look, which only aroused a smirk from her companion. The guard pretended not to hear them as he began fumbling with the steel gate. He swung it open with a rusty creak, dragging it with all his weight behind it.

Wind chimes rustling on the wind greeted them as they passed the threshold to the lord's estate, a sweet floral scent assaulting Nevia's nostrils. She quickly saw the source of the lovely fragrance,

Chickasaw plum trees in full bloom and clustered together in a lovely garden in front of the manor.

The clearing of a throat diverted her attention from the iron archway and violets to a middle-aged man whose arms were folded over his chest at the doorway. He didn't bear the Asturian uniform, instead donning a simple black suit, an imperial crest pinned on one of his jacket's lapels.

"We're here to see Lord Torquil," Nevia stated.

The man stiffened. "His Lordship is not here."

"Well, then we'll wait until he returns." Nevia proceeded forward, the man looking down at her over his bulbous nose.

He raised a bushy brow. "Can you not come back later?"

She lifted her chin. "You would demand your empress to 'come back later'?"

A long pause stretched between them, a muscle twitching in his jaw. Nevia could see his mind spinning, likely taking in their less than comely appearance, their dirt-stained tattered clothing. "Right, yes, yes, of course. Forgive me, Empress. Right this way." With large gloved hands he opened the oaken door for her and granted her entry, entirely ignoring Ardan. "My name is Andrei, butler to his lordship. Should you need anything, please call upon Lenna. She would be happy to assist you."

The manor was modest, with little finery despite the outward appearance of wealth and splendor. Mauve runners stretched the length of corridors, with portraits and tapestries lining each ivory wall, some paint missing and exposing bare drywall. One portrait in particular arrested Nevia's attention, featuring Torquil in all of his finery, along with a lovely dark-haired woman and a small red-headed babe in her arms, eyes blue as the sea. She stood before the portrait longer than necessary, realizing much later that she was left behind.

"I didn't know that Torquil had a child," Nevia said to Andrei's back, catching up with them.

The butler's shoulders visibly stiffened. He ran a hand over his balding head. "They do not talk about her much. The child is . . . eccentric."

Nevia could only wonder what he meant.

They were led to a formal sitting room. A plush floral sofa rested before an unlit hearth, a tall bay window half-curtained at the furthermost wall behind it. Andrei gestured to the seating before uttering, "Lady Ailish requests that all remove their shoes before stepping on the rug."

It was a suggestion, not an order, yet Nevia chose to respect the lady's wishes, having no desire to incur the wrath of the nobles whom she hoped to enlist. She unlaced her boots elegantly, while Ardan merely kicked off his and collapsed onto the sofa with little grace. Andrei curled his nose, but said nothing. Instead he directed his attention to Nevia as she seated herself beside her companion.

"Is there anything that I can get you while you wait?"

Both shook their heads, and with that the butler bowed, shutting the door behind him with a snap. Save for the ticking of a clock behind them, the room was silent, the gears of the pendulum groaning as it swung back and forth, back and forth. Many, many times.

CHAPTER 33

Torquil did not return that day. It was Lady Ailish who had come to them after hours of patient waiting, her silvery gown cascading about her in a shimmering pool. Her chestnut-brown hair shone in the candlelight, and upon witnessing her Nevia thought the family portrait did not do her justice. She was a sight of true beauty, and age did nothing to tarnish it.

"I'm sorry to have kept you waiting so long, Your Highness." She shifted over toward them, her smile gentle and serene as she lowered herself into a curtsy. What Torquil radiated in ice, his wife made up for in warmth. Immediately she put Nevia at ease, her irritation under wraps as she turned a smile to the lady of the manor.

"It's quite fine. I understand that Lord Torquil is busy."

"He was supposed to return today, but it seems his business has kept him away longer than expected." Her eyes shifted uncomfortably between Nevia and Ardan, as if something was amiss. "Would you be willing to return tomorrow?"

Both guests exchanged a glance. They certainly could, though time was precious, and they didn't account for delays. Nonetheless, Nevia couldn't force Torquil's return, and, as much as she wanted to press Ailish about the details of Torquil's absence, she refrained.

"Very well. We will stay at the local inn."

"Try the Flowering Hyssop," Ailish offered. "Tell them that I sent you for free lodging."

"That would be very kind, thank you."

She offered another bow, hesitating before slipping outside the room. Nevia stretched, swiveling in her seat to steal a glance at the swinging pendulum, performing its precise dance.

Surely delaying their journey by one day wouldn't be too problematic.

◇ ※ ◇

A week had passed of staying at the Flowering Hyssop when they received word that Torquil returned home from his business. They were summoned to the manor with all haste, to return to the sitting parlor that Nevia had put many miles into when pacing its length.

The invasion was to commence in one week: nowhere near enough time for them to return to Zenoch, even if they smuggled aboard a cargo steamship that migrated upriver toward the cliffside trade cities. Everything banked on Torquil's acceptance of her plight. If he did not . . . she shuddered to think of the consequences.

The door creaked open, causing her to sit bolt upright upright in her seat, brushing back strands of blonde hair and smoothing down her collar. Her gaze flickered up to meet the Lord of Asturia's. Auburn hair draped over his shoulders, his face drawn into a pinched frown at the sight of her. He offered her a bow, however slight. "Your Highness."

Nevia tugged at the hem of her tunic. Despite the fresh garments they had purchased in town, she still felt underdressed in Torquil's presence, devoid of her jewels and finery from the palace. "Lord Torquil."

"Your visit is . . . a surprise, to be certain." Torquil flashed a glance over at Ardan. "And your companion is . . . ?"

"Ardan," the Zenochian supplied. Deftly springing to his feet, Ardan crossed the room in a mere few strides to extend a hand to the lord. Torquil looked down at it as though offered poison and looked back to Nevia, his own hands clenched into fists at his sides.

"What is going on?" he asked. Direct and to the point.

Nevia ran her tongue over dry lips, assured this wasn't going to be as easy as it was with Vladios. "I came to talk to you about the upcoming invasion of the Feishin Kingdom."

Silence. Torquil's dark eyes were critical and calculating. "Go on."

All else that Nevia could hear was the thrumming of her own heart. "I am not sure if you received word of the speech that I gave, or its contents—"

"Yes." He scratched at his cheek, suddenly looking uncomfortable. "Yes, Empress. You will find that your words echoed to all corners of Danaeca, and they didn't earn a positive reception. If that was what you were expecting."

His words were sharp and pointed. Nevia visibly winced, quickly shattering at Torquil's hostility. "I wasn't expecting a positive reception. I only wanted to spread the truth. The people deserved to know."

Torquil didn't look convinced. He folded his arms over his chest. "Mmm, yes. And I don't suppose you thought of the consequences of sharing this 'wealth of truth' to the general public? There has been civil infighting, Nevia. Bloodshed and violence in the streets. Plunders and murder. The list goes on and on following your wonderful little speech. The emperor has had quite the mess to pick up ever since you left, which, might I add, didn't exactly paint a positive picture of you."

"He was going to have me killed."

Torquil's lips twisted. "Do you really believe that?"

"Yes!" Panic dug its claws into her heart. She glanced over to Ardan for support. While his expression remained stoic, his fists were clenched so tightly his knuckles turned white, and his gaze remained fixated on Torquil as though he wanted nothing more than to punch him. Nevia hoped he'd refrain.

The too familiar creaking of the clock pendulum reminded that time was still going, despite the conversation grinding to a halt. Torquil sighed, running a hand down the full length of his face. "So, why did you come? To preach your speech to me personally?"

Nevia's fists curled defeatedly at her sides. Quickly she was realizing it was a mistake to come; Torquil wasn't going to be open-minded. It would be a miracle if he let them go unscathed.

"I just wanted to"—Nevia closed her eyes, pain etched plainly on her face—"needed you to know that some of the Zenochian clans know the truth."

Torquil strode over to an armchair and sank into it, propping his forearms over his knees to study her. "Not surprising. This truth seems important to you."

"Torquil!" Hot tears filled Nevia's eyes. Despite her imploring expression he sat there, expressionless and uncaring. "Please, I need your help. Darius is playing you all. He told me so himself. Verrine knows the truth, just ask him."

"Verrine seems just as clueless to *this truth* as I am," Torquil responded, tone icy. "In fact, he laughed after hearing about your speech. I won't iterate his exact words as I find them unsavory, but he wouldn't agree if I asked him, no."

The door creaked open again, attracting Nevia's attention. She half-expected guardsmen to emerge, ready to cart her away, or perhaps even a servant with appetizers. Instead it surprised her to meet the startled gaze of a young girl, no older than eleven years of age. Her thin red hair hung limply down her back, and those eyes. They shook Nevia's very core, and it took her a moment to realize what was so unsettling about them.

Her irises were nearly white.

Torquil's shoulders visibly tensed at her arrival. He glanced over at the girl, as if trying to will her away. "Not now, Orla, dear."

"I heard talking." The girl shut the door behind her, pale nightgown fluttering about her. She leaned against the door, studying Nevia. "You're the empress."

The girl from the portrait, Nevia thought, sure they were one and the same; how many other children would be housed within Lord Torquil's manor, after all?

"Your daughter," Nevia said softly, turning a smile toward the child. Orla studied Nevia passively before her pale lips formed words spoken so softly that Nevia briefly thought she imagined them.

"A bed of arrows. The carpet soaked with blood."

"What?" Nevia looked disturbed. "What did you say?"

She opened her mouth to speak again, but before she could continue Torquil leapt from his chair and rushed over to Orla's side. "That's quite enough. You know better than to interrupt my private councils. Go on to bed now. I'll read to you in a moment."

His hands shook as he reached for the doorknob, swinging it open and giving the girl a shove. Ardan and Nevia exchanged quizzical glances, surprised at his erratic behavior. Before leaving, Orla gave Nevia one last haunting stare. The door nearly caught her skirt with how quick Torquil slammed it shut, his face contorting into something ugly and angry.

"Do not speak of her to the emperor." His words were lethal, eyes feral. Nevia had never seen Torquil like this. She should've used this as leverage, to blackmail him into helping, but she couldn't bring herself to.

She thought she understood but probed further. "What was she talking about?"

"She's not in her soundest state," Torquil said tritely.

She sat back in her seat, clearly doubtful, but was unable to disagree. The girl did seem odd, perhaps chronically ill. Her skin was too translucent, and her limbs too thin and brittle. Nevia questioned if her health was even the best.

"How many others do you insist on hiding her existence from?" Nevia challenged.

"As many as I feel would threaten her." He squared his shoulders, nostrils flaring. "Is there anything else that you have to say, or is this the part where I send you on your way?"

This was it. Her last chance. She rose from her seat and strode over to him, looking up into his eyes. "I won't bore you with the details. You already know the story." Nevia reached for his lithe and bony hand. To her surprise, he didn't wrench it away. "But please know I'm just trying to do what is right and save a peaceful nation. The Feishin Kingdom isn't perfect, but that doesn't mean we should invade and change its government. Please, please do the right thing and align Asturia with us. Darius has been led astray. I fear that pressure is eating away at him, and he is becoming his father more and more."

She felt like she uttered everything in a jumbled blur, afraid that Torquil wouldn't allow her a chance to speak again if she paused. His expression tightened as he finally recoiled from her touch.

"Give me time. I need . . . to think." Torquil rubbed at his temples, adorned with new streaks of silver since Nevia last saw him at Saavis. He turned on his heel to leave, and she couldn't help noticing the newfound exhaustion in the way he moved. He paused in the doorframe.

"Why don't you stay a night here in the manor, and I will give you my answer on the morrow?" Torquil suggested over his shoulder. "I'll have Lenna set up a room."

Nevia gave a start of surprise. "Well, we have been staying at the Flowering Hyssop, which has suited us fine—"

"No, please, I insist. It's the least I can do."

His hospitality stunned her into silence. Biting her lip, she dipped her head, not finding it within herself to refuse. "That would be very kind, thank you."

Torquil opened the door to leave, and Nevia didn't know what possessed her to reach out and grab his brocade sleeve.

"And thank you, Torquil, for thinking about what I've said. I know that it must be hard to hear."

His throat bobbed as he nodded, shifting away to close the door behind him. Her hand fell limply to the side.

Ardan still reclined on the couch, knee bobbing with unspent nervous energy. His head rested against the back of the couch as he inhaled sharply. "Would you say that it went well?"

"As well as could be expected, I guess. At least he's considering it. Torquil always had a level head. If he thinks about this logically, he'll come around."

I hope that he will, she thought mutely, pressing a hand to her forehead. It was hot to the touch. She hoped that a fever wasn't developing. While the old wound on her shoulder occasionally pained her, it had been healing well with no outward signs of infection.

The door slowly opened, and the serving woman from before entered. She glanced at the two of them before frowning.

"Milord said that you would only be needing one room, Your Highness." She glanced Ardan up and down. "He didn't mention that you had . . . company."

Queasiness began to sink in as she glanced over to Ardan, whose grin could not be wider.

"Oh, it was intentional!" He waved a hand carelessly in the air. "Don't worry. You don't need to prepare another room."

"What he means is," Nevia started, gritting her teeth, "he doesn't mind sleeping on the floor. He's my guard and can't bear to leave my side. Isn't that right, Ardan?"

Bemusement flickered in his eyes. "Of course, Empress." He jerked his head at Nevia pointedly for emphasis. "What she said."

The serving woman seemed unconvinced. "Mmm, very well. Right this way, Your Highness. I will show you to your room."

They passed the familiar portraits as they returned to the same hall whence they came. For a manor of this size, it was relatively quiet, having passed only a handful of guardsmen, something which struck Nevia as curious.

"Are you the only maid?" she asked.

Her question gave Lenna pause as they halted before a worn door, its white paint peeling along the edges. Her hand hovered on the discolored brass knob. "I am. Lord Torquil prefers a modest staff."

"That must be a lot of work," Nevia murmured.

Lenna gave no answer as she entered the room beyond. It was entirely shrouded by darkness. When Nevia drew a tentative step inside she was immediately greeted by a strong musty odor, and it soon became evident that this room hadn't been in use for some time. Lenna struck a match and a flame danced to life on its end, casting long shadows behind her back. One by one, she lit a candelabra, illuminating the space. The room was smaller than Nevia had thought, with barely enough room for a simple bed, bureau, trunk, and chair. A distressed wardrobe rested along one wall, a knob missing with a gaping hole left in its wake. Nevia frowned.

"Is there anything that I can get you, Your Highness? Perhaps a warm meal?"

"That would be nice, thank you." Nevia glanced over her shoulder at Ardan, who ran a finger along the bureau and rubbed off a thick layer of dust with his thumb and shrugged. "And please bring a meal for my guard as well."

"Of course, Your Highness." Lenna bowed and left.

The bed groaned under Nevia's weight as she sank onto the floral bedspread. A plume of dust filled the air in response, forcing a cough from her lungs.

"Great housekeeping here, huh?" Ardan murmured, echoing Nevia's thoughts. "For a lord, he has pretty lousy accommodations. This place is so unkempt. Can't he afford to hire more help?"

"It is odd," Nevia agreed.

Ardan crossed the room, considering for a moment before sitting on the bed alongside Nevia. The mattress sank so that both were pulled toward its center.

There they sat, shoulder-to-shoulder, silent as the trio of flames swayed and danced on, until the empress sighed heavily, inclining her head against Ardan's shoulder to rest. She felt his muscles tense, then shift before he slowly, hesitantly, wrapped an arm around her shoulders. She didn't pull away.

"So," Ardan began slowly, swallowing hard, "am I really sleeping on the floor?"

A giggle escaped Nevia as she shoved him, her palms splayed against his chest. A hearty laugh escaped him as he fell backward. A whimsical smile was planted on both their faces, perhaps the first true smile that graced Nevia's lips since her father's passing. "That depends. Will you be good?"

"Oh, I don't know." He rolled onto his side, propping his head on his fist. "What constitutes 'good' by your definition?"

She leaned over, her thick hair brushing his shoulder. One hand was still splayed against his chest, his heart roaring underneath her fingertips. Nevia wondered if her own heart outmatched its pace.

"Well, I don't know. Can you keep your hands and feet to yourself if you share a small corner of the bed?"

"Is that all that I must keep to myself?"

"You're awful!" Nevia swatted his shoulder, even though he was still laughing. She folded her arms across her chest, grateful that the dim lighting concealed her reddening cheeks. The butterflies began to flutter in her stomach again, those flutters that screamed desire, guilt, and shame. She turned her gaze downward, biting the inside of her cheek so hard that she could taste the metallic tang of blood.

Ardan must've sensed her tension. He rubbed his hand up and down her arm, soothing the gnawing guilt with a smile tender and full of reassurance. "Truly now, I can sleep on the floor, or ask the servant for another room," he offered, as if that was all that plagued her. "I'm sure they have one somewhere, though I'll admit that I'm frightful to see its condition if this was deemed acceptable for their empress."

The temptation of pushing him away was real. It would've been the easiest solution, yet Nevia couldn't bring herself to do it. She had taken such comfort in his presence, something she seldom felt over the past month. She leaned forward.

"No, stay."

When he didn't seem convinced, she further added, "I . . . want you here with me."

His hand covered hers, a bubble of warmth and security amidst the raging sea of chaos. "Then I will stay with you. I am yours to command, Nevia."

"I don't want to command you to do anything." She pressed her forehead against his, basking in his presence, drawing strength from it. "I just . . . don't want to be alone. Not right now, not with everything happening."

There was more to it than that, but she couldn't admit that to herself.

They brought little in the way of belongings, but Torquil was hospitable enough to provide the basics. A fresh change of clothes smelling strongly of antiquity and mothballs could be found in the wardrobe. Nevia wondered to herself how long her nightgown had been in storage as she yanked the garment over her head, snagging it on a stray barrette lodged in her curls.

Ardan had politely left to allow her to change, and she was grateful for the moments that she had to herself. Suddenly she cared more about her appearance than she should've, cursing herself that she hadn't shaved her legs in weeks or properly brushed her hair. She snuffed out the candles with care, as if each carried a prayer on the wind, leaving one lit by her bedside for Ardan to find his way back.

It's just Ardan, she reminded herself. They were simply friends. Adventurers, fellow countrymen who were questing together. Surely no harm would come to them for sharing a bed.

Right?

The door creaked open as Ardan slid back into the room, propping his spear in the corner before kicking off his boots. Nevia was already tucked neatly under the covers, hands folded over her stomach. While the hour was still young, every muscle in Nevia's body ached and her consciousness begged to shut down, the mental exhaustion of the past month overbearing.

Ardan leapt onto the mattress beside her, donned in linen pants and with his shirt pulled overhead, exposing his bare chest. A blush crawled over her cheeks. She took in the strong muscles that rippled across his abdomen as he shifted, the shrouded, enigmatic tattoos lining his chest. She assumed that one of them was his own Kindred Spirit, but she couldn't detect it in the darkness.

If Ardan noticed her staring, he didn't acknowledge it. He kicked up the covers, patting her shoulder and murmuring a quiet "goodnight." She turned expectantly, thinking there would be a discussion, a hug, something, *anything,* but he rolled onto his side and remained there, back to her.

Nevia heaved a relieved sigh, grateful for the invisible partition he'd created between them and lessening the intimacy of sharing a bed. Yet despite her relief she was disappointed. A forbidden part of her wanted to be held, cradled against his strong chest and feel his breath rise and fall rhythmically, lulling her into a comfortable slumber. Her lips tightened; she could request it. She doubted that Ardan would deny her, especially with his subtle suggestions that he felt something for her, but she wasn't sure if that was a boundary that she was ready to cross.

A tear rolled down her cheek as she blew out the remaining candle and pressed her back against Ardan's. She took comfort in this small way, being close to one who accepted her true self without any expectation of how she should behave or perform.

He truly cared, something that felt both alien and so very wonderful.

And she cared for him back, despite hating herself for her divided, traitorous heart.

CHAPTER 34

Nevia awoke in a cold sweat, kicking off the covers and rising on the bed. Her gaze flickered toward the heavy draperies concealing the window, making it difficult to gauge the hour. No sunlight peaked through the narrow gaps between drapes. It was still dark. She blinked several times to make out details in the room, but it was too dark to see past the outlines of shadows.

One of which moved.

Her breath hitched. Ardan remained sleeping soundlessly against her back, so she knew it wasn't him. Then the sound of a stretching bowstring assaulted her ears. Her heart hammered in her chest as she flattened herself on the mattress, an arrow embedding itself in the wooden headboard where her heart had been.

Cold dread seized her as another arrow was released into the soft weave of the mattress at her side. Nevia rolled off the bed and onto the ground, pressing her body against the uneven floorboards. She held her breath as one of the assailant's footsteps rocked the wood under her cheek. The metal springs above her groaned as Ardan shot up. She hoped he realized they were armed and ready to kill them.

Along with Nevia's fear was fury. Who would assault them in their sleep?! Was Torquil's security this poor?

She heard the shuffling of feet and the door creak open, allowing light to pour onto the floor. She caught a glimpse of their assailants: three, each donning familiar lavender uniforms.

Torquil's men.

The lord's hospitality had been a ruse. He wanted them dead —but why? Why kill them when he could've shackled them and handed them over to Darius' men, their capture all too easy in his estate?

Hands seized her from under the bed, dragging her by the upper arm. A flicker of silver caught in the light, and a bone knife wielded by Ardan was thrust into her assailant. With a cry the grappling hands retreated, replaced by the familiarity of Ardan's calloused hands that yanked her out, bringing her to his side and pressing her close.

Their enemy circled them, clad in leather armor with bows cast aside in favor of sharp steel swords. They stood facing each other, their silhouettes barely visible in the darkness. Ardan was equipped with only a knife, his spear still propped in the corner and inaccessible.

After a tense moment of stillness, both parties sensing and gauging, Ardan moved first, lunging towards the closest soldier and knocking the air from his lungs. A further shove occupied another, but the last grappled Nevia and spun behind her. Just as quickly, a bead of crimson formed at her bobbing throat, where the sharp edge of his blade bit into her flesh. Ardan whipped around, spear in hand, at Nevia's whimper as she was forced to turn around. He froze.

The soldier jerked his head upward in triumph, voice deep as he said: "Move and the empress dies."

Ardan stiffened his shoulders, sizing up the opposition before relenting. His lax grip on his spear prompted the guard he rammed to jerk it away. He raised his hands in surrender, hazel eyes resting on Nevia's captor.

"Much better." His grip tightened around the empress as he nodded to his companions. "Bind him."

Nevia knew it was now or never. She allowed her body to slacken, catching her captor off-guard. She then threw her head back, her skull crashing into his nose. The pain caused him to buckle, and she wasted no time in grabbing his sword arm and twisting it backward. He let out a piercing cry as she heard the bones release a wet snap.

Another brought his sword down across her bicep, her nightgown proving to be defenseless against the steel of his blade.

It drew blood, a hiss rising from her throat, yet the wound was thankfully shallow. He raised his weapon to do more, but stopped, body jerking and eyes widening from the spear budding from his chest. Ardan quickly discarded the man and dragged Nevia up to the windowsill, tearing the draperies open.

Nevia swallowed hard as she stole a frightful glance out the window. The drop stretched far, at least ten feet into the wiry hedges below, their twisty limbs fearsomely entwined and foreboding.

She drew in a breath and leapt, wind whipping up in her ears as her nightgown fluttered. Her feet made first impact with the hedges, next her side. Pain shot through her joints and muscles, but it paled in comparison to the cut on her arm. Hot liquid ran down the length of her forearm; she didn't need to glance down to know it was blood. Groaning, Nevia started to untangle herself from the brush.

The hedges rustled beside her as Ardan followed, though he was up in seconds. She bit back her envy as she stumbled, trying to gain her footing on wobbly legs that felt like gelatin. Worry arched Ardan's brow as he drew his attention from her face to her bloodied arm, but the voices above kept him silent. Arrows arched through the air and landed about them, though thankfully none sang true. Every muscle in Nevia's sore body protested as they stumbled forward, yet they had to press on. They were simple targets remaining as they were. They skirted along the manicured lawn, scrambling down the hill and away from Torquil's estate without looking back.

If they were followed, it wasn't for long. Nevia's heart pounded in her throat as they ran into the outlying trees to lose themselves rather than tempting fate in the streets. They were moving in the direction of town, Nevia knew, though she thought it better to leave Palthesi altogether. Their business here was done.

"Well, so much for the warm welcome." Ardan cast a dark look over his shoulder. "Has he always been this two-faced?"

Nevia turned her face toward the heavens, morning's first light tinting the sky, stars blinking out from existence. A comfortable chill hung in the air, caressing her locks and cooling her skin. "It was odd, but I think I know why he tried to have us killed. The child. Torquil's daughter is a seer, and he didn't trust me with his secret. Quietly eliminating me before I got to Darius made the most sense."

Ardan grew deathly quiet. He let out a low breath, the warmth of it fogging the early morning air. "But that's stupid. You clearly oppose Darius; why would he think you'd prattle this off to him?"

"I don't know," Nevia admitted, the pit in her stomach festering into something hideous. "I really don't know."

She braced her throbbing arm. Everything in her body protested, yet she knew they couldn't stop to rest. They were running out of time. She turned her gaze onto Ardan, who looked as sickly as she felt, and extended a hand. He obliged, weaving his fingers into hers and giving her hand a reassuring squeeze.

A reminder that she wasn't alone, that everything would be okay, even if it felt impossible in that moment. Torquil, someone else she respected and thought a friend, tried to have her killed, and it bruised her more than she would've liked to admit.

CHAPTER 35

Despite Nevia's better judgment, she allowed her exhaustion to prevail, succumbing to Ardan's coaxing of finding some place to stay in Asturia. They did not dare return to the Flowering Hyssop, as that would've been nothing short of a death sentence. Instead they found a rustic farm along the outskirts of the city. A chicken coop stood to their right encased by a wired fence, with colorful roosters milling within it. One crowed noisily as they passed, alerting anyone who would listen that dawn was upon them. They ignored the rooster's call and continued along gravel to the barn, climbing over a fence containing several goats to scamper up their ramp and through a window. Nevia collapsed in a fresh pile of hay, surrounded by manure and livestock, and remained there until midmorning.

Her sleep was broken and fitful, her dreams so lucid that, at times, she didn't think them dreams at all. The prickling of hay against her cheek roused her after a few short hours, opening her eyes to the point-blank muzzle of a horse that brushed her face. Its breath tickled, and the sight alone was enough to brighten her mood. She drew herself up on her elbows, lifting a hand to its velvet head. Her fingers traced the white star along its forehead, its coat a fine silver that shimmered in the early morning light infiltrating from the slatted barn windows lining the ceiling.

"You really are an animal whisperer, aren't you?"

Nevia spun around to find Ardan running a towel over his hands with a smile. The empress rose to her feet, dizzy from the blood rushing to her head. She tried and failed to brush the hay from her nightgown. "I suppose, maybe."

He tossed the towel aside, stepping carefully over a manure pile to make his way over to her. His movements reminded Nevia of a cat; long, sleek, and silent. Hazel eyes wandered over her, as if taking in her every feature, every curve. He reached up. For a moment Nevia thought that he was going to touch her in affection, but instead he plucked a strand of hay from her hair. He spun it between his thumb and index finger, gaze never leaving hers.

"You are more talented than you would like to believe, methinks." He stood close enough that Nevia could feel his breath on her face.

"I'm not sure why you're trying to flatter me." Nevia bit her lip, tearing her gaze from his eyes to take in his smooth, broad lips. Her heart thrummed wildly in her chest.

"It's not flattery. It's just the truth. Over these past couple of weeks I've watched you downplay yourself constantly, always putting yourself last and even casting yourself lower to make people feel better." He leaned in, bracing a forearm on an overhanging beam. "Why all the humility?"

"Why not?" Nevia was flustered now, heat rising into her cheeks. Ardan wore a boyish smile, which only accentuated his striking facial features: the point of his chin, his high cheekbones and hollow cheeks. Her hand betrayed her, reaching out to cup one of his cheeks. He leaned into her touch as she ran a thumb over his jawline, feeling the short stubble on his otherwise smooth, flawless skin.

His hand raised her chin so that their gazes locked. She lost herself in the twin swirls of green and gold, so much so that when Ardan leaned in her lips met his without resistance.

Their kiss felt fiery enough to send sparks throughout the barn. His arms encircled her waist. She felt her body press against his, which she further leaned into. A burning desire coursed through her core, into her lower abdomen. She wanted to be closer, to feel what his skin felt like against hers. She ground her hips against his thighs, inwardly cursing their height difference. Within moments her fingers dipped into his hair, his dark locks as silky as she had imagined.

Time seemed to stop as she was lost in that kiss. It was Ardan who pulled away, jerking his head to the side so that Nevia's lips met with his jaw. She felt his facial muscles tense as she placed a soft kiss there, causing her eyes to widen in alarm.

"Ardan?"

"I'm sorry," he murmured distractedly. He still wasn't looking at her, but he had yet to release her from his grasp. "You probably didn't intend for this. I—"

Before he could continue, Nevia placed another kiss on his jaw, her lips soon traveling further downward to his throat. A moan of pleasure escaped him, his gaze hungry as his eyes met hers, then drifted lower over the rest of her, still in her disheveled nightgown.

Their lips met again, their hands traveling to places they dreamed of but wouldn't have dared to explore before. Ardan's hands were twisted up into Nevia's unbound hair as he kissed her passionately, his lips traveling down her neck, lower, to the space between her breasts, her lower abdomen—

A gasp escaped her at his touch. She held on to him tightly, one leg wrapped around his waist, nuzzling her nose into the crook of his neck and getting lost in the heat of the moment.

Sunlight infiltrated her closed lids, causing her eyes to snap open and tear away from him. Her mouth fell agape as a narrow figure appeared in the barn entrance.

The ranch hand was a youth, perhaps no older than fourteen years of age. Looking just as shocked as Nevia felt, his grip on his pitchfork slackened as he gaped at them.

"You two s'pose to be in here?" he asked.

A smirk crossed Ardan's face as he pinned Nevia to his chest. "Needed to find a private place with my lady," he stated roguishly with a wink. "Surely you understand."

This eased the ranch hand considerably, the boy's smile slowly stretching in the light. "Aye, that I do. I mean, if you two need a room, my friend Cian's place is just down the road. I'm sure that he—"

"No, that's alright," Nevia said, perhaps too quickly. "We need to get back to my mother's place soon, anyway."

Ardan, however, seemed as though he'd been contemplating the boy's offer, earning him an elbow to the ribs. He rubbed his side ruefully, expression twisting from a grin into a grimace. "Yeah . . . and I need to get to work."

"Some other time, then. My name's Rob, by the way."

Nevia studied him momentarily, wondering how often he casually offered up his friend's home to complete strangers to do . . . . Goddess knew what. "Well, thank you for the offer, Rob," said Nevia. "We'll . . . certainly keep it in mind."

Ardan strode forward, punching the ranch hand playfully in the shoulder as he passed.

"You stay out of trouble now."

Rob looked gleeful, as if he were inside some great conspiracy between two lovers and their opposing families. "Same to you two."

A short, rough laugh escaped Ardan. "I'm always in trouble."

Trying to will the flush from her cheeks, Nevia dipped her head and moved past the stablehand to follow along behind Ardan, adjusting her nightgown to conceal her breasts. The morning sun greeted them; not a cloud present in the cerulean sky. She let out a breath as the fresh air brought a swell of relief.

"That was a close one."

Ardan dug his spear into the soft earth of the path. "Luckily I know my way around young men and what they want to hear."

"You're horrible!"

Ardan only smirked. "I know."

Nevia felt Ardan's fingers brush hers, prompting her to open her hand, and a great part of her wished to let him in, to pick right back up where they left off. But instead she swallowed hard, closing her hand tightly into a fist and holding it close to her side.

She cursed herself for caving to his affection, succumbing to her innermost desire. Guilt gnawed at her, her stomach twisting into unbearable knots and causing a wave of nausea to roll over her.

"We can't let that happen again." She hated herself for the words that escaped her lips, yet she felt it prudent. She was empress, still wed to Emperor Darius by law, and yet she had no intention of returning to his side. He'd dealt her wounds that permeated beyond flesh, cleaving bonds that could never be mended. Any chance of rectifying their grievances was tarnished when he'd killed her father, and that was when she knew—with the utmost certainty—that they were through. Forever.

Ardan's face fell at her words, disappointment clearly etched in the grooves of his brow. "I understand. Forgive me, Nevia."

She cringed. "It's not your fault. You tried to resist, but I urged you on. I—I wanted to."

His lips tightened, but he said nothing. She wondered what he must have thought of her.

Clambering down a set of hills, they left the countryside of Palthesi behind, with nothing but the clothes on their backs and the spear in Ardan's hand. Everything else had to be left behind. The majority wouldn't cause Nevia much grief, though the loss of her mother's pendant pained her. They would need supplies before they ventured north. While they had little to offer, Nevia was certain some form of trade could be arranged, even if in the form of physical labor. She was no stranger to bartering, having been raised in the north.

"We need to plan," Ardan said, breaking the silence as they crept across the smooth blades of grass. "Clearly, negotiations with your lord didn't go smoothly."

"No." Nevia's gaze fell to her feet. "No, they did not."

Ardan shrugged and rubbed his nose with the back of his hand. "And we have already wasted so much time waiting for the lord to return. I don't think there's any way to get back to the north in time."

"That is for certain."

"Now, I've been giving this a lot of thought," Ardan started slowly, "and I think we should board Torquil's ship setting sail for the Feishin Kingdom."

She opened her mouth to retort, but Ardan held up a hand to silence her.

"As stowaways. It wouldn't be that hard."

Nevia could think of all of the reasons why it *would*. "I don't know, Ardan. There's security, and being at the right place at the right time, and—"

"We escaped an entire manor that was out for your blood, didn't we?"

"Yes, well, that was getting out, but infiltrating a warship? *Torquil's* ship?"

"They always say that getting in is easier than getting out."

Nevia rubbed at her temple. "Yes, but we'll have to get out of this, too."

"Simple. We'll get off the ship the moment everyone's left for battle. It'll be fine."

A groan escaped Nevia as she slumped forward, deep in thought with her palms trailing over her nightgown. While irrational and insane, Ardan's plan was perhaps the only viable option they had. Not being present was something that Nevia could ill afford. The Zenochians were counting on her to be there, not for her skill but for her voice.

Something she never thought she'd be able to use.

"All right," Nevia relented. "But it isn't going to be as easy as you claim. There will be watches preventing us from simply sneaking aboard. Torquil will know that something is amiss, and for that we need to be ready."

Ardan weighed her words carefully, expression thoughtful. "We'll indeed have to be careful. But worry not; this isn't my first time sneaking somewhere I wasn't supposed to be. Just follow my lead and everything will be fine. You'll see."

An ember of hope welled inside her chest, but it would be a stretch to say he completely pacified her. She knew Torquil better than him, and she felt any experience that Ardan had would pale in the face of whatever lay ahead.

"First thing's first, I need something else for me to wear."

Ardan arched a brow. "Why's that?"

Nevia scoffed, snatching up fistfuls of her nightgown and shaking them. "I can't very easily go to war in this, now, can I?"

Both of his brows rose now as he studied her long enough to make her cheeks go pink. "I honestly don't see why not."

"Ardan!"

"Just kidding, Empress. Just kidding. Shopping for fine warrior garb will be made a priority. I promise."

To see the tension ebb from Ardan's shoulders, the way he carried himself lighter, eased her. Perhaps they had already been able to patch things up, and yet she still saw the desire that lingered in his gaze, the way that his fingers inched toward her. She so greatly wanted to snatch up his hand and bask in his presence, soaking in his love and affection, but she couldn't.

And she told herself that the rest of the way back to Palthesi.

CHAPTER 36

Infiltrating Torquil's ranks proved more difficult than they assumed for one reason that Nevia hadn't considered: all of his soldiers were male.

This left them with fewer options, though ultimately it was decided that Ardan would blend in with the warship's crew while Nevia would have to stay hidden, a herculean feat as every square inch of the ship appeared traversed for any one reason. At last he'd been able to stash her in a broom closet belowdecks an hour before departure, and that is where she remained.

For hours. And hours.

And hours.

The slight rocking from waves striking the warship drifted her in and out of sleep, and she soon lost track of how long she'd been stashed away. She wondered how much longer it would be before they arrived, how much longer she could stand it. A terrible cramp seized her thigh. She gritted her teeth against her discomfort, fighting the urge to reposition herself until she nearly cried out from the pain. She was loathe to disturb the delicate balance that was the broom closet, lest everything go tumbling out the improperly latched door and arrest the attention of the sailors.

Wherever Ardan was, she hoped that he would come for her—and soon.

"Hard to starboard!"

Bodies littered the deck, the stench of sweat masking the slight sea spray of the ocean. Ardan, head ducked low as he swabbed the deck, kept himself busy throughout the day, blending in with the crew seamlessly. His northern garb was exchanged for a sailor's striped tunic and black pants, his head wrapped with a red bandana that aided in masking his nationality. It turned out that such precaution was rather unnecessary as the crew was diverse, and Ardan recognized some from as far as the southern country of Kikioni. Even still, if he was to cross paths with Torquil he would need to exercise caution. The lord had seen him once and would likely recognize him again.

He dipped his mop into a tin bucket to slosh onto the weathered floorboards, but the facade was hardly needed; no one paid him any mind. The majority of soldiers were rosy-cheeked from drink, their words crude and slurred. One middle-aged man with a steely-gray beard—a general if gauging from his uniform—bragged in explicit detail about what he'd do with the Feishin princess after they conquered the kingdom, revolting Ardan so greatly that he relocated to the other side of the deck, mopping even more furiously than before.

The crowd started to thin, the promise of a warm meal belowdecks beckoning the men. While Ardan's stomach growled, it wasn't the hunger that sent him with the crowd, but the promise of retrieving Nevia.

Eight hours. Ardan hated himself for stashing her in the insufferable confines of that closet space. He hoped that she wasn't struggling, that she hadn't been found, but all that he could do was swallow down his anxiety as he blended in with a dozen other sailors, clambering down the stairs to follow the aroma of fried chicken and spices.

The dining room was impossibly loud, dozens of voices reverberating against the stark white walls. Ardan stood on tiptoe to make out a long table against the leftmost wall, surrounded by a cluster of men reaching over one another like ravenous beasts. The line leading to the table snaked around the room and outside—yet it didn't stop him from ducking and weaving, remaining obscure as he picked his way toward the front.

Now close, it became clear that rations were being carefully divvied out to ensure that there would be plenty to go around.

Five kitchen hands distributed the meal from mounding piles of soggy vegetables, bread rolls, and refried chicken so greasy that Ardan wouldn't even dream of feeding it to his wolves. When his turn came he accepted his portion and moved away, past a cluster of soldiers that were trying to barrel ahead for seconds. As Ardan left he could hear shouts and swears, shortly followed by a fist meeting with bare flesh. He dared not linger to see the result of the encounter.

The weathered staircase leading down to the sailor's quarters was deserted, filling him with hope. Maybe, just maybe, that big oaf manning the barracks would be absent—

His hopes were soon shattered at the sight of the surly steward from before, sitting on a box of crates, snarfing down his meal without any sense of decency. His bald scalp gleamed from sweat under the candlelight as he wiped the back of his mouth with thick, greasy fingers. He turned irritated eyes toward Ardan.

"Back again so soon?"

"Uh, yeah." Ardan held up his meal in one hand, the mop in the other. "Needed to return this. Can't mop well in the dark up there."

The steward looked wary. He drew in a rattled breath, nostrils flaring. Ardan schooled his face into indifference, yet he couldn't help wondering if the steward could hear his racing pulse.

Nevia was right: trying to board Torquil's ship as stowaways was a terrible idea. The steward's scrutiny made him hold his breath, awaiting his final judgment.

The steward posed no physical threat to him. Ardan was ready to kill him if necessary, but he really didn't want that. He was sick of mopping, and the thought of sopping up this man's sticky blood sounded grossly unappealing.

"Don't put it away yet," the steward said finally. "Someone decided to piss against the closet. I need you to clean it up."

Ardan shuddered, from both relief and horror. It seemed that his cover held, but poor Nevia in that closet. . . .

He tried not to think of it.

"Umm, yeah, okay."

The steward grunted in response, then decided Ardan didn't deserve his attention any longer. He resumed chowing down on his meal, the unsettling slurps continuing. Ardan sidestepped around him and steadied gait as he moved to the broom closet, suppressing the urge to break into a sprint the rest of the way.

Ammonia caused Ardan's eyes to water the moment he arrived. He held his breath as he leaned over the wet planks to wrench the closet door open. For a moment he stood there, heart racing, until he saw her.

Her platinum hair blended perfectly with the overhead mop, body curled into a tight ball against a crate. Slowly she lifted her head, her eyes and face puffy from dust and filth. She winced as she moved one arm, then the other, before finally stretching her legs. She let out an uncomfortable hiss, causing Ardan to press a finger to his lips, throwing his head in the direction of the hall.

"Not alone," he mouthed, before extending the food out to her.

She shook her head, splaying a hand on his chest and forcing herself to standing. Her legs gave way, causing her to tumble onto the floor. Ardan feared it would only be a matter of moments before the steward came to investigate. Thinking fast, Ardan let his mop fall, its handle landing with a clatter. He threw a bucket out of the broom closet for good measure.

"Sorry! I'm a klutz!" he called out.

Tenderly he knelt, scooping up the empress and cradling her in his arms. She burrowed her nose into the crook of his neck, and he could tell by her sharp inhale that she was taking in his scent. His smile was bitter, lips fixed into a grim line. He shouldn't have left her for so long, should've found any excuse to reach her sooner.

"Okay, I'm okay. I think I can feel my legs now." Her voice was raspy from lack of use. Ardan hesitantly released her. Her legs shook under her weight, but they didn't slip out from under her again. Her glassy eyes flickered toward the food, then him, questioningly.

"For you," Ardan whispered, extending the tray over to her, but one look at the dish made her shake her head. He could hardly blame her, but added, "You need to keep up your strength. We will be on the outskirts of the Feishin Kingdom in about two days, and if you want to stand upright you need to eat something."

She relented, seating herself on a bucket and seizing the bread roll with trembling fingers. While she did this, Ardan fetched some water from the crew's fresh supply in the opposite room, filling up her three water flasks they had wisely stashed with her. At least she wouldn't suffer from dehydration. When he returned she was finished, shooting a darkened glance toward her personal prison.

"I don't want to go back in there."

The despair in her voice, the anxiety in her glassy eyes. He let out a slow, long breath and knelt before her, slowly wrapping her in a tight embrace. For a moment she remained still, and Ardan wondered if he'd made a mistake. He started to shift away, to apologize, but she wrapped her slender arms around his neck, pulling him in closer. He ran his palm up and down the length of her back, massaging the taut muscles in her shoulders.

"I can't get you out yet. But once the steward goes to bed I'm getting you out of here. I think I know where I can put you." Truthfully he had no idea, but he would figure it out. He had to. "Until then, sit tight and hang in there. I am so sorry. If I could trade places with you, I would in a heartbeat."

She drew in a quivering breath, facing the closet as one would going to war against a dragon, a fierce determination kindling in her eyes. It took all of his willpower to refrain from pressing her to his chest again, to take in the sweet, gentle taste of her lips. Instead he cupped her cheek, thumb tracing her jawline. "I'll be back soon," he whispered.

Taking in her beautiful visage one last time, he closed the closet door, sealing her in as if it were a coffin.

With a heart heavier than lead, he forced his feet to shuffle away, his tray untouched save for the missing bread roll. The steward chuckled darkly as he passed, causing Ardan to pause at the stairwell. He was quickly becoming his least favorite person.

"Took you long enough. Had fun over there?"

It took all of his willpower not to punch the disgusting man in his rotund, obnoxious face as Ardan whirled on heel. Instead he glared daggers at the steward. "The time of my life," he said sardonically before storming away, marching up the steps and back onto the deck.

How far that was from the truth.

CHAPTER 37

The crown prince drew a sip from his porcelain cup, savoring the sweet blend of jasmine and honey in his tea. Dark clouds swirled outside his bedroom window. It looked like a winter storm was brewing. A fresh snowfall hadn't befallen the Feishin Kingdom in weeks; Qirin didn't mind the thought of a fresh snowfall to conceal the old.

A gentle rap at the door behind him arrested his attention. "Enter."

A serving girl swept in and immediately knelt, folding her legs underneath her as she pressed her head to the floor. His lips curved along the golden rim of his cup, conveniently hiding his frown. "Please, you don't need to do that for me."

It embarrassed him, and made him feel like he was just a chip off the old block. Like his mother.

The thought sickened him.

"Your Majesty." The girl rose, brushing at the fine wrinkles of her modest black skirt. "The queen has requested your presence urgently."

Qirin quirked a brow. How unusual. He set the cup down, striding toward his dressing table to retrieve a robe of midnight blue. "Of course. Where is she?"

Wrapping the robe over his bare torso, he followed the maid into the dimly lit hallway, their slippered footsteps soft as they migrated to the throne room. A deep heave escaped him as he thrust both doors open.

Nobles flittered through the chamber, the buzz of their rushed, low tones echoing off the walls. His brow wrinkled as his dark eyes darted from Lady Teniel to the head of security, to finally his mother, who was locked in an intense conversation with a man Qirin recognized but didn't know by name.

The queen, usually a figure of order and beauty, looked terrible. Smudged eyeliner lay around her eyes. Her skin revealed wrinkles and her complexion was splotchy without the thick layers of powder adorning every inch of her face. She waved a hand to silence her companion before turning to her son.

"Oh, good, you're here." Her fingers grazed the folds of her black coat. "Excuse us for a moment, Bintu, please."

Ah, Bintu, Qirin thought idly, considering the wizened man whose salt-and-pepper beard dipped to his chest as bowed lowly to his queen, long emerald robes cascading onto the marble stone of the dais. Queen Arethusa strode away, her footfalls loud as she directed Qirin away to a corner of the room so that they could speak without garnering as much attention.

"What is all of this?" Qirin gestured to the crowd. "I doubt that you called them all in for a teatime social."

Queen Arethusa turned a weary glance his way, raking her worn face with long red nails. "They've come for me."

Her gaze penetrated the opposite wall, as if peering into the nether planes far beyond their physical existence.

"Who was come for you?" Qirin finally prodded when too long a silence lapsed. "What are you talking about, Mother?"

She burrowed her face in her hands as her shoulders shook. "I knew this day would come. I knew ever since that crazed barbarian woman came and butchered dozens of our own, claiming that we hurt them. I wanted to believe enough time had passed that they wouldn't, but now—" She lifted her gaze, revealing eyes wild with panic, not unlike a caged animal desperate to escape its confines. "They have come to take everything from us."

Qirin remained silent. He, too, knew that this day would come, in ways that his mother did not. His thoughts fled back to the solitary message sent by one of Zenoch's messenger birds. It came over a month ago, but he hadn't divulged its contents to his mother. No, he knew her response would be dissatisfactory; he would need to do things his own way, make the preparations that he saw fit. Ones she would never approve of.

Even still, his heart ached as he watched his mother mourn, having never seen her this broken in his life. He should've comforted her and offered reassurances that no harm would come to their family. Perhaps a good son would've even insisted on protecting her. But Qirin instead clamped his hands at his sides.

"When are they coming?"

Arethusa's eyes darkened. "My son, they are already here."

"Your Majesties."

Both turned to Teniel Rumaar, hair drawn into a messy bun atop her head. Her coral pantsuit sported deep wrinkles, as though she had slept in it. "It would seem not only Zenochian ships charge toward our shores. Those of imperial make accompany them."

"How long before they arrive?" he asked with a frown.

Teniel hesitated before replying, "Within the hour, Your Majesty."

Qirin whipped around to look at his mother, her complexion ashen.

"Evacuate the city into the underground shelters," she ordered. "Prepare the rest of the guards to shield the city."

The prince grimaced. He gently laid a hand atop his mother's, stroking her knuckles with the pad of his thumb. Leaning in so that only her ears could hear, he whispered: "Please think this through carefully. The empire is bringing an entire army. They will break through our defenses within a matter of minutes."

The queen grew very still. For a moment Qirin listened to his pounding heart, hoping that her silence meant that she saw reason. Maybe she would agree with him, maybe—

"It is all we can do," came her reply, causing Qirin's heart to sink. "And besides, we have the wall."

He gave her a cool look. "Which will be obliterated with their cannons."

Her eyes met his, glittering with a danger that he had never before seen. "We will not retaliate."

"But, Mother, if we choose apathy, pacifism as we know it will crumble anyway." He slammed his fist into his open palm. "We have the weapons and the technology. Let us surprise them while they are still at sea. Maybe they would be caught so off-guard that they wouldn't invade. Maybe—"

"Enough." Queen Arethusa marched away, not looking back at him. "I do not ever want to hear another word of wielding arms from you. Understood?"

Qirin drew in a breath, saying nothing.

"That is not the image that your father would want for the kingdom, nor our nation's founders. We will stand for what we believe in and then, only then, will we have the favor of the gods to turn away our attackers," she concluded.

Ah, and it dissolved into the religious mantra. It took all of Qirin's willpower to stifle the sarcasm that tried to escape his lips.

From the corner of his eye he saw a blur of pink; rushing into the room was his sister. The prince's eyes narrowed. If his mother had seemed disorderly, Princess Mila looked like nothing shy of devastation. Her eyes were puffy and red, burgundy hair in a massive tangle that Qirin didn't know was capable from his sister's otherwise silky mane.

"Mother, is it true? Are we being invaded?" Hysteria laced her tone, eyes wild as they darted frantically about the room of nobles. The throne room had started to empty, now that a direction had been determined and orders were placed. Only a handful of individuals apart from the royal family remained.

Queen Arethusa's lips tightened. "Darling, everything will be alright. Everything is going exactly as intended."

Disbelief etched itself on Qirin's face as the queen's composure grew a bit more collected, as she stood proudly before her children.

Relief flooded Mila at her words. She rushed to snatch up her mother's hands. "Really? You think so?"

Arethusa wrenched one of her hands free to smooth down her daughter's hair. "Yes, everything is according to the gods' design. Whatever will be, shall be. So long as we remain steadfast and pray, everything should be fine. Our kingdom will prevail—"

Qirin couldn't help letting out a snort. Sternness crept over Arethusa's features as her eyes narrowed on him. "Do not lose faith! The moment that you do, all hope will be lost."

"I'm sorry," Qirin scoffed, scratching his cheek. "It's just that it astounds me you actually believe yourself. Do you really think everything will be alright if we sit here and do nothing but twiddle our thumbs? Really? Do you not think that the gods would want us to fight for what is ours rather than let some greedy empire swoop in and claim it for themselves?"

The throne room fell silent. Even the nobles stopped in their chatter. Teniel along with another man filed out of the room, perhaps thinking it would be best to leave the royal family alone to deal with their affairs. Qirin thought they weren't wrong.

Rage contorted the queen's jaw. She drew a step closer, and for a moment Qirin thought that she wanted to strike him. He secretly wished that she would—perhaps it would ease the guilt that burrowed itself into his heart. Instead she shook her index finger at him, hand laden with rings.

"I never want to hear you speak like this again," she spat.

The prince crossed his arms over his chest, meeting his mother's gaze unflinchingly. "Very well, Mother."

"Good." She took Mila's hand, who didn't resist her mother's touch. "You need to get yourself to the underground shelter. To be safe."

The princess blinked, turning her wide, innocent eyes unto her mother. "You're not coming?" Anxiety drew the color from her round, youthful face.

Arethusa wrapped her arms tightly around her, tucking her head underneath her chin. "I must greet the emperor," she said gravely. "But do not fret. You're strong, and you have a heart of iron. The Feishin Kingdom will prevail, no matter what happens next."

She kissed both of Mila's cheeks before giving her daughter a bitter smile. Neither Qirin nor Mila was foolish enough to think she wasn't bidding them farewell. Instantly Mila's gaze flickered over to Qirin, who remained standing impassively.

"What about him?"

"He will go with you."

Qirin gave a start. "Excuse me?"

"Take your sister down to the shelter." Arethusa's voice was thick as she turned her face from them. Qirin suspected she was on the brink of tears.

"With all due respect, Mother, I would very much like to accompany you."

"No, you will stay where you are, safe from harm."

Qirin was struck dumb, forced into submission. He dipped his head, his long ebony hair pooling over his shoulder. If he knew one thing, it was that no argument could be won with his mother. Striding forward, he braced her shoulders before planting kisses on both cheeks.

A bitter smile twisted her lips, so pale in contrast to their normal hue. She placed a slender hand against his cheek, running her thumb along his jawline. He felt numb, devoid of emotion. Words came to mind, yet nothing escaped his lips before his mother's hand slipped away. He watched her dark silhouette disappear down the hall until the doors were closed behind her.

The winter storm rolled across the seas and collided with the island, clouds so heavy they seemed to cloak the upcoming battlefield from the heavens above. The Feishin guards' turquoise tunics whipped in the chilly wind, their plaited dark hair streaming behind them like kite strings. They stood shoulder-to-shoulder on the beach outside the gates in a long line, bravely facing the enemy fleet dotting the horizon. Despite their lack of weapons, each wore a face of confidence and determination, including, at the very back, their queen.

Cold rain pelted their faces and shields, percussive plinks echoing throughout the shoreline. The gates to the city remained closed at the soldiers' backs, a final line of defense should the imperial troops get through them.

The queen frowned at the sky, the weather not ideal for the modest blowgun she permitted her men and women to use. One prick of a dart and a solitary soldier would be asleep for hours. The issue was timing and the feasibility of landing a clean shot. Cold and miserably windy, the conditions were less than amicable.

Arethusa's heart sank at the sight of the fleet penetrating the fog. There were a lot of ships—and a lot of men. Panic threatened to consume her, but she swallowed it down, instead allowing herself to glide through her ranks, virtually all that the kingdom had to offer. She stood regally before them, forcing her back to the incoming fleet and the waves that caressed her heels.

"Brave men and women of the Feishin Kingdom," she thundered, words clear and commanding over the crashing waves, "today you are here to defend our beloved nation, the finest country in all of Danaeca, and perhaps all of Gaia. For the past five centuries we have known peace thanks to our Father, King Feishin. It is through love, peace, and faith that we prosper, and thus the only path is through pacifism.

"Our enemies come at us with weapons of death and hatred in their hearts. We will greet them not with swords, but words. This is the true way. The gods have not let us down before, nor will they today. We must remain steadfast and true to what we hold dear in our hearts, and defend this beautiful country we have worked so hard to preserve. Your families and friends are counting on you."

Arethusa tilted her head to the heavens, bathing in the rain that kissed the apples of her cheeks. She turned to her brave defenders and smiled. A true, genuine smile, knowing that it may be the last she ever gives them.

The imperial ships halted at the docks, throwing down their mighty anchors and pulling back their sails. Men from the ships scrambled off their decks, flooding the shore as they approached the kingdom. Together the Feishin guards remained, expressions stoic as their eyes studied the opposition warily. Arethusa was flanked by soldiers at either side, shields at the ready to defend their queen should the need arise. She remained still as a statue, regal and proud.

At long last the man of the show arrived: Emperor Darius himself. He strode down the ship's ramp in long strides, boots sinking into the wet sand. Their eyes locked as he stood before her, surrounded by his own loyal men. An army vastly outnumbering her own.

"Young emperor," Arethusa greeted, nostrils flaring.

Darius' jaw clenched. "Queen Arethusa."

"I bequeathed a gift, and this is how you repay me?"

The emperor remained unfazed, eyes unmoving. "Queen Arethusa," he repeated, tone hardening further. "You are charged with war crimes, including but not limited to the destruction of twelve Zenochian clans, leading unprovoked attacks which took thousands of lives. How do you plead to these charges?"

Arethusa's lower lip quivered, uncertainty flickering across her face. "Darius, you and I both know it was not I who launched those attacks. You know my position on peace, and yet you dare accuse me of such a heinous act? Why, I did not even raise a finger at the clanswoman who came here demanding recompense. What makes you think that I would ever initiate such violence toward Zenoch?"

His hand reached for his sword, a movement not unnoticed by Arethusa's guard. The guardswoman raised her shield adroitly, creating a barrier between them until Arethusa gestured to have it lowered.

"I see you are denying your crimes." Darius' face hardened. "And tell me: where will it stop? After Zenoch, will you go on striking? After conquering their territory, will you stop there? Or will you not rest until all of Danaeca is under your dominion? We already know you hold your nation above all others."

"My gods, do you not hear yourself?" Arethusa threw her hands up in the air. "Darius, this is madness. When you came to me all those months ago, I saw a young man aspiring for a new era of peace and unity, someone so unlike Emperor Rufus. And now? Why, I cannot tell you two apart."

Darius' lip curled in disgust. He spun on heel and marched away, summoning Prometheus to his side. Their heads were bowed together, voices low, exchanging words that Arethusa couldn't catch, and yet their demeanor caused her fists to quiver at her sides. What outrage! How could she have been so foolish in believing in this childish man? She should've learned her lesson when her husband tried to offer their gifts to Zenoch and died doing so, should've recognized the nature of humankind and how it was impossible to change. And yet, the damage had been done —nothing could change that now.

Slowly Darius turned, burgundy cape whipping around him like a flag. "Queen Arethusa, it has been decreed that you must abdicate from the throne and come into our custody immediately, where you will be tried for your crimes."

Arethusa scoffed. "And if I resist?"

Darius folded his arms over his chest. "Then I'm afraid we will have to force your surrender ourselves."

Thunder roared in the distance, rain falling in sheets. The ocean waves swelled fatter and higher, leaving even the Feishin guards to stand in freezing water. Arethusa tilted her chin, eyes afire with indignation. "Then we will stand strong."

A darkness passed over Darius' face, and it was then that Arethusa saw weariness and sorrow. As quickly as it appeared it was gone, replaced by the hardened mask of a man who knew naught but conquest.

And power.

He snapped his fingers and threw out his arm, summoning the soldiers of Zenochians and imperials alike. "Let us bring the queen to justice, then, and those who stand beside her. Charge!"

The troops poured forth like water from a floodgate, weapons drawn high and light glinting from their smooth, steel armor. Their footfalls were like miniature thunder booms as they moved to strike at the Feishin front line.

The Feishin were ready, the back line raising their blowguns and steadily aiming at their targets before letting darts fly. Struck between shoulder and neck, soldiers fell flat in the water, to be trampled by their none-the-wiser comrades who did not check to see if the fallen were alive or dead.

The crack of a cannon stole the queen's attention, diverting her gaze to a distant ship outfitted with the imperial flag. Her heart sank. *They must be after the wall,* she thought, crestfallen. If the wall was destroyed the queen knew no amount of faith or prayer could save them from whatever chaos would follow.

The cannonball vanished in the heavy rainfall, but, instead of colliding with the wall as Arethusa so greatly feared, it crashed headlong into Darius' ship. Water flooded the vessel, and, while it was too far ashore to sink, it would not sail again without great repair. The queen stared in confusion. Was it a misfire? How could their aim be so far off the mark?

The distraction was enough of an opening for another barrage of feathered darts to fly. They sang through the gusty air, making their mark on at least a dozen imperial men who toppled and, doing so, caused others to topple too over them, sowing disorder within their ranks.

An arrow whizzed past Arethusa's ear, striking a Feishin guard's neck. Blood streamed forth as though a pipe had burst from the wound as he fell backward into the water. He would be dead in seconds, departing to the afterlife without even a final word.

A volley of further cannonballs sounded across the beach, colliding into dozens of imperial troops. Their lives were made forfeit by their very own men. This was the second time that the rogue ship had come to her aid, and Arethusa couldn't fathom why.

She didn't have much time to ponder over this, however, when an imperial soldier, face bloodied and feral, brought his blood-stained sword down over her head. Swiftly one of her guardsmen came in to defend her, shield catching the sword and keeping it firmly in place. Both men gritted their teeth, trying to overpower the other in a battle of strength and wit. Arethusa thanked all the gods when a dart sank into the side of the imperial soldier's neck, causing him to slump forward into the shield and be cast aside.

"Your Majesty!" her guard called out, wet hair plastered against his forehead. "You must retreat behind the wall! We cannot guarantee your safety for as long as you're out here."

A grimace set her jaw. While it was foolish to stand in the open, so vulnerable with neither weapon nor shield to defend her, her place was here. Her people needed her for strength, for inspiration. If she was not willing to lay down her life in the name of pacifism, how could she request it of others?

The enemy lines advanced, while the number of Feishin guards dwindled rapidly. Soon the shore was stained with more blood than the waves were capable of washing away. Arethusa swallowed hard, reality starting to sink in. She thought up a silent prayer, but even she, the devout queen, was starting to have doubts on their victory.

A hand clamped down on her wrist, raising her eyes to her defender. His lips moved mutedly, Arethusa unable to make out the word over the cries of dozens.

She glanced over her shoulder, watching in surprise as a volley of cannonballs were fired from the rogue ship. Now closer, she could discern the blue-and-yellow Malabrian flag flapping in the gusty current. Men started to disembark from its deck, their uniforms replicas of the other imperial soldiers save for a blue ribbon draped over their chests.

"Long live the empress!" a decorated soldier cried, raising his sword.

Baffled, the queen turned to glance at the emperor, whose face was a mirror image of her own. The men flew along the ship's ramp, clashing weapons with their imperial brethren as soon as their boots hit the ground. Clearly these imperials were allied with the Feishin army, but why? Just what was going on?

Two other ships of Zenochian make arrived shortly thereafter, broad in bow and of crude fashion. Troops of various Zenochian clans engaged in combat as soon as their boots hit the sand, fighting imperials and fellow Zenochians alike.

Leaving the Feishin untouched.

A closer cannon blast rumbled deeply when another cannonball hurled into the gate. With a smash and grind of metal, the tall gate buckled but Arethusa realized that, thank the gods, the gate still stood erect. Her gaze flickered toward the source: Darius' ship. While crippled, its cannons were still intact, and were being reloaded.

Alarm filled Arethusa. They could *not* penetrate the city. If her civilians were threatened. . . .

Her thoughts were pierced by a spear that struck her left side, sending white-hot pain to course through her. A strangled cry escaped her throat, her breath stolen and failing to return. She glanced down to see the spear from her left side all the way to her right. The sight made her dizzy, her tongue numb.

"This is for my kin that you killed." The eyes of her attacker glittered cold and cruel, his bronze face contorted with rage. He removed his spear, blood spraying over his face. She gasped for breath, but oxygen didn't manage to reach her lungs. Her vision began to tunnel. Within the maelstrom of voices that cried her name, one stuck, somehow recognized.

"Stay with me!"

Arethusa blinked, trying to force her vision to right itself. Barely could she make out a familiar face—Khatalia's face—dirt-stained and teary over her. Her cracked lips moved.

"I'm sorry," Khatalia murmured, lifting the queen into her lap and cradling her close to her heart. "I am so, so sorry. You were right, and I was a fool. Please, please forgive me."

A weak smile stretched the queen's lips as she extended a shaking hand into open air. The movement pained her, taking all of her effort to focus on that one action. Finally her fingers met Khatalia's mane, willing her palm to cup her cheek.

Arethusa opened her mouth, her voice coming in harsh rasps. "I . . . forgive—"

She tried to suck in a rattled breath. An agonizing fire burned within her as she tried to cough and couldn't. She stared at Khatalia without really seeing, feeling a rush to her head, her lips, as her body grew cold. She could see light beyond Khatalia, which she clutched. She accepted it, and felt her body grow weightless as she rushed toward it. Faster, and faster.

And then she was gone.

CHAPTER 38

The ship's rocking finally ceased, sparing Nevia the monotonous clatter of rattling buckets at her ankles. She tilted her pained neck, listening. Footfalls echoed through the barracks as sailors and soldiers stirred. They must have arrived on Feishin shores. Soon she would be free.

Her heart thundered as she waited, listening for what felt like forever. She thought they had left—they would have by then, wouldn't they?—and dared to crack open the closet door.

Its hinges groaned as she stole a glance out into the room. The barracks were as she remembered: stale, blank, and desolate, with storage crates littering each corner of the narrow room. Not a soul could be seen, and it was a good thing. She was desperate to get out. It was a long time coming.

Nevia let out a sigh of relief, allowing herself a smile. What awaited her wouldn't be pretty, but at least she wouldn't be confined to a broom closet anymore.

She stepped out, eyeing the waste buckets and considering doing her business before trying to find Ardan somewhere above deck, when footsteps approached. She swallowed, waiting again. Could it be him? She doubted it. The footfalls were wrong, the boots ringing too deep to match his gait. Not waiting to find out, she slipped back inside the closet, folding herself tightly against the wall and bringing her knees to their familiar placement against her chest.

Outside the unknown walker paced the length of the room, halted, and issued a relieved sigh as she heard a trickle meet with the waste buckets on the farthermost wall. It was not Ardan, but Nevia remained hopeful. She would just remain there, just a few more minutes, and then she would be free.

The footfalls resumed, and she thought he was leaving. She allowed her shoulders to slump, getting ready to wait a few moments, until dread filled her, the footsteps halting outside her door. Fear clawed at her throat, her heart throbbing as it beat furiously. The door swung open, and standing there was a man who smiled down at her ominously. He was big and tall, with broad shoulders and a wide, sleazy grin.

"What have we here?" he wheezed, his breathing labored, a hand reaching out toward her. She tried to think fast, to push past him through the now narrow opening of the door, but she failed.

He caught her in his thick arm. "Going so soon, before we've even gotten acquainted? Why, Empress, I'm so sad! I'm your biggest fan."

His dark chuckle and dangerous glint in his eye made her think otherwise.

And then another cold reality hit her.

"You know who I am?" she blurted stupidly, tossing blonde hair from her eyes as she stared up into his broad face.

"Of course I do. You're the traitorous empress. Even I, a humble steward, would recognize you. It's an honor to see you, Your Highness, though I wish it was in different circumstances."

"Then I command you to release me," she said, yet was unable to remove the waver in her voice. "This is unacceptable."

For a moment he considered her, then laughed, a loud, full-belly laugh that sent chills down her spine. "Oh, I will, I will, in due time, My Empress. You see, I hears that you and His Highness aren't exactly on the best of terms right now, so I will be taking you to him after you and I watch that war of his together. We'll have front-row seats, you on my lap. Won't we have a nice time?"

He rubbed her upper arms, giddy at the prospect. She could see the lust in his eyes. He started to shift her from the closet, and she had no choice but to comply, his strength overwhelming her and making it impossible for her to get away.

"Darius will not tolerate your dismissal of my commands." She knew it was a lie, but she hoped the steward would believe it. One look at his face told her that he wasn't easily fooled by her empty threats. His lip curled upward.

"This is going to be so much fun."

This was not going well at all. She let out a scream, one loud and piercing enough to morph his face from glee to fury. He clamped a hand over her mouth.

"Oh, now, now, none of that. We don't want to arouse the attention of your boyfriend now, do we?"

Her eyes narrowed. He must've meant Ardan. But how would he—

"Don't look so surprised." He turned her to face him with his crude grin. "He came to see you *so* many times. At first I wondered what he could've possibly been doing down here, what fascinated him so much about the broom closet, but now I know, and, I must say, I'm rather offended that he didn't invite me to join in."

Horror wrote itself on Nevia's face, realizing what this man must've been insinuating. "Oh, no, no, it was nothing like that. He was bringing me food, and water, and—"

"It's alright, no need to explain yourself," he soothed. "We can add infidelity to your list of sins when we hand you over to the emperor."

Fury contorted her features. His words couldn't have been farther from soothing. "You have no right to pass judgment on me. You don't know my personal life or circumstances. Back off."

"Oho! The tribal girl snaps her jaws, does she? Well, this old man knows a trick or two himself. I know how I can get you to be quiet."

The steward's hand flashed to his waist, where Nevia spotted a narrow dagger being unsheathed by its worn leather hilt. Alarmed, she didn't wait to see what he was going to do with the blade. His other hand still gripped her upper arm, but his tension on her had grown lax, as if assuming she was too stunned or afraid to try anything.

She went for his face. With a ferocious roar she raked her nails across his cheeks, pleased to leave angry red marks where his flesh was scratched away. He let out a furious wail, bringing his dagger across her arm, drawing warm blood. She flinched, refusing to cower or make a sound, to give him the satisfaction. He readied his other hand to backhand her, but she was quicker, and, with both his hands off her, she threw herself back into the broom closet and slammed the door shut.

Her heart hammered against her rib cage as she fumbled with a broom, propping it just right to effectively serve as a lock. The handle rattled as he tried to wrench the door open, only to no avail.

"It's only a matter of time before I get my hands on you!" he shouted, voice muffled through the door. "And you're going to regret giving me a hard time. I was going to go easy on you, not make you go through too much, but now you've made me angry. You're not going to like what happens next. Why, I'll bind and gag you, and do everything I want to you, and your precious emperor and boyfriend won't be there to save you."

She squeezed her eyes shut, not wanting to envision or picture what sort of twisted ideas he had for her. For *them*. One thing she knew for certain: she would rather die than let him touch her.

The broom started to slide as he jostled the door handle more furiously. The pounding on the door continued, and she could only picture the moment when the door gave way, revealing her position and taking away any safety she felt behind the solidly made door. If only she had a dagger, or some method of protecting herself—

And then she remembered Ardan's spear, propped next to the mop beside her, and smiled.

She clutched the weapon in both hands and drew in a deep breath to steel her nerves. She had never taken a life, had once sworn that she never would. All living things, good and bad, human or otherwise, held value to her, and the thought of what she was about to do sickened her. But the flip side was what he was going to do to her if she didn't.

He brought this upon himself.

She moved the broom, allowing the door to fly open when he least expected it. He staggered back, losing his footing so that he nearly fell. That was when the opportunity presented itself, her fingers curling along the shaft of the spear in her palms. She didn't know how to use it, but for this she didn't need to. She understood to aim with the pointed end, and drive it clear through his chest with all of her weight.

To say whose face held more surprise—hers or his—was difficult.

Enfeebled hands reached to the weapon embedded in his chest, but only briefly. Rasped breaths escaped him as his legs gave way, slumping forward. Nevia couldn't manage his weight, having to release her grip and allow both weapon and body to clatter to the ground. Nevia fell to her knees, the gravity of her deed seeping into her.

She killed him. Blood would now stain her hands forever.

A scream escaped her lungs as she stared at the pool of crimson extending from his body along the wooden floorboards. Footsteps echoed down the hall, someone clearly alerted by her girlish scream. She didn't care; it didn't matter anymore. A forbidden part of her wished someone would come and make her pay retribution for what evil she'd committed. She was ready to pay with her life.

She wasn't prepared for Ardan to come charging down the hall, face pasty white. He took one look between at her and the steward before darting forward to scoop her into his arms. Both shook from nerves. Nevia's emotions unleashed in full, the tears pouring from her fast and hard.

"I did it—I did it—I shouldn't have—I can't believe I—"

Ardan only clung to her tighter, her cheek pressed against the buttons of his loose tunic.

"Shhh, it's okay." He soothed her in every way that he knew how. He brushed his hand along her thick mane, planted kisses atop her head. He ran a hand down the length of her back, and yet nothing could erase the way she saw herself, the monster she was. The atrocious act she committed.

Eventually her tears slowed, some semblance of reality returning to her. Ardan must've sensed her start to calm, his hands running down her back and eventually releasing her so he could peer into her face. She nearly lost herself in the sea of green and gold swirls, the eyes she'd come to love despite making her feel like a traitor. Shakily Nevia drew in a breath, turning her gaze to the bloodied floor.

"You did what you had to," he reminded her, even if he didn't know this to be fact.

She heaved an inhale. "But I didn't even hesitate," she blurted. "Not really. He was on the other side. Ardan, I don't know what he was going to do to me. I was terrified, I—"

"You did what you had to," he repeated, firmer this time. He released her and strode forward, and she shut her eyes as he knelt to retrieve his spear. Even still, hearing the squelch of tearing flesh was nearly enough to undo her again.

"We should go," Nevia said, rising shakily and motioning toward the hall.

He swallowed nervously, following her. Before they crossed the threshold, however, he finally found the words that were trying so hard to escape him.

"And Nevia, before we go out there . . . "

Her fists were clutched tightly. "Yes?"

"This might be putting you on the spot, but I need to tell you this." Sweat beaded on his brow from effort. "I want you to know I love you, even if you're not ready to love me back."

He paused, and she noticed his hands quiver at his sides. Nevia's mouth felt dry, and no words felt right at that moment. The steward's accusation not long ago lay too close to the truth.

"I just want you to know that. No matter what," he finished.

Tears welled in her eyes. She opened her mouth, and Ardan waited, eager to receive her affection or rejection.

But nothing came. Nothing at all.

She spun on her heel and fled, long powder-blue cloak sailing behind her as she ascended the stairs, not once looking back.

CHAPTER 39

Gray skies greeted Ardan as he emerged above decks, icy rain showering relentlessly from the heavens. Within minutes Ardan's garments were soaked, chilling him to the bone and plastering his dark hair to his face. The battle cries rang out to greet him, the bloodstains upon the sand deep and ominous. Wordlessly he scraped off the empty vessel, footsteps mute amidst the sounds of clashing steel on either side of him. Icy water greeted his back, a fresh wave of cold against already chilled flesh.

He thought back to his conversation with Nevia and cursed himself. Why did he have to make things complicated? Why, out of all the women he'd ever met, did he have to fall for the empress of the Androvich Empire, whose husband they were about to encounter on the battlefield?

What a fool he was, and how far he'd fallen.

He'd never known love or what it felt like to care so intensely for someone, but after traveling with Nevia for weeks, watching her struggle, fall, and get back up, he knew that it was love which swelled in his chest.

But he was a fool if he expected that love to be requited.

But she kissed me, he reminded himself. And then he realized that no, he had kissed *her*. There was a difference. While she didn't reject him, and even kissed back, it was not the same. All of those glances, those touches—maybe it was just human nature, that organic, primal attraction between two people in close proximity to one another that caused her to respond as she did.

Perhaps he never would know.

Ardan was no stranger to death and combat, but the sights of infighting were enough to make his stomach revolt. Imperials running one another through, kinsmen locking axes and eyes brimming with hatred. He tried to avert his gaze as he searched the sea of heads for Nevia, but the woman was nowhere to be seen.

"Nevia!" He cupped his hands around his mouth to bellow at the top of his lungs. "NEVIA!"

"You have business with my wife?"

The voice, smooth as velvet, caused him to turn, and he didn't need confirmation to know who it was that stood before him. The dark glint in his chocolate-brown eyes, the hard lines drawn across his visage. A golden circlet rest elegantly upon black locks, which were drenched and slicked from his face. A longsword was gripped in one hand, blood dripping from the blade and into puddles of saltwater mixed with rain. A shield emblazoned with the imperial crest lay strapped to his opposite arm, bedecked with gold and glittering jewels. The man fixed his lips in a straight, disapproving line. "Don't tell me that you were foolish enough to bring her here."

Ardan refused to be threatened. He stood straighter, fixing him with a cool stare. "You must be Emperor Darius."

"How observant of you."

"As for Nevia, she is a free woman who can be where she pleases. Unlike you, *I* don't keep her locked away in a cage to showcase only when it profits me."

The job didn't ruffle Darius' feathers as much as he anticipated. Instead, Darius smiled coyly. "Oh, that's nice. I imagine instead you'd give her pig's skin to wear, have her freeze in some cave somewhere and fend for herself in the wilderness. Because I agree, that is *so* much better."

Ardan's fingers tightened around his spear, the freezing steel biting into his palm. He was itching to wipe the sneer from the emperor's face. And yet, he wouldn't attack him unprovoked. As much as Ardan would've delighted in being the one to run him clean through, it wasn't his place to end the life of the man who ruled over half of Danaeca. There would be consequences for such an action.

If not with the people, then with Nevia.

"You're fighting a losing battle," Ardan uttered through gritted teeth. "Once Nevia tells everyone the truth, all the Zenochians will turn against you, and you and your imperials will go running home with your tails between your legs. There is no way out for you."

That was the end of their civil discourse. Darius let out a roar, sending a wide arced swing of his sword in an attempt to cleave Ardan's head clean off. The lithe clansman leapt backward, parrying the blow. He swiveled, making a thrust which was met by his shield.

"She will never be yours to control again," Ardan growled. "And I personally will make you pay for what you've done to her." Ardan didn't know what overcame him, why he was making this statement. Perhaps it was because he hated Darius, or perhaps it was because he loved Nevia more.

Fury ignited the emperor's eyes. He swung his sword, twice, thrice, the clash of steel reverberating around them. Their bodies were locked in a rhythm of testing movements, not unlike a dance, through the sea of combatants. Darius was too quick, cunning, and agile—a contradiction to his stockier build. With each jab that Ardan made, Darius was able to steal in three, and soon Ardan realized that he was gravely outmatched.

Their battle led them further along the coast, Ardan finding his feet collide with jutting rocks that climbed up to a cliff face overlooking the sea. He leapt up, seeing an advantage to seeking the higher ground. Darius pursued, undaunted, seemingly tireless.

Ardan picked up the pace, scaling higher. If he could only manage to spring down upon Darius—

There. He saw his opening. His long legs sprang underneath him, spear extended and ready to run Darius through.

Darius, yet again, was too quick. He shifted slightly with his sword extended, its pointed tip gleaming moments before it would greet Ardan.

The clansman's eyes widened. Falling, he had too much speed, too much momentum to dodge—

And then he felt it, the snag of steel ripping through his leather armor, followed by the pain lacing up his side. He couldn't tell how deep the wound was, but it didn't feel lethal. Ardan fought against the pain, colliding his head into Darius'. The emperor cried out and staggered back, and in went Ardan's spear, clean through Darius' left shoulder.

Blood mixed with rain as it spattered the jagged rocks. With a grimace, Ardan ripped his spear free, preparing to continue his assault when an arrow pierced him through. Shock contorted Ardan's features, all breath escaping his lungs. His unarmed hand reached for the arrow jutting from his torso.

Darius kicked his spear out of his slackened grip, towering over him with a smug grin adorning his features. He lifted his blade. Ardan couldn't move, not fast enough; he prayed that Darius would make it quick.

"No! Stop! Please!"

Nevia's cry pierced through the sounds of combat, halting the emperor's fatal blow. The empress clambered over, falling to her knees at Ardan's side, tattered cloak billowing around her form. Her pants were torn at the knees, tunic dark and wet. From blood or water, Ardan couldn't tell. Darius lowered his sword, his expression bewildered at the sight of her.

The empress' hands hovered over the wound at his stomach, horror carved on her features. Her slick fingers wrapped around the arrow shaft, but before she could wrench it free Ardan gently placed a hand over hers.

"It's better left there," he rasped. "Bleeding could get worse."

Nevia pressed a kiss to his lips. To say that Ardan was surprised was an understatement. Her lips were wet and salty, and yet he savored it more than any other kiss they shared, if only because she initiated it. He blinked away rain droplets, finally wrenching his gaze from her over to Darius.

The emperor had backed away from them, standing a few feet away and watching them with cold indifference, his jaw set.

"I see that you have moved on." Darius's words were deathly quiet.

Nevia's throat bobbed. She whipped around to face Darius, opening her mouth to speak, but he held up a hand to silence her. "Don't. Just . . . spare me the excuses, the reason. I-I know already, and I don't want to hear it."

The arrogance fled his features, shoulders dipping in defeat. It wasn't guilt that Ardan felt when he looked at him, nor was it pity.

It was sorrow. He saw a man so broken that he destroyed everything he cared about, including himself.

No word escaped Darius as he trudged back to his army, leaving them there. To die or to live, but their fate was no longer in his hands. It was theirs to dictate.

"Ardan."

His name on her lips brought his eyes back to her face, specifically to the warm reassuring smile she wore. He let out a long, weary sigh of exhaustion. "You shouldn't have bolted off ahead of me," he said. "See what happens when you leave me to my own devices?"

"I love you too."

He blinked back his surprise, staring at her as if for the first time. The empress carefully wrapped her arms about him, helping him to a sitting position.

"You think I'm dying, don't you?"

"No, it's not that. It's just . . . I never did answer you." She clasped both of his hands in hers. "I left, and I'm sorry. I guess . . . I just wasn't ready to admit it to myself. I have cared about you for a while, but it was all complicated because I still felt bound to Darius. But I know where I stand now, and I know how to move forward."

He smiled at her, and she returned it, a true, genuine smile reserved only for him. She placed her forehead against his and he leaned into it, caressing her nose with his own.

"You should go," he said finally, words he hated himself for. "They need you."

She looked as though she was fighting back tears. It took all of his willpower not to kiss her again, but, if he did, he feared that she wouldn't leave—or that he would be unable to let her go. He stroked her thick, damp hair gingerly.

"Promise me that you'll live," she ordered.

His hoarse chuckle morphed into a cough, blood pouring from his chest wound at an alarming rate. He settled back against the rock, taking in her face, her eyes. If he was to die, he wanted her image to be the last thing he remembered. Just as wet, disheveled, and perfect as she was in that moment.

"I will do everything that I can to stay alive." It was all he would offer, as he refused to lie to her. Death, while not imminent, was not far off.

"I *will* see you again," she asserted, teary-eyed. Whether she was reassuring herself or him, Ardan couldn't tell. "Just wait a little longer. I will send someone to get you. I will—"

"Nevia."

She stopped, meeting his gaze. He swallowed hard and dipped his head.

"Just go, and stay strong. Your people—Zenochians and imperials both—need you."

CHAPTER 40

Tears stung Nevia's eyes as she shuffled down the face of the cliff and onto the beach, nearly losing her footing on the slick surface several times. Ardan was a fighter, and she knew that he would hold on as long as he could. But his blood loss was significant, and she feared for the worst.

She was a fool. Choices, decisions, even feelings—all had been stolen from her for years, and it had taken her a while to realize her marriage with Darius had been a sham for some time. Missing him and being bound to him: these were constraints that she was placing on herself, continuing her imprisonment long after she broke free from her chains.

And now, she realized the truth: while she could pity him, she didn't have to be under his thumb anymore. He changed, and she needed to accept that she did too.

They were over, and that was okay.

The boom of a cannon sounded, causing her entire body to shudder. She watched a cannonball arch through the air, soaring through the sky before colliding with the kingdom's copper gate. It held, but barely, its metal frame dangerously bowed and hinges separating from the surrounding stone wall. Nevia knew it wouldn't hold for much longer.

Her boots sank into the saturated sand as she rushed past individuals locked in combat, none taking notice of her. Fallen bodies littered the shoreline, some claimed by the waves as they crashed and relented. Her gaze found a fierce, muscly Zenochian warrior with short-cropped pale hair bracing his spear in front of him. His thick biceps shook under the weight of three imperials which he was fending off singlehandedly. Not far from this man stood Khatalia, her back to the empress as she charged toward an enormous man who easily towered over her. Nevia hoped her friend hadn't met her match, but she couldn't give herself pause. She had to somehow garner their attention, to inform them that this entire war was a ploy for the emperor to claim the Feishin Kingdom's resources for his own. They were all merely pawns in his sick, twisted game.

"The queen is dead! The queen is dead!"

The phrase was being sung by dozens of voice, striking up panic in her heart. And there, in front of the gate, lay the queen's lifeless body, her face beautiful even in death. Two guards stood sentinel over her, treating her corpse as though sacred. Bloodstains were visible on their turquoise uniforms—her blood, Nevia realized.

For a moment the fighting ceased, the words prompting an unspoken truce. The armies parted to permit Darius to stride forward, his face a mask of stony indifference. His cape was missing, along with his shield and one of his sleeves. At the front he raised a hand, calling for attention.

"Citizens of the Feishin Kingdom! Your queen has fallen."

Silence trailed his words. The Feishin soldiers cowed back, clustering together in front of the copper gate. To see a people devastated by the death of their queen was heart-wrenching, their love for her clearly great.

"Come and kneel before me," Darius continued. "Enough blood has been spilt on this day, and I'd rather not see more. Let me help you. I will appoint a new, just ruler for your country and reunite it with Danaeca, as it was once before. If you will but only submit to me."

He extended a hand: an order disguised as a peace offering. Moments of tension lapsed and nary a person moved or said a word. Two Feishin guards began to stumble forward, as if to accept his terms, until they parted so that another could force through. The prime minister, Teniel, appeared and marched up to the emperor, head held high in haughty defiance. Nevia almost didn't recognize her in her leather armor, a stark contrast to her usual silks.

"We have our ruler," Teniel declared. "And we refuse to bow down to a tyrant such as yourself. Our Crown Prince, Qirin, son of Athilan, will assume the throne and guide us."

The damaged gate groaned as it was drawn open, the strain resulting in more than its hinges could handle, resulting in their breakage. Many frantic Feishin guards cried out, scrambling out of the gate's path before it collapsed with a deafening thud. On the other side stood Prince Qirin, face stoic, surrounded by a handful of guards. His long hair was drawn from his angular face, his black leather armor pristine. Gasps sounded through the crowd, and it took Nevia a moment to realize why: his right hand clutched the leather hilt of a katana.

The prince pointed the curved blade's tip at Darius. "I am King Qirin, ruler of the Feishin Kingdom and son to the late King Athilan and Queen Arethusa." His eyes narrowed dangerously. "We will stand to oppose you, forsaking the tradition of my forefathers to do so. I promise to take you apart limb from limb for what you have done to my people, most especially my dear mother."

An electric hum filled the silence following Qirin's words. A Feishin locomotive rolled down the rickety path on large wheels toward them, bedecked with an arsenal fit for a medium-sized army. Where they had come from, Nevia had no idea, though she partially wondered if the rumors about a secret military was true, or at the very least a vault of weaponry existing somewhere on the island. Qirin gestured toward the prime minister, whose face grew deathly pale at the vehicle's arrival.

"Teniel, begin distributing the weapons," he commanded.

The woman's face tightened into a grimace. "Your Highness, the queen would never—"

"Well, she's not here," Qirin spat with such ferocity that it made Teniel recoil.

Armor clinked as Lord Verrine emerged from the rear, his steel breastplate reflecting what little light pierced through the thick stormy clouds. The hilt of his sword shimmered like dozens of tiny emeralds.

"You would discard tradition to ward us away?" Verrine challenged.

Qirin was unperturbed. "As you can see, pacifism didn't serve us." He gestured to the many bodies surrounding them. "The gods didn't save us for being steadfast, did they? No, force is necessary to preserve what is left of our country."

A dark chuckle escaped Verrine. "Spoken like a true warlord." He spread his arms wide, mouth stretched into a mocking grin. "My dear Feishin people, do you really accept this man, this *child*, as your king with his foolish notions? He would have you go against your beliefs and pick up weapons of war. Is that what the First King would have done? Your late queen died defending pacifism, and here's her very own son: willing to cast her sacrifice aside so callously. Don't tell me you condone him."

Murmurs dispersed through the crowd. Nevia noticed a Zenochian clansman flex his fingers around the hilt of his axe, appearing eager to resume fighting.

"This is absurd," Teniel interjected. "You have no right to march onto our soil and lay claim to our kingdom, let alone tell us who we should follow and why. According to Feishin law, the heir to the throne assumes leadership immediately after the monarch's passing. Therefore, Qirin is our king. There is no room for debate."

"Yes, yes, king in name." Verrine waved a hand impatiently. "But that doesn't mean you have to accept him. Our offer still stands, but not for much longer. Bow to His Imperial Highness, and we will take care of you."

Two Feishin soldiers strode forward, standing before Darius and kneeling, plaited hair falling deftly over their shoulders as they dipped their heads in subservience. Others followed suit, the number of Qirin's subjects dwindling to a mere dozen.

Shock was evident on Qirin's face as he wrinkled his nose in disgust. "You would turn against the crown?!" he seethed toward his own.

"You would have us abandon our faith," one of the Feishin guards said, voice high. "We must remain steadfast to the Way. Forgive us, Your Highness."

The emperor laid a delicate hand on the Feishin woman's shoulder. "You have done the right thing," he reassured. "No further harm will come to you. I commend you for standing up for your beliefs." The words, while kind, were sickening. If Nevia was closer she would've spat at him.

The emperor rose. "You have seen a great tragedy on this day, and it is no fault of your own. Let me help you. I will make things right. Of that you have my word."

"Enough!" Qirin raised his katana, this time in more than posturing. "You will pay for your crimes against humanity. Not just for the death that you have brought here, but that which you caused in Zenoch, as well."

Darius scoffed, folding his arms across his broad chest. "Don't tell me that you believe the stories."

"They are not stories."

The words left Nevia's lips before she could stop herself. She emerged from the heart of the crowd, only then realizing how unlike an empress she appeared. Her tunic was tattered, hair askew, and dirt mixed with blood smudged her skin. Yet she stood tall and proud as all eyes fell upon her.

The empress—who finally built up the confidence she needed.

She moved to Qirin's side and turned her face to the people, chin lifted, refusing to cower or be afraid. "Everyone, you have all been played. You've been nothing but puppets for Darius to gain power from the Feishin Kingdom through core shards that only they harvest. This war was merely a tool for an invasion, to take what he wants. My Zenochian friends," she turned a pitying glance at her fellow kin, "those attacks were a ruse, created by imperial soldiers donning Feishin uniforms to rally a cause for this war. The Feishin people are innocent."

"Silence, you!" Verrine shoved his way toward her, nearly trampling a Feishin guard groveling at his feet. "Like anyone would listen to a two-timing snake."

Nevia raised a pale eyebrow. "My point exactly."

Qirin's mouth gaped open, staring at Nevia as though she were mad.

"Regardless, my position stands," Qirin said, disregarding Nevia and her claim. "Continue to defend this monster and you will pay with your blood alongside him."

Nevia threw a glance over her shoulder at the new king. "Must you resort to blood? Don't you think enough has been spilt? Maybe—"

"No, he dies for what he's done." There was a cold finality to Qirin's words, and behind them a bloodlust unbecoming of a Feishin royal.

A handful of imperial soldiers strode before Nevia, their burgundy uniforms drenched from the earlier downpour. Their swords hung limply in their hands, and it surprised her when they burrowed their blades into the sand at their feet. They dipped their heads in respect, pressing a fist to their chest in subservience.

"We are yours to command, Your Imperial Highness."

Nevia nearly fell over in shock. They were submitting themselves to *her*. Their empress.

Because they believed in her.

Gratitude made her eyes water. Dozens more flocked over, and Nevia recognized their blue-and-yellow uniforms to belong to Malabria. They, too, bowed to her, followed by none other than Lord Vladios himself, offering her a wink as he lifted his head. She smiled, making a mental note to reward him with the finest liquor from her private stores later. Many Zenochian warriors also drifted to her, leaving only a handful of Zenochians and the vast majority of imperial soldiers at Darius' side. Despite the new uncertainty in their eyes, none dared to turn on the emperor, and Nevia couldn't fault them. He was their rightful ruler, son of Emperor Rufus I; to leave his side for hers would've been treason to the highest degree.

Verrine threw back his head in dismay. "Oh, for the love of Saava!" He unsheathed his sword and charged her army, others following his lead.

Qirin extended his sword arm. "Attack!"

Feishins, imperials, and Zenochians alike clashed against their common enemy: Darius and his army. An onlooker would not be able to discern friend from foe, as they were all divided in their allegiances, their beliefs on what really happened the day of the avalanches.

This is it, Nevia thought to herself. *This is the end.*

They would either win or lose this war, but one thing was certain: if they were to die, they would die trying.

CHAPTER 41

Blades locked and cries echoed; the sounds of war. It was clear the Feishin only learned the art of swordsmanship for sport and not combat. Their flurries were too graceful, too impractical. All too quickly the Feishin soldiers were disarmed and brought to their knees, either to surrender or die. Nevia watched this with an aching heart, feeling personally responsible for this bloodshed.

Despite the loss of the Feishin military, they still had the majority of the Zenochians and some imperials. They could still win this war, however slight their chances were.

Suddenly Nevia was knocked clean off her feet. One of her palms collided with jagged rock, slicing it wide open. She spat out a mouthful of sand, rolling onto her back to find a blade pointed at her, wielded by none other than Lord Verrine. Fury contorted his narrow face as he glared down at her, wielding a hatred so fierce that he seemed capable of tearing her apart with only his teeth.

"You had to ruin *everything!*" He lifted his sword, and Nevia had to roll to avoid his blow. He wrenched it from the sand effortlessly and rounded on her, footsteps soft. Quickly she scrambled to her feet, scanning the ground for any abandoned weapon to defend herself with. She was no fighter, but she would not go down without a fight.

Especially not to Verrine.

The rapier wildly sliced through the air. "Darius values you too damn much!"

She threw herself behind a boulder moments before his blade clattered against the unyielding stone.

"I told him over and over that you're in the way, that you need to be stopped. But he never listens!"

Nevia stopped listening to bolt, and he followed, much to her dismay. And he would not. Stop. Talking.

"The blasted fool. I should've tried harder to do away with him, but things became a little messy after you left that I didn't dare try again."

His words brought Nevia to a sudden halt, and instead she whirled on him. "What in the world are you ranting about?"

The point of his rapier traced a sigil in the sky with no effect. "Oh, don't tell me you didn't figure it out. The assassin, my attempt at making you look like the suspect, which, I confess, was a disappointment. No one seemed interested in thinking their sweet, naive little empress had anything to do with her father's friend trying to kill the emperor."

These words gave her pause, long enough for Verrine's blade to bite into her thigh. She let out a yelp and stumbled back, only to be greeted by a coarse stone digging into her spine. The shells of barnacles dug under her fingernails as fury seized her.

"It was *you*!" she spat. "You're the one who sent the assassin!"

Verrine rolled his eyes. "Well, obviously. Who else would've done it? Surely you don't believe he would've had the gumption to do it himself, do you?"

Her mind was spinning as she tried to make sense of it all. "Beiyo was so kind. He never would've harmed Darius without a reason."

"You would be surprised what lies can do, Nevia." His eyes glittered cruelly. "Oh, but wait—you *do* know what they're capable of! But unlucky for you, *I'm* the better storyteller, and it looks like I might just get my way after all."

Running a hand through damp curls, he tread toward her again, exhibiting no signs of fatigue that would've given Nevia an advantage. "Right now it's just you and me, Nevia, and I can finally eliminate you from the equation." His serpentine smile stretched wide. "Who knows? Maybe His Highness will even thank me."

Spinning on heel, Nevia tried to make a run for it, but he was faster, grasping a fistful of her hair and throwing her back. Her head collided with the boulder at her back, causing her world to spin. She barely heard someone call her name as Verrine readied his blade to strike again. She closed her eyes, accepting her fate, knowing she could not move fast enough to escape.

A body barreled into hers, giving her a sudden jolt. She felt herself cast carelessly to the side, and her eyes snapped open to find Darius, his face pale and drawn. Blood began to soak through her tunic, and it took her a moment to realize it was not hers.

"Neve—I—"

Nevia forced herself upright, fighting against her confusion. This did not make any sense! She grasped Darius by the shoulders, searching his body for the gaping hole she knew must be somewhere. She then noticed his unsheltered side and the blood that jutted from it. Her fingers fled to it before she could stop herself. "Why would you—"

Verrine clicked his tongue, interrupting before she could finish forming a sentence. His smile was infuriatingly bright. "Well, well, well. I was right." His sword glistened with the emperor's blood, which he ran a finger along. It seemed he was savoring the moment. "Love really is going to be your downfall. And now I'll get to kill you both together. No one will ever know. And besides, it would be quite romantic, would it not?"

"You sick son of a bitch," Nevia murmured through gritted teeth, hands burrowing into the sand at her sides. Her fingers met with something jagged: a rock the size of her head. She continued talking to keep Verrine distracted. To buy her some time. "Did you plan this from the beginning?"

"Were you not listening? Of course I planned this! All of this! I didn't decide to help this man from the goodness of my heart. I thought I would be serving under this pathetic excuse of an emperor until an unfortunate accident befell him. Thankfully it happened a little sooner than I expected. All thanks to you, Nevia."

A roar of fury escaped Nevia's throat as the rock at her fingertips came free. She charged straight for Verrine, surprise flickering in his eyes as he flung out his sword defensively. She stopped short of his blade, launching the massive rock toward his head. Their range made it hard to miss, the rock striking him in the temple. Cloudiness filled his eyes as the hilt of his rapier slipped from his bloodied fingers. He sank to his knees before collapsing face-first into the sand, unconscious. Briefly Nevia considered the rapier, its emerald hilt beckoning. It would have been all too easy to end his pathetic life, but she felt a simple death was too forgiving of a sentence for a man so sinister. He would be tried in court, she decided, to receive the public humiliation and shame that he deserved.

A groan escaping Darius' lips diverted her attention, causing her to swivel. A pool of blood spread from underneath his dying form. Something in her snapped at the sight.

He saved her—at the cost of himself.

Moments passed as she stood there, motionless, unknowing of what to say in his final breaths. She would've died had it not been for his sacrifice, and yet she felt it didn't atone for all the evil he had committed. He had harmed her, killed thousands, including her father. Despite it all, she found herself on her knees beside him, staring at the gaping wound in the vulnerable place between breastplate and pauldron. Hot tears welled in her eyes, despite her internal struggle. Darius still cared, and, as much as she hated herself for it, a small part of her did, too.

"Darius, why—" Her tears etched pathways on her dirt-stained cheeks. "Why throw your life away? Why save me?"

The rain started to ease as thick gray clouds parted, allowing the sun's rays to cast over her shoulder and beam down on the emperor's face. His eyes met hers, pale lips curving upward.

"Because it was the right thing to do." His breaths came in slow and shallow, the effort of speaking almost too great. "Neve, remember when I said—when I said that I had to make a choice—of who I was?"

Nevia found her throat restricted, unable to speak. Instead she sought his hand, clutching it tightly in both of hers.

"Well, I-I realized it—when he was going to kill you—I had made the wrong one. Please—" He broke into a coughing fit. Nevia propped him up in her lap to make him more comfortable, his breathing less laborious. He was able to speak again, his words more broken as the minutes ticked by.

"Please—forgive me, Neve. I—love you."

A sob finally wrenched itself free from her aching throat. Her tears plinked on his breastplate as they rolled freely from her cheeks. She bent over to brush her dry lips over his forehead. "And

I love you, too." She surprised herself that she meant it. Never could she forget what he'd done, but she no longer hated him. The young woman within her had once fallen in love with him, and that woman, while no longer her, still lived on inside her. "Always."

With a trembling hand he managed to cup her cheek, running the pad of his thumb along her jawline.

"I'm glad—" He closed his eyes. "that I leave—my legacy—with you."

"Darius, no, listen, I—"

But he didn't listen. He never did. "I succumbed—but—you meant most—always—"

His entire body grew heavy in her arms, his hand falling from her face. The light left his eyes, and she knew in that moment he was dead. Never would he look at her lovingly again.

With a shaking hand she lowered his eyelids. One could have mistaken him for sleeping. "I'm sorry, too," she whispered. "For hurting you. It was unfair to us both. Maybe things would've been different if forces weren't working against us."

She bit down on her knuckles in an attempt to keep the sobs from escaping, but it was no use. She had to mourn. She had lost so, so much.

Darius. Ardan. Her father. The thousands who perished during this bloodbath. A war that never should've started.

Encroaching footsteps tore her from her anguish and forced her gaze upward. Lord Torquil towered over her, his plate mail stained with blood splatters. One hand rested on the hilt of his sword as his eyes shifted uneasily from Verrine, facedown in the sand, to Nevia, and finally the emperor in her arms.

"Torquil. . . ." What was there to say? She bowed her head, gaze returning to Darius. His face was pasty white and his lips were drawn tight, and yet he looked oddly peaceful. "Do what you must, but I would rather you kill me now than blame me for this."

Long, tense moments lapsed as his dark gaze scrutinized her. "You're right: it would be all too simple for me to say you did this and allow my Orla's secret to die with you. But"—cold fury was evident on his face as he shot an ugly glare at Verrine—"as much as I don't trust you, I trust *him* less. To realize he was behind this, that everything you said was true. . . ."

To Nevia's great astonishment he knelt beside her, resting a gloved hand on her damp shoulder. A touch both tender and imploring. "Will you tell anyone about my daughter?"

Her response came easily, as she vowed to this long before Torquil's request. "Not a soul. She doesn't deserve to die for powers beyond her control."

The Asturian lord appeared thoughtful. "Perhaps someone like you in charge is what the empire really needs." He lifted his chin. "Would you change the law so that Orla could live free?"

Her lips tightened. "Change is hard. I-I don't know if I can."

"But would you at least try?"

It was a lot to promise. Magic had been outlawed long before Emperor Rufus founded the empire. The prohibition kept them safe, but at the cost of many. Removing such laws would create more scrutiny to befall her, and she knew obliterating the laws banning magic wouldn't be without consequences. Even still, she believed there must be another way to deal with those who abused their powers if it meant innocents such as Orla could live free. Torquil deserved that much.

She dipped her head in assent. "You have my word."

Torquil shifted his weight to kneel before her, a fist pressed against his heart. "Then I shall testify as to what I witnessed, Empress Nevia. Consider me your loyal subject."

A relieved sigh escaped her lips, but the feeling was short-lived. Sounds of combat echoed over the beach, and she knew lives would continue to bleed out until none were left. Slowly she rose, allowing the emperor to fall from her arms—for the last time.

She lifted her chin, turning her gaze toward the horizon as the wind whipped her face. Both the emperor and the Feishin queen were dead, and she was left to pick up the pieces.

"Carry him. We must show the people and spread the word. This war ends now."

Torquil tossed his head in the direction of the Ivalian lord. "And him?"

No trace of pity could be found on Nevia's hardened face. "We'll bind him and come back for him. He'll be brought back to Velspire and be tried for his crimes before all."

"Very well, Your Highness."

Binding him was short work, as Verrine offered no resistance. They bound both his ankles and wrists so that even if he regained consciousness in their absence he would not be able to get far. There was no more room for him to run, no more conniving his way out of the chaos he sowed. Nevia would ensure that he paid this time.

Never again would he hurt her.

CHAPTER 42

It felt like they entered a graveyard. Bodies littered the coastline, their fallen weapons caressed by the waves. Nevia plowed through the carnage, trying to convince herself that this bloodshed was not her fault. What little fighting remained was reduced to feeble strikes and parries, with less vigor, less vehemence behind them. Defeat shadowed the soldiers' faces, as if awaiting death to finally halt them.

Her gaze found the new Feishin king locked in combat with a member of the imperial army. His raven hair was slicked to his face in sheets by a mixture of rainwater, sweat, and blood. His footwork held promise, but his lack of prior combat was evident in his movements.

She deftly stepped between Qirin and his opponent. A foolish action, as they all too simply could have cut her down, being as unpopular as she was. Thankfully they did not choose this course of action. Qirin's eyes widened, shocked, as he lowered his blade, his opponent following suit. The king shot her a glare, as though irritated that he couldn't finish what he started.

"Darius is dead," Nevia informed him, voice flat.

Suspicion was evident on his face. "You killed him?"

Nevia shook her head, gesturing to Torquil who wove through the tangled web of bodies behind her. In his arms was the emperor, head bobbing lifelessly. "It was Lord Verrine who killed him. In his final breaths he left me this empire, and I'm ending this conflict. You have to stop fighting. Now. Please."

Doubt clouded Qirin's gaze as his eyes flickered to his opponent. Both gave a curt nod, accepting her terms. The imperial soldier meandered away without sparing her a glance, weaving into his ranks and gathering men together, no doubt spreading the news. Soon the battlefield grew silent, combatants dispersing. Some looked disgruntled, while others seemed optimistic.

Qirin cast a sideways glance at the empress. "You cared for him, didn't you?" His tone was soft, not unkind, despite the accusation of his words. Nevia shot him a meaningful glare and walked away, deeming her response unnecessary. The answer should've been obvious.

She regally strode through the ranks, held held high, yet inside she was broken. She would have sooner crumbled in tears than face these people who had already lost so much and did not deserve to lose more. But alas: this was her place, her responsibility. She had to do this.

"Everyone." Her voice came out soft, yet all turned in attention. "It is over. Emperor Darius has passed on, fallen at the hands of the traitor, Lord Verrine of Ivalia, who caused this whole mess. In his dying breaths he left his empire to me, to do as I deem fit.

"As my first decree I command all of my imperial troops to stand down, and I wish to wash our hands of this grave misunderstanding. Let us learn from this tragedy and start anew. King Qirin, please grant me this."

Qirin's jaw clenched, and for a moment Nevia thought he would refuse. However, he relented, dipping his head in silent acknowledgement.

The war was over.

CHAPTER 43

The red sun dipped below the horizon, cloaking the coastline in darkness. Despite the icy waves bathing the battlefield, the scars of war still lingered. Nevia thought the next time she saw Feishin shores would be too soon.

Strong winds ripped through her hair, whipping her face. On either side of her stood Khatalia and Ardan. Their survival filled her with immense relief, yet the remembrance of what the war had cost them remained burdensome. Nevia was saddened to learn that Risanna had fallen, leaving Ardan without a chief and Khatalia without a sister. Nevia barely knew her, but found her death still gnawing at her insides. The chieftain had shown her nothing but kindness when she could've easily regarded her as the witch the imperials claimed her to be.

They held a small funeral for Risanna the night prior. Her fellow clansmen and women gathered to offer formal prayers and offerings, pleading to their gods to grant their fallen leader safe passage into the nether planes. Her body was then laid upon a bed of hay, and Ardan set it aflame. Never would Nevia forget the pain reflected in his eyes, the darkness which engulfed his features as the flames devoured her corpse. He had already lost much, and it grieved her that he lost another. While he had been Risanna's second, he had also been something more: her friend.

The price they paid for peace was steep.

The emperor's body was carefully preserved over a bed of ice and then wrapped in linens to be brought home. He would receive a proper burial and be laid to rest alongside his father. The date of his memorial was to be determined, but making the proper arrangements was a high priority to Nevia upon her return. The imperial people needed this opportunity to bid Darius one final farewell—as would she.

She greatly dreaded that day.

Ardan's fingers folded over hers, bringing her back to the present. Soon she would be leaving them. The *Dauntless* was deemed irreparable after the cannonball's heavy blow, but this hardly impacted them. There was plenty of room aboard the other ships ferrying the imperial military, especially after the loss of so many men.

"I wish you didn't have to do this alone," Ardan murmured, planting his chin atop her hair. His wounds had healed remarkably well, and Nevia considered his condition nothing short of a miracle. It would be a while before he did any heavy lifting, which would prove challenging for him, but Nevia knew he would manage. He would survive.

She permitted herself to lean into his warmth one more time, closing her eyes against the sea breeze. "I won't be alone. I know that you'll be thinking of me, even if apart."

She knew it was a lie. Without Darius and her father in Velspire, she wouldn't feel anything but alone. She hoped to find Elante, but even that held little promise. Her former handmaiden had likely embarked on something new in the time she had been dismissed. Even if she had not, Nevia was unsure if Elante would want to come back after everything that had happened. She could not blame her if she didn't.

Ardan lifted their entwined hands and pressed a kiss to her knuckles. "Always. And I will come and see you soon."

The promise filled her with joy—an alien emotion. "Don't rush things. Sanen needs you now more than ever, and I'm sure it's considered bad form for a chief to leave his people."

The breeze almost masked his shudder, but Nevia well knew he took no joy in his new position. She squeezed his hand in reassurance. "Risanna would be proud, as would your father. You will make a great chief."

A low sigh escaped Ardan's lips as his eyes scanned the glittering sea. "Only time will tell, but it's what she would want."

It saddened her to see Ardan so willingly cast aside his own desires for the good of his clan, to accept a role he wanted no part in. None else could replace Risanna like him. His choice to step up was the most practical one, even if he resented it. Their roles were similar in that regard.

Footfalls in the sand caused Nevia's fingers to slip from Ardan's. She whipped around to meet the gaze of the Feishin king. He was still dressed in his ceremonial black garb, silver tassels of his obi belt swaying in the breeze. He folded his arms in his wide bell sleeves and offered a bow. "I was hoping to find you before you left. I wanted to thank you for staying for Mother's ceremony. It would've pleased her."

The empress dipped her head in acknowledgement. They laid Queen Arethusa to rest that afternoon in the Shrine of Everlasting Peace alongside her ancestors and husband. The ceremony was held in the great halls of the Wind Palace, its walls barely enough to contain their number. Nearly all citizens came to pay their final respects to their beloved queen, including Nevia, whose presence was symbolic of the peace Arethusa laid down her life for. At first she thought it improper to attend when her nation was responsible for the queen's demise, but Qirin had insisted upon it. She did not regret it, especially when it meant she could prolong her stay for a week. To be with Ardan during his recovery was something her public officials would not have understood.

"It was my pleasure," Nevia offered, clasping her hands and returning his bow. His shoulders stiffened, but he did not protest. "Your mother was a fine woman, and I will miss her dearly."

"I'm glad you feel that way." He drew a step forward and clasped one of her hands, his fingers ice cold. "The Feishin Kingdom will always welcome you, and I look forward to the prosperous future we'll build together."

Nevia placed her other hand atop his. "As will the empire welcome you. You will always have allies in us."

A smile creased Qirin's forehead. "I thought as much, especially with the core shards I'm sending back with you."

Nevia blinked in confusion. "What?"

"Nephyl—the core substance—whatever it's called." He waved a hand carelessly. "I spoke with Teniel, and I've chosen to distribute the material."

Nevia's jaw slackened. She might've fallen over had it not been for their clasped hands.

"I don't believe it's a blessing from the gods like my mother did," Qirin clarified. "I've disagreed on this ever since their discovery. Your late husband was right on one thing: the people *do* deserve to know about this material, as it affects not only my country but the world at large. This has to be done if we're going to build a world on trust."

"But Arethusa was worried about taking from the source and what it may do to Gaia." Nevia fumbled for the right words. "Will this not jeopardize your own production of Nephyl?"

"No, it will not. I appreciate the concern, but there's more than enough to go around."

This would change everything. Not only would it provide a solution to the empire's energy crisis, but it would grant technological advancements throughout the world. A part of her wondered if the world was ready. But it was Qirin's decision; it was not her place to offer her unwarranted opinion.

A grunt came from her left, reminding Nevia of Khatalia's presence. Qirin's sharp gaze flickered to the chieftain, whose appearance was even more haggard than usual. Her hair was unkempt and her eyes bloodshot. Her tattered clothing still held bloodstains from the war.

They merely stared at one another for several tense moments, neither coming up with words. Perhaps they felt there was nothing left to say.

"What will you do now?" Nevia asked, piercing the awkward silence. "Will your country still uphold to pacifism after all this?"

Qirin rubbed his brow, a frown forming. "It's not something that will easily disappear. Pacifism will always hold a special place in the hearts of my people. And as you saw, there's those who so heavily oppose weapons that they would force my abdication. However, I think a no-weapons policy is an unrealistic extreme in the modern world, and I don't intend to hold us to such strict confines anymore. I never want to see such tragedy befall my people again."

The empress found his words both reasonable and disconcerting. From her experience people did not like change, and the change he proposed was plentiful.

She tucked stray strands of hair behind her ear, smothering her doubts rather than voice them. "Thank you for your generous gift and hospitality, Your Highness. I will not forget this."

He lifted a hand. "Please, just call me Qirin. No need for honorifics between friends."

Nevia hesitated briefly. She was uncertain if she considered him a friend, but he was certainly no enemy. "In that case, Nevia suits me fine, as well."

An approving smile stretched his lips. "Right then, Nevia. Safe travels."

He turned to leave, but he did not get far before Khatalia threw out a hand and caught his shoulder. The glint in Khatalia's green eyes was feral. "Be careful. The path of blood is steep, and the cost you'll pay may be more than you're willing to part with."

Qirin tilted his head, briefly considered her warning before laughing in her face. "I will keep your words in mind." He smiled, yet there was something dangerous behind it. "Though I find this coming from you slightly ironic."

The muscles at Khatalia's temple twitched. He started to move away again, and this time she allowed it. Discontent appeared to settle over the chief as her eyes narrowed on his back. "The arrogance of that one is rich," she said lowly. "Be careful with him, Nevia. There is something foul about him."

The empress threw a glance at his disappearing figure, hoping he hadn't overheard. Her worry must have been evident on her face, as Khatalia leaned over and threw an arm around her shoulders. "You look troubled."

Nevia shifted to wrap her arms around her torso in response. For a moment Khatalia stood there, too stunned to move, before finally returning the embrace and pinning her close to her chest.

"Thank you, truly." Nevia burrowed her face into Khatalia's thick winter furs, choking back tears that threatened to fall. "I would be nowhere without you."

"Nah." Khatalia stroked her back, with an uncharacteristic tenderness. "You would've been just fine. Might not have made so many great friends, though." She drew her away to an arm's length, offering her a wink.

"You and I both know that's not true. I would be dead if not for you."

"Doubtful, just married to the bastard still."

Sorrow dug its claws into Nevia's heart anew at the mention of Darius. What he did was wrong, but the way she handled things was wrong, too. She could finally see that now, even if it was too late to do anything about it.

Khatalia seemed to misunderstand Nevia's silence, as she gave her a pat on the head and said, "Don't worry, you'll see my face again soon enough. Your lot owes me for damages, after all."

Damages? Her face fell as understanding slowly dawned on her. "Oh, yes, of course. How insensitive of me. You must be expecting compensation for the damages that have incurred from the . . . the avalanche."

Khatalia's face blanched. "No, nothing like that. What I meant was my clothes, my things. They're still in your palace." She punched Nevia's shoulder, and she couldn't tell if the inflicted pain was intentional. "I would never hold you accountable for Darius' actions. I thought you knew me better than that."

Relief flooded Nevia in the form of tears. They welled in her eyes, beading before she could blink them away. She bent over, offering a deep bow to the chieftain. "Thank you. You're a good friend, Khatalia. I'm so grateful to know you, and I'm going to miss you so, *so* much."

Khatalia grew impatient, swallowing hard and blinking furiously, as though fighting back her emotions. She clicked her tongue. "Come on, none of that. You need to stand tall and be empress. See your guards looking at you funny over there?"

Nevia's gaze followed Khatalia's index finger to the two imperial soldiers standing at attention by her vessel, as stoic as ever. She wanted to correct her and explain that was how they always looked, but she didn't have the heart to. Instead she nodded, allowing her arms to slip from the chief and take a tentative step toward the ship. Before she got far a hand caught her own. She lifted her eyes to meet Ardan's.

"I'm really going to miss you." Sorrow laced his voice as he looked down at her with fondness.

Nevia stiffened. The guards were watching everything. What would they think if they saw her display affection for a man so soon after her husband's death? How did *she* feel about it? Her emotions were a mess, especially when it came to where her affections laid.

Her breath hitched as his fingers grazed her jaw. She decided to damn the consequences; life was too fleeting. She flung herself into his warm embrace, pressing her head against his pounding heart. His arms cradled her, perhaps for the final time.

"I love you, Nevia."

The words made her knees weak, words that she very much yearned to hear. And yet, memories of a different man in a different time using those same words surfaced, and guilt flooded her anew.

Return his affection, a small voice said in the back of her mind. *Tell him that you love him. Don't make more regrets.*

But when she opened her mouth a choked sob emerged instead. She recoiled, shaking her head frantically and bringing trembling hands to her mouth. "I-I'm sorry. It's just, I—"

Concern washed over his features, a reaction differing from the anger she anticipated. He gently lowered his arms, releasing her with a whisper. "Hey, it's okay. I get it. Grieve him, sort your feelings. You owe yourself that much."

He wiped a tear from her eye, one that she very much hated shedding. "Besides, this is not goodbye. You cannot get rid of me that easily, Nevia Bylilly."

A promise. This is what Nevia clung to as she followed the imperial soldiers off the coast, aboard the vessel that would cart her back to the empire, to the stifling walls that were once her prison —and would be again.

Her crown a shackle, her title a sentence.

She was not cut from the same cloth as Darius. The past few months of travel solidified it. She was meant to be wild and free— to soar as her Kindred Spirit, the Roc, did. And yet her bonds restricted her to remain in Velspire, to clear the ashes of a fallen empire. It was the least that she could do after role in its demise.

The sun had set, ending the longest week of Nevia's life. She stood at the stern as her ship set sail, gaze never leaving the silhouettes of her friends on the Feishin coast. The ship's steam engine roared to life belowdeck, propelling them out to sea. Both Khatalia and Ardan waved until they became stick figures in the distance, and Nevia was grateful to the distance for concealing her tears. Their paths dissected here, and she didn't know if they would ever cross again.

The following two days were long, likely because Nevia chose solitude over companionship. She would remain in her quarters by day, and once darkness settled she would emerge, seeking the companionship of the stars, observing the constellations that pointed her in the right direction many times in her life.

This time, however, was different. She knew the right direction, but she wasn't moving toward it.

The night air fogged her breath, and her garments did little to stave off the chill in her bones. Thought of her return did nothing to warm her. Already she missed Ardan. She told herself that she shouldn't. It was wrong to desire another when her husband just died, and for her. Despite this, her feelings were impossible to wield. Perhaps it was time she stopped trying.

The hairs at the back of her neck stood on end. Someone was watching her. The empress stilled, reminding herself that she was safe, that no one aboard would wish her harm. Upon turning, Nevia was unable to conceal her gasp.

A face as white as death greeted her, pupil-less gaze boring into her soul.

"Greetings, Nevia Bylilly of the Androvich Empire."

All remaining color drained from Nevia's face as she backed away, hands gripping the frosted railing behind her. "Yune?" she asked in disbelief. "It can't be. How did you escape?"

She tilted her head, her many facial piercings reflecting the moonlight. A green pendant worn around her neck and newly glowing painted her pale skin a sickly hue. "Yune is but one of many like me," she said. "We are one and the same. I came to issue you a warning, Nevia Bylilly. Trust not the warlord or the chief, as together they will bring the death of Gaia."

Cold dread filled Nevia at the familiarity of receiving a prophecy and the destruction that followed. Her life was forever altered that day in the square, and she didn't think she could bear it to happen again. "No, that can't be true." She shook her head, panicked. "Qirin and Ardan . . . they're my friends. We attained peace together. They can't bring the death of Gaia. They never would—"

"I speak only of what I saw." The seer shuddered, and for a moment Nevia feared she would collapse as Yune had. The empress started to reach for her, yet stopped mid-motion. Unable, unwilling. "Whether you will heed my warning is up to you, but I suggest you do—for all of our sakes."

Nevia closed her eyes. She could now see why Darius hated prophecies. Perhaps he had been right: perhaps they were self-fulfilled. If she had not chosen to defy him, ultimately choosing war, could the outcome have been different?

Did she have a choice now?

When she opened her eyes she found herself alone. No trace of the seer could be found.

Save for the necklace, still aglow at Nevia's feet. A dark impulse suggested she kick it into the black depths of the ocean, but she couldn't. She picked it up, finding the chain lighter than it appeared. A familiar energy hummed within the crystal, and when Nevia closed her eyes visions swam in front of her. Beyond her comprehension and control—both hopeful and terrifying.

She gasped, her fingers involuntarily allowing the necklace to fall onto the deck, the steel railing the only thing separating her from the ocean's unyielding waves.

"No, I refuse to believe it," she whispered, eyes wide as they locked onto the necklace.

As if in response, the core shard glimmered back.

Acknowledgements

There are so many people that assisted me in creating this marvelous book, who I am so grateful for in many ways. First and foremost, I want to thank my husband and best friend, Ross, who has supported me and all of my dreams. Without him, this book would not exist. He is also my editor, who really made my so-so words shine on paper.

A huge, huge shoutout to my beta readers who worked hard to bring me feedback and ways to improve my story to what it is today. Rachel Spitzer-Firliet, Loony, Jake, and Heartland, words cannot express my gratitude for the invaluable feedback that you've shared.

Massive shout-out to my street team. You all rock, and I am so grateful to you for your support in bringing Nevia's story into the hands of readers.

Thank you to my cover artist, Christian Bentulan, who made a stunning cover and really made my book stand out!

Another huge shoutout to Teresa at *The Art Armature*, who has helped me with figure out graphics and created stunning official artwork for this book. Thank you for bringing my earliest visions to life!

I spent a great amount of time researching the publication and editing process, and there are some amazing tutorials out there from some indie authors that share fabulous information. Some which I found particularly useful were from Mandi Lynn, Natalia Leigh, and Bethany Atazadeh. Thank you for publishing such content for authors such as myself, who dream of getting their words out there into the hands of readers but have no idea where to start!

I want to thank those special friends who supported and encouraged me through my writing, which are too many to list by name but include my entire D&D group, Eva, Jess, Rachel, and my beloved Granny who we lost while I was in the process of finishing this book. We would discuss writing (as she is also a published author), crafting, and so much more. Such an amazing lady she was, and I would love to aspire to be like her.

And last but not least, I want to thank you, my dear reader, who journeyed with Nevia and stuck with her to the very end.

About the author

Madison has lived all over the United States, now residing in the Northeast with her daughter and husband, who she loves with all her heart. Both are an inspiration to her to pursue her dreams and career of writing.

Madison has wanted to pursue a career in creating stories since she was four! She asked her mother what a person was called that created pictures for books, and from that moment decided that she would be an illustrator. While she still has a love for drawing, she has gravitated more toward writing the stories in her heart rather than drawing them. She wrote her first short story at nine years old, and has been writing stories ever since.

Find Madison on the Web!

Want to know more about Madison's current projects and interact with her on social media? You can join her newsletter on her website: www.MadisonReneAuthor.com, as well as follow her on the following social media platforms:

Instagram: https://instagram.com/madisonreneauthor
Twitter: https:/twitter.com/madireneauthor